GN

CONS,
SCAMS
&
GRIFTS

CONS,

SCAMS

&

GRIFTS

JOE GORES

Published by Warner Books

A Time Warner Company

Copyright © 2001 by Joe Gores
All rights reserved.

 Mysterious Press books are published by Warner Books, Inc., 1271 Avenue of the Americas, New York, NY 10020.

Visit our Web site at www.twbookmark.com

For information on Time Warner Trade Publishing's online program, visit www.ipublish.com.

 A Time Warner Company

The Mysterious Press name and logo are registered trademarks of Warner Books, Inc.

Printed in the United States of America

First Printing: August 2001

10 9 8 7 6 5 4 3 2 1

Library of Congress Cataloging-in-Publication Data
Gores, Joe
   Cons, scams & grifts / Joe Gores.
     p. cm.
   ISBN 0-89296-594-0
   1. Daniel Kearny Associates (Imaginary organization)—Fiction. 2. Private investigators—California—San Francisco—Fiction. 3. San Francisco (Calif.)—Fiction. 4. Art thefts—Fiction. 5. Romanies—Fiction. I. Title: Cons, scams, and grifts. II. Title.

PS3557.O75 C64 2001
813'.54—dc21
                                                2001030637

This Novel Is For
My Beloved Dori

Upro pcuv hin but Pcuva;
Kás Kámáv, mange th' ávlá!
Bárvol, bárvol, sálciye,
Brigá ná hin mánge!
Me tover, too pori,
Me kokosh, too cátrá,
Ádá, ada mi bezèti!

On the road.

          Jack Kerouac

On the road again.

          Willie Nelson

The road to hell is paved with good intentions.

          Anonymous

All roads lead to Rome.

          Voltaire

CONS,
SCAMS
&
GRIFTS

Prologue

It was Easter. From his exquisite one-story art deco building in the 9100 block of Sunset Boulevard, Victor Marr talked on the scrambler phone with the Yakuza gangster named Kahawa, in Hong Kong on his behalf. Marr was a mid-60s granite block of a man, with a stud-poker face not easily bluffed, a bold nose, and pale eyes that held no mercy. Tall and wide, still with the unruly hair and whipcord muscles of the Okie oil drill rigger he had been, summers, while attending the Colorado School of Mines. Then geologist for Standard. Out on his own. The first massive wildcat strike . . .

Now West Indian Oil was one of the Big Five.

"Were you able to close the deal?" he demanded.

From Hong Kong, Kahawa said in accented English, "A man in Europe put money down. Brantley says a number of cutouts were used, he does not even know the buyer's real name. But I saw the contract. It is of iron."

"Of course you outbid this man." The Hong Kong silence was eloquent. Marr's face tightened. "You *did* get it from Brantley."

"I stole it. But moving it safely out of Hong Kong undetected poses certain . . . problems. It might take time . . ."

The tension left Marr's face. His steel-shaving mouth turned up at the ends. He thought he was smiling. For the first time, he used a title of respect in addressing the Yakuza.

"Most satisfactory, Kahawa-*san*. Make sure no harm comes

to it. I need the time to beef up my security arrangements at Xanadu anyway. Tell Brantley to keep news of our acquisition from the man in Europe until it is in my hands. And he must *never* tell the authorities about this. Not ever."

"Both will be difficult. Brantley is a man of honor."

"Until it is in my hands—and never. Understood? If he refuses to cooperate, quote Falstaff to him: 'Honor . . . who hath it? He that died o' Wednesday.' "

Marr hung up. His tastes had been refined over the years. Now, he could quote Shakespeare. Now, no truck stop waitress could satisfy his sexual urges. Now, no work of art except an original by a grand master could excite him.

But one could possess only so many women, could own only so many grand masters. One wanted . . . *more*. The archetypal. The unique. Hence this little gem of an office building on Sunset instead of a Century City penthouse suite. Hence . . . *it*.

No need to show his prize to others. Enough to know no one else had one like it because there was no other like it.

Marr speed-dialed Xanadu, his hilltop estate three hundred miles up the coast in the Big Sur wilderness. He asked for, and despite the holiday got, R.K. Robinson, his head of security. He gave Robinson very specific instructions without telling him why: never let a subordinate know too much.

He made the call because there was always the possibility that the unknown European, upon eventually hearing of the theft, might try to reclaim his prize. But Victor Marr, in that secret inner place other men might call a soul, did not believe for an instant there was any actual danger. Who else in this ruthless world was as ruthless as he?

He was right—but also wrong. He was forgetting that in this ruthless world there is also sly.

one

On that Easter Monday at Universal Studios, just over the hill from Marr's Sunset Boulevard office, a shaggy black bear came down a flight of stairs with the shambling side-to-side gait of an animal not used to walking upright. In front of him half a dozen orderly queues of Easter week vacationers waited for open trams that would take them on the last of that day's famous Universal Studios backlot tours.

Among them was a small black girl of about five, pink dress, matching pink shoes, with pink-beribboned pigtails sticking straight out from each side of her head. When she saw the bear, her eyes flew wide, whites showing all around, even as her face scrunched up to deliver a wail of urban terror.

The bear stepped off the curb in front of her, tipped his Smokey Bear forest ranger's hat down over one eye, and did a soft-paw shuffle as he sang in a fine bear-i-tone voice.

"Smokey the Bear wears a hat,
But he doesn't know where it's at!"

The child's face was illuminated by a radiant smile. The bear did the old vaudeville head dip so his hat rolled down his arm on its rim to land in his wide clumsy bear's paw.

"Br'er Bear's chapeau's awful silly,
Why, that's entirely gilding the lily!"

And by some strange magic it wasn't a hat anymore, it was a magnificent paper lily all of gold.

> *"A lily, a rose, by whatever name,*
> *Is the very point of this silly game!"*

And somehow his lily had been transmogrified into a paper rose.

The bear stepped back to do a clumsy bow for the laughing children, lost his balance, and went sprawling over the curb right in front of them. As they OOOHHH'ed in alarm, he clambered clumsily to his feet, opened his arms, and finished his song:

> *"To fashion a crown in this way,*
> *For our beauteous Queen of the Day!"*

And yes! His single paper rose had become a small circlet of tiny, real, red tea roses with green leaves and interwoven stems. Which fragrant crown he balanced on the little black girl's pigtails. Somehow, for a moment, wearing her tippy crown, she was the regal woman she would become.

The trams were there. The bear hugged the little kids and even their mommies, and posed for pictures with them all. He ended up sitting on his haunches with his upside-down Smokey hat rematerialized in his hand. This gave the jovial, invigorated people the chance, should they so desire, to drop change into it as they boarded. Many did.

Br'er Bear shambled away from the deserted tram stop. He stepped over a waist-high barrier to slip into the janitors' shed where he had hidden his vinyl satchel. In a few moments he had become just a shaggy puddle of fake fur on the concrete floor out of which Ephrem Poteet emerged as butterfly from chrysalis.

Poteet was an almost-swarthy gent in his late 30s, with dark eyes he could make glisten like those of Antonio Banderas. He was still handsome despite new fine lines etched into his face by weeks of strain. Strain indeed. Terrible things had been done up in San Francisco, but that was all over now. He was once more *wuzho*, pure and unashamed, back where he belonged, his secrets safe. No one knew he was here, especially not his wife, who was utterly ruthless and had strange powers that he feared.

All the time he had been cavorting around, Poteet's long-fingered hands had been busy through slits under each front paw of his suit. Now he dug into the long, hidden pockets he had sewn down the outsides of the bear's legs. Lo and behold, here were wallets rich with cash, here were credit card folders and a poker hand of phone cards, here even was a folded sheaf of old-fashioned traveler's checks. All of them lifted from purses and wallets and handbags and back pockets.

The wallets would go into a series of convenient trash cans on the way home; their credit and phone cards, soon to be traded for cash, would temporarily rejoin Br'er Bear in the satchel. The cash would go into his pockets; through a series of small purchases he would convert the traveler's checks into more cash.

Half an hour later Ephrem Poteet, satchel in hand, strolled Universal's CityWalk like any other tourist. Past Gladstone's, with sawdust on its floor and open barrels of salted peanuts in the shell. Past the thirty-foot-high King Kong scaling the wall of the video store. Past Wizard's Magic, the magic-themed restaurant under the high-glassed dome roof. Finally, past the fountains that sprang up randomly to wet down those who challenged them.

In the back of a foyer housing several ATM machines was a door with DO NOT ENTER above it and a red light beside it. A notice warned that a bell would sound if the door was opened. Poteet opened it. No bell sounded. Parked under a NO PARK-ING sign outside in the alley was a golf cart. He putt-putted down the same winding road up which the daytime trams had toiled laden with sightseers, left the cart among several others parked behind Building 473 by the creative types from the Editorial Building.

A bus dropped Poteet on Highland in an area of Hollywood where no tourist from the Universal tour would venture after dark. On North Whitley, next to a distributor of naughty underwear, he entered the Hurly Burly. The saloon stank of illicit smoke, stale beer, and fresh urine. The juke was wailing a 1940s song about a lady they called the Gypsy. She could look in the future, said the song, and take away all your fears. Unless the Gypsy was Yana of fear and longing, of course.

A very fat woman in a fuzzy red sweater sat at the left end of the bar, swollen feet hooked over the rung of her stool, massive thighs stretching her stretch slacks to their utmost.

"Buy a girl a drink, dearie," she simpered, gap-toothed.

Pointing at her glass, Poteet chose the opposite end of the bar. There was no one in between, nor in any of the four booths along the side wall. The Hurly Burly's solvency obviously did not depend on its booze sales.

The bartender slid another drink down to the fat woman. He wore a gold hoop earring in one ear and a knife scar on one swarthy cheek. Blue veins stood out on his temples. His eyes had seen all that his particular world had to offer.

"Ephrem the Dip," he said, "long time no."

"Not long enough," Ephrem said, glad to see him. "Draft."

He slid one of the purloined credit cards across the stick to the bartender. The man regarded it, nodded.

"How many and how fresh?"

"Twenty-two—maybe five hours old." Poteet mated the credit card with a phone card. "And seven of these."

"I'll move 'em back east tonight. What price we talkin'?"

Twenty minutes later the deal was struck, and the cards and a good deal of cash surreptitiously changed hands. Ephrem barely wet his lips with beer. When he drank, he drank too much too quickly with generally disastrous results.

*   *   *

Etty Mae Walston was a small-boned but wide-beamed widow lady with slightly bowed legs and bifocals and wispy dead-white hair piled atop her head like shaving cream. She had lived in the 2800 block of Marathon in L.A.'s Silver Lake district for enough years to register the neighborhood's distressing decline. Heavens to Betsy, these days your car could be stolen right off the street and the police might not show up until the next day.

Since TV, save televangelists and infomercials, had little on it a decent body wanted to watch, Etty Mae spent much of her time spying on her neighbors from between front-room lace curtains washed thin by time. Her binoculars had been bought by her late husband, God rest his soul, for Dodger home games.

About two weeks earlier an almost-swarthy gent had moved into the paint-peeling white-frame house next door. He was very frustrating to Etty Mae; because he received no mail, she could not get his name from the postman or by snooping in his mailbox. He seldom came home before midnight, and seldom stirred outside before noon. Why, only the good Lord knew who he really was and what he was up to.

A terrorist planning to bomb Parker Center? A white slaver seeking to abduct teenagers for the vile uses of Saddam Hussein? One of those rapists who drove around after dark in a closed van grabbing innocent women right off the street?

Tonight, just after *The 700 Club*, her vigilance was rewarded. As on the previous night, the underdressed woman came clicking up the sidewalk in her high heels to pause under the streetlight. This time Etty Mae's binoculars were ready to bring her into focus: long black hair, oval face, strong nose, red-gleaming lips. Tight dress, white gloves.

Just like last night, the hussy went up the steps of the terrorist/white-slaver/rapist's unlighted house to meld with the shadows on his porch. Why, oh why, wasn't the front door angled so Etty Mae's binoculars could probe whether she went inside?

Just after midnight, Ephrem Poteet unlocked his front door to go yawning into the echoing, half-empty house. The way to the single bedroom lay across the living room and down the short hallway. He didn't bother with lights; there was almost no furniture to run into anyway.

Perfume stopped him dead in the bedroom's open doorway. Familiar perfume. Lights blazed to squint his night-adjusted eyes. She had been sitting on the bed in the dark, waiting for him. Young and beautiful. Rich curve of breast and hip emphasized by a thin, clinging dress that showed extravagant cleavage. What powers had she used to find him so soon?

"My beloved wife!" he exclaimed ironically, carefully schooling superstitious dread from face and voice.

"The title papers," she purred. "I want them. And the money. Everything is mine."

He knew he would give her what she wanted—all of it. He would give her today's take, too, if it would get her out of his life. But to give in too easily would make her suspicious.

"The money is spent," he lied. He hadn't been able to bring himself to touch a cent of it. Why had he even taken it?

She stood with a lithe movement, advanced on him even while smoothing the skimpy fabric down over her hips to emphasize their curves. Her eyes twinkled as her mouth made a *moue*.

"All of it gone? Every penny? *Bad* Ephrem!"

She slid her arms around him, pressed her open mouth to his. Her tongue darted. Her hips ground against his. She triggered his arousal as she always did. She giggled.

"Aha, my Ephrem, I feel that you are glad to see me."

"Yes. But still, I should get something for the papers."

"So you shall, my Ephrem. Here." Her hand came out of her

purse to slide razor-sharp steel into his belly. She jerked the blade sideways and up. "Like it?"

He gasped and fell, wide-eyed, as she skidded the straight-backed chair over under the ceiling's old-fashioned light fixture. Even then, going into shock, he tried to outwit her.

"An old fox . . . doesn't use . . . the same den twice . . ."

"But you are a stupid old fox, my Ephrem. I made sure last night that it was all hidden right up here in the ceiling."

"If you knew . . . where it . . . was . . . then why . . ."

"I thought you understood, my sweet—I want you dead."

"Mister?" The voice was old and quavery and full of dread, but it called again, "Mister, you all right?"

"In . . . here . . ." Ephrem managed to get out.

By squinting he could see the old white-haired lady from next door, for once without her binoculars. Her mouth was slack with fright: who could blame her? Here he was, bleeding on the floor, with his pockets turned out and a knife buried in his gut.

So your nosiness overcame your fear, he thought. Nothing new there. All his life he had known women like that.

All his life he had known women . . .

Known women . . . known . . . women . . .

"It was my . . . wife . . . from . . . 'Frisco . . ."

The old woman's face was down close to his. Not *just* nosiness. At the end, *Rom* thief and lonely old *gadja* woman.

"Oh, you poor, poor man!"

The room was darkening. He felt an overwhelming sadness, a sense of loss, the loss of what should have been.

"Yana," he croaked. Despite all, he now knew, he still loved her. He cried, "*Yana-a-a-a-a . . .*"

Nevermore.

two

On Tuesday's beautiful early spring afternoon in Rome, Willem Van De Post was behind his desk getting a phone call from Hong Kong. He was a heavy man but obviously athletic, with shirtsleeves rolled up over muscular forearms, a square Germanic head, sandy hair, and piercing blue eyes. What he heard robbed him of all tranquillity, made him lean forward across the desk, made his hand whiten around the receiver.

"Stolen?" he demanded in impeccable Italian. He listened, then burst out, "I don't care who threatened who with what, we have a valid contract, the renovation is almost complete . . ."

He looked diminished in his swivel chair. This acquisition was to have been the crowning achievement of a long and honorable career: how he had fought the board of directors to allocate the funds on the argument that it would bring them international fame!

"Is there any indication of whom—" He listened. "A Japanese?" He paused, said, "What good does it do me if you send my deposit back? I won't have the—" He stopped again. "I . . . I will have to call you later."

He sat staring sightlessly out the window at the green sweeping vistas his office overlooked. Call him back? Why bother? The prize had been stolen by, Willem knew as surely as if he had seen it in a crystal ball, international financier Victor Marr. He'd always known Marr wanted it, but never dreamed he would use the Yakuza gangster Kahawa to steal it and to threaten Brantley with ruin, pain, perhaps even death, to ensure his silence. Only because of their long friendship, he was sure, had Brantley dared call him at all.

Willem could go back to the board of directors, of course, the ministry, even, but what could they do? The facility to house it was nearly complete. So what? Marr would laugh at Interpol, laugh at governments. Would say, Prove I have it.

Then the frown lines eased on his handsome, lived-in face. He could never prove Marr stole it, and he could never match the man for sheer ruthlessness. But . . . in the wild days of his youth he had done some things to stay alive, and thus already had a wonderful connection in California: his wife's uncle, Staley Zlachi, King of the Muchwaya Gypsies.

Offered a sufficiently tempting prize, Staley might just be persuaded to do some work on Willem's behalf. For the first time since hanging up the phone, Willem Van De Post began to smile gently to himself. *Devèl* knew, Uncle Staley was not ruthless. But he *was* sly.

Willem Van De Post was suddenly ready to call Brantley back in Hong Kong.

Because of the time zones, that warm afternoon in Rome was a chilly 5:47 A.M. in San Francisco's foggy Richmond District. Dan Kearny was parked in the Coronet Theater's no-parking zone on Geary Boulevard. Around the corner behind him, on Arguello, three leased car transports roped exhaust into the chilly dawn air. Ahead, beyond the Almaden intersection, Wiley's UpScale Motors was crowded with costly sports cars and restored classics.

Kearny was a compact man in his early 50s, heavy of face, massive of jaw, hard of eye, his thinning curly hair gone silver. He unhooked a clumsy handful of mike from the dash of his Ford Escort to thumb the red button on its side. For an operation like this, give him the good old outmoded C/B radio every time.

"This is S/F-One. All units check in."

Giselle Marc was tall and lean with wicked thighs, blond hair in loose easy waves around her face, blue eyes alight, big brain ticking over. Excitement thrummed in her voice: this was her first time in the field on a dealership raid.

"S/F-Two. A block away on the other side of Geary."

Next to check in was O'Bannon, the redheaded Irishman with the freckle-splashed leathery face, gargling his Rs as usual.

"Faith an' BeJaysus, an' 'tis a frosty mornin' for poor auld S/F-Three to be up here on Lone Mountain."

He was in place at Rossi and Turk, two blocks uphill. A couple of years Kearny's junior, when he left the booze alone O'B was the best all-around field man DKA had after Dan himself.

"S/F-Four, check in," said Kearny.

Bart Heslip's heavy baritone growl wore the field-nigger patois it amused him to put on and off at will like an old and treasured sweater. He had a stylishly shaven pate and a thin mustache. "S/F-Four mos' surely be on Palm below Euclid, waitin' fo' word fum de Great White Father, yassah boss."

When he had quit the ring with still-unscrambled brains to become a repoman, Bart had been a rising middleweight with thirty-nine wins (thirty-seven by KO) out of forty fights put into the record books.

Larry Ballard was next, thumbing his mike with a stifled yawn. "S/F-Five on Anza between Stanyan and Loraine Court, over."

Not boredom, Kearny knew: probably out chasing some skirt all night. Despite his love of the ladies, despite sun-bleached hair and surfer good looks and a recent black belt in karate, Ballard, Kearny had to admit, was a damned good field man.

Next came a thin and reedy voice so unlike Trin Morales's usual breathy Latino tones that Kearny barely recognized it.

"S/F-Six, in place by Mel's Drive-In."

Morales was just back from a prolonged medical leave of

absence after an outraged Latino and three *amigos* had beaten him to a pulp because Trin had messed with the man's teenage sister. He had lost much more than forty pounds and his bully-boy manner; he was almost timid now. Kearny had never liked him much, despite his being a tough, treacherous, amoral, first-rate repoman. Now, maybe, not even that. Ballard actively hated his guts.

After waiting in vain for Ken Warren's check-in, Kearny said, "S/F-Seven, what's your twenty?" Ken was silent. Kearny repeated his question. "Are you in position, S/F-Seven?"

Finally there came two double-clicks as Warren thumbed his mike on and off twice. Which meant his Dodge Ram was squatting right on the Wiley UpScale Motors front gate with a long-handled chain-cutter waiting open-jawed on the seat.

Dan Kearny checked his watch and said "Go!" into the mike.

The DKA hands burned rubber to close in on UpScale from all sides. The drivers of the auto transporters snapped away their cigarettes while trotting back to their trucks. Ken Warren was out of his Ram to snip the padlock chain on the gate as if the case-hardened steel was Silly Putty.

Big John Wiley threw back the covers in their bedroom a mile or so away on El Camino del Mar to stumble bare-ass across the room and cut the alarm. He had rounded shoulders, a sunken chest, a watermelon belly. Wings of lank black hair hung down on either side of his face. His blue eyes were shrewd, his mouth sensual, his nose well-shaped.

Big John punched 911 on the bedside phone. "My name is John Wiley and somebody is breaking into my auto dealership on Geary at Almaden!"

He listened, cursed, and hung up. Still abed was Eloise, his wife of thirteen years, a pretty blonde who had put on weight but could still turn the boys' heads when she was all dolled up. He jerked the covers down from her bare shapely shoulders.

"Get dressed, baby," he said. "We don't have much time."

Most classic car dealerships take their restored autos on consignment, or buy them outright. Big John didn't have the cash for that, so Cal-Cit Bank lent him the capital needed for the stock to attract high-tech Gen-X buyers, using the cars themselves as collateral. As a car was sold, Big John was supposed to pay off the bank loan on that particular vehicle.

Lately he'd sort of forgotten about those repayments, until Stan Groner, VP Business Loans, got tired of missing cars and missing cash and being out on a limb. He told Kearny to raid UpScale, grab all the cars on the lot, and auction them off.

Eloise was awake by now. "What's the matter, Johnny?"

"Cal-Cit Bank is hitting the dealership."

She was out of bed, throwing on her clothes.

"Those shits! What do you want me to do?"

"Drive the 'Vette down to Pacifica and lock it in your sister's garage and forget it's there. Get her to drive you home and tell her to forget it, too. I'll drive to UpScale in your heap with some bucks—repomen were born with their hands out."

"What about our salesmen?"

"Screw the salesmen, they're on their own."

"Of course screw them. But they're all driving cars from your lot as demos. If we can hide those cars too until—"

"Good thinking." Big John paused in the doorway. "Warn them from your car phone on the way down to Pacifica."

At UpScale Motors, the first of the auto transporters was backed into the open gate with its ramp down. Kearny's crew was opening cars and firing them up. Giselle plunked down into the icy leather seat of a sweet little red '88 Alfa Romeo Spider Quadrifoglio with personalized plates reading STATO. She keyed awake the dashboard's bank of red and yellow lights. The engine growled. She *liked* this car!

Kearny was standing beside the transporter ramp, clipboard in hand, marking them off. Heslip and Morales had the first two aboard; Ballard waited his turn in a Maserati Bora Coupe. Kearny came over to the Alfa, leaned down as Giselle opened the window.

"When this one is on the truck, Giselle, sneak into Wiley's office and get the names and addresses of his salesmen. We'll grab the demos they're driving before they can hide 'em."

Ballard, whose flooring reports of cars out of trust at Up-Scale had stirred Groner to action, grinned and jerked his head at a Corolla rolling to a stop beyond the fence.

"Do it the easy way—here's Big John himself."

Kearny walked through the gate to meet Wiley, who was out of his car and waving his arms and yelling.

"Get those cars off that transporter! Just last night I person-ally handed Mr. Groner a check for—"

"I spoke with Mr. Groner eight minutes ago," lied Kearny blandly. "And . . ." He made a slashing motion across his throat.

Big John drew him away to where the transporter shielded them from the others. "There really is some mistake here."

"Yeah, and you made it. You're out of trust with Cal-Cit Bank on twenty-seven cars worth over seven hundred K."

Big John's hand brought out a roll of greenbacks, casually.

"Several of these cars are already sold—they just need final detailing before delivery." He pressed a fistful of bills into Dan Kearny's hand with his deal-closing smile. "I just bet you're a man who likes a few bucks under the table."

Kearny grinned like a wolverine, but his eyes were sud-denly the coldest Big John had ever faced—and, being in the used-car trade, Big John knew his cold eyes. Kearny opened his hand. The ocean wind coming up Geary whipped away the dead presidents like a politician's promises.

"You bet wrong," Dan Kearny said.

Benny Lutheran, a heavy-bodied blunt-faced man of Ger-man heritage, bragged that he could close a deal with a dead man. As he came down Geary his car phone buzzed. He picked up.

"Benny Lutheran."

"Benny—Eloise Wiley."

Benny was passing the Coronet Theater. He put on his turn signal and his oiliest salesman's voice. "Eloise!" It was the first time she'd called him since last year's Christmas party when she was drunk in the storeroom and let him put his hand down the front of her peasant blouse. "Meet you in the storeroom?"

"The bank is closing down the dealership," she said.

Benny had already started his turn into UpScale. "Later," he said, dropped his cell phone, slammed on his brakes, hit reverse, and squealed backward out of the open gate.

Ken Warren was already running for his Dodge Ram. He had recognized the sporty little vintage 1975 280Z from the hotsheet. A salesman was driving it as a demo and was trying to keep it as his own. No way, man!

Benny Lutheran made a screaming right turn off Geary into the first street he came to, Beaumont Avenue. Beaumont dead-ended a block uphill at Turk. Turn left, and Turk was a straight shot to Divisadero. Jink over a block to Golden Gate, and he'd be one-way inbound all the way to Market Street.

So he whipped left into Turk, accelerated—and stood on the brakes in a scream of smoking rubber. The cross-walk was flooded with students on their way to early classes at the Lone Mountain Campus of U.S.F. A black-haired pixie-faced girl in a red warm-up jacket gave him an exuberant finger.

Pissed off, Benny twisted to look over his shoulder before gunning the Datsun in reverse. Three inches from his back bumper hulked the repoman's truck. Benny's door was opened, a vise-grip hand reached in; suddenly he was standing in the street beside his car with his shirtfront rumpled. The students had stopped to watch. The girl in the red jacket jeered at him.

"You gonna take that? Paste him one in the mouth!"

At the same time the repoman said, "Ahng taktin nat cah!"

Hey, this guy was some kind of retard! Retards, Benny knew from five minutes of a PBS special he'd caught, were gentle souls and stupid besides. He was as tall as the retard, and outweighed him by thirty pounds. And Miss Pixie-Face was watching.

So he threw a looping right hand at the retard's jaw. It was a good right. It connected. It hurt his hand. It didn't seem to hurt the retard's jaw.

Thunk! Bright colors. Benny, feeling sick, was sitting on broad tan steps leading from Turk Street up to the lofty spires of Lone Mountain College, holding Miss Pixie-Face's handkerchief to his broken nose. His tear-blurred eyes saw a wavery form standing over him. It waggled a finger in his face.

"Hnew hnit—an htay ner!"

Again, Benny didn't understand a word the guy said, but he just knew, in his heart of hearts, that only an idiot would stir from that spot just then. And Benny Lutheran was no idiot.

Nor was the retard. Not even a retard, in fact. Just one hell of a tough carhawk with a speech impediment, helping to put Wiley's UpScale Motors out of business.

three

On the other hand, San Francisco's Homicide Squad was never out of business. Their cup was always full, pressed down and overflowing. But even Homicide cops have to eat, right? So at ten-fifteen that same morning, Rosenkrantz, the bald one—the only way, somehow, that Beverly could tell him from Guildenstern—was at Jacques Daniel's Saloon waiting for salami and Swiss on a French roll, lettuce, mayo, pickles, hold the mustard.

Beverly and Danny got together while working at the St. Mark as cocktail waitress and bartender, bought a failing neighborhood bar on 21st Avenue and Lincoln Way, and renamed it Jacques Daniel's because of their names, Beverly Amy *Daniels* and *Jacques Daniel* Marenne. They had taken it from fern-and-Tiffany-glass back to new old-fashioned San Francisco saloon: polished brass bar rails, a C/D player masquerading as a juke-box, a clientele that talked IPOs despite the March Nasdaq meltdown.

Meanwhile here was bulky Rosenkrantz: round unremarkable face, shirt unpressed as usual, herringbone jacket, dark slacks. A tie, askew, like spaghetti in tomato sauce dropped on the floor. A 9mm Glock 17 bulging his jacket over his right hip.

"I got a joke," he said.

"You always do," Beverly replied sadly. "Always awful."

She was slightly above five feet, size four and triumphantly blond, with sparkling blue eyes that could turn sensuous when

Danny was around, a tiny waist, beautiful dancer's legs, and a bosom too full for the ballerina she had once aspired to be.

"These two whales are swimming along when they see a sailing ship. The first whale says, 'That ship killed my father! Let's swim under it, blow as hard as we can, and turn it over.' The second whale nods his head okay."

Beverly put the sandwich down in front of him, and started to make another one just like it.

"The whales swim under the ship and blow as hard as they can, and the ship turns over. The sailors are in the water, floundering around, yelling. The first whale says, 'That's not enough revenge. Let's go eat up all of those sailors.' The second whale shakes his head, saying—"

" 'I was willing to give you a blow job,' " smoothly inserted the big, bulky, unremarkable man coming through the door, " 'but you didn't say anything about swallowing the seamen.' "

Guildenstern had a full head of sandy hair and an unpressed shirt; his tie, also askew, was like an anchovy pizza dropped on the floor. His herringbone jacket had leather elbow patches. When he took the stool adjacent to his partner's, his 9mm Glock 17 bulged his jacket over his left hip. Beverly slid the second sandwich across the stick to him with a couple of paper napkins.

"Salami and swiss? Lettuce? Mayo? Pickles? Hold —"

"Hold the mustard," agreed Beverly.

Guildenstern was surprised. "Yeah. Hey, what do you tell a blonde with two black eyes?"

"Nothing," said Rosenkrantz. "You've already told her twice."

An assistant D.A. who was into community theater—he always played Felix, the neat one, in *The Odd Couple*—had first called them Rosenkrantz and Guildenstern. Now, new SFPD men didn't know their real names; some whispered their wives didn't, either, but they had the highest case-closure record in the Homicide Squad.

"We got a call from Harry Bosch, the Hollywood Homicide cop," said Guildenstern around his sandwich. Rosenkrantz blew on his coffee and nodded to go on. "Seems a guy got knifed down in LaLa and died in the arms of the snoopy old broad from next door. His dying words were that it was his wife did the nasty to him."

"Heavens! A wife killing her husband? I'm astounded."

"Harry said both the vic and the perp were from up here. Ephrem and Yana Poteet. Even had a local address where we can start." He turned to Beverly as if she had asked a question. "Victim and perpetrator—guy who got did, guy who done it."

"In this case, *broad* who done it," said Rosenkrantz.

Both big men pulled ten-dollar bills from their pockets and laid them on the bar. Beverly started to shove one of them back, but Rosenkrantz made such an evil face at her that she stopped. Guildenstern finished his sandwich in one big gulp.

"How can you tell when an auto mechanic's just had sex?"

Covering her ears, Beverly said, "I don't want to know."

"One of his fingers is clean," said Rosenkrantz inexorably.

After they left, she picked up their tens, dropped their plates and cups and silver into the double sink's hot soapy water, then burst out laughing. They would have to do something much more heinous than tell dirty jokes to make themselves unwelcome here. A few months ago, Danny disappeared; she got him back damaged but repairable only because Rosenkrantz and Guildenstern had galloped to the rescue, jokes flying.

She started cutting French rolls for the lunch trade. Yana and Ephrem Poteet. The names rang faint bells. Something Larry Ballard had been involved in a year or two ago. Gypsies, maybe?

Yes indeed, Gypsies. During the 1,500 years since they were booted out of their native India, the Gypsies have existed in other lands by doing the things those societies' citizens can't or won't do. In Western Europe and the Balkan countries and Russia, unless exterminated, they have been forced to abandon their nomadic ways to live in slums at the edge of big cities.

But in America, land of the free and home of the brave, they still wander at will, these days usually by Cadillac rather than the horse-drawn *vardo*, and work the welfare and benefit systems for all they're worth. Ironically, in an age where computers and Internets and electronic snooping diminish all freedom, these last free people on earth still bind themselves by traditions and taboos as strict as those of Orthodox Judaism.

There are at least two million Gypsies in this country, of at least four recognized nations: Kalderasha, Muchwaya, Tsurana, and Lowara. But they keep so far outside the population mainstream that they are missed by the census-takers and anyone else who might try to curtail their way of life.

Gypsies don't mingle with *gadje*, they don't look back, they live only for today, and one thing is certain: they cause all sorts of mischief. Because Christ Himself, dying on the cross, gave them dispensation to con, scam, and grift from the *gadjo*—the outsider, the non-Gypsy—with perfect moral impunity.

Ramon Ristik, a swarthy, bright-eyed man of about thirty, was a member of the Muchwaya nation and much given to the con, the scam, and the grift. His last time in San Francisco he worked North Beach, where topless was born when Carol Doda removed her bra while dancing atop a piano at the long-gone Condor.

Because the *ofica* of his sister Yana (professionally, Madame Miseria) was around the corner and up a steep narrow alley known as Romolo Place, Ramon favored the Columbus/Grant/ Broadway intersection for his work. After convincing the marks of great impending evil in their lives, he steered them to Madame Miseria, who stripped them clean. He impartially conned gullible tourists, local warm-blooded Italians, and superstitious Chinese.

During Ramon's subsequent wanderings elsewhere, Madame

Miseria went out to the Richmond District's cold fog-blown Avenues. Here Ramon, upon his return, found gullible Chinese, but few warm Italians; few hayseed tourists, but many recently immigrated Russians. Russians could be *tough*.

The Troika on Clement had a silver samovar in the window; guttural Slavic tongues vied with English at a crowded bar thick with forbidden cigarette smoke. Ramon slipped onto a stool just as the manicured hand of a short tousle-haired bespectacled man slapped a rare $500 bill down on the bar.

Catching Ramon's surreptitious glance at the bill, the Russian demanded, "You—something?"

"I have been rude, forgive me," said Ramon. Then he turned over the unresisting hand to see its palm. "Back in Mother Russia . . ." He paused diffidently. "I had a certain facility with . . . seeing things . . ."

"Reading palms?"

"Among other . . . abilities. As you know, your left hand suggests what your road through life might be. Your right hand shows what road you have actually taken. Perhaps I might . . ."

The Russian said silkily, "What does this service cost me?"

"There is no charge," Ramon replied with offended dignity.

Light glinted off the Russian's glasses as he opened his right hand under the strong cylindrical back-bar lights. "Then tell me all, my friend."

Something in the man's demeanor made Ramon uneasy, but after all, bogus palmistry was his basic profession. So he began tracing the central line that cut across the muscular palm.

"This is your life line. See, it is long and strong. That is good. But here . . ." He indicated the place where another line crossed it at an angle. "See that . . . intersection?" He bent closer. "There is almost a break there. It could mean an illness, or . . ." His eyes widened. He swayed back slightly, casting a sharp glance at his companion. "Or . . . or danger."

"Danger?"

"A psychic disturbance, a . . ." He paused again, then said, carefully, "Back in Matroushya, were you ever exposed to . . . influences that might have been connected with . . . evil?"

"No. I had a very important job with the government."

Ramon took a handkerchief out of his pocket and wiped his brow. He shook his head. "Then it is better that I stop here."

"You cannot stop," said the man with emotion. "Not now."

"But this is too . . . too heavy for me. I am of but limited skills, perhaps I misread . . ." He looked up into the disks of light-reflecting glass that hid the man's eyes. "I wish you . . . no, I beg you, come with me and see my sister. She has the second sight, she is nearby . . ."

Suddenly Ramon felt a most dreadful agony. It was the Russian's hand. The bastard had grabbed his testicles in an iron grip! Ramon's hands scrabbled ineffectually at the bartop.

The Russian's voice was low. "Yes, I had an important job with the government. I was with the KGB. We knew what to do with lying, cheating, conniving Gypsy scum like you. We would rip their balls off." He twisted viciously before letting go. "A pity we two did not meet up in Matroushya before the fall."

Ramon staggered outside to the laughter of the Troika's other patrons, almost throwing up with the waves of nausea passing through him.

Tough, those Russians. Very tough.

He turned quickly up the nearest of the Avenues and thus away from Clement Street: the Russian might quit chortling with his buddies too soon and glance at the bar in front of him. It had taken all of Ramon's fortitude, while the Russian was twisting his balls, to lift that $500 bill off the bartop.

four

The great classic car grab by Daniel Kearny Associates (Head Office in San Francisco, Branch Offices throughout California, Affiliates Nationwide) was over. Wiley's UpScale Motors was out of business. Or was it? Kearny and his people met in the empty second-floor reception area of DKA's converted red-brick laundry building at 340 Eleventh Street, in the City's SOMA District.

Kearny sat on the scarred edge of the old desk, clipboard in hand. Behind him was the old-fashioned waist-high partition and gate that led to the head of the back stairs. Faintly from below came the clack of computers, the shrill of phones, a waft of exhaust fumes from the storage area behind the building.

Larry Ballard was tipped back in a straight chair against the wall, blue eyes sleepy, surfer-blond hair looking windblown. Far from chasing a woman last night, as Kearny had thought, he had been at a karate dojo on Ninth Avenue until midnight, working with the *yawara* stick the medieval Buddhist priests had called, rather fancifully, the lightning bolt of Siva. O'B and Bart Heslip were sitting on chairs under the windows.

"Eight to go," O'B said.

"Seven," Ballard objected. "We got twenty cars."

Giselle was sitting in what had been the receptionist's swivel chair, facing Kearny. Beyond the wall behind her were the row of small, neat cubicles, facing the street, in which the field operatives did their paperwork. She brushed a long strand of golden hair back from her forehead.

"Nineteen until we know how Ken made out with that 280Z."

"Ken doesn't miss," said Ballard.

"Where's Morales?" asked Bart Heslip.

"He went home," said Kearny. "He felt sick from—"

"Aw, poor guy," said Ballard.

"Give him a break," said Giselle.

"Forget about Morales," rumbled Kearny. "We've got to find those missing cars and drop a rock on them."

Giselle was handing out the list she had printed up.

"These are the ones that are still out there."

1962   Corvette roadster, white/red interior, $28,500.
1995   Panoz kit car, dark green/black interior, $39,995.
1982   Ferrari 400I convertible, gold/black interior, $34,900.
1970   Aston Martin Volante, black/leather interior, $95,000.
1990   Jaguar XJS convertible, champagne/black interior, $17,995.
1966   Mustang convertible, red/parchment interior, $12,500.
1995   Acura NSX, black/black interior, $62,000

The Datsun 280Z Ken had gone after was not on the list. Keep the faith, baby. Kearny did the math in his head.

"I make it $290,890 out of sight and out of trust. I have to go back east for the national convention in Chicago this week. Giselle will coordinate from the office, Jane Goldson will assign your current files to the other field men. *Get those cars!*"

Larry read from the list, "1970 Aston Martin Volante, black with a leather interior. Not many of those tooling around—"

"Not the point, Reverend," said O'B. He hadn't had a drink of anything except nonalcoholic beer for almost two months, so his blue eyes were clear in his leathery freckled Irish face. "You know the salesmen are trying to keep those demos for themselves. We gotta get into the UpScale personnel files for their names and addresses and hangouts."

Ballard gave a skeptical laugh. "Big John would love to catch us trying a little B and E so he could yell for the cops."

Heavy shoes tramped up the uncarpeted back stairs. Ken Warren's tough face and big shoulders appeared above the landing.

"The 280Z?" Giselle asked him.

"Hnit'n hnin na mbahn."

In the barn—meaning, in the bank's storage lot.

"That's one guy we won't have to check out," said Bart.

"What if they hide another one in his garage just to finesse us?" asked O'B. "We need that salesman list—"

Ken Warren's big hand slapped a sheet of creased, greasy, lined yellow paper down on the desktop, half a dozen names and addresses scrawled on it. "Hne odtha hnthnailsmn," he said.

*   *   *

Backward on the storefront window in the lower-rent fringe of San Francisco's sunny Noe Valley was

TED'S TV REPAIR
VCRs, Computers, Major and Minor Appliances

Sitting with Lulu in the little apartment behind the shop, Staley Zlachi, King of the Muchwaya, looked anything but the stereotyped Gypsy. No brilliantined locks here, no swarthy skin, no golden earrings or twirled mustachios. Late in his seventh decade, Staley was white of hair, benevolent of belly, ruddy of face, everyone's ideal Santa Claus. Lulu looked like Mrs. Claus, a jolly round-faced *hausfrau* up to her elbows in flour.

Together they could have conned the stripes off a tiger.

Almost. Last month in Tennessee they sued a clan of Tsurana Gypsies over a farm equipment deal that had gone sour. Each group had been conning the other, as usual using the *gadjo* legal system to settle their intertribal differences. But the Tsurana whispered in the judge's ear that Staley was a *Gypsy*—and the case was thrown out. Staley paid all costs. A disaster!

Now here they were in Baghdad by the Bay, one of the best places in the country to score big bucks in a hurry because here minorities ruled. By Gypsy law, San Francisco belonged to the Kalderasha. The least that dominant tribe's *Baro Rom*—Big Man—might expect was a courtesy call, gifts, some quid pro quo. Staley had been left unable to offer any of those things. But Rudolph Marino, his heir apparent, was on his way across the Bay from Richmond. He would know how to raise money.

The phone rang. Without salutation the recognized voice of Willem Van De Post spoke to Staley in *Romani*.

"What are the Muchwaya doing to celebrate Millennium year?"

"We have many projects in hand," Staley said untruthfully.

"So. As I thought. Nothing. Come to Rome. It is the two thousandth birthday of our Holy Mother Church. We are having year-long celebrations, festivities, huge crowds . . ."

Staley had thought of it, of course. The hordes of believers, the urgency of their spiritual needs . . .

"But the cost!" he exclaimed prudently.

"I can guarantee you will recoup it in a week in Rome if I can use your people for an operation there in California. Here are the facts as I know them . . ."

When Staley finally put back the receiver, he said, "That was the man in Italy who is married to your niece. I have never appreciated him before."

"Willem? Willem Van De Post?"

"Yes, Willem. On the side of the angels, and a saint to protect us! Almost, we will have the Italian government behind us."

But to do what Willem asked they were going to have to

poach on Kalderasha territory in a big way, and pool all of their enterprises to raise money besides. Somehow he would have to convince his tribe to do it, and avoid the cops at the same time.

Just then the spring bell on the front door jingled merrily. Lulu went smiling out into the shop and instantly tagged as cops the two bulky men who had just entered.

She chirped, "What can I get for you gentlemen?"

"Ted Terrizi," said the bald one.

"Ted, better known as Staley," said the other.

Lulu tilted her head quizzically. "Staley?"

"Staley Zlachi," sneered Guildenstern, "as in Gyppo."

"Papa," Lulu called in a musical voice.

Ted's business really was fencing hot electronics rather than repairing them. Staley came through the curtain still clutching the hastily snatched-up *Chronicle* sports section. His reading glasses were down on his nose, an old-fashioned watch chain glinted across his ample belly. He had kicked off his shoes on the way, a nice touch: who committed crimes barefoot?

"Papa, they call you some other name I don't know . . ."

With a protective arm around her shoulders, he gave them a saddened, significant Alzheimer's eye-roll above her head.

"Mama, she don't always get things so good these days."

"What she can get us is the present whereabouts of one of your people," said good-cop Rosenkrantz as bad-cop Guildenstern slapped a faxed photo down on the countertop.

"You know this guy here?"

"He looks dead," said Staley.

"Dead as disco." The two old people hurriedly crossed themselves. "The question ain't whether he's dead. It's whether you know him."

Lulu's left eyelid twitched. Staley immediately said, "He is one of our people, yes, God rest his soul. Ephrem Poteet."

"He's got a wife, Yana," stated bad-cop Guildenstern.

"Oh, her we wouldn't know nothing about."

Lulu spoke over him. "She once was of our *kumpania* but she has been declared *marime*." She addressed herself pointedly to good-cop Rosenkrantz. "You know *marime*, mister handsome policeman?"

"Yeah. You tossed her out on her can. What for?"

"She stopped following the ways of the *Rom*."

Though Gypsies were seldom involved in murder cases, both Homicide cops had picked up enough lore over the years to know that this ritual rejection by the tribe could be for anything from breaking a sexual taboo—showing too much thigh, for instance, as opposed to breast, which didn't count—to working a straight, *gadjo* job. In one famous case, a girl's whole clan had been declared *marime* because she had joined the Peace Corps.

"So we don't know where Yana is," Staley was going on. "Don't nobody keep track of people who've been tossed out."

"But you know whether she's in town or not."

Staley nodded unwillingly. "I hear maybe she is." Lulu's right eyelid gave a slight twitch, so he added smoothly, "She's a fortune-teller when she's working, I hope that helps you out."

"Calls herself Madame Miseria," nodded ever-helpful Lulu.

As Rosenkrantz and Guildenstern were leaving, a lean, very handsome man with gleaming black blow-dried hair brushed by them in the doorway without apology. His high-cheekboned face had the piratical lines of a mob attorney of Sicilian heritage, and his suit definitely wasn't from the Men's Wearhouse. The cops appreciated expensive clothes as only honest men who can't afford them do; they knew it took a K or two, easy, to waltz that grey wool number out the door.

"Looks like a Mafioso," said Rosenkrantz, "so why's he goin' in there? In that suit he didn't fall off a potato truck."

"Gonna put a horse's head in their bed," Guildenstern wheezed. "He wasn't carrying anything he could fence, and besides, we're Homicide." As they were getting into their plain sedan, he added, "You catch Mama's twitching eyelid?"

"Alzheimer's," said Rosenkrantz wisely.

"Yeah. Guy goes to the doctor, doctor says, 'I've got bad news and worse news. You got cancer and you got Alzheimer's.' "

" 'Thank God I don't have cancer,' " said Rosenkrantz.

Guildenstern chuckled, then sobered. "Madame Miseria. At least we got a name to give Dirty Harry down at Bunco."

Staley hung up the phone and sat back down at the kitchen table. The fragrance of Lulu's thin stogie filled the room.

"The L.A. cops refuse to release Ephrem's body and they're holding his possessions as crime-scene evidence."

"I'm still gonna hold a *pomana* for him," insisted Lulu. A *pomana* was a ritual feast for the dead at which only fruits and grains are served. "Even if we don't got his body."

"We can hold it at my place on High Street in Point Richmond," said Rudolph Marino. "Big brown shingle house with a great view across the bay. The owners are on a world cruise and the neighbors think I'm their nephew." He changed the subject. "Why'd you tell 'em that Yana reads fortunes as Madame Miseria?"

"Why shouldn't I of told 'em?" Lulu was just short of defiant. "They wanted to notify her that Ephrem had been killed, that's all. You got a problem with getting her into trouble with the cops? She's been declared *marime*, what more do you need?"

Staley said cautiously, "How much trouble we talkin' here?"

"They're from Homicide, not General Works," said Marino.

"How d'ya know that? They didn't say nothing like that."

"Mama, they showed us a picture of Ephrem—dead," Staley reminded her. "And then started askin' about Yana."

Rudolph added, "Ephrem fingered her as his killer before he

died. He said, 'It was my wife from 'Frisco.' And at the last second he yelled her name, '*Yana-a-a-a* . . .'—just like that."

"How you know all this stuff?" demanded Lulu in a suddenly subdued voice. If Yana was guilty of preplanned murder, she had broken one of the most deeply held *Rom* taboos.

"The bartender at the Hurly Burly in L.A. is a Kalderasha with a pipeline to police headquarters."

"*Why* would she kill him?" asked Staley. "Ephrem never had no money. He always drank or gambled away everything he made."

"This time he had money."

"From where?" asked Lulu with a new gleam in her eye.

"He made a big credit and phone card score at Universal Studios and cashed it in at the Hurly Burly two hours before he died. Bragged that he'd taken a lot of cash and traveler's checks, too. After Yana stuck him and emptied his pockets, she took apart the ceiling light fixture."

"How'd she know he might of hid anything up there?" asked Staley. "They ain't lived together for six-seven years, right?"

"Yana's got the second sight," said Lulu decisively.

No one could challenge this. Staley fell silent. He felt momentarily old, happy to have an heir apparent. Rudolph could do the heavy thinking.

"Whatever she did," said Rudolph, "we have to try and get to her before the *gadje* cops."

Staley took control of things again. "Call to make sure she's there, but go in person, Rudolph. Phones got ears."

five

At forty-three, Dirty Harry Harrigan (his red hair faded to pink by the gray that Just For Men somehow didn't quite hide), had pond-scum eyes and a brass plaque on his desk: FEEL SAFE TONIGHT—SLEEP WITH A COP. He already had in his twenty with the SFPD, and during his years on the force had never fired his weapon at anyone. But his gun, sheathed in latex, was another matter. He fired that at anything hot, hollow, and female he could find.

He tried for Giselle once when she came to Bunco with questions about Gypsies, but she turned him down. He went to what he thought was her apartment anyway; she'd slipped him the address of a radical lesbian women's-rights martial-arts self-defense collective. His evening had ended badly.

Rosenkrantz sank with a sigh into one of the chairs across the littered desk from a brass INSPECTOR HARRY HARRIGAN nameplate that had *Dirty Harry* underneath the name.

"Dirty Harry," he said. " 'Cause they give you all the shit details, right?"

These two guys only came to him when they wanted to pick his brains. He snapped, "You fuckin' guys say that every time you come in here. Say what you want, and leave."

"Madame Miseria. We wanna talk to her."

"Talk to her about what?"

"Police business," said Guildenstern in a cold, dead voice.

Harry felt the chill. "Yeah, well, she's Muchwaya, and I hear they're back in town. Fact is, a Russian barkeep I know out on Clement called to report a Gyppo-looking guy took one of his regulars for half-a-K after trying to steer him to a lady fortune-teller." He shrugged. "Coulda been Madame Miseria."

"Her old man got aced down in LaLa Land last night, died sayin' his wife did him."

That changed things. "Yeah, I remember now. Madame Miseria's supposed to have a mitt-camp out on Geary Boulevard."

"Geary," said Guildenstern flatly, "which runs parallel to Clement—where a guy tried to steer someone to a Gypsy fortune-teller. How come we know more about that than you do?"

After the two big Homicide men had departed, Harry went out to a pay phone. If Poteet's wife had killed him, she now had the money and papers he had run off with two weeks earlier. Goddam her, she hadn't bothered to tell Harry. Probably thought he'd never hear about it.

Yeah, well, he had. He savagely punched out her number. He wanted his cut *pronto*. And she'd better be wearing that see-through red lace bra and those red crotchless panties when he came to collect.

In a suddenly deep, growling voice, the young, beautiful, brightly clad Gypsy woman calling herself Madame Miseria intoned:

> *"Tré báct me çáv*
> *Tré báçt me piyáv,*
> *Dáv tut m're baçt,*
> *Kâná tu mánge sál."*

The merest hint of incense made the air slightly heavy. Yana raised her head to look deep into the eyes of the woman across the table from her. Meryl Blanchett was matronly, mid-50s, but fighting it with a too-short skirt and bright blouse and jangly jewelry. Round face with tuck marks in front of the ears, warm eyes that crinkled at the corners when she smiled.

They were in Yana's *ofica* on Geary Boulevard, in the *duikkerin* room where she did her *boojo*: crystal-ball gazing, psychic reconstructions, and Tarot card readings. The walls were covered from floor to ceiling with blood-red plush drapes to soak up street noise. The only light came from a cantaloupe-size crystal ball glowing between them on a three-foot-square table covered with black velvet.

Back against one wall, a museum-quality Greek icon of St. Nicholas, alive with gilt, shared its tabletop with a ceramic springer spaniel, minus a leg, won at a carnival midway. A cheap ceramic fat grinning Buddha from Chinatown, acrawl with ceramic children, wore a rosary of exquisite Danish floating amber around its neck. Red, blue, and gold votive candles softly lit an acupuncturist's chart that mapped *chi* points of the human body.

Madame Miseria translated in a softer, more feminine voice:

> *"I eat thy luck,*
> *I drink thy luck;*
> *Give me that luck of thine,*
> *Then thou shalt be mine."*

"Yes!" cried Meryl in her soft, I-want-to-please-you voice. "I want to give Theodore back his luck."

"Then go to the place where you two first met—"

"Julius Kahn Playground inside the Presidio Wall just down from my apartment," Meryl interrupted breathlessly. "Theodore has a wonderful schnauzer, Wim, and my little Milli—"

"Your white miniature poodle."

"How did you know who Milli was? I never told you . . ."

Yana thought, Because you flashed its picture when you took out your wallet to pay me last week. She leaned forward to lock eyes with the woman across the gently pulsing crystal ball.

"I know many more things than I wish to know."

Yana was not yet 30, full-bosomed, with lustrous, shining black hair that, let down, reached nearly to her waist. Her oval face was truly beautiful: small, full-lipped mouth and short, straight nose. Her long-lashed, dark, deep-set liquid eyes could be stern or melting, could seem to pierce to the very soul, or fill with all of this world's saddest wisdoms.

More things than I wish to know. Where had that come from?

"Should *you* know them, you would never sleep again." The phone call had changed everything; now she had to rush to the client. "At the playground you will select a blade of grass and take it in your mouth. Then you will turn first to the east and then to the west, and say . . ." And she deepened her voice again to chant:

> *"Kay o kám, avriável,*
> *Kia mánge lele beshel!*
> *Kay o kám tel' ável,*
> *Kiva lelákri me beshav."*

Meryl exclaimed despairingly, "I'll never be able to learn either one of those. I'm terrible with languages."

"I have written out translations for you to memorize."

In her mind's eye she could see Theodore and Wim: a pair of handsome devils. Theodore with touches of bogus grey at the temples, Wim with a magnificent walrus mustache. The pair of them trolling the Presidio Wall for foolish females. A scoundrel, Theodore. He would take Meryl for much more than Yana ever would—including her happiness. Yana would have liked to crush this Theodore like a grape. Or *really* bind him to Meryl.

She sighed inwardly, softened her voice to warm and melodious as she gave Meryl the chant's translation.

> *"Where the sun goes up*
> *Shall my love be by me!*

Where the sun goes down
There by him I'll be."

She said sternly, "You must cut the blade of grass into small pieces and put it into his food—a salad is best. When he eats of it, he will be moved to love you, to be truehearted."

Meryl laid five $100 bills on the table, belatedly kept her hand on them as if fearing that mere money would not buy her what she so desperately sought. Yana was counting on this.

Meryl began, "You are sure this will . . ."

"Nothing is ever sure in this world. Well, I have one other potion that *never* fails, but it is dangerous . . ."

"Oh please! I want it! Anything!" Meryl quickly, anxiously, released the money as if it had suddenly become hot beneath her fingers. "I'm sorry if I seemed to doubt you . . ."

"My grandmother taught me the spells to chant while making it." Yana touched the dimmer switch under the rug with the toe of her narrow black boot. The crystal ball began to glow with a cerulean tinge apparent in its depths. "Those who practice the black arts use their version of this potion to destroy—"

"It mustn't hurt Theodore!" Panic in Meryl's voice.

"Then you must use it exactly as I instruct you." She touched the switch again. The crystal began to fade. Her voice faded with it. "If I give you this potion, then on next St. John's feast day I must go to Golden Gate Park and catch a green frog to put, alive, in an earthen pot pierced with small holes."

"So it can breathe?" Meryl was a gentle soul who belonged to Best Friends, PETA, IDOA, Wild Care, HFA, and ALDF.

"So when I bury it in an anthill they can get in through the holes and eat it alive down to its skeleton."

Meryl shuddered at the deliberate brutality of the image. Pinpoints of light cleverly directed through the nearly dark crystal ball made Yana's eyes glow with an unearthly fire.

"This skeleton I will grind to powder, and mix this with the blood of a bat and dried, ground-up bluebottle flies . . ."

Actually, Yana concocted the potion from a paste of black bean powder, toasted tofu, and water. Her toe moved. The crystal began to pulse rose-pink. Yana put her hands on the table, fingers spread and touching each other, then suddenly drew them back and up and opened her arms wide, materializing a tiny dark and misshapen loaf like a breakfast sausage link.

"This will tie Theodore to you for life. *For life.* Use this and there will be no extinguishing his love for you. Wrap it in your handkerchief and take it home—if you dare."

Resolve tightened Meryl's usually indecisive features as she gingerly picked up the little sausage with her handkerchief.

"I . . . I dare anything for Theodore's love."

"So be it. At your supper for him, serve split pea soup, very hot, then slip this loaf into his bowl so it will dissolve."

"I . . . I don't have enough cash to . . ."

"A check will be acceptable. Five thousand dollars."

This was the carefully weighed escalation, the moment of truth. But Meryl asked, almost timidly, "To Madame Miseria?"

"To my birth name, Yasmine Vlanko." Meryl started writing the $5,000 check. Yana said, "One more thing. You must give him the blade of grass and the potion on the night of the new moon."

Leaving just enough time to open a Yasmine Vlanko account and close it when the check had cleared; in case of trouble, there would be nothing to link Yana to the mythical Yasmine.

She walked Meryl out through the miniature anteroom she had fashioned for possible waiting clients, dimly lit by a *faux* Tiffany lamp with cut-crystal rectangles dangling from the shade to tinkle with the slight wind of their passage. Here the incense was only a shadow on the moving air.

Yana was closing the recessed street door behind Meryl

when she saw two bulky men getting out of a plain sedan three doors down toward Eleventh. They put no money in the meter. The sedan was too plain. The men were too bulky.

The check between her teeth, she made six silken moves to be free of her voluminous parrot-bright soothsayer's gown.

six

Rosenkrantz and Guildenstern paused on the Geary Boulevard sidewalk just off Twelfth Avenue to examine a blue
sandwich board in front of a yellow-brick apartment house. It
bore a yellow outspread hand, palm forward, and the words:

ADVICE ON

PAST   LOVE

PRESENT   MARRIAGE

FUTURE   BUSINESS

"Follow the yellow-brick hand," said Rosenkrantz.

They didn't see the black Cadillac Catera sliding into a parking space across Geary, nor did they see a tall lean man in a
grey suit get out. They were too busy reading lettering on a
draped-off first-floor window overlooking Geary.

PSYCHIC & TAROT
CARD READINGS!
$5 SPECIAL READING!

The narrow entrance was arched in a vaguely Moorish way.
Two steps up in a small vestibule was an inset door with an

OPEN sign hanging on the knob and more lettering on the opaque glass:

MADAME MISERIA
KNOWS ALL . . . SEES ALL . . . TELLS ALL . . .
No secret too DEEP . . . No Future too BLEAK . . .
MADAME MISERIA Can Help **YOU**

"She ain't exactly hiding out, is she?" mused Guildenstern.

Cut-glass teardrops tinkled softly on the Tiffany lamp's phony stained glass shade when the two cops entered the tiny waiting room. A young woman reading a magazine started eagerly from her chair, then subsided in obvious disappointment.

"You're waiting for Madame Miseria?" asked Rosenkrantz.

"Yes." She shot a quick look at the tiny gold wristwatch just above her white-gloved left hand, and added in a low, well-modulated voice, "I had a three o'clock appointment."

Golden hair shone under her white tam-o'-shanter, big round glasses gave her small face an almost scholarly cast. She was slender yet full-bosomed under a white sweater and grey flannel jacket. Slim ankles and narrow black shoes peeped out from under a pleated grey mid-calf skirt. A thin attaché case rested on the floor beside her chair. For a fleeting moment, Rosenkrantz wished he had a daughter like her.

"Maybe Madame Miseria is inside," he suggested gently.

"I used the bell-pull. There was no answer. And the inner door is locked."

Guildenstern said, "Yeah? Let's give her another jingle."

He jerked several times on the silk-tasseled bell-pull. A bell bong-bonged inside. He rattled the door. No response.

"See? She doesn't answer." The blonde stood up, almost theatrically. "What if something has . . . has happened to her?"

"Why would you think that?" snapped Guildenstern.

"One hears . . ." A vague gesture. "Gypsies . . ."

"Just why are you seeing her?"

"*Consulting* her," she corrected. Her eyes, behind their glasses, were abruptly icy. "And I can't conceive of any circumstance under which that would be any of your business."

The cops belatedly hauled out their shield wallets.

"Police officers," they said in unison.

"I see. I do not wish to embarrass Madame Miseria by being here at such an awkward time," said the blonde. "So, good day."

As she picked up her attaché case, the door was opened by a man in a thousand-dollar suit. He bowed gallantly as she swept by him with a distant nod. The door closed behind her. Guildenstern bore in on the chivalrous dude.

"We saw you out in the Mission this morning at a Gyppo hot-TV storefront place."

"Now we see you here at a Gyppo mitt-reader's camp," added Rosenkrantz. "We wanna know why."

Guildenstern held out his hand. "And we wanna know who."

The man slapped a business card down on the open palm.

"Angelo Grimaldi, Attorney at Law. My firm represents the Catholic Archdiocese of San Francisco in—"

Guildenstern said, "What do you call twelve lawyers falling out of an airplane?"

"Skeet," said Rosenkrantz.

Grimaldi went on smoothly, ". . . In certain legal matters. I am trying to serve papers on the woman who, I learned at what you so colorfully call the Gyppo hot-TV storefront, operates here as Madame Miseria. She received a large sum of money from one of the Archbishop's parishioners under dubious circumstances—"

"Pardon my French," interrupted Guildenstern, "but why would the Archbishop give a shit whether one of his flock got scammed by a Gyppo fortune-teller? Ain't going to crystal-gazers against the precepts of Holy Mother Church, like that?"

"Hate the sin but not the sinner," said Grimaldi. "This Madame Miseria was posing as . . . well, as a Catholic nun. In habit. At the cathedral. The victim, an elderly parishioner, believed she was contributing to Renew 2000, and even though her money is gone, she still refuses to believe that, um, Madame Miseria was not a genuine nun. As a result, she is rethinking her very considerable generosity to Mother Church."

"So the Archbishop brought you into the picture to help maintain the cash flow?" Rosenkrantz guffawed. "Sounds like a clear case of assault and barratry to me."

Grimaldi gave him an icy look. "Since Madame Miseria is obviously not here, I bid you gentlemen good day."

When he was gone, Guildenstern said, "Why don't flies buzz Italian lawyers?"

"Even flies got some pride." Rosenkrantz frowned. "You think maybe that guy's a little slick for the holy-water crowd?"

"We'll soon find out." Guildenstern punched out a number on his cell phone. "And since this Yana Poteet is our number one suspect for scragging her husband, at the same time we'll get us a search warrant all proper-like to enter the premises."

Before a uniform arrived with the warrant, they learned that the Archdiocese had never heard of anyone named Grimaldi. When the landlord opened the apartment, they found an expensive crystal ball glowing with an eerie blue light in the *duikkerin* room. On the kitchen stove they found a frying pan full of incense smoldering on low heat. Guildenstern turned it off. In the bedroom, Rosenkrantz opened the closet door with his fingertips. A diaphanous dress in brilliant red, yellow, and purple hung from a rod facing the room. He held it up in front of him on its hanger.

"Is it me?" he asked.

Guildenstern, dragging a chair under the old-fashioned light fixture in the middle of the ceiling, snorted in disgust.

"Get useful. Gimme a hand here."

Rosenkrantz steadied the chair. Guildenstern studied the fixture at close range. He grunted. "Dust, not dollars."

Only dust in the other light fixtures, too. They took turns washing their grimy hands at the kitchen sink. They did not find either Madame Miseria or Yana Poteet.

"That blonde rubbed me the wrong way," said Guildenstern.

"I liked her. The daughter I never had."

Belated alarm scrunched up Guildenstern's features.

"No back door to this dump, we're comin' in the front, and this blonde is sittin' in the waiting room." He suddenly snarled, "The daughter you never had! Between us, forty-five freakin' years on the force an' we watch our suspect waltz right past us out the door in a blond wig. Now I'm pissed."

Rosenkrantz nodded. "What do you call two policemen buried up to their necks in sand?"

"Not enough sand," said Guildenstern hollowly.

Yana rode a 38 Geary/Fort Miley Muni bus away from her invaded *ofica*. It stopped to let an old woman off where the great onion-shaped spire of the Russian Orthodox Cathedral of the Holy Virgin glinted gold in the sunshine. A little priest with a black habit and a bobbed grey ponytail used a big carton of candles to push open one of the twelve-foot-high gilded doors.

Three wise-eyed recent-émigré Russian teenagers got on the bus. They would have been baiting Madame Miseria in an instant; Yana, in her business suit, glasses, blond wig, and attaché case, drew only indifference. They were foreigners, but they had one another. She had nothing. She could no longer be Madame Miseria. She could no longer be Yana Poteet. Since she had been ejected from the Muchwaya, she could no longer even be a Gypsy. At times like this, yearning for the *kumpania* was like a lingering terminal illness. She had made a fateful decision when she learned to read. It had been a skill like any other, something that would enable her to *go* somewhere in life, win a place of honor in the tribe, and some of the advantages of the *gadjo* world. Instead, the *gadjo* knowledge had put a barrier between her and the Muchwaya. They had become uncomfortable with the change in her, and called it ambition. Whatever it was, she could see herself how far it had removed her from tribal wisdom and racial cunning. They had been *gozever* to ban her.

Now Ephrem was dead, his poor, sad silly cache above the light fixture rifled. And she had no nation, no tribe, no clan, no *kumpania*. Her brother, Ramon, would help her if she asked him, not because she was his sister but because he feared her powers. At heart he would always be a loyal *Rom*. Why endanger his standing with the tribe? It was up to her to make the final break from them or be swept under.

But she was so weary. The words of the dying Gypsy came back to her. "Bury me standing—I've been on my knees all my life."

seven

It was dawn. Trinidad Morales, barefoot, nude, carefully pulled aside dusty cream drapes with little roses on them to look out into Florida Street. *Madre de Dios!* He never really expected it, but there *was* someone sitting in a car outside . . .

One of them? He swiped a hand down his smooth brown face. Until the beating, a well-fed, round face with a gleaming gold tooth and hard little eyes that missed nothing. The tooth still gleamed, the eyes still missed nothing: but were they hard?

Down inside, where it mattered, *he* was no longer hard.

And without that, what was he? A *conejo*, a scared little rabbit. Even, perhaps, a *cobarde*—a coward. He'd always heard that a really tough professional-type beating took away something that you never got back, but he'd never believed it. Now he did.

The four of them had jumped him outside this apartment. He remembered the husky Latino opening the car door in front of him . . . The terrible blows to the kidneys . . . Dimly, the kicking boots, the wash of blood on the concrete . . .

And the face, brown like his own, so close to his as he lay bleeding on the sidewalk. Whispering the words . . .

You touch my sister, man, ever again, you with the dead.

Might as well be. With the dead. He hadn't touched any woman since then, because she might be *the* woman. Who had she been? Junior high school girl? Wetback *chica*? Neighborhood kid? *Taquería* waitress? Any of them, no matter how vulnerable to a man like Morales, might have a tough, fanatic, vindictive brother with a posse of his own.

It was not knowing which way to look that unmanned him.

That and the brown, whispering face so close to his.

With the dead, man.

He went into the bathroom, shivering in the morning chill, to reach around the plastic shower curtain and turn on the hot water so the stall would get good and steamy.

He'd told Kearny after they'd hit the auto dealership that he had to go home because he didn't feel good. That had been a lie. Physically, he'd never felt better. The lost weight, the convalescent's diet, the months of rehab . . .

But deep down inside, he was scared. Before the beating he would have looped back on his own backtrail, followed them until he had identified them, then dealt with them, one by one; for each, a beating for a beating. In fact, when the medics thought he was going to die, hatred of a face and a name—*Esteban*—pulled him through. But later hatred turned to fear. Coming back here late from repo work some night, would he find them outside this apartment waiting for him in the darkness?

Stop, Esteban! Stop! You have killed him!

The girl's voice. But not her face. Not her name.

Trinidad Morales, unfeeling, cold-eyed, cold-hearted tough guy, once one of the best dam' repomen around, was too goddam scared to go looking for the man who had done this to him.

Because this Esteban, whoever he was, had many *amigos* . . .

While Trin Morales had none.

Receptionist Jane Goldson's desk was by DKA's front door, Kearny's at the far end of the office. In between were the skiptracers and clerical staff who faced the street through steelmeshed windows. In case of legal trouble, Jane could stall while Kearny slipped upstairs or out the rear door to duck service.

Giselle was stuck behind Dan's desk while he was out of town and the rest of the field men were out running down those scrumptious classic cars. As office manager she recognized the necessity of it: as a field agent she didn't have to like it.

Ballard plunked down in the client's seat across the desk.

"I noticed the look on your face when you were behind the wheel of that sweet little red Alfa," he said. "What d'ya think that STATO license plate stands for? Status symbol?"

" 'Stato' is 'state' in Italian, the car's an Alfa Romeo, *ergo,* Alfa State, and you're right, that's what that little car puts me into, a state of bliss." She sighed. "I can't afford it."

"It'll go for only six, seven K at auction, and I bet Stan the Man would give you terms, maybe even knock down the price."

She shook off her longing. "You have anything for me?"

"Like a classic car repo?"

"Exactly like that."

They'd worked together for some nine years; there had been a time when they'd thought . . . but friendship and professional regard were better in the long run. The moment passed long ago.

"We got no paper trail," said Larry.

She lifted resigned shoulders while indicating the files open on the desk in front of her. "You get behind this desk and find one, Hotshot. I'll go into the field and have some fun."

"Yo mama," he said. He hiked his chair closer. "I talked with Stan at the bank yesterday. For some reason, they don't want to auction off the classics we've already brought in."

"He wants a full set. I'd love to have 'em all in the barn by the time Dan gets back from Chicago."

Ballard's frown drew vertical lines between his hard blue eyes and above his hawk nose.

"Wiley lives in a nice 'hood. What bothers me is him show-ing up in that Toyota at the dealership. I thought he'd be driving a classic."

"You're a genius, Larry! The Corolla's gotta be his wife's ride, bought and paid for. They switched cars." She grabbed the phone. "I'll check the registration and run them both through a credit rating service for relatives and references."

Larry was on his feet. "I'll go out and chat up his neighbors, then call in for whatever you dig up."

"Call in? You?" She laughed. "That'll be the day."

The hunt was on; suddenly she felt fine. She didn't even miss her cigarettes. She forgot she was still behind a desk.

The Wileys' brown-shingle two-story at 313 El Camino del Mar had an under-the-house garage and the steeply slanted roof wore a brass weather vane in the shape of a frisky whale. Two square bays gazed out through white-curtained double windows.

Ballard wore a drab tie with a small, tight knot as hard as a Calvinist's mercy, and a nondescript blue suit five years out of date. Unneeded clear-glass specs peeked out of his breast pocket. He carried the private eye's greatest prop, a clipboard.

Plod up terrazzo steps, ring-ring. A dissatisfied woman in her thirties, obviously just got husband and kids off, sitting down with the newspaper and her third cup of coffee.

"Good morning, ma'am. I'm with the Underwriters Bureau. We're conducting interviews in selected upscale San Francisco neighborhoods about the make and model of automobile each member of your household drives . . ." And her neighbors' cars? Nothing.

Buzz-buzz. A seventy-something retiree with bristling eye-brows.

"Good morning, sir, here's my card—the Underwriters Bu-reau of the National Auto Agency. We're surveying . . ." No.

Knock-knock. A brown face, tight, reserved, watchful.

"Good morning, ma'am . . . Oh. *No habla inglés?* The lady of the house is . . . Yes, I see, thank you . . ."

On his seventh house, across the street and down three from Wiley's, he caught a break: a lanky teenager with a spotty chin and an almost-shaven head was home with the flu, Classic Coke in hand. Jeans three sizes too big just barely hung on snakelike hips. Loud rap music came to the door with him.

"I've been watching you work the street for the last hour, and you never write anything down on that clipboard."

Little brother is watching.

"Between you and me, I'm a repoman after information."

"Cool! Remember that movie on cable—*Repo Man?* This one scene, Harry Dean Stanton is hiding out in a hospital room and he gets away just before the cops bust in. One cop says, 'Where is he?' just as the preacher on the TV over the bed says—"

" 'He is risen.' " Ballard had his arms spread wide like the Sermon on the Mount. They both burst out laughing.

"So whose car are you after?"

"Big John Wiley's."

"That jerk? He drives a '62 Corvette roadster, white body with a red interior, 327/auto trans, Wonderbar radio, all original. Yesterday morning he went off in his wife's Corolla, she left in the 'Vette. 'Cause of you, right?"

Bingo. "Have you seen the Corvette around since?"

He shook his head. "Another lady looked like Mrs. Wiley only younger drove her home about noon in a 2000 gold Saturn so new it still had paper plates. She stayed a couple of hours."

Larry shook the boy's hand. Smart kid. Observant kid.

"You ever want a job as a private eye, give us a call."

"I'm going to college in the fall." The boy said it in an almost disappointed voice. "Harvard."

They usually were, though not always Harvard.

Larry called in. "Like you thought. They switched cars."

"Terrif!" said Giselle, sounding just like Kearny. "Eloise has a sister in Pacifica, Mrs. Ellen Winslett. A week ago she registered a new—"

"—gold Saturn?"

"I *told* you that you guys always have all the fun."

"Seven'll get you twenty Wiley's wife tucked the '62 'Vette in her sister's garage to leave us scratching our—" He stopped. "What's that Pacifica address?"

"Just a sec, something on Palmetto Ave—"

"North Pacifica. This isn't one of those houses red-tagged when the bluffs started sliding after all that rain in January and February, is it?"

"Palmetto is back from the bluffs." She gave him the number, then added the favorite line of Kathy Onoda, who had been her predecessor as DKA office manager until a CVA had cut her down at the ripe old age of twenty-nine. "Go gettem, Bears!"

eight

The delegates to the annual convention of the National Finance Adjusters, Investigators, and Repossessors crowded the sprawling new Congress Plaza Hotel and Convention Center on South Michigan Avenue in Chicago, toddling town, meatpacker to the world, fog on little cats' feet, etc. A plush air-conditioned conference room insulated them from the unseasonable May heat wave.

Over the decades the National had gone respectable. In the early years it had been skits that made fun of deadbeats and racial minorities in smoke-filled back rooms. When the dawn came up like thunder from Kalamazoo across the lake, you woke to a horrible, splitting, hangover headache with a woman from some raucous after-hours Rush Street strip-joint sharing your bed.

Now, Dan Kearny just wanted to get back to San Francisco so he could oversee the recovery of the missing classic cars. Maybe he could slip out, find a phone . . .

But the man at the podium said, "And now, with no further ado, I give you our featured speaker, DKA's own Dan Kearny . . ."

No heat wave at Pacifica. Plenty of sun, but a strong onshore breeze to bring in chilly air, and soon, an afternoon fog bank unusual for May. More like August. Slanting Palmetto had some of the most breathtaking ocean views anywhere in the

Bay Area, but the developers had, as usual, built the houses facing each other across the street instead of the blue Pacific. Duh.

The wide slanting driveway of the ranch-style Winslett house held a 2000 gold Saturn with paper plates. The attached one-car garage was shut. Because the Corvette was in there?

Larry pulled a U-ie, parked, got out with his repo order in one hand, in the other a set of pop keys, two heated and bent screwdrivers, and a three-prong hotwire. Tools of the trade now almost as classically outmoded as the '62 'Vette itself.

No kids playing in the street, no curtains twitching on the windows facing Larry from the far side of the road. He cupped his hands to peer in through the Winsletts' garage-door window.

Yeah! The Corvette was between him and a washing machine against the back wall making dissonant slosh-gurgle harmony with the adjacent dryer's thunk-whirl. He swung up the overhead door to slightly spronging springs. Give him sixty seconds . . .

Not to be. The inside door was nudged open by the hip of a very pretty blonde of about twenty-five who backed in toting a double-armload of dirty laundry. When she saw Ballard, she dropped her laundry. He almost held up crossed forefingers to ward off evil: pregnant women were dynamite, and she was extremely pregnant. But the best defense was always a quick offense.

"Mrs. Ellen Winslett?"

At her name, the panic began ebbing from her face. "Y . . . Yes?"

He dug out a DKA card, remembering too late that it was one of Kearny's; he'd run out of his own. "I'm, uh, Dan Kearny, here to take physical custody of this Corvette. It is out of trust and California-Citizens Bank has put out a recovery order on it."

"I'm . . . I can't . . . It isn't our car . . ."

"Exactly. Out of trust and in the hands of a third party. I'm

glad you understand." The washer stopped. Against the contin-
uing thunk-whirl of the dryer, he said, "Can I get those clothes
out of the washer for you, ma'am?"

"No, I wait until the dryer's stopped before— Say, are you
allowed to just come onto someone's property like this—"

"Oh, yes, ma'am"—making it up as he went along—"under
California chattel-recovery rule 19350E we can enter any unlocked garage to effect recovery of the bank's legal property."

She gave a rueful little laugh and shrugged prettily.

"I'll go get the keys."

She returned with not only the keys but two cups of tea.
They sipped and chatted like old friends. She even stood outside on the sidewalk watching him put the Corvette on the towbar. She smiled ruefully.

"I'm glad Garth isn't home. He tends to get . . . physical."

"Then I'd better be gone before he gets here."

Irate husbands defending pregnant wives he didn't need.
But he went back to shut the overhead door for her. Even big
with child she was aware of herself as a woman, and he liked
her.

As he topped the hill, the Corvette riding comfortably behind his truck on the towbar, a red Cherokee passed him going
the other way. He caught a heavy-faced, stubble-bearded profile behind the wheel. Something in that red face made him
keep his eye on the rearview. *Garth tends to get physical.*

The Cherokee stopped, the man turned to stare intently at
either Larry's truck or the Corvette on the towbar. At thirty yards
and moving, Larry couldn't tell which. Then he was over the
brow of the hill; too late for the husband, if that's who he was.

Bart Heslip had drawn an UpScale Motors salesman named
Romeo Ferretti. Romeo was supposed to be living in an old Victorian clinging to steeply slanting Elizabeth Street, which, half a
block above, banged its pretty nose on Grand View Avenue.

There probably was a grand view down into Noe Valley

from the second-floor bedroom windows; certainly the willowy young man—"that's Chuckie with an 'ie' "—seemed eager to take him up for a look. Bart declined.

"Do you know when, Mr., ah, when Romeo will be back?"

Chuckie made a pouting face. "Well, I hope never. He just moved right out with my absolutely divine 33 1/3 RPM set of Wilhelm Furtwaengler's *Götterdämmerung*."

"No! To take *anybody*'s recording of *Götterdämmerung* is *Götterdämmerung* cheek, but to take *Furtwaengler's!*"

Chuckie with an "ie" started to giggle.

"Oh, make fun, I deserve it. But the Berlin Philharmonic *is* the best recording. He took our cat, too." A sly sideways look from long-lashed eyes. "Pussy Galore."

"I saw the movie."

"Are you a . . ." Chuckie repeated the eye-thing. "Friend of Romeo's?"

"Never met him." Bart half-pulled an envelope from his inside pocket, thrust it back down again. "Insurance. He reported an accident, some damage to his car . . ."

"Oh no! Not that *adorable* old Ferrari convertible!"

"The very one," said Bart quickly. It figured. What would someone named Ferretti try to embezzle except a Ferrari?

"But Romeo's *such* a careful driver!"

"Ah . . . do you know where I might find Romeo now?"

That's when Chuckie started to cry.

As the AIDS threat became old hat because new and more powerful drugs were prolonging sufferers' lives, attractive young gay males with no sense of history started a new party craze in the Castro District. They assembled at someone's apartment with the understanding they had to leave three things at the door: their clothes, their condoms, and all talk of HIV.

Romeo became addicted to such gatherings, and at one met "a simply *devastating*"—Romeo's very own words—older man, a doctor recently retired from U.C. Med Center. Just like that,

Romeo had gone to live on the medico's big estate down in the very expensive Peninsula community of Woodside.

"The Marcoses used to have a home there," said Chuckie in a wistful voice as he dried his tears.

"If the shoe fits . . ." began Bart, decided the joke was too obscure, unthinkingly added, "and now Romeo lives there."

More boo-hoos. Bart felt like shedding some salt himself when he checked out Chuckie's gold address book that had a lascivious Proteus frolicking with some suspiciously male-looking nymphs on the cover. The doctor's name and Woodside address were smeared over with black ink. All Chuckie could remember was Herbie-something on—could it really be?—Bare-Something Road. Or maybe, he giggled, it was on Bare-Everything Road.

Bart tried U.C. Med Center with his cell phone, got told by Personnel that they never gave out the names or addresses of anyone who worked there or had ever worked there or might be contemplating working there in the future.

He called it in to Giselle for some skip-tracing. Perhaps because she had an M.A. in history from S.F. State, she took the long view of the Castro District's heedless gay sex parties. It was the doomsday scenario, she told Bart, and then launched into a psychological explanation that to him explained nothing.

When she ran down, Bart said, "The last millennium ended with a whimper so I'm going to do the same to start this one?"

"Exactly! *Fin de siècle.* In 1900 tuberculosis—what they called consumption then—was the romantic death. In Y2K it's AIDS. Up two-point-three percent in San Francisco."

"Yeah, romantic as hell. But you're still just as dead. Now, how do we go about finding Dr. Herbert-Something?"

Giselle giggled. "Bare Something . . . maybe Bare Mountain?"

"Naw, that's Bald Mountain and it's in San Anselmo."

"Come take me to lunch, Bart, I'm getting cabin fever. I bet I'll have something for you by the time you get here."

Though DKA had long since entered the computer age, Giselle immediately came up with one of the old standbys she still secretly preferred: the crisscross directory that listed by address rather than name. She had it by the time Bart arrived.

Herbert Greer, M.D., 72 Bear Gulch Road, Woodside.

Now, to find out whether Romeo, his Romeo, really wert in Woodside. Or rather, if the Ferrari wert. After dark for that.

Lulu picked up the ringing phone and musically told it, "Ted's TV Repair, if it ain't broke, we can fix it anyway."

The strong, rich, well-known voice of Willem Van De Post said in *Romani*, "Lulu! How is my favorite aunt?"

Lulu chuckled. *"Me ávri pçándáv čoreskro báçht!*—I tie up the thief's luck!" Then she added, "It must be very late in Rome. How is Stanka? How are the little ones?"

"Not so little. Rita runs an office here *a Roma* and is planning marriage, Nani will graduate from university in June, and Giuliezza just started her first year at Bologna."

"University," Lulu said disparagingly. "And marriage to a *gadjo*, I bet! You are ruining those children."

"Times change, Aunt Lulu. To be *Rom* in Europe right now is a hazardous thing." He lowered his voice. "Is Staley there?"

Staley was in the shop, selling three VCRs that had fallen off a truck right in front of a fellow Muchwaya the night before.

"This is Ted."

"I have information best given in person. I will come to California. We must meet discreetly. It is all very delicate."

When he heard Willem's voice, Staley switched instantly to *Romani* and leaned closer to the phone, even though the two *gadje* buying the VCRs couldn't understand a word he was saying.

"The zoo is always a safe place to meet."

Willem laughed. "You have a sly mind, uncle."

They set the day and time, then Staley hung up and met the

inquisitive eyes of the men buying VCRs at a price that made it obvious they were hot.

"What was that lingo you was using?" asked one of them.

"Arabic. My people are originally from Lebanon. My nephew want to borrow money." He chuckled merrily. "Is what relatives are for—to borrow money."

nine

Heslip was buying Giselle lunch at a new fancy SOMA restaurant. Ballard was dropping off the Wiley Corvette at the Cal-Cit Bank storage lot below Telegraph Hill. And salty old repoman O'Bannon was across the Golden Gate getting himself lost while searching for an UpScale salesman named Timothy Bland. Lost in the Marin County community whose local fire truck he had once repossessed for a truck-sales company. Oh shame! Oh woe!

Bland was supposed to be living on Toyon off Currey. What could be simpler, even on Tam Valley's steep, heavily wooded, impossibly twisty house-crammed streets?

Except Currey Avenue didn't intersect with Toyon after all. O'B decided, after a lot of map study, that Toyon came off Currey Vista. It didn't. Then it had to come off Currey *Lane*. No, Currey *Lane* came off Currey *Vista*.

So Toyon had to come off Curry Vista. It did. Except its street numbers didn't come anywhere near the number Ken Warren got from Benny Lutheran of the broken nose. But on a narrow blacktop lane called Toyon Court that dipped discreetly downhill off Toyon, O'B found the number he had been given for Tim Bland.

It was a two-story redwood duplex clinging to the downhill side of the street with steel fingernails. The concrete floor of the empty double carport beneath the duplex wore an encouraging puddle of oil. A classic would lose more oil than a new car.

Nobody home at Bland's lower apartment. Nobody home upstairs, either, except a grey and white tabby cat O'B could just hear meowing through the double-glassed front door.

Work the neighborhood, ask questions of everyone in sight. Except there was no one in sight, and Tim Bland could be driving any one of the seven missing classics—or none of them.

Pardon me, sir, I'm looking for a guy driving a car. Sure.

The next house downslope was a typical California hillside cantilever: the carport on the roof and the bedrooms in the basement. An old woman with mad eyes held up her cell phone just inside the door and repeatedly pantomimed punching 911.

O'B went away. She's somebody's mother, boys, you know.

The next cookie in the jar was a heavyset guy who answered the door in mid-afternoon wearing only morning breath. He would never star in a porno flick, that was for sure.

"Yeah, whadda fuckya wan'?"

"I'm trying to get in touch with Mr. Bland—"

"Earn a hones' livin' you come aroun' knockin' on my door."

"Could you tell me what kind of car Mr. Bland—"

"Push a hack nights, pay my taxes, don' beat th' wife." *Wife?* Loneliness could do strange things to a woman. "Summich sold me a lemon of a Honda once. Summich ain't home."

Slam! Sound of sliding deadbolt. And nobody home at either of the other two houses. Sometimes it went that way.

Go get some lunch, scattering corn behind him so he could find his way back again. Then just keep checking the address until Tim Bland showed up. Or, abysmal thought, didn't show up.

O'B climbed wide wooden stairs to Houlihan's restaurant on Bridgeway, and sipped nonalcoholic O'Doul's in the bar while waiting for his table. Until 1937, Sausalito was a sleepy little Portagee fishing village with only the ferries connecting it to

San Francisco across the Bay. Then the Golden Gate Bridge went and ruined everything by making it accessible by auto.

A voice at his elbow eerily echoed his thoughts.

"Things descend to awful goddam hell."

Zack Zanopheros was a private eye who organized court cases for prominent defense attorneys. He was a grinning bearded compact man O'B's own age, whose bright, zestful eyes crinkled up at the corners when he smiled. He wore a cashmere sports jacket, dark slacks, and shiny black loafers with tassels. He plunked his half-emptied bottle of Beck's down on the polished mahogany.

"Let me buy you a beer."

O'B returned his grin. "Sure. How's tricks, Reverend?"

"I let the computers do the work and I play a lot of tennis. How's the repo business?"

"We still get to go out and thug cars."

Zack nodded sadly. "You can't do that by computer." A half-hour later he was still toasting "the good old days," when the loudspeaker intoned, "Zack, party of one."

"Let's make it a party of two," Zack said quickly.

Only when the maître d' led them to one of the front-window tables that faced the far gleaming tumble of San Francisco across the Bay did O'B realize that Zack had been buying him full-bore Beck's instead of O'Doul's.

Aw, *shucks!* What was a fellow to do?

Staley Zlachi strolled with other midday patrons through the turnstile at the San Francisco Zoo—still called by old-timers the Fleishacker Zoo—and paused at the top of the concrete steps. He watched glowing pink flamingos dip black scimitar beaks into the wading pool. The hot grease from the concession stands smelled good to him, as did the clean, rank animal smells. From the primate house came the booming *hoo-hoo-hoo-hoo* of a howler monkey. He moved on to the orangutan habitat, where the dominant male, hulking and dish-faced, was out on the ramp leading to their concrete house.

"Magnificent, isn't he?" asked an accented voice.

The man was bulky but very fit, early 60s, dressed with European punctiliousness in a dark solid-color suit, somber tie, white shirt, and highly polished black shoes. He had a large square head and ashy hair slightly thinning over the forehead. His blue eyes were sad and piercing and merry all at once.

"Orangs were mentioned in the Linnaeus classification texts of 1766, but the first individual was not brought to Europe until the nineteenth century. Now they are extremely rare in the wild, even though extremely intelligent." He sighed. "Habitat destruction is making them extinct."

Only then did Staley turn so they could shake hands. As he did, a woman and three small children bundled up against the chill ocean breeze came up to the railing near them. The two men immediately switched to *Romani.*

"How are you, Willem? What is this I hear about Rita?"

Willem chuckled. "It is true. In the fall she will marry a *gadjo*, a fine Italian lad. I know, I know, you do not approve. But remember . . ." The bundled-up family moved on. The two men returned to English. "I am *didâkâi*—half-*gadjo*—myself. All *gadjo* by blood, but by upbringing—"

"The story is legendary," said Staley. "You were an orphan, six years old, on the open roads of Holland during the war. *Mami* Celie scooped you up and made you part of the *vitsa.*"

"Grandma Celie." Willem shook his head fondly. "How I loved that woman! She taught me how to live with one foot in the *Rom* world and the other in the *gadjo* world. She dealt in the G.I. black market at Porte Portese so I could go to school. But I forget my manners. How are you, Staley? And Lulu?"

"We're fine." He paused sadly. "Well, we got a situation. One of our *kumpania* killed her husband in cold blood. We think there's a lot of money involved."

Willem crossed himself while shaking his head. "Money is

good but murder is bad, very bad, bad for all *Romi* everywhere."

"We gotta deal with it. To do that we gotta find her first.
Trouble is, she's living in the *gadjo* world and knows how to
avoid us. She's very smart."

"You need some *gadje* to help you look."

Staley's eyes suddenly flashed. "Hey! Maybe you got something there! I know this guy . . ." He paused. "But hey! What
about *my* manners? You're here for our help with a recovery
problem of your own."

They ate cheeseburgers and fries and drank coffee at one of
the little round tables near the concession stands. The hot
grease not only smelled good, but tasted good to Staley, too.
Willem told him all about Robin Brantley in Hong Kong, and
Victor Marr, and the Yakuza gangster named Kahawa.

"What could Robin do? The Yakuza threatened his life."

"And now Marr has it here in California."

"At a fortified mountaintop facility near Big Sur." He told
Staley all he had learned about Xanadu. "Brantley says he is
willing to help. But will he stand fast and not falter, not go to
Marr through his fear of physical violence?"

"We gotta bigger problem," said Staley. "The way you describe this Xanadu, my people just don't have the sort of training and expertise ya need to get into a place like that."

"Ah, Staley, there is always a way," said Willem gently.

And sure enough, there was. Another hour of talk between
these two sly men, and they had it. A crazy way. A brilliant
way. A *Gypsy* way.

Ballard meant to go right back to the office after dropping
off the Corvette, he really did. But he'd been at the dojo again
until 2:00 A.M. the previous night, practicing for his first-degree
black belt, then had been up early to check out Big John
Wiley's neighborhood. The day had snowballed from there.

So he decided to go home to his two-room studio apartment facing Golden Gate Park across Lincoln Way, make himself a pot of his signature coffee, grab a shower and shave and change of clothes. Then he could pull an all-nighter if he got any hot leads.

As he started up the hall wrapped in a cloud of steam and a big shaggy towel, Midori Tagawa came in the street door behind him. For two years he had shared the shower and bath with this porcelain-doll Japanese exchange student who rented the tiny back apartment. During those same two years he intermittently waged a gently unsuccessful seduction campaign against her.

"Hello, Larry, no see you, long time." In her high little voice, soft as eiderdown, it was more like, "Herro, Rarry."

He bowed elaborately. "Ah so, long time. How's school?"

"Cost a lot. I got part-time job now."

He had lent Midori a semester's tuition, hoping she'd maybe pay him back in exquisite golden flesh. But her bookkeeping was scrupulous and her body remained inviolate. A few months ago they came close. He caught *her* coming from the shower wrapped in just a towel, which slid down her body just as she disappeared into her apartment. Accident? Deliberate? He'd been involved elsewhere at the time, so he'd never tried to find out.

"Menswear," Midori added obscurely.

"Menswear?"

"Nordstrom's, Stonestown. Sell menswear."

Ballard had on very little menswear. Just his towel. And there was a draft in the hallway of the old two-story Victorian. A shiver ran through him.

"You cold," Midori said quickly. "You come fo tea."

"I'm not dressed for it," said Ballard.

That's when *his* towel fell off. Through no conscious agency of his own, honest. But still, revealing the tumescence of long abstinence and the remembered tantalizing glimpse of Midori's taut ivory haunches and glowing golden thighs all those months ago. She put a hand up over her mouth and giggled.

"You come as you are, Rarry."

Then that exquisite little hand reached out and took hold of Rarry's distended handle and led him down the hall to mutual ecstasy in her tiny, scrupulously neat apartment.

ten

The intercom on Kearny's desk buzzed. Giselle flicked the switch. Jane Goldson's clipped British voice came tinnily from the other end of the room. She was speaking in low tones.

"There's a Mr. and Mrs. Winslett here to see Mr. Kearny and they have their knickers in a twist."

Watching them come down the office toward her, Giselle heard a lot of alarm bells going off.

Winslett was a big bristling man, six feet and over 240 pounds, with a red lined face and a stubbly brown beard and the wide mouth and glittering blue eyes of a blustering, first-class bully. A not unfamiliar type in the repo trade.

The woman was petite, big with child, with long straight blond hair and a face that normally would have been very pretty. But she had a split lip and a swollen purplish jaw and a black eye and a feverish look. Her short-sleeved maternity dress was grease-smeared on the left hip. Her left elbow was skinned. Giselle could almost smell the fear coming off her.

A *lot* of alarm bells.

"I wanna see a fucker named Kearny!" yelled Winslett. "Look what he did! My wife is eight months pregnant and—"

"You're saying he assaulted her?" Giselle was furious.

"Punched her out, knocked her down—after he took an axe to my garage door. Then he stole my brother-in-law's car." He slapped down a sheaf of Polaroid photos on the desktop. "I got pitchurs. So what're you gonna do about this?"

Giselle turned to the almost-cringing blonde.

"Mrs. Winslett, are you saying our field man did this to you in the course of effecting a totally legal repossession?"

Her good blue eye—the one not swelled shut—met Giselle's steely gaze with a sort of panic. She spoke in a half-whisper. "I . . . it happened like my husband says."

As Giselle started out of her swivel chair imperiously, Winslett's ham-size hand came up to push her back down. But his arm was halted in mid-movement by a hand as large as his own. He was staring into Ken Warren's slate-cold eyes.

Ellen touched Giselle's arm, her face pleading. "Please."

They looked at each other, woman to woman.

Giselle said, "Kenny. It's all right."

Warren released the arm, jerked a thumb at the door.

"Hnowt!" he barked. "Hnah!"

Winslett wavered, then grabbed his wife's wrist, yanked her after him so hard she almost cried out. As they went through the back door that led to the street, Ken Warren started after them.

Giselle called sharply, "No, Kenny, let it lie!"

"Na'll knust mnake hsnure hney gnow."

Make sure they go. She sat down shakily. She desperately needed a cigarette, but didn't have one. What in God's name had Larry done down there in Pacifica? And where was he?

Larry parked in the fenced lot behind the office. He felt loose and easy and had a foolish grin on his face. Two hours with Midori. He went in to sit down across from Giselle.

"What did you *do* down there in Pacifica?" she demanded.

The look on Giselle's face got through even his post-Midori euphoria. "Do? The Corvette was there so I took it."

"Street-parked?"

"In the garage. What—"

"Garage locked?"

"No. The overhead was down but it wasn't—"

"Mrs. Winslett was in the garage with you?"

"Yeah, she came in with a load of dirty laundry just when I was hooding the Corvette. Why the third degree? Did I forget to genuflect when I came in?"

"Why did you use Dan's name?"

"I gave her one of Dan's cards 'cause I was out of—"

"Winslett says you took an axe to the garage door, which was locked, that his wife walked in on you during the repo, and that you beat her up so you could get away with the car."

Well, hell, and he had liked the woman, too. "Did she show you any bruises or scrapes or anything?"

"Larry, she'd been beaten up, believe me. Really bad. A black eye and a split lip, bruised jaw, skinned elbow . . ." Giselle was thinking like the office manager of a hard-nosed repo agency again instead of an empathetic woman. "We're in trouble. They've got our card, they've got photos of the axed garage door, I bet they've got photos of her all banged up . . ."

"I'll go down and talk to the neighbors tonight. Somebody'll have seen him chopping at that door himself—"

"You'll not go near that place, Larry Ballard! You'll not go near Pacifica. And you're off the classic cars right now."

"Hell, I don't want to back off those classics, I—"

"She's Wiley's wife's *sister*, for God sake! You stay away from that house and those cars!"

In the early years of the last century, word of something like Ephrem Poteet's murder, probably at Yana's hands, would have traveled up and down the highways and byways in the old Gypsy *patteran* (leaf) or trail language.

Are the campfire ashes still warm? Has rain partially obliterated footprints and wagon ruts? Drop a handful of grass at a crossroads. Draw a cross with chalk or look for one made with two sticks (always check which arm is longer). A notched stick, a woven pattern of twigs in a low bush, feathers stuck on a tree, hairs from a horse's tail, a strip of bark, a rag . . .

Nobody used *patteran* anymore, not in the States, but the phone was the Gypsies' new trail language. Most still defiantly could not read or write, but all of them could talk. *Devèl*, how they could talk! And the talk was of nothing except Ephrem Poteet's death at the hands of his wife, Yana. Then word went out that a *pomana* would be held for Ephrem in Point Richmond.

He died in L.A., they had no body to bury, and since his meager possessions had been impounded as evidence, they could not be burned or smashed in the traditional *Romi* way. But still they would have their ritual feast of fruits and grains in his honor even without a body to lie in state with gold pieces on its eyelids.

Just at dusk before the streetlights came on, they drifted up the hill to Rudolph Marino's dark-shingled house in Point Richmond across the Bay from San Francisco. They were relatively few in number, maybe a dozen, with no small children; the event was solemn and few of the *kumpania* had known Ephrem personally.

Rudolph was living in Point Richmond because most of the permanent Muchwaya residents of the Bay Area lived in Richmond, and because his Florida hotel scam collapsed and he had to get out of Palm Beach quick. He was wary of leaving his footprints across the plush carpets of upscale hostelries for a while.

Point Richmond, once called East Yard, was the oldest part of that East Bay city. In the 1970s, its houses, stores, restaurants, and churches were repainted, restored, and revived. It was sandwiched between the San Rafael–Richmond 580 skyway—beyond which lay the Chevron oil refinery—the railway yards, and the slowly awakening Richmond harbor.

In matters of ritual, nobody was more exacting than Lulu. It was she who had organized the *pomana*. But Staley wanted to use the occasion for his own purposes after his conference with Willem. What he planned was for the good of the *kumpania;* but like any monarch, he knew that his subjects needn't always know everything he was doing on their behalf. This was the ideal time to unveil the plan. The most influential members of the tribe were here.

Yana was a major if covert topic of gossip among the *Romni* preparing the traditional meal.

In the modern appliance-filled kitchen a willowy teenage girl named Pearsa Demetro began to lay out the Tarot cards, softly chanting an old Gypsy incantation from Tuscany in a clear high voice:

> *"Venti cinque carte siete!*
> *Venti cinque diavoli diventerete . . ."*

Lulu shushed her, and to the accompanying giggles of the other teenagers added sternly, "Yana's husband is dead, so a song about cursing your husband is close to *marime*."

But as soon as Lulu turned away to tend the stove, Pearsa laid out another card, studied it, then started another stanza.

> *"Diventerete, anderete*
> *Nel corpo, nel sangue nell anima."*

"No more!" exclaimed Lulu, really angry this time. "You don't know how powerful that is!"

"But *Mami*"—she used the honorary term for grandmother—"I don't have a husband. I'm just practicing."

Like Yana, Pearsa had been born with a caul over her head, which gave her many powers—the second sight among them. So Lulu could not bring herself to object when the girl chanted the final stanza.

> *"Nei' sentimenti del corpo*
> *Del mio marito . . ."*

eleven

After the ritual fruits and grains, the *pomana* grew boister-ous, as wine loosened tongues and limbs and sharpened memories of the deceased. The *zengin saz* played, weaving a long road of melody back to a time and place only the oldest of them remembered, but where they, and Ephrem Poteet, had nevertheless been together. The men danced their souls, heav-ily, but with grace. Women set down their dishes and reached for their *daires* and tambourines. Staley, sensitive to the mo-ment, signaled the musicians, who called to the dancers with a *Bibke bibke bibke romke udt!*, bringing them together to the strains of *naçti uçava*. He cannot get up. Ephrem had fallen on the *Longo Drom*, but they were people of the road. If they lis-tened, they could hear his *darbuka* made of clay playing now.

Staley, *Baro Rom* of the Muchwaya, nodded the band to si-lence, and began to speak a ritual opening in *Romani*.

"By your leave, *Romale*, assembled men of consequence, heed my words. A journey lies before us. In my hand I hold an invitation from the Holy Father himself. This year marks the two thousandth birthday of Holy Mother Church. We were in Rome before the Church was born. We were among those who built it. And now our *tabor* shall be there for the canonization of one of our own, Ceferino Jiminez Malla!"

He had used the word *tabor*—a large group of related Gyp-sies traveling together in horse-drawn wagons—deliberately, and was gratified that many responded to the dream. There was a buzz of astonishment in the room. Few of them knew the saint-to-be, but none would admit it. The first ghost of a challenge was raised by Josef Adamo, who scammed the *gadje* as a paving contractor. He had an important stomach and greying ringlets and black eyes that missed nothing.

"We should have been planning this a year ago. Nearly five months of Millennium year have passed. We should be there now."

Sly Lulu had asked him to raise the question to forestall other challengers. By arrangement, Rudolph Marino answered for Staley. Being the heir apparent, he was listened to as closely as the King himself.

"We will be there next month, believe me. With six months to carry out our plans. There is the promise of a very quick and very large score."

"Promised by who?" Adamo asked bluntly.

Staley smote himself on the chest with a clenched fist.

"By your King."

There was a smattering of appreciative laughter. Nobody was better than Staley at finding ways for the Muchwaya to score.

"I am satisfied," Adamo said formally, and sat down.

But then Wasso Tomeshti said, "We must go in style as befits American Gypsies returning to the homeland."

When not working, he was the most traditional-looking of Gypsies: a day's beard, twirling mustachios, a red bandanna around his thick neck. When working, he shaved and wore suits and bought electronic appliances with checks that bounced, then sold them with phony service warranties at cutthroat prices out of storefronts rented by the week in big-city low-income areas. The government never saw the sales taxes he collected.

"To this end, I can offer all of my brothers the very best deals on cell phones, beepers, pocket calculators, travel clocks, earphone radios . . ."

Staley waited for someone to question him about the myriad details attendant upon such a move, details he might have forgotten himself, which was not so uncommon these days. Again it was Adamo who obliged him.

"How do we finance such a journey?"

Before anyone else could speak, a female voice asked, "And what will we do once we are there?"

At this last, silence fell over them. Pearsa Demetro, who had sung the incantation over Lulu's objections, had so far forgotten herself as to speak out in a formal *kris*.

"GO!" Staley roared at her. "Go, wash the dishes!" He waved a peremptory arm. "All of you *cshays*, go!"

The four teenage girls fled into the kitchen in frightened silence. Staley turned back to the adults.

"The voyage will pay for itself once we are there. But . . . to get there . . ." He paused dramatically. "I have a plan. It is based on the trust the Muchwaya have for their King."

"I will hear my King!" declared Nanoosh Tsatshimo.

His specialty was bogus electroplating. He operated in Jewish neighborhoods and indeed, looked more Semitic than *Rom*. It was he, backed by Sonia Lovari, whose scam was as a Native American, who first called for a formal *kris* to declare Yana Poteet *marime*. His reasons, unlike Sonia's, were traditional.

Staley let his eyes flash with delight, patted his paunch.

"Good! Then I will tell you what will be necessary if we are to succeed. Each Muchwaya clan—Johns, Millers, Costellos, Ristiks, and Steves—must contribute one-third of all the money they make to our common travel fund for the next month."

"How can we do that?" Voso Makri asked softly. He was a startlingly handsome blue-eyed Greek Gypsy with a great shock of golden hair, recently arrived from Thessaloniki. Not yet well known in the *kumpania*, he was said to have computer skills equal to those of Rudolph himself. "The Bay Area is Kalderasha territory. We can barely eke out a living here, let alone contribute a third of our meager gleanings to the *tabor*."

Perhaps encouraged by his objection, Sonia Lovari spoke up. She wore buckskin and a long plait of black hair down her back because her con was as the last living member of Ishi's tribe.

"I can go on my own much cheaper than to share with—" She stopped abruptly, then finished up almost lamely, "With some who do not carry their own weight."

"But Sonia," said Staley, "who are we individually, you and I, without our *kumpania*, without our *tabor*?"

Rudolph said bluntly, "I am already working on our travel plans. We will all go together, as the nation of Muchwaya."

Staley reminded them of the millions of pilgrims already in Rome for the year-long Catholic celebration of the Church's 2,000th birthday. The Holy City overflowing with celebrants from every nation on earth, many of them deeply religious, more of them country bumpkins, most of them ignorant of credit cards and even traveler's checks. There they all were with money in their pockets—and with their arms upraised in praise of God.

Immaculata Bimbai, who was blond and looked like a countess, spoke up. She was 32 and looked 22, and her scam was fainting in jewelry stores.

"*Baro Rom*, what of the Italian *Romi*? We are American Gypsies, will they not resent us?"

Staley spoke sagely.

"Are we not pilgrims like any others? For fifteen hundred years the *Romi* have been going to Rome for pilgrimages and canonizations. Our people were the Papal envoys across the face of Europe during the Middle Ages."

Posing as Papal envoys, thought Rudolph as Staley pontificated in English, but why put too fine a point on it?

"That is another reason we gotta raise a lot of money quick—so we don't work no hardship on our European brethren. I have many plans, plans which will astound you. But first—do we have agreement? If so, you all gotta see Lasso here to get passports, and you gotta pay for them yourselves."

Lasso looked pleased. The Gypsies glanced at one another. They hated to pay for anything, but their imaginations were fired. Were they not all in accord? All but Sonia Lovari, on her feet once again.

"*Baro Rom*, we cannot leave this city until the soul of our dead brother, Ephrem Poteet, has been consoled. What are we going to do about his wife, Yana Poteet—the woman who murdered him? I spit upon her shadow, I would curse her progeny except the syphilitic whore will never be able to bear children."

Everyone knew that Sonia hated Yana for telling a *gadjo* repossessor where to find the Cadillac Sonia was driving. Letting her initiate a witch-hunt would only interfere with their search for Yana on the sly. Lulu rose to speak in council for the first time that night.

"Yana Poteet is a disgrace as a *Romni* and no longer a member of this *kumpania*. We have already in solemn *kris* declared her *marime*, so leave her to the *gadje* justice. Murder is a blasphemy that breaks even their teeth. They will avenge our dead brother for us."

Staley had them in the palm of his hand. He spread his arms wide in benediction, every inch the King.

"Now go, my children, to bring glory upon this tribe!"

The three of them were at last alone in Rudolph's kitchen. By candlelight, Lulu looked old and worn.

"Best way to go to Rome to bring this glory on our tribe is find Yana and get back for the *kumpania* the money she stole from Ephrem's body," she said.

"Or for ourselves." Rudolph made a deprecatory gesture. "We shall not forget Yana."

"We don't know the *gadjo* world well enough to find her in it," Lulu said.

"Since we can't find her ourselves," said Staley, "we have to get someone to look for her who *does* know the *gadjo* world."

"Who?" demanded Rudolph with surprise in his voice.

"The repossessors with whom we dealt in the matter of the thirty-two Cadillacs. Daniel Kearny Associates."

Rudolph started to chuckle; it grew into open-throated laughter as he savored the irony. Lulu, lost in her fears of retribution should they break the *marime* curse laid on Yana, hadn't yet caught on. She finished the last of the memorial mixture of wheatberry, cinnamon, honey, and sultanas before objecting.

"How we gonna get them to do our looking for us? Last time around they was hunting us down like dogs."

"This time around we're gonna *hire* 'em," chortled Staley.

twelve

The spring fog came over the crest to flow down the eastern slopes of the Coast Range, and it was a dark and stormy night.

Well, not stormy, but man was it dark. And foggy. Bart Heslip pulled into a closed Standard station on Woodside Road to study his battered *Thomas Guide Atlas* for San Mateo County. Keep on Woodside right through town, maybe a mile, and Bear Gulch Road went off to the right.

Beyond town it was inky, no streetlights: horse country, big-tree country, sprawling-estate country. Most of the roads and lanes and drives leading off Woodside didn't seem to have any street signs on them, at least not street signs that Bart Heslip was able to see.

Out near Sears Lake, Woodside Road just . . . ended. He got turned around and went back, his wipers on intermittent, driving five miles an hour with his flashlight angled out the open window so he could eye every track and driveway and road coming in from, now, his left. Cold wet early-hours air brought grass and horse smells and beaded his face and sent a shiver through him.

Finally. A brush-obscured sign: BEAR GULCH ROAD.

He backed up, turned in. Narrow blacktop, twisting and turning up the slanting side of a tree-covered hill. Dark, dripping foliage, drifting fog. A quarter of a mile in, the road widened to a flat area the size of a basketball court, with a black steel gate set in concrete and flanked by chain link fences. By the gate was a board with a number pad beside an intercom phone. No good without the correct combination.

Bart sighed, backed into the rear right corner of the lot, and settled down in the forlorn hope of somebody coming in or going out of Bear Gulch Road at one in the morning.

The 1995 Panoz kit car, sleek and low and gleaming ($39,995 on Giselle's hotsheet), made a hard right past a red-headed guy asleep in his car on Toyon and into the carport to park over the oil stain O'B had noted earlier. The car was one of the greatest tools in Tim Bland's seduction kit, but not the only one. Tim was in his early thirties with dark good looks and crisp shiny black hair and bright very direct blue eyes that sold many used cars to female customers; many found him handsome and slightly dangerous and went to bed with him. One would tonight.

Bypassing his apartment, he walked down the blacktop in the drifting mist, his shoes scraping subdued echoes from the tarmac. He had sold the woman's husband a Honda, one thing had led to another, so now he had something juicy and frustrated and available waiting right on his doorstep.

He'd called ahead, so he went by the unlocked door and into the living room already rock hard. The night taxi driver's blond wife was waiting for him, leaning forward over the back of the davenport wearing only black lace crotchless panties and a lascivious expression. He entered her from behind, spent almost immediately. They went into the bedroom and Bland sat down on the side of the bed to unlace his shoes. He had plenty of time to finish her off before her old man's shift ended at 6:00 A.M.

She knelt on the bed behind him.

"You'll get a kick, Mr. Wonderful said some redheaded guy woke him up in the middle of the day with a lot of questions."

"Yeah?" Bland spoke with scant interest. He had long since decided that you only had to *seem* to listen to women.

"Questions about you."

Bland was suddenly all attention. "About *me?*"

"What kind of car you drive, where you were, like that. Jake ran him off." She reached around him with eager fingers. "Hurry up, honey, you got my motor running . . ."

Bland was indeed hurrying. He was already off the bed, pulling up his pants. He had no doubt at all that the redheaded man asleep in his car up on Toyon was after the Panoz.

"Listen, Vix, I gotta go. Be out of town for a few days."

"Whadda ya mean, outta town?" Anger was clouding her face. "You got *your* rocks off, what about *my* rocks?"

Bland knotted his shoelaces. "Save 'em till I get back."

"Save 'em?" she shrieked. "Why you rotten . . ."

Her curses followed him out of the house. There were a thousand Vixens in this world, only a few Panoz cars. Twenty minutes later he was swinging the sleek shiny auto up out of Toyon Court past poor slumbering O'B, who obviously had overpoured during his late lunch with Zack Zanopheros.

Bart Heslip, out of his car to shadow-box beside the front fender, had just knocked out Oscar de la Hoya with a really nifty combination when approaching lights and swelling engine noise swung the Bear Gulch Road gate silently inward. Immediately after a Lexus exited, Bart drove through as the gate swung shut.

The blacktop hairpinned back upon itself half a dozen times in the first mile of steep, heavily wooded hillside. A big mule deer buck, eight nascent points of velvet-covered scimitar antler adorning his head, poised on the edge of challenge in Bart's headlights for two breathless heartbeats. Then he threw his black nose into the air and bounded off down the slope.

Around another hairpin, so tight and steep there was a mirror set at its apex to let drivers see approaching vehicles, a pair of fat-butt raccoons scuttled across in front of him. Their masked bandit faces wore sneers and their beer bellies rolled from side to side as they scrambled up the slope with their thieves' honor intact.

Bart parked a dozen yards beyond the luminous numbers 7 and 2 tacked to a tree on the right-hand side of Bear Gulch. He killed engine and lights, sat listening to the night sounds and the creak of the cooling engine. Then, leaving Giselle's hot-sheet on the front seat, he locked up his DKA Taurus and started back toward the driveway, disappearing down the hill-side carrying only his repo tools and a flash.

A petite orange tiger-stripe cat was sitting in rapt attention beside a decorative koi pond in front of the rambling redwood-and-stone house. Obviously the Pussy Galore purloined by Romeo Ferretti from his former partner Chuckie up in San Francisco. Big slow drifting submarine shapes below the dark surface held the cat enthralled. The good life, cat-style.

Yeah! Bart's careful flashlight showed the Ferrari parked in plain view, its nose against a stone-and-concrete retaining wall at the end of a widened-out parking apron. The top was up; moisture had collected on the sleek coachwork.

No visible lights in the house, but their bedroom might be over the two-car garage facing the driveway. Bart boldly tried the driver's side door. Unlocked. Didn't even have to use his picks on the old-fashioned wind-wing such cars sported. When he opened the door, the light under the dash showed him a stubby between-seats gear shift. He reached in, popped it into neutral. Hand brake already set. He swung the door almost shut without slamming, so the interior light would go out. Piece of cake.

That's when the rude beast inside the garage started roaring and slamming itself against the closed overhead door. But Bart already had the Ferrari's raised hood resting on his back, lean-ing into the engine compartment with his flashlight between his teeth. He clipped the hotwire to the distributor, found the hot post of the battery, laid the third prong of the wire against the double posts of the solanoid.

rrrRRRrrr rrrRRRrrr rrrRRRrrr VROOOOOOOOOM!

A window went up. He stepped back and slammed the hood.

"Stop! Thief!"

Stone chips flew behind his right shoulder, *crack!* and *crack!* again. Something touched his left ear with a hot finger. A third shot merely spattered more stone chips.

A voice shouted, "No! Herb! My God, don't shoot my car!"

Bart had dropped and rolled in tight against the side of the Ferrari away from the house. Ablaze with excitement, he swung the door open above him and snaked himself into the driver's seat. He'd never been shot at before—not in earnest. It was terrifying and exhilarating.

He couldn't back the low-slung Ferrari up to the street without bottoming out, and the bank wanted its car back in one piece. He did a classic bootlegger's turn on the concrete apron to end up facing the steep driveway for his run up the slope.

A two-hundred-pound Rottweiler, obviously raised on raw liver—raw *human* liver—raced from the garage to launch itself at his still-open door. Bart kicked out savagely just as the massive beast left the ground. His heel slammed into the short crinkled nose, the dog spun away going *yowp! yowp! yowp!* in astonishment. People didn't do that to him: he did that to people.

Bright-beam lights shone in Bart's rearview and another powerful engine roared behind him. Coming up into slanting Bear Gulch Road, he swung right, *uphill,* running without lights, racing past his own parked car. Over the crest, out of sight, *stop!,* kill the engine, hope they turned downhill.

Downhill, his pursuers might catch up with him before the gate could open at his approach. Since the Ferrari was on no cop's hotsheet, only DKA's, they could shoot him and get away with it—*but officer, we thought he was a car thief.*

He went on, using his lights now. Away clean. After a mile, he became aware of a dull throb in his nicked ear. Lucky the upholstery was leather. Easy to clean the blood off it.

O'B came up behind the wheel of his car with a start. Four A.M., two hours after bar-close. Head full of ache, mouth full of the all-too-familiar dirty sweatsocks. He checked the carport. Empty. He groped in the glove-box for his emergency flask, tipped it up to his lips. Empty, too. Damn!

Tim Bland wasn't coming back tonight. Time to go find a twenty-four-hour gym with a sauna, soak out the alcohol. His wife, Bella, was going to be really pissed. O'B drove away into the fog.

thirteen

The fog had broken early; sunshine blessed the Marina District's wide quiet morning streets. When Harriet Nettrick's doorbell rang at North Point and Broderick, she saw on her terrazzo stoop two young nice-looking men she took to be Latino. Each carried a workman's long metal toolbox. The panel truck in the driveway wore the familiar Water Department logo.

She opened the door. The one with FRANK sewn above his tan uniform's pocket said, "Mrs. Nettrick? We're from the Water Department. A chemical contaminant has gotten into the pipes for this area and we have to eliminate it. Can we come in?"

She opened the door. "My goodness, I hope it isn't—"

"The kitchen, ma'am?" He was all business. "Syd, you go check the upstairs bathroom."

Syd went up the stairs as Frank followed Harriet to the kitchen and across its old-fashioned inlaid white tile floor to the sink.

"Could you get me a water glass, please, ma'am?"

While holding the glass under the cold water tap he let a fragment of crumbled Alka-Seltzer slide down its inside, then turned to her with the glass of foaming liquid in hand.

"This isn't the way your water usually looks, is it?"

Harriet put her hand to her breast in shock. "Oh my Lord!"

Down on his knees in front of the sink, Frank opened his toolbox. It held wrenches and screwdrivers, rolls of soldering wire and electrician's tape, and any number of odd-looking tools. For the next twenty minutes he was under there, twisting things, grunting, tapping metal tubing with the back of his small pipe wrench, having Mrs. Nettrick hand him a variety of objects from the tool kit. Finally Syd appeared in the doorway.

Frank demanded, "Were the bathroom pipes corrupted?"

"Level three."

"Same here. We got it in time!" He went back under the sink, tightened something, gave a couple of grunts, backed out awkwardly, stood up to wipe his hands on a maroon cloth from his back pocket. He rinsed out the glass, filled it anew, and held it up before Harriet's dazzled eyes.

"See that? Crystal clear." And he drank it down to show her how innocuous it had become.

Because they were such nice boys, who had saved her from who knew what lurking chemical horror, Harriet wanted to tip them even though they solemnly assured her it was not necessary.

Several hours later she realized all her cash and credit cards from the purse she had left beside her easy chair in the living room were gone, as was the money from her bedside table. So were her silver and jewelry.

At about the same time the *kumpania* took its share of Frank and Syd's take.

While Mrs. Nettrick was calling SFPD Bunco—much too late, of course—diminutive Midori Tagawa was almost selling sweet old Mr. Stabler the wrong size shirt.

This was at the menswear department of the big fancy Nordstrom's department store in the Stonestown Mall way out off 19th Avenue. The shirt was a red and black check lumberjack with a brown cloth log cabin sewn to the back of it. Midori was still heavy-lidded and almost languid from yesterday's lovemaking with Larry Ballard, still unfocused.

"Midori, are you sure that's the right size for him?" asked a low voice in her ear.

For a second Midori thought it was an *inner* voice, a Zen sort of thing, then realized it was the other saleswoman on the men's department floor, a Guatemalan of Baltic origins with the exotic name of Luminitsa Djurik.

Midori blushed and put her hand over the lower part of her face. She giggled nervously. "I no so good at sizes yet."

"I am," said Luminitsa. She was a long-legged, slenderly voluptuous woman with long black shiny hair and dark exotic eyes and an oval face. She raised her voice so Stabler could hear her. "This shirt is preshrunk, sir, so there is no need to buy a size too large against shrinkage in the first wash."

"Say again, miss?" He gave them a small, sweet smile. He was short and shaky, but his faded blue eyes behind severe gold-rims bubbled with good cheer, and his silvery hair had an absolutely stunning pewter sheen. "The hearing's the *second* thing that goes when you get old."

Luminitsa moved in for the kill, a warm big-sister smile on her gleaming red lips. Midori knew this was a common tactic, taking over the sale a new salesperson had already made and grabbing the commission. But she was secretly grateful: it was so easy to lose face by not pleasing a customer.

"Grab those two young guys just coming in," urged Luminitsa *sotto voce* as she turned away with the old man firmly in tow, her arm through his. Her dark eyes gleamed, her almond skin glowed. "You come over here, Mr. Stabler, I have some other things you're just gonna love."

"Mr. Stabler, that was my dad," he said spryly. "I'm Whit, that's short for Whitney . . ."

After she had sent Whit Stabler away with a shopping bag full of menswear, Luminitsa asked Midori, "How'd you do with those college kids?"

"They no buy anythings. They just keep asking to take me out fo drink after work."

"You gotta be more aggressive, kid. You won't even make

your draw unless you get in there and make people want to buy. I put everything Whit bought on your number, by the way."

Midori's hand started up to cover the bottom part of her face. "But I only talk to him about that one shirt . . ."

Luminitsa pulled the hand back down.

"You aren't in the land of the rising sun here, kiddo. People think either you got bad teeth or you're hiding something. Fair is fair, he was your customer. But next time he comes in he's *mine*, girl!"

"How you know he come back, Luminitsa?"

"Once they've seen Luminitsa, they always come back."

Larry Ballard, he come back for more of Midori last night. Maybe he come back again tonight, too. He say he come back. Maybe he no able to get enough of Midori. But to be safe, she better make sure he didn't see Luminitsa.

The intercom buzzed. Victor Marr said curtly, "Yes?"

"Hong Kong is on the scrambler phone, sir."

Marr picked up to hear Kahawa's flat, dry, sibilant voice.

"Marr-*san*, Brantley has heard rumors that the man in Europe is planning to try and recover what he considers his property."

"Does he know this man's identity?"

"No," said Kahawa. "But he suggests you beef up security . . ."

"My security up on the mountain is excellent," said Marr coldly.

"Mr. Brantley has a great deal of experience in security matters—before the Colony was reunited with Mainland China. He has used a security specialist from Germany and found him very satisfactory."

"Couldn't hurt," said Marr. "Get his name for me, and I'll hire him to double-check our precautions."

*   *   *

Josh Croswell was a tall, slim man of 31, with a ready hand-shake and a smile full of wonderful teeth. Cultured and elegant outside of business hours, he had cried when Evelyn Cisneros retired as *prima ballerina* of the San Francisco Ballet. But when the young couple entered the store, he circled like a shark smelling blood in the water around a crippled seal. A *pair* of crippled seals; a *lot* of blood.

Croswell's jewelry patter was like the man himself, precise and practiced and *so* sincere. He knew little about fine gems, but the upscale tourists shopping this Post Street store knew less.

This pair was almost laughably perfect. Computer types up from Silicon Valley to the big bad city to celebrate either an engagement or a wedding; and either way, ready, nay, *eager* to pledge their troth by spending some of that Internet IPO money. Almost as eager as Josh was to help them spend it.

The man was maybe twenty-four, with dark hair parted in the middle and slicked straight back to give his face a surprised look. His glasses were heavy horn-rims and his fingernails were manicured.

The girl could not have been over twenty-two, slight and honey-blond and shy, clinging to his arm as they came through the door. Life had not yet written any interesting messages on her perfect face, but she had a figure that deserved a porno Web site of its own. Not Josh's gender of preference, but he could go either way. Right now he was strictly business, at his smarmy best.

"May I be of assistance?"

"I . . . we . . ." The girl colored, and the man picked it up. "My, ah, fiancée . . . Ah, we would like to see some, ah, rings."

"Diamonds, of course?" Josh was already indicating two trays of their most expensive items. "I think you will find—"

"Oh Donny, they're all so gorgeous!"

"Yes, ah, they sure are, darling. We'll make the final choice together, but I want *you* to come up with the possibles."

Donny moved farther down the counter with a slight head-jerk. Josh followed. The girl was so engrossed in the locked display case of rings that she barely noticed them.

"My fiancée's name is May," Donny said in a low voice.

Josh almost said, And the month is May. So? But he merely kept his expression of polite interest. Donny was impatient.

"She was *born* in May. Her birthstone is the emerald."

The light dawned. "You want to get her an emerald ring."

"No." Donny made a quick negative gesture. "May will be using her grandmother's diamond wedding set, but I want to surprise her with an emerald. A *good* emerald."

"All of our gemstones are of excellent quality," said Josh, thinking of one they had in the safe that looked wonderful but that . . . well . . . according to Mr. Petrick, had some hidden flaws not apparent to Josh himself. "I have something in the office that I think might be exactly what you're looking for."

A relieved and boyish smile lit up Donny's features.

"Cool. I'll be looking at rings with May."

The emerald was impressive and *big*—15 carats. Josh kept an eye on the surveillance camera as he extracted it in its chamois bag from the safe, but May and Donny were heads-together over the diamonds, oblivious to all about them.

Donny said to Josh, "We can't make up our minds over three of these, so if we could see them together . . ."

Josh unlocked the cabinet, set out the trays with their choices. He kept keen-eyed watch as May examined the rings with awe and wonder on her face.

"Can we . . . can you set aside . . . ah . . . hold all three of them for us until I can get my mom in to help us decide?" Anxiety filled her face and voice. "I mean, if you sold one of them before Mom saw them, well, then I'd always wonder if . . ."

"We will put them safely aside for you, madam."

"May darling, you'll be late for the bridal shower if—"

"Oh my God!" She hugged Donny, kissed him so quickly that she got the air an inch from his face rather than his lips, and careened out of the store on her teetery high heels, one hand holding her ridiculous red hat on her head, calling behind her, "That little bar off the St. Francis lobby at five o'clock."

Donny leaned eagerly toward Josh. "Okay, let me see it!"

With the solemnity of a medieval bishop bringing out a local saint's miracle-working gallstone, Josh removed the chamois bag from his pocket. He opened the drawstring. The 15-carat emerald slid out across the felt on the glass top of the display case to lie winking like an idol's eye in a Sax Rohmer novel.

"Is it all right to pick it up?"

Josh gave him a calculatedly condescending chuckle.

"Certainly. Body acid from your fingers cannot damage a gemstone." Donny had laid it reverently on his open palm. "It has a typical emerald cut—rectangular girdle with truncated corners. But . . ." Josh took the stone back, turned it over so it looked like a tiny Aztec pyramid. "See the cuts like steps from the girdle, the flat top of the stone, to the culot at the point? A Portuguese step cut, giving the maximum number of facets when you look down into the stone. Most unusual."

Josh had expended his emerald expertise. He didn't know that the low price his boss put on the stone was because of a slight yellow tinge and an occlusion hidden within its depths. But his scanty knowledge seemed all that was needed.

"How . . . ah, what does it cost?"

Mr. Petrick, Josh knew, would be delighted if he could sell the stone at $12,500 retail. But if Josh could move it for more, Mr. Petrick needn't hear of the extra money.

"Twenty-five thousand dollars," he said decisively. "As is. Of course a setting would cost—"

"No, no setting," exclaimed Donny with a sort of alarm, "I don't want it made into a ring or anything. Just the emerald itself. So May can choose exactly how she wants to wear it."

Josh could barely keep the glee and greed from his voice.

"Then you wish to purchase it?"

"Do I . . . Oh, yeah, *sure!* It's so great!"

Josh would not only collect commission on the $12,500 of the sale he was going to tell Mr. Petrick about, but also pocket the entire $12,500 he wasn't. Now came the sticky part.

"How did you wish to . . ."

Before Josh's astounded eyes, Donny jerked up his shirt to show a canvas money belt strapped around his lean middle. From its pockets he began pulling great wads of fifties and hundreds.

"We'll take the money over to your bank so you can make sure it isn't counterfeit . . ." He paused, obviously struck by a thought that alarmed him. "You *do* gift-wrap, don't you?"

fourteen

By day, Woodside wore a much more benign, bucolic aspect than on a dark and stormy night. Green and rolling fields stretched forever, white-fenced, dotted with expensive show horses and rambling homes like English country estates.

Everything bucolic except Larry Ballard's big mouth.

"I can't wait to see where you got shot in the rear," he said from behind the wheel of his truck, not for the first time.

"That's *ear*, not rear," gritted Bart. Man, it would almost have been worth it to *walk* down here from the City to retrieve his car, rather than have to listen to Ballard.

"But the blood on that Ferrari's leather driver's seat suggests you were sitting on your wound—"

"Slow down, slow down, it's right up here," snapped Bart.

The Bear Gulch sign seemed quite visible by daylight. A BMW convertible was just turning in. Larry put on his blinker.

"In the inky darkness the owl of death hoots. Blood spurts from Curt Hero's shot rea—"

"I'm warning you, Ballard."

They followed the BMW through the opened gate and up the road. Bart's eldery DKA Ford Taurus was still in the turn-off beside the road. Larry pulled in behind it.

All four tires were flat.

Bart sighed and started to get out. "Don't say anything, okay? Just call me a tow truck."

"Now?" Larry got out and punched the Triple-A button on his cell phone. Then he told Bart, "Okay, you're a tow truck."

"Hyuk, hyuk, hyuk." Bart crouched to examine the tires. He straightened up. "Tell Triple-A we've got four slashed tires and only one spare. Tow truck driver's gonna have to bring an extra wheel so he'll have two tires to tow it in on."

"How the hell did they know it was your car?"

Bart grimaced in near-agony. "I left Giselle's hotsheet in plain sight on the front seat." Before Larry could open his mouth, he added, "Don't even think about saying it."

"It," said Larry, and started laughing so hard he had to re-peat everything twice to the Triple-A road service agent.

Never ever live this one down. Never in a thousand years.

Trin Morales plunked himself down across Kearny's desk from Giselle. Hadn't slept worth a damn last night.

"What do you have for me?" asked Giselle crisply. She liked Trin a bit better now that some of his cockiness was gone.

"Colton Lewis has skipped from the Russian Hill address," he said. "No wife, no kids, he was renting furnished." He made a fly-away gesture with a stubby brown hand. "Vroom. Oklahoma stickers on his suitcase."

"I doubt that. If he's driving one of those classic cars, Lewis will be lying doggo somewhere in the City with it. I bet Big John Wiley still thinks of all of those demos as his."

Actually, she knew how hard this kind of assignment was. Even *if* this guy Colton had a missing classic, which one?

"I'll get one of the girls to do a DMV check for any cars Lewis might actually own. Meanwhile, get on the neighbors, see if they know what he drives."

For a moment his old superior smirk almost curved Trin's thick lips. "I did that yesterday. Nobody could remember."

"So write a field report about it, Hot Shot."

Morales grunted and levered himself from his chair. As he disappeared up the stairs, Kearny's private line rang.

A thick male voice asked, "Kearny there?"

"Not at the moment. If I could take a message—"

"You know when he will be?"

"If you could tell me what—"

Click.

The voice had sounded like that of Staley Zlachi, the King of the Gypsies. But why would he be in town? And why calling Dan? She shrugged. If it was important, he'd call back.

Josh Croswell was on top of the world. He had sold a flawed emerald for twice what it was worth and was going to report only half the take to his boss. But then super-nerd Donny walked into the store with a worried look and no May on his arm. Josh found a suitable expression to paste on his face.

"I guess you've come to a decision about which diamond ring you want . . ."

"No, I'm here about the emerald. We've got big trouble."

"Ah . . . the store policy is, ah, no returns after—"

"Returns?" Donny was frowning. "Oh, no, no, I don't want to return it. I want to buy another one just like it! May says she wants to set them side by side in a platinum brooch."

A huge jolt of adrenalin whirled through Josh. He thought: I can hit some of the gem-exchange Internet Web sites that Mr. Petrick uses. There have to be 15-carat stones around, maybe even one or two with that unusual Portuguese step cut. *I can fill this order.* Donny was still talking.

"You find me an emerald that May's Mom can't tell from the other one, and I'll pay you $75,000 for it. In cash."

Seventy-five thousand! And Mr. Petrick *wasn't due back* until next week. Find that duplicate stone, sell it to Donny for 75K, *and keep the net money for himself!*

He couldn't get Donny out of the store fast enough. After

he put up the CLOSED sign, he rushed back to the office, and started scanning the gemstone Web sites on the net for emeralds at offer. Finding nothing even close, he put out his own message:

Wanted immediately: single emerald, rectangular, 15 carat, Portuguese step cut . . .

Geraldine Tantillo exited through the impressive inset portico—flanked by four double sets of Ionian Greek pillars—of Brittingham Funeral Directors. She was a somewhat overweight woman in her late 20s, and could hardly wait to get to a lesbian bar on 20th off Castro for her nightly glass of white wine. She was *beat*. Came from hating your job. She lived just a few blocks away from the bar and it had become her local. She could nurse a single white wine through a whole evening, the girls were friendly, and the bartenders knew her name. Just like *Cheers*.

Sappho's Knickers was a warm, narrow place that kept the lighting dim, the drinks strong, and the old-fashioned juke loaded with romantic oldies made for dancing cheek-to-cheek. The dance floor was so tiny that while dancing with one girl you'd be rubbing butts with another. A turn-on indeed for a lonely lesbian lady from Dubuque.

Not that Geraldine did much dancing with anyone: she was too shy to ask and not pretty enough to often get asked. But tonight she had been there only a half an hour when the most beautiful woman she had ever seen sat down across from her.

"I am Yasmine Vlanko," the woman said.

Yasmine Vlanko was ageless: she could have been 18, she could have been 48. Her hair was long and black and lustrous, her eyes deep pools, her teeth small and gleaming between beautifully rounded lips. Her lithe full-bosomed figure was

clad in skintight black leather, like Emma Peel wore in the old
Avengers show that sometimes still appeared in rerun.

"And I'm Geraldine Tantillo."

Poor Geraldine knew instantly that she was in love. As if
sensing this, Yasmine leaned toward her across the table.

"Please, do not form fantasies about me, Geraldine. I am
celibate because I have dark and powerful energy fields that
shift in dangerous ways when I have sex with anyone." Indeed, Geraldine could feel that energy enveloping her. Yasmine continued, "I felt *your* energy from across the room. You
are troubled. I often can help those in trouble. A year ago you
came to San Francisco from . . ." She shut her magnificent eyes
for the moment, opened them. "Somewhere in the Midwest . . ."

"I . . . Dubuque, Iowa," Geraldine heard herself saying. "I
had a good beauty salon job in Dubuque, and I had a secret
lover—Ariane. I was happy. But Ariane said she . . . yearned
for the open minds and heady freedoms of the west."

"And she betrayed you."

"On our second weekend here." Geraldine realized that
tears were running down her cheeks. "She ran off with a hot-
eyed Latina salsa dancer and my seven thousand dollars in
savings."

"So you were stranded," murmured Yasmine Vlanko.

"Yes. And finding a job was horrible." She gestured at herself. "I'm shy. I'm overweight. I have no color or clothes
sense. Not a problem in Dubuque, but here, all the beauty salons are run by Vietnamese or French or Italian women who
hire by nationality or percentage of body fat, I'm not sure
which. Not one of them would even take my app. I finally got
a job in a funeral home doing cosmetic and hair work on
corpses."

"And you have hated every minute of it," said Yasmine. She
reached across the table to take both of Geraldine's hands in
hers. She closed her eyes. She crooned something under her

breath. She opened her eyes again. "Quit your job," she said. "Then meet me here a week from tonight at ten o'clock—and I will change your life forever."

She let go of Geraldine's hands. She stood. Geraldine stood also, impelled by forces she couldn't understand.

"Here," said Yasmine. "One week from tonight. If you have quit your job, your life will be changed forever."

And, somehow, she was gone.

fifteen

The Ferrari was in the barn, safe and sound. But the Great White Father was going to be unhappy when he saw *this* month's expense account, thought Bart Heslip as he zipped north on the beautiful Junipero Serra freeway. A tow job, four new tires—all had been slashed too ferociously to be saved. He fingered his discreetly bandaged ear. It was itching.

The Taurus started missing. He checked the gas gauge. Half-full. Now backfiring. It was a repo out of Minnesota that Kearny bought as a company car after the client balked at transporting charges back to Minnetonka.

He swung the now badly limping car into the Trousdale off-ramp in Burlingame, which took him down through tree-crowded residential tracts to El Camino Real, the Royal Road of the old Spanish missions. Eventually he found a gas station with an attached garage. He told the mechanic what to look for.

The sandy-haired kid was wiping his hands on a bright red cloth as he came back into the office where Bart was gulping down a Diet Pepsi because he liked the bubbles going up his nose.

"Yeah, well, you were right. They sugared your gas tank. Sugar got carried to the distributor, the plugs, the pistons—everything. It formed a glaze. It's like rock candy in there. You'd have to pull the engine, dismantle it, steam-clean it—which costs a hell of a lot more than that old car's worth."

*   *   *

Meryl Blanchett had just returned to her Chestnut Street flat from taking Milli on her morning walk to the Presidio Wall. The phone was ringing when she entered the room. It was an unlisted number, so Meryl picked up immediately. A wonderfully remembered voice spoke.

"Meryl, it is I."

"Madame Miseria!" she cried. "Thank God! I keep calling you, but nobody answers. And you haven't cashed my check yet."

"I am not going to cash it—ever—because of the wonderful thing you are going to do for me. You have your hair done once a week at JeanneMarie Broussard et cie."

"Yes, but how—" Meryl broke off with a surprisingly girlish giggle. Yana could picture the flush of embarrassment mantling her pleasant cheeks. "But of course, you can see anything you want to see in your crystal ball . . ."

"And many things I do not wish to see," said Yana. "I also know that you have great influence with JeanneMarie."

"I have gotten quite a number of the other docents at the Legion of Honor to patronize her shop, it is true . . ."

"Here is what you must do," began Yana. As it was not quite new moon, Meryl could not yet know that Yana's spells and potions were worthless in binding the feckless Theodore to her.

Meryl instantly agreed. Of course.

Dan Kearny stepped through the front door of DKA wearing his new blue suit, bought in Chicago, and a lightning-pattern tie a saleswoman had told him was the latest thing. Jane Goldson came out of her chair behind the reception desk. She was slight and slender, with a veddy British accent and a skirt that stopped a foot above her knees. Her legs were excellent. To the eternal sorrow of the field men, she would never go out with any of them. She held out an inch-thick stack of phone messages.

"Welcome home, Mr. K. These are the ones who wouldn't

talk with Giselle. Only Mr. K for them. And Mr. Groner has been doing a bird over the missing classic cars from UpScale Motors."

He thanked her while starting down the busy office past the mostly female skip-tracers and credit checkers and phone workers. It was good to be back. Giving that keynote speech at the convention had been a bearcat. Standing ovation, but still . . .

"Dan!" Giselle was looking at him from across his own desk. "Great suit. Killer tie. How was Chicago?"

He reclaimed his swivel and tossed his batch of messages down on the blotter. "Terrif. Listen, Giselle, what's this Jane tells me? That Groner's on the warpath?"

She sat down across from him. "Nothing like that, Dan. He just keeps calling for reports so he'll know when to set up the auction of the classic cars. He wants to move them all at once. Last night Bart got the Ferrari convertible down in Woodside. They took a shot at him, but didn't hit the car." She told him of Bart's adventures, ending with, "Anyway, he and Larry had to call a tow truck—"

"If he thinks he's going to stick the tires on his expense account, after pulling a stupid stunt like that . . ." His private line rang. He snatched it up, said, "Yeah?" into it.

"They sugared the gas tank, too," said Heslip's voice.

After a strangled pause, Kearny said with disgust, "Maybe you can raise one of the other field men and bum a ride in." He threw the receiver in the direction of the phone. As Giselle was replacing it correctly, he said, "How are we doing otherwise?"

The young, taffy-haired woman in the old-fashioned pinch-waist yellow and brown plaid suit and run-over black pumps paused on the sidewalk in front of Brittingham Funeral Directors. Tugging at her mid-calf skirt, she stared up at the impressive inset portico flanked by four double sets of Ionian Greek pillars. Brittingham's had been serving San Francisco from the same location on Sutter Street between Larkin and Polk since 1850, and to date, not one of their clients had ever come back to complain about their work.

Carter Brittingham IV, great-great-grandson of the founding Brittingham, was standing in the hallway outside the crowded Evergreen Room waiting for the Reverend Dickson, who was, of course, *pro forma* late. Dickson was a difficult man of God— indeed, in his darkest, most secret moments, Brittingham thought of him as the Reverend Dick*head.*

Seeing an Arkie-looking woman enter, Brittingham glided toward her, speaking in a deep, soft, almost sepulchral voice.

"If you could tell me your Loved One's name, madam—"

"Loved One?"

Her voice had some sort of regional twang; apart from lips smeared a garish red, that small oval face should have had a dusting of freckles across the bridge of the nose but didn't quite. Slanty eyeglasses that had gone out in the 1970s gave her the slightly goofy, off-kilter look of a tipsy church organist.

"The, ah, Departed whom you wished to—"

"Oh, no, I'm looking for Mr. . . . ." Her voice had an upward inflection that made it a question. "Brittingham?"

"I am he," said Brittingham with admirable brevity.

He was a slightly soft, fulsome man over six feet tall, impressive in striped pants and cutaway dark coat, gleaming plain-tip black Oxfords, and black silk tie knotted in a full Windsor.

She stuck out a firm hand which he found himself taking.

"Becky Thatcher," she said. "From a little bitty town in the Ouachitas Mountains of Arkansas. I'm looking for a job."

Brittingham shuddered inwardly. "I'm very sorry, Ms. Thatcher, but we have no openings of any—"

"Isn't anybody better'n me on hair and makeup for corpses."

This stopped Brittingham cold. It was very difficult to find cosmeticians who could—or would—adequately wash and set the hair of the Departeds, let alone make up their poor, cold, dead faces. And the girl he'd had for almost a year had, the day before, suddenly quit.

He considered Becky Thatcher's taffy hair piled in curls on top of her head, the pigeon-toed stance in the scuffed shoes, the garish lipstick, the jangly costume jewelry. Any corpse this little hillbilly sent up to him might well come out looking either like a strumpet or a gigolo. But he needed someone *now.*

"So, um, what . . . er . . . qualifications?"

"I've been to beauty school—didn't graduate, Mama took sick and we needed the money so I went to work for the local undertaker. Mr. Toombs. He taught me to make up corpses real pretty for God. Toombs, isn't that just the name for a man who buries people, though? Anyway, he was the coroner, too, so I've worked on every sort of people—fell off of a silo, mashed flat by a semi, gut-shot by someone thought they was a deer—"

"Oh my," he said, "we don't get many Departeds like that at Brittingham's." He paused. "Well, I don't suppose it would do any harm for you to fill out an employment application . . ."

The Reverend Dickhead chose that moment to come in from the street bearing several layers of unction.

"Carter, Carter, my dear man, may God bless, sorry I was detained, but a man of God is at the mercy of . . ." His eyes focused on Becky Thatcher, surreptitiously caressed the body accented by the pinch-waist suit. "Ummm, whom have we here?"

Becky dropped him the hint of a curtsy.

"Reverend, I know you and Mr. Brittingham are gonna be real busy, so if you could spare him for just one teensy second . . ."

With one small hand she drew Brittingham a few feet down the hall, out of the Reverend's earshot.

"I'll fill out them forms and all later, but couldn't I just sort of . . . try out today? I really need the work." Her eyes turned merry behind the slanty glasses. "You don't like what I do, you don't owe me a thing. What can you lose?"

What indeed? His assistant, Harvey Parsons, would be there to see she didn't do anything *outré* to one of their Loved Ones.

Giselle Marc had hitched her chair closer to Kearny's desk, and had been talking steadily. Since DKA's life's blood was finding people who had defaulted, defrauded, or embezzled from banks, bonding companies, lending institutions, or insurance conglomerates, and taking their unpaid-for chattels, she had a lot to go over with Kearny. An hour later she was down to a final folder. She opened it on the desk.

"Okay, the classics from UpScale Motors. We started out looking for seven of them after Ken scored that little 280Z. Larry got the Corvette roadster out of Wiley's brother-in-law's garage down in Pacifica the day after you left."

"Any trouble?"

"Not with the repo, no." She already was losing her enthusiasm at his return. "But, ah, Dan, something happened that might come back to bite us. A few hours after Larry took the Corvette, the brother-in-law and his very pregnant wife stormed in here with a bunch of Polaroids they said showed—"

She was interrupted by the arrival of three men through the back door. Two of them were cops who now and then shagged cars through police records for DKA. The other . . .

"You Kearny?" snapped the one she didn't know.

He had strands of thin black hair combed sideways to cover a spreading bald spot and his small black mustache looked pinned to his sallow face like a tail pinned to a birthday party donkey.

Kearny said, "Tom. George. How are the families?"

The stranger yapped, "I'm the one you gotta worry about, wise-ass. Sergeant Willis Franks of the San Mateo County Sheriff's Department. You're under arrest for aggravated assault and wanton destruction of property. On your feet, buster."

Tom and George winced. Kearny said, "Let's see some tin."

Franks pulled out his shield wallet and displayed his badge. Kearny nodded and stood up.

"Pacifica?" he asked Giselle as if the cops weren't even there. She nodded. "Okay, get Hec Tranquillini on the horn and have him meet me at the San Mateo County Courthouse." He looked at Franks. "The holding coop's still in South City, isn't it?"

Franks nodded, taking the cuffs off his belt.

"You don't need those," said Tom.

Franks got a mean cop look in his eye. "Assistant D.A. Scarbrough said to bring him in *fast* and bring him in *hard*. I don't know what that means to you pussies up here, but in San Mateo that means the cuffs."

"You ain't in San Mateo," George pointed out.

Kearny winked at Giselle, said, "Hec, pronto," and went out with the San Mateo cop firmly holding his arm.

sixteen

Hector Tranquillini was small and neat and nasty, like a scorpion in your shoe. Five-four in his artfully constructed high-heeled boots, an invariable 145 pounds *before* a session of handball at the YMCA on Golden Gate. *Handball*, not racketball. And no sissy soft inflated blue handballs: the little black hard rubber ones that made red swollen catchers' mitts of your hands.

Hec was waiting in the interview room when Dan was brought in prior to his arraignment and bail hearing before the judge. Hec shooed out the guard while flicking his eyes around the room to indicate the D.A. might have it bugged. Illegal, of course, and it couldn't be used in court; but bugs were a useful tool in scoping out the defense attorney's strategy. Fat chance, fella.

"Another fine mess you've gotten me into," Hec said with the joviality of a miniaturized Al Capone once the guard was gone. He slid the Accusation and Complaint across the table. Dan read, suddenly looked up to meet Hec's twinkling eyes. His own hard blue eyes were bright with suppressed laughter.

But in deference to the possible bug, he said in a defeated voice, "Do you think you can get me out of here on bail? I . . . I don't know if I could handle a night behind bars."

"I can try. And I think I'd better demand a preliminary hearing as soon as possible so we'll know how bad it is."

* * *

Assistant D.A. Philip Scarbrough was just 30 years old and just six feet tall, straight, single, with the sort of clean-cut good looks that often came out of Stanford. And like so many other Stanford men, he was on the rise. Important People were beginning to notice him. He would work up to District Attorney of San Mateo County, springboard to state Attorney General—after that, who was to say how far his ambition might carry him?

He didn't have the interview room bugged. He didn't have to. When Ellen and Garth Winslett brought in their complaints against Daniel Kearny, he knew he had a winner. A crowd-pleaser. A vote-getter. The brutality of the assault, the brazen smashing of the garage door, the purloined Corvette, the business card, those damning Polaroids of the battered Ellen . . .

That's why he'd told Sergeant Willis Franks to bring Kearny in fast and hard, show him who was in charge from the git-go. He first eyeballed Kearny in Judge Valenti's modern but pleasant South San Francisco courtroom overlooking Mission Road, with San Bruno Mountain lurking in the background. Kearny was a tough-looking fifty-something, with a square jaw and slightly flattened nose and cold eyes. All bluff. He was scared. Had to be.

Looking at the reddened marks on Kearny's wrists from the tightness of the cuffs clapped on as they'd crossed out of San Francisco County, Scarbrough thought maybe he shouldn't have told Franks to be so enthusiastic. But slimeball repossessors were never popular with jury members driving financed cars.

"Mr. Scarbrough?"

Judge Anthony Valenti was a burly 60, with a wealth of his own grizzled hair and the huge hands of his Italian grandfather, a fisherman in the days when Monterey's Cannery Row had been the sardine-packing capital of America. Rimless specs perched on his broad fleshy nose.

"Ready for the People, Your Honor."

"Is the defendant in court and represented by counsel?"

"Yes, Your Honor." Tranquillini's voice suddenly bore the subtle Italian lilt of *his* ancestors from northern Italy's Lombardy district. "Ettore Tranquillini for the defense."

Ettore? Kearny suppressed a grin. Hector was Ettore only over a plate of Mama's pasta—or in front of an Italian judge.

Scarbrough almost felt sorry for the defendant. *This* was Kearny's attorney? A little pipsqueak with not much black curly hair, and so *short.* Surely not even marginally competent.

Hector was on his feet. "Your Honor, I would like to bring to the court's attention the treatment my client has received. He is a respected San Francisco businessman, yet a San Mateo deputy sheriff dragged him from his office in handcuffs—"

"He assaulted a pregnant woman!" Scarbrough burst out.

Judge Valenti said mildly, "Surely not proven yet, Mr. Prosecutor. And I want to hear you on the subject of handcuffs."

Scarbrough said defensively, "He's a repossessor, he—"

"Your Honor!" Tranquillini was on his feet again. "Those handcuffs were ratcheted down brutally tight—look at Mr. Kearny's wrists." Dan held his arms aloft; the reddened, scraped skin showed up nicely against the muted courtroom colors. "All of this without even a courtesy call to my office so I could surrender my client in the usual manner."

"Is this true, Mr. Prosecutor? Was no attempt made—"

"We . . . didn't know who his counsel was, Your Honor."

"And you didn't ask?" The judge heaved a deep sigh. He said to Kearny, "How do you plead, sir?"

Dan stood up respectfully. "Not guilty, Your Honor."

"So noted. And in the matter of bail?"

Scarbrough said quickly, "A hundred thousand, Your Honor."

"Did the complainant lose her baby?"

"Well, no, Your Honor, but—"

"Was she hospitalized?"

"No, Your Honor, but we have Polaroid photos showing—"

The judge gaveled him silent. "Those are for the trial, not here. Bail is set at ten thousand dollars, cash or bond."

"Your Honor," said Hec, "we request a speedy preliminary evidentiary hearing, so the court can determine whether the state has sufficient evidence to bring my client to trial."

"Sufficient—" The judge stopped himself. He expected delaying tactics by the defense, not a rush to judgment. He said thoughtfully, "I see." He looked over at Scarbrough. "Any objections, counselor?"

Scarbrough was secretly delighted. He had planned to ask for a fast prelim himself, giving Valenti a chance to eyeball Ellen Winslett in court before her bruises faded and before she gave birth. Beat up and pregnant. A dynamite combo. He had more than enough to bind Kearny over, and at trial the jury would convict without leaving the box. Tranquillini was a clown.

"None at all, Your Honor. We are happy to oblige the accused."

"All parties will be advised of a court date," Valenti said formally. "Defendant is released subject to bail being posted."

Next morning at Brittingham's Funeral Parlor, every viewing room was occupied, with several more Departeds on the runway, as it were, like jets waiting for clearance to depart. Two Rosaries tonight, three Viewings, in the morning *four* Funerals.

One result of all the hurry and worry was that Brittingham forgot all about Mrs. Karposki until a scant hour before her Viewing. He had left her hair and makeup to that strange little female person who had come around asking for the cosmetician's position. Oh my!

He rushed down to the sterile, brightly lighted embalming area to find Harvey Parsons passing the time with eighty-three-year-old "Tex" Watkins. Tex was supine on a stainless steel table, nude, staring up into the round overhead lamp with indifferent eyes. Harvey was about to drive a thick hollow steel spike down into his solar plexus to start the embalming process.

Nowadays they made a small incision above the clavicle and used an aneurysm hook to fish out the main carotid artery, put in an insertion tube, and pump in some formalin solution such as PSX. But Brittingham had trained Harvey himself in the old ways he secretly felt were still the best ways, and now couldn't spare him for the time it would take to retrain him.

"Harvey, did that new girl, Miss Thatcher, come in today?"

Harvey was a strapping young man with a clean-featured, almost ascetic face, a shaved head, and *no* instinctual empathy for Bereaveds. But what that lad could do with viscera . . .

"She's in the Readying Room, sir, with the Jones baby."

Brittingham felt a thrill of anxiety. A baby! He trotted, slightly knock-kneed, across the cold, sterile embalming room to the pastel colors and soft lighting of the Readying Room. A place of preparation, a place of—dare he think it—*hope?*

A stranger in a white floor-length smock turned at his entrance—and was Becky Thatcher transformed. Gone under her crisp white cap was the mound of taffy curls. Gone the slanty glasses, gone the Day-Glo dress, the run-over shoes, the jangly jewelry, the garish lipstick. In their place, a doe-eyed refined-looking young woman of remarkable beauty and serenity. Only the soft voice with its tinge of accent remained the same.

"Oh, Mr. Brittingham, I'm so glad to see you, sir!"

And she stepped aside so he could view the infant. He almost cried out, My God, we've made a terrible mistake, that child is alive! But then he realized it was just her remarkable skill. Life glowed in the little cheeks, the chubby hands seemed to reach out for a hug, surely any moment childish prattle . . . He felt salt tears start in his eyes. Becky spoke earnestly to him.

"Babies is easy, Mr. Brittingham. Ones this small, they's not much been did to them before . . ." She paused. "Now Mrs.

Karposki, poor woman, she seen some rough things in her day."

An abusive spouse, for one. Brittingham turned to the other wheeled gurney. All the physical bruises and psychic pain of assault were gone from the dead woman. She was surely only sleeping. And her hair! A silver halo around that thin, finally serene face.

"Miss Thatcher, what can I say?"

Becky suddenly giggled. "How about, 'You're hired, Miss Thatcher'? You say that, I'm one happy little hillbilly lady."

She was infectious. Brittingham chuckled himself.

"You're hired, Miss Thatcher."

It wasn't until noon that Hec could get away from court to join Dan Kearny and Giselle Marc for a council of war in the guaranteed privacy of DKA's upstairs reception area. Hec listened attentively as Dan asked Giselle, "What did you do with Larry after the Winsletts showed up?"

"Took him off the classic cars right away," said Giselle. "Tomorrow he'll be back on his regular cases—"

"No. I don't want him coming into this office at all until this thing is settled. Not even at night to type reports. Find him some work where he doesn't have to show up for any reason."

"Okay. For what it's worth, he says the Winslett woman was totally cooperative, gave him the keys, even served him tea in the garage. The man he described coming down the street as he left matches Winslett himself."

Hec perked up. "The beating was about the tea," he said. "But wily Wiley showed Winslett how to make it pay big time."

Giselle began, "Garth Winslett beat her up."

"And Wiley set this up," said Hec with a shake of his head. "This is about DKA and the cars. He sends 'em to an ambitious D.A. who files a *criminal* assault case against Dan personally. Once Dan gets convicted of *that*, the Winsletts'll bring civil suit against him personally and DKA as co-conspirator, and take you all down."

Giselle flipped the pen with which she had been taking notes neatly across the table to land by Hec's fingers.

"I hate him. So what's our strategy on this? Dan's in all sorts of trouble and—"

"—and Hec is here on his white horse to save me."

"Maybe," said Hec. "In a jury trial you never know."

Which didn't make Giselle feel any too nifty about it all.

seventeen

What's this message on my machine?" demanded Ballard when he finally got hold of Giselle. "Get in touch with you immediately, don't come into the office under any circumstances? And then you're too busy to call me back?"

Actually, Larry was taking his ease in his broken-down easy chair with the phone to his ear, sipping a cup of his truly superb coffee; but trying to reach Giselle at the office for over two hours had gotten a little old, so he was passing it on.

"Yeah, busy on a mess of your own making," said Giselle. "Dan gets back from Chicago yesterday, and two hours later gets arrested on a complaint brought by the Winsletts, thanks to Casanova. Now it's *criminal* charges—aggravated assault and a bunch of other things. You're to keep out of sight as long as it takes, and that doesn't mean sneaking off up the coast after abalone, or entering some karate tournament somewhere."

"Arrested? Dan? Criminal charges? Dammit, I *told* you I should go down to Pacifica and nose around for witnesses."

Her tone changed. "Listen, Hot Shot, you've done enough damage already. This is straight from Mr. K: don't come in, don't even call in except on the unlisted number as Joe Bush."

"Just great! I get laid off because the Winsletts are a couple of liars."

"For the time being you're still on payroll. But stay in town in case I come up with something for you to do before the evidentiary hearing. If I can't get hold of you, these days all will come off your accrued vacation time."

"Hey," he said in a hurt voice, "Giselle Marc says stay in town, Larry Ballard stays in town. What do you think I am?"

"I think you're twisty as a snake and slippery as an eel."

"Okay." He was now self-pitying. "Whatever you say."

He hung up the phone and was on his feet with such energy that he knocked his coffee cup off the arm of the easy chair into the wastebasket he had learned to leave there for that purpose. Pulling on his jacket, he headed for the door. Maybe, if he went out to Stonestown and bought Midori Tagawa lunch, he could talk her into taking the weekend off. Then they could just stay in bed together until Monday morning, doing what they did best.

Trin Morales parked on slanting Filbert Street on Russian Hill. He locked up, trudged farther uphill to the narrow yellow apartment house where Colton Lewis had lived until just a few days before. Going around and around yesterday with the hostile old battleaxe landlady had got him nothing at all. Now, he was looking for a way to bypass her and snoop Lewis's former apartment without her knowing anything about it.

There was a truck from a commercial cleaning service parked three spaces down from the building. Just as Trin climbed the terrazzo steps from the street, a tenant came out. Trin caught the door just before it closed.

"Thanks," he said. "Cleaning service."

He didn't look back to see if the man was watching him; that kind of guilty behavior gave you away every time.

Trin puffed his way up the carpeted stairs to the third floor; someone had eaten sausage for breakfast. The smell made him hungry. As he hoped from seeing the cleaning service truck, the door to Colton Lewis's evacuated apartment stood open. In the living room, a uniformed Latino was haphazardly running a vacuum cleaner over the wall-to-wall. Trin boldly strode across the room as if he belonged there. But before he reached the hallway to the bedroom, the cleaning man called at his back.

"Hey! Morales! Where's my twenty bucks?"

Trin stopped dead. Hell, he knew that voice. Carlos Feliu. A stocky serious-faced man with a fat wife and six kids. He and Trin used to sometimes drink in the same bar on 21st Street. Trin's gold tooth sparkled in his grin as he opened his arms wide to give Feliu a big *abrazo*. He stepped back to dig in his pants pocket and hand over the $20.

"I would of paid you back long ago, Carlos, but I been sick. I'm just back to work."

"I can see you lost a lot of weight, man."

"Listen, I really need to find the guy used to live here—he skipped out with a car isn't his. If you go down and tell the landlady you found a gold ring with an opal in it—and want to give it back, maybe she'll give you a forwarding address."

"What if she wants to see the ring I didn't find?"

Trin twisted the gold ring with an opal in it off the finger of his own left hand. He handed it to Feliu. "Then you show it to her, Carlos. You found it under the bedside table."

"She's gonna tell me she'll see he gets it back."

Maybe Carlos wasn't the man for the job. But Trin still thought it was his best shot.

"Act suspicious. Let her think you suspect she's just gonna keep it herself. You think there might be a reward and you want it." Trin grinned his most engaging grin. "It's worth the try—and another twenty."

Fifteen minutes later Feliu returned with a forwarding address for Colton Lewis on Gellert Drive in the City.

"Hey, man! It worked. I acted real suspicious-like, didn't trust her, see, and she got sort of mad. Like maybe she was sore because she hadn't thought of the reward thing herself. But I just stood there playing the dumb Mexican *peón*, and finally she gave me the address and told me to get out of there."

Trin gave Feliu another $20 and slipped the ring back on his own finger. "Man, you'd make a good private eye yourself."

Driving back down to the Mission District with the address safely in his pocket, he thought, with an elation he hadn't been able to feel in months, the Cisco Kid is *back!* And Colton Lewis is dog meat. Being cute and shifty, Lewis was still in town just as Giselle had surmised.

But who was cuter and shiftier? Trin Morales. The Cisco Kid. And who was about to treat himself to a pizza rather than the Mex food he usually ate? Right again. Trin Morales.

Since it was only 11:00 A.M., the pizza joint on Mission off 19th wasn't yet crowded. Trin slid into a red-vinyl booth with a sigh of satisfaction. The slender, pretty Latina waitress came over with silverware and a napkin and a glass of water.

"Can . . . can I help you, sir?"

She had a quavery little voice like the squeak of a mouse, and stared at him as if he were a boa constrictor gonna swallow her up. He could smell shampoo on her long gleaming black hair, something flowery. Like her face, it was vaguely familiar.

"Oh, ah, yeah. Gimme a small double-cheese double-salami thin crust. Individual. And a Diet Coke, too."

Forty pounds ago it would have been an extra-large thick crust with double *everything*, and he would have washed the whole thing down with draft beer. But his stomach had shrunk.

Instead of writing down his order, the girl leaned down close to almost hiss, "Are you crazy, coming here? If Esteban hears you came to see me, he will—"

Esteban! This was she, his sister! Milagrita! It all came back in a rush, her name, everything. He met her at a Cinco de Mayo dance, poured a lot of beer down her so she would pass out in his car. Then he took her to a hot-sheet motel out by the Cow Palace where he could always get a room for free because he had something on the guy who managed it.

She got sick in the toilet a couple of times that night. Afterward when she started to sober up, there had been blood on the sheets. That excited him, and he banged her again.

As he slid hurriedly out of the booth, she pressed a crumpled scrap of paper into his hand. Her voice was low.

"Just leave a time and place on the answering machine at this number—I have to tell you things."

Outside in the colorful, bustling Latino crowds of Mission Street, Morales feared he might throw up into the gutter, like Milagrita that night in the motel room when she cried and told him that she'd been a virgin.

Stop! Esteban, stop! You have killed him!

He got into his car, slammed and locked the door. Did she think he was nuts? They set up a meet, Morales walks in with a big shit-eating grin on his face and his dick in his hand, there's Esteban and all his buddies waiting, Morales goes home with his dick in a paper bag. If he goes home at all.

He pulled out into traffic and drove toward his Florida Street apartment. She must have seen him around the neighborhood after that night, gotten his real name, and told her *loco* brother about him. *Puta.*

But even as he muttered the word, he thought, *Madre de Dios*, how young had she been? Even now she looked only about sixteen.

He hadn't trusted anyone since his eighth birthday, why should he be stupid enough to start now? And a woman besides? Especially *this* woman. He wasn't *loco*. Was he?

eighteen

When Midori saw Larry Ballard's tall form threading its way toward her between the display tables, she shot a quick look around and relaxed: no sign of Luminitsa Djurik. Larry came up to her with his big sexy grin that made her go weak in the knees.

"You wanna buy somethings? Big sale today."

He leaned close. "What I want to do is take you into a fitting room and toss your skirt up over your head and—"

"*Rarry!*" She put a hand over the bottom half of her face and blushed bright scarlet, giggling.

"But I'll settle for buying you lunch at the Olive Garden."

Her face wreathed itself in smiles. She checked the tiny watch on her slim wrist. Ballard could feel himself getting hard just looking at her. Last night in bed, she had . . .

"Just fifteen mo minutes, then I got a whole hour."

"Hey, Midori, where you been hiding Mr. Dreamboat?"

Midori turned, worst fears realized. Luminitsa! Of the long legs and big firm breasts and gleaming red lips and glowing almond skin. And good English, too. It was all over, because once they'd seen Luminitsa, they always went back for more.

"Is my friend, Rarry." To Larry she said, eyes miserable, "Is Luminitsa. She work with me, she teach me everythings."

Ballard nodded and smiled. "Luminitsa." She reminded him of someone, he couldn't think who. Didn't matter.

A little old man with cheery faded blue eyes behind gold-rimmed spectacles popped out from behind Luminitsa.

"I'm Whit Stabler." As he and Ballard shook hands, he added, "Anything you want, these ladies'll take care of you."

"*Anything*, Whit?" asked Luminitsa with a throaty chuckle.

Ballard tucked Midori's arm through his to lead her across Nordstrom's gleaming floors toward the front door and the Olive Garden, and away from Luminitsa. Midori sighed.

"Luminitsa very beautiful."

"And old Whit reminds me of my grandpa. So what?"

"You no want Luminitsa?"

"Jesus, no. I know her type. If she's nice to someone, it's because she thinks she can use him. I bet she takes old Whit for a bundle before she's through with him."

"You no want Luminitsa!" she repeated. "I very happy."

At 760 Golden Gate, the DKA clerical staff was stuffed into what had been a one-floor flat. The field men's cubicles and Dan Kearny's private cubbyhole and makeshift storage boxes for personal property removed from repos were all stuffed into the under-the-building garage. In a pinch, the garage could also temporarily store two sedans or three compacts.

Here at 340 Eleventh Street, each of the two ground-floor rooms was bigger than the whole setup at Golden Gate. The field men were upstairs and there was room for twenty repos in the fenced lot out back. Giselle shared the windowless back room with the C/B, the fax, and the Internet computer. After school, teenage girls came in to churn out collection demands, legal notices, and skip letters; but their giggles and gossip were no more distracting than the twittering of a flock of sparrows. It was how Giselle herself had started out, more years ago than she liked to recall.

Two men came in from the storage lot through the locked back door behind her without tripping the alarm. With a casual finger, Giselle pushed the intercom button that sent a silent

CODE RED signal to Kearny in the front room. Then she saw they were Rudolph Marino and Staley Zlachi. Alarms would not slow them down. After the phone call where he didn't identify himself, she should have expected the Gypsy King to drop by.

"*Piccina! Come va?*" asked Marino with a big smile.

Marino was using his Angelo-Grimaldi-the-Italian-lawyer persona today. Gleaming hair, gleaming oxfords, $2,000 suit, Patek Philipe watch. They had conned themselves into a brief but intense affair when their paths had crossed a couple of years back, then parted without permanent damage to either one. Giselle returned his smile.

"*Va bene,*" she told him, then turned to scold Staley. "You hung up before I could say hello the other day."

"The last time I laid eyes on you, Giselle, you was all dressed up as a young Gypsy lad."

"A *ternipè*, you called it, right? In Stupidville, Ohio."

She was laughing at the memory when Dan Kearny came through the door from the front office hefting a tire iron. He skidded to a stop. He nodded casually to Staley.

"Why didn't you come in the front door like regular folks?"

"Is serious business, the police are already involved."

"If they're involved, we don't want to be." Then Kearny shrugged. "Aw, hell, come on in, this ought to be good."

Rudolph took Giselle's arm. "You and I are not needed, *cara*. I only came along because I hoped to see you."

"You came along to get me out of the way so Staley can con Dan into doing something he'll regret for the rest of his life."

He didn't deny it. "I will buy you lunch at MC-Squared."

"Do they even serve lunch at MC-Squared?"

"To us they do."

Josh Croswell was eating his lunch in the office, keeping his eye on the scanners, when a burly mid-50s Jew entered the jewelry store. He had Semitic eyes quick with intelligence, a grey-shot patriarchal beard, and an unobtrusive black skullcap.

His blue suit was rumpled; his narrow tie was carelessly knotted.

"I am addressing Mr. Joshua Croswell?" he asked.

"You are," piped Josh in his best customer's voice.

"Good." With his heavy guttural voice, it came out as
"Goot." "Solly David from the Los Angeles Gemstone Mart."

"Am I glad to see you! Your e-mail message said—"

Solly waved a small quick hand. "I hadda be up here today
anyway, I thought I'd drop by, see can we do a little business."

Josh locked the front door, flipped the OPEN sign over to
CLOSED, and led Mr. David back to the narrow cluttered office.

"Pretty soft, retail, three hundred percent markup—you
must be rakin' it in. Me, I deal in fine gemstones, wholesale
only, for the trade." With a thick finger, Solly opened the flap
of a small folded envelope. "Fine gemstones like this here one."
A glittering emerald slid out across the desk blotter. "Fifteen
carats, rectangular, Portuguese step cut."

Josh stared at the stone, trying to pretend expertise.

"Ah . . . are you sure that's fifteen carats?"

His very beard seemed to stiffen. "Get out the scales."

"Oh, no, no, no need of that," Josh said quickly. "Um . . .
how much are you asking? For the trade."

"It's a bargain at seventy-five K," said Solly carelessly.

Seventy-five thousand! That was as much as Donny was of-
fering Josh for it. He had to talk this guy down. With a jeweler's
loupe he peered intently into those brilliant depths.

"Am I seeing an occlusion in—"

Solly snatched the emerald back, highly offended.

"This stone is not from outta Africa, it's from Colombia,
where all the best emeralds come from. Smuggled out from a
mine in the mountains the Colombian emerald cartel don't
know about."

"Yes, it's beautiful," interrupted Josh, almost desperately,
"but I've got a client here who'll only go so high."

"Not my problem. Look at the color! That brilliant green

comes from the high chromium content in stones from this mine. Seventy-five, first, last, and only offer."

"I was thinking more like thirty-seven-five," said Josh.

Solly shook his head sadly, took out his little envelope.

"Forty-two-five," said Josh.

Solly paused. He checked his watch. He sighed. "Okay, fifty K an' I don't gotta take it home with me on the plane."

Josh sat down behind the desk, got out the corporate three-tier checkbook. He'd have the money back into the account before Mr. Petrick's return. Fifty K against 75K: a net of $37,500 for him from the sale of the two emeralds, tax-free, plus his commission on the $12,500 half of the first sale that he would let Mr. Petrick know about. It was dead easy.

"So Ephrem is dead," mused Kearny.

"You knew Ephrem?" Staley let his surprise show.

"He'd hear things about the Lowara, the Kalderash, pass 'em along." Dan added the lie glibly, "Never about the Muchwaya."

"Yeah, well, now he's dead and the cops think Yana killed him. We gotta find her fast and first."

"I've got no problem with that."

Staley repeated with new emphasis, *"We* gotta find her."

"Jesus, I can't believe this! You're trying to hire DKA to find a missing Gyppo girl before the cops do?"

"You find people all the time."

"For banks and big corporations."

"Finding is finding."

"I trust banks and big corporations."

Staley tried to look hurt, then they both had to chuckle.

"Look, Mr. Kearny, act like Yana is one of those Cadillac cars you chased all over the country to take away from us. We'll even pay you a repo fee for her on top of time and mileage, just the same as if she was a automobile. Full load. No discount." He took a big roll of greenbacks out of his pocket and dropped it on the desk. "A good deposit up front."

It was the goofiest idea Dan had ever heard of, and it came from the twistiest man he had ever known. But he *liked* Staley, there was a hell of a lot more going on here than saving a Gypsy girl from a murder charge, and he wanted to find out what it was.

"Okay. I can put one man on it full-time—"

"Who? Who you gonna put on it?"

Kearny could see no harm in telling the truth. "Ballard."

"Wonderful! He outwitted Rudolph Marino, how many men ever done that? I couldn't ask for no better recommendation."

"Okay," Dan said. "Now we gotta talk terms."

That took another hour and sadly depleted Staley's roll of coarse notes thrown so confidently on the desk. When the haggling was complete, they shook hands on the deal.

Giselle, hearing all about it after her return from her lunch, asked a bit snidely, "You're going to let Larry start up all that stuff with Yana again?"

"He's gotta find her first."

Giselle shrugged, then chuckled.

"I wish I could have been here to take a photo of it."

"Photo of what?" demanded Dan suspiciously.

"You and Staley. The devil shaking hands with himself."

Dan Kearny was not amused.

nineteen

A sober, rejuvenated O'B was questioning people on Toyon Court as they got home from work. At the naked taxi driver's house the door was flung open by a slender pretty barefoot blonde in tight jeans and a scoop-neck sweater that advertised her lack of a brassiere. Her lean face almost burned with intensity.

"You're the redhead was askin' questions about Tim Bland."

"Guilty."

In the living room, that morning's *Chronicle* was a paper blizzard across a sagging chintz couch facing the TV. She swept the paper to the floor, sat down, gestured at O'B to join her. The couch smelled of chips, stale beer, sweat, tobacco.

"Jake's sty," she said. "He's a fuckin' pig. Oink oink." On the coffee table was a shaker and a full martini glass. "I'm Vix as in vixen. You want a drink?"

"I'm O'B as in I'm on the wagon."

"I oughtta be." She shook out a Virginia Slim, lit up, blew smoke from the corner of her mouth away from him, took a hefty slug of her drink. She blinked. "Whew! I musta forgot to wave the vermouth bottle at this one. You a friend of Tim's?"

The moment of truth so often faced when you were trying to get information rather than just thug a car. Take a chance.

"I want to take his car away from him."

"That dark green Panoz kit car?" she demanded avidly. He'd

chosen right. She said, "No wonder he took off when I mentioned you'd been askin' Jake questions about him."

"Any idea where he might have gone?"

She stood, drained her martini in a single gulp, began walking with quick, angry strides about the living room.

"When Jake's working overtime, bastard Tim likes to drive me in his precious car up to his old man's cottage in Sonoma so he can spend the weekend shoving that cigarette-size dick of his into me." She hurled her martini glass into the fireplace, shattering it, yelled, "G'wan, get outta here, ya nosy bastard!"

O'B got out before she threw the martini shaker at him. He could be in Sonoma by 11:00 P.M. Check on a phone listing for the father. Cruise the grid of downtown streets. He didn't know what a Panoz looked like, but Sonoma wouldn't have more than one.

Geraldine Tantillo nursed her glass of white wine in Sappho's Knickers. One week ago, at this very table, strange, exotic Yasmine Vlanko told her to quit her job and promised to show up tonight at ten and change Geraldine's life forever. Geraldine had quit the job, the hour had arrived—but no Yasmine. Geraldine sighed. Ariane all over again.

"Hello, Geraldine," said the deep, rich, contralto voice.

Dark, beautiful, mysterious Yasmine, sexy in her skintight black leather, was sitting across the table from her.

"How did you . . . I . . . I thought you weren't . . ."

"I said I would be here."

Geraldine tamped down her hopeless passion: Yasmine had to remain celibate if her strange powers were to be effective.

"What . . . what happens now?" Geraldine asked timidly.

Yasmine leaned toward her. Her perfume was more like an incense than a scent. "Now I help you," she said. "As I promised. Then you will not see me again."

"No!" Geraldine was aghast. "You can't just—"

"If I am here for you to lean on, you will never develop

fully as a woman. You will never find another lover who will nourish you." She sang in a low, liquid voice:

> *"Predzia, csirik leja,*
> *Te ná tráda m're píranes."*

She then sang the translation:

> *"Fly my bird—fly, I say,*
> *Do not chase my love away."*

"I . . . I don't understand."

"It refers not to a real bird, but to a cloud in the east on Whitsunday—which would mean you would find no lover that year. Should I stay, I would be that cloud in the east for you."

She slid a sheet of paper across the table.

"That is the address of JeanneMarie Broussard et cie, a beauty salon on Spruce Street in Laurel Heights. They will expect you there at nine on Monday morning to start work at ten."

Geraldine cried, "I know this place! I tried to apply for work there, they wouldn't even talk to me. How did you—"

She looked up from the paper, sudden dread constricting her throat. Rightly so. Yasmine Vlanko had vanished.

Yana Poteet sank back in her seat on the almost empty downtown Market Street streetcar. A light raincoat hid the tight fuck-me black leather. Her slumped position and the scarf swirled around her head added fifteen years to her age. But inside she was jubilant. She'd pulled it off! She had an honest job in the *gadjo* world and a safe place to live in that same world.

Deciding she should work at a mortuary, following Geraldine from work, scoping out which of Geraldine's buttons to push. Conning Meryl Blanchett into getting Geraldine a job at JeanneMarie Broussard et cie. Easing Geraldine out of the job she hated and into the new one with JeanneMarie. Geraldine might even find the new life Yana had promised her. Who could know?

She pulled the cord, left the streetcar at the transit transfer point on Seventh and Market so as to not walk too directly to Columbine Residence for Women on Breen Place above the old Main Library. Single women only, no men above first-floor administration, and you had to check in before midnight, no matter what your age.

White-haired, stern-faced Mrs. Newman was already behind the check-in table set four-square across the entryway.

"Good evening, Mrs. Newman," said Yana gravely.

"Good evening to you, Miss Thatcher," Newman said, beaming at the taffy-haired Yana. Such a wholesome girl.

Working in a mortuary was unclean employment for any *Rom*, but the women's residence was spic and span. No cop, no Gypsy, no husband in L.A., if still alive, would ever think of looking for her at either place. In many ways she was more comfortable right now as a hillbilly lady named Miss Becky Thatcher from Arkansas's Ouachitas Mountains than she would be as a Muchwaya *Romni*.

In her room, she removed her raincoat and saw Yasmine Vlanko in the mirror. She felt anger. She could thank Ephrem Poteet for putting her through the last two weeks. He was causing her even more trouble dead than alive.

By an effort of will she calmed herself. *Za Develesa*, Ephrem, she whispered. Go with God.

twenty

Stroll south from the Ferry Building on the once-proud Embarcadero, and you will run into a new, gentrified waterfront of high-price condos and inset-tile walkways and lampposts with wrought-iron scrollwork. Stroll north, and you will run into the almost-desperate carnival-house gaiety of Pier 39, and, beyond that, Fisherman's Wharf crowded not with the crab and salmon fishermen of yesteryear, but with tourists.

Midway between these two extremes, shoehorned in between two empty piers abandoned as the shipping moved away to other ports, is a tiny, forgotten waterfront bar called the Marlin Spike, where it is always 1947. You drink straight shots with longneck beer chasers, you eat steak sandwiches on crusty French rolls with a side of fries, and nobody has ever heard of cholesterol. Above the bar is a faded ten-foot-long photo of thirty naughty bare-butted women wearing only sailors' caps and middy blouses, winking bawdily over their shoulders at the camera.

It was nearly midnight when Nanoosh Tsatshimo slid into the high-backed booth in a corner overlooked by no windows. This con, as this city, was new to him: he usually worked silverplating schemes in Chicago's teeming South Side where the Jewish working-class ghetto rubbed elbows with the black working-class ghetto. He took a long, grateful gulp of the proffered icy beer.

"You have chosen well," he said.

Immaculata Bimbai was in her foreign countess mode tonight.

"We can speak freely here. The bartender is one of us."

In Immaculata's jewelry-store cons, youthful Lazlo, her little brother, usually carried luggage as a bellboy, or carted around empty boxes from upscale shops. Immaculata had made him a major player for the first time; he could no more contain his excitement than a puppy can contain its wriggling.

"How did it go?" he demanded eagerly.

Immaculata said to him sharply, "Show respect, Lazlo. This is an important man in our *kumpania*—an elder."

Lazlo muttered his abashed apology; Nanoosh merely grinned.

"My children, let me tell you. First, I was never any closer to L.A. than Rudolph's house in Point Richmond."

Lazlo said, "How did you make the jewelry-store guy *think* you were there?"

"Rudolph did it with his computer. He says e-mail responses on the Internet can seem to originate from wherever you say they originate."

"So he sent the guy an e-mail that was supposed to come from that Los Angeles Gemstone Mart you made up?"

"Exactly, Immaculata. He was *kuriaio*—he was greedy, he wanted to make all his money at once. I told him I wanted seventy-five thousand dollars for the emerald, and he offered only thirty-seven-five. Then . . ."

And with exquisite timing, Nanoosh fell silent.

"Don't do that to us, Nanoosh!" pleaded Immaculata. Her life was jewelry-store cons; if this one came off as hoped, she foresaw great things in it for her and Lazlo.

Nanoosh, milking his moment, said, "Then I took his check."

"His *check?*" exclaimed Immaculata, appalled. "No! Cash!"

Was this how he conned 'em back there in Chicago? If so . . .

"Certified," said Nanoosh.

And started to laugh as his thick fingers upended his crumpled Safeway shopping bag. Thick sheafs of banded greenbacks spilled out on the tabletop.

"How much?" Lazlo asked. He looked even younger than he had while playing Donny, the nerd from Silicon Valley.

"Fifty thousand," said Nanoosh in phony indifference.

"Take out my twenty-five thousand seed money, and that's twenty-five net," breathed Immaculata. She was still as beautiful as she had been while playing May, the putative bride; but with her own character back in her face and eyes, she looked closer to her real 32 than to May's 22. "That's eight thousand two hundred and fifty for the Muchwaya—"

"And five thousand, five hundred eighty-three and change for each of us three," supplied Nanoosh.

Immaculata, her busy fingers already opening the packets, said with a sort of wonder, "And we didn't break a single law."

Several vineyards around the small wine-country town of Sonoma have tasting rooms that bring throngs of tourists and Bay Area locals during daylight hours. Flowers are everywhere. General Vallejo's home and grounds have been rigorously preserved. The bakery's French bread lures San Francisco insomniacs to Sonoma at 6:00 A.M. so they get it hot from the oven. Picturesque shops and restaurants try to hang on to tradition while catering to the tourist buck. It is a mostly successful attempt.

But now, on these small-town, weeknight streets, everything was closed except a lone bar facing the town square. No car moved, no pedestrian strolled. To O'B, parked on the far side of the square from the bar and staring across its ponds and playground, dominated by the 1800s town hall, Sonoma looked like a 1950s movie set. He felt frustrated. He had already checked the only phone directory available, back at the crossroads leading into town; no Blands listed. And he couldn't really ask anyone questions anyway. If Tim Bland had local ties, a question might inspire a phone call that would alert him to the search.

A patrol car pulled up beside O'B. The lone cop stuck a square, tough, sleepy-looking face out of his window.

"You need any help, sir?" Both question and voice were courteous; but the eyes were the cynical cop's eyes issued with the uniform at every police academy's passing-out parade.

O'B took a chance. "You know a guy named Tim Bland?"

"Don't ring a bell. Why you lookin' for him?"

Just what he didn't want, a curious cop. He said quickly, "Tim and my kid sister had a fight. She's damn near forty, he's thirty, and now she's sorry, and she wants me to find him *tonight...*" ·

The cop yawned involuntarily. "Family," he grunted, and departed. O'B sighed. He hadn't eaten anything since lunch.

After thinking long and hard, Trin Morales left his apartment in his usual circuitous fashion, at DKA surreptitiously switched into a 1997 Honda Accord repo awaiting transport back to Skokie, Illinois. Driving repos, ever, was strictly against DKA policy; but who cared about the rules? Trin was maybe talking his life here. He left a phone message for Milagrita to catch the Mission Street BART—Bay Area Rapid Transit—at the 23rd and Mission station in time to reach the Ocean Avenue station at 2:00 A.M. Take the covered walkway to Geneva Avenue. Be alone.

Trin got to the Ocean Avenue BART station, way out where Geneva passes over the 280 freeway, at 12:30 A.M. Drove the whole neighborhood, noting every pedestrian, checking parked cars for heads backlit by the headlights of approaching vehicles.

Nobody had the station staked out.

By 1:15 A.M. he knew every parked car, every shadow that could hold a man, every possible approach. He parked on San

Jose facing Geneva, where he could see the BART station pedestrian overpass with a turn of his head. He slumped behind the wheel and waited.

With a start, O'B sat bolt upright behind the wheel still slant-parked on the Sonoma square. Not again! Asleep just like last time—not booze, at least, just exhaustion—but just like last time, Tim Bland could have driven by him a dozen times.

He checked his watch with bleary eyes. One-fifty A.M. Bar-close time. Bland wouldn't be driving by this night. Just time to walk across the park for an O'Doul's and a couple of bags of pretzels at the General Vallejo to sustain him on the long frustrating empty-handed drive home to the city.

The pseudo-Spanish mission bar had lots of old drawings of Vallejo's *hacienda* when it had been that Spanish officer's stronghold, and of San Francisco's Presidio when it still had been a Spanish fortification. Old muskets and sabers were crossed on the walls; there were Bowie knives, *sombreros, serapes,* and, hanging from a cross rafter, a pair of cracked Spanish leather officers' boots complete with big-roweled spurs.

All that was missing was the mark of Zorro, and a husky man with a deeply lined face was trying to put that on the tall lean blonde behind the bar. His deep tan stopped in an abrupt line two inches above his eyes; obviously, out in all weather with a wide-brimmed hat pulled down on his head.

As O'B slid onto a stool, the guy said, "Aw, c'mon, Sonja, it's Friday an' I know your old man's out of town until Monday. It's party time!"

Sonja had high cheekbones, blue eyes full of mischief, and thin red lips curved with humor. She was dressed frontier style: tight jeans, high-heel boots of tooled leather, a red-checked cowboy shirt with the top three buttons undone, a bandanna around her shapely brown throat. Hmmm. Just Tim Bland's type.

She leaned across the bar and stuck her face quite close to that of the husky man.

"Gus, I don't know what the hell gave you the idea that I cheat on my husband, but if I did it sure as hell wouldn't be with you." She winked at O'B as she pointed Gus toward the door. "Closing time, big boy. Go home and give Carmen my love."

"She's at her ma's place in Salinas for the weekend, that's the trouble."

"Then go home and lock yourself in the bathroom with a *Hustler*." As Gus shambled out, she gave O'B an apologetic smile. "Sorry, Red, but last call is already past."

O'B put a ten-dollar bill on the bar.

"A couple of bags of pretzels and an O'Doul's? The ABC can't bust you for that. I'll even drink from the bottle."

"Nonalcoholic O'Doul's? Oh, what the hell—okay."

She got the bottle from the cooler under the back bar, flipped off the top, set it down with two bags of pretzels. He drank deep as she went around turning off lights and the jukebox and brought the house phone up from behind the bar. O'B spun his stool around back-to-the-bar to give her the illusion of privacy.

"I'm closing up now, the last guy's just leaving," Sonja said behind him in a low, throaty voice. "When you get here, stick your head in and I'll come out. I don't want to stand around outside waiting, Tim—you don't know what this town's turned into."

Right on. Tim didn't know Sonoma, liked tall lean blondes, and screwed other guys' wives. O'B drained his O'Doul's, picked up his pretzels, waved off his change, and headed for the door.

"Thanks, Sonja," he called as he went out.

Sprint across the square for his car? No. Play the odds. He stepped back into the shadows of a narrow alley that led to a courtyard of small shops and cafés.

Seven minutes brought the throaty growl of a sports car. It stopped with its dark green hood just visible from O'B's ambush. Panoz kit car. Left in the street with the motor running as Bland crossed the sidewalk.

Tim Bland pulled open the door of the General Vallejo to stick his head in, and O'B walked unhurriedly out of the alley. He slid into the cockpit of the low gleaming green car crouched like a leopard in the street. Slamming it into gear, he fishtailed away around the square with Tim Bland's shouts of outraged astonishment shredded by the wind of his passage.

twenty-one

Milagrita came across the BART station's pedestrian walkway at 2:01 A.M. She was wearing jeans and a 49ers warm-up jacket and had her hair tucked up under a Giants baseball cap. She was alone. Nobody crossed behind her. Morales was still in place on San Jose Ave, across Geneva from the old Green Muni Center crammed with antique trolley cars. He squealed the Accord around the corner and skidded to a stop right in front of her.

"Get in!" he yelled.

He was away so fast the open passenger-side door slammed shut behind Milagrita on its own. Only where Geneva merged into Ocean Avenue did he look over at her. She had opened her jacket and removed her cap and shaken out her long black hair. Red letters on her black T-shirt said SUPPORT MENTAL HEALTH OR I'LL KILL YOU. Her eyes were very big, but her voice was strong.

"You had us meet way out here because you do not trust me."

"I don't trust nobody."

"Then indeed I am sorry for you."

"You gonna get in trouble being out this late?"

"I am almost nineteen," she said proudly. "The phone number I gave you is an apartment I share with another girl. Esteban does not like it, but . . ." She shrugged. *"Mi madre* trusts me so he can do little about it."

Almost nineteen. When he had nailed her in that Geneva Avenue motel room, he had thought she was sixteen, a juvie. It hadn't bothered him: before Esteban's attack, he had started to look at fourteen-, even thirteen-year-olds. Now he had been without a woman for so long he didn't know what he'd like.

There was little traffic as they drove west on Ocean Avenue through a neighborhood of small businesses.

"Uh, I'm sorry what I did to you, Milagrita."

It was the first time he could remember apologizing to anyone except in a sort of half-assed way to a giant iguana in Baja's desert north of Cabo during the great Gypsy Cadillac hunt.

"It was wrong," she agreed gravely, "but it is finished."

"Not for your brother. He still has guys watching me."

"Verdad," she said seriously. "It is why I had to talk to you. When you came into the pizzeria today I meant what I said. He will try to kill you if he knows you have seen me."

"I didn't even know who you were!" Morales blurted out.

"I have always told Esteban that. After a time he saw you had no interest in any woman, so he was satisfied and would have given up. But one of Esteban's *amigos*, Jorge, says I have been dishonored and that you must *really* pay for what you did."

"Uh . . . do you . . . how do you feel about this Jorge guy?"

She was silent for a moment, her dark sleek head lowered.

"I hate him. Someday, because you have had me and he has not, he will try to take me the way you did, and make me keep silent about it afterward. But he feels you have challenged his *machismo*, so he wants you dead first. That is what I wanted to tell you. Esteban would give up, but Jorge, never."

"Yeah, well, I ain't so easy to kill."

Big words for a *cobarde*, he thought. A man who hides behind closed blinds, and now hides behind a girl's skirts. A girl he couldn't protect from this Jorge even if he wanted to.

He asked, "Can you drive a car?"

"Cómo no?" The touch of pride was back in her voice.

"This one?"

She checked for auto trans, nodded. "*De vero*. But why?"

"I'm working. I might need you as a driver."

"What sort of work does one do at two in the morning?"

"I'm a repoman."

They crossed 19th Avenue into Merced Manor. A long block north, beyond broad Sloat Boulevard, was Stern Grove where the free summer concerts were held. Morales had never been to one. He wondered if Milagrita had.

"What kind of car are you looking for?" she asked.

"Don't know," he grunted.

She giggled. Her teeth were small and very white in her brown face. When she laughed her whole face laughed. She was a pretty young woman about to plunge into beauty.

"What sort of repoman does not know what he has to repo?"

Morales handed her Giselle's folded skip list from behind the visor. The Corvette and the Ferrari were lined out.

"It'll be one of these other five cars. We start by finding Gellert Drive, just before Sunset, and go from there."

They went by the broad flat-topped grassy mound of a Water Department reservoir built after the '06 quake. The fog was in, out here near the ocean the night was cold and damp. They had not passed another car in either direction since crossing 19th.

"There! Ahead to the right!" Her voice was excited.

On this side of Ocean, Gellert was just a block long and the numbers were wrong. They recrossed Ocean and followed Gellert to the address, 492, that Trin had gotten from Carlos Feliu. It was a well-kept two-story salmon-colored house with green and white trim. A Jeepster was parked in the driveway.

"Maybe it is hidden in the garage," Milagrita said.

By jumping up repeatedly, Morales could see through the glass along the top of the overhead door. Empty. Walking back toward his still-running car, he thought it would be a good trick on him if Milagrita drove off and left him. She didn't.

"Nothing," he said when he was back behind the wheel.

"So we have failed."

We? Had that been real disappointment in her voice? He told her the story of the dealership raid and the salesman whom Trin thought had taken off with the demo he was driving.

"*Es claro.* He has no right to the car," she agreed.

They drove a grid of two-block streets within walking distance of the residence address checking out every long shot they saw. It was nearly three-thirty and Milagrita was yawning by the time all the possibilities were exhausted.

"There's a little pocket of streets over beyond Sunset where he might have hidden it," Morales said doggedly.

He hadn't realized how much he wanted to look good in front of Milagrita.

"Let's go," she said gamely.

One block beyond Sunset, Ocean hit a circular court called Country Club Drive. They cruised slowly. As they passed a remarkably ugly green and yellow San Francisco row house in the 400 block, Milagrita suddenly exclaimed aloud.

"Wait! Stop! Back up! There is one from your list!"

It was a black moisture-covered 1995 Acura NSX, obviously parked there for hours. Jesus, was he so tired he had missed it?

"It is truly worth sixty-two thousand dollars?"

"If it's the one we want. They ain't makin' 'em anymore."

He left the Accord running as he got out his flashlight and opened his door. They were scant yards from Skyline Boulevard; beyond that sprawled the San Francisco Zoo. Fog-laden ocean wind carried the wild mingled smells of the animals to them.

"Is this really it?" Milagrita demanded. She was like a ferret after a rabbit. He almost started to laugh at her.

"I think so. Lemme check the VIN."

Yeah! Right number. He started working his filed-down

skeleton keys on the door. The third one fit. In her excitement, Milagrita started yipping and jumping up and down. Then she started pounding Trin on the chest. Finally, she embraced him.

He opened the Acura's door, started to get in. Lights went on in the second floor of the green and yellow house. A window went up over the inset garage. A voice yelled.

"Hey, you out there, I'm calling the police."

Morales stepped back out, shouted at him, "This your car?"

"No, but—"

"Then shut the hell up and go back to bed." To Milagrita he said, "Let's get out of here—he's gonna call the cops, so I'll drive this one and you follow me to our office in the Accord. It's Daniel Kearny Associates at 340 Eleventh Street."

It was after 4:00 A.M. when they got to DKA. He wanted to send her home in a cab, but she wanted to see the whole process: notifying the police of the repo, removing and cataloging the personal property, making out the condition report, finally writing a field report that also noted time and mileage and expenses. Trin included $25 for a driver, which he solemnly offered and which she solemnly accepted.

Only then would she let him call a taxi. They parted wordlessly after another of her brief impetuous *abrazos*. He paid the cabbie, stood watching the Yellow disappear down Eleventh Street toward Bryant and her Mission District apartment.

Would he ever see her again? Not if he wanted to stay healthy. Probably wouldn't be able to stay healthy even then.

Getting back into his own car, he realized this had been the best night of his life. And he couldn't even say why.

twenty-two

Larry Ballard woke at eight on Monday morning with the heady smells of Midori still on his body. He unsuccessfully groped for her in the bed beside him before sitting up under the twisted bedclothes. Swinging his feet to the floor, he padded through into the living room with its pathetic kitchen alcove.

"Midori?"

Then he remembered. *Monday morning.* She had promised Nordstrom's she'd be back to work on Monday. Feeling at once almost frail and like the biggest stud in the world, he crossed the living room to twitch aside the bulbous bay window's oft-mended lace curtains to look out across Lincoln Way into the green depths of Golden Gate Park.

No green depths. Just a solid bank of early fog swirled and whipped by icy gusts off the Pacific. Out here in the ironically named Sunset District there was usually fog in the morning and evening with a four-hour window of milky sunlight in between.

Ballard let the curtain fall back. Not only would Midori be riding the streetcar out to Stonestown in her thin coat—the only one she had—she still had classes to attend. She'd go right from her half-day at Nordstrom's to S.F. State.

Forgetting his naked state, he strode down the hall to her apartment and crossed her tiny living room calling, "Midori?" She was in the bedroom, in bra and panties, just dropping a black dress with a mid-calf skirt down over her head.

She turned. "Rarry! I try not to wake you. What is—"

"It's cold out, you've got classes this afternoon, I want to drive you to work."

"Like that?"

He looked down. Whoops.

Midori was already giggling and sliding her panties down and off under her dress. And just like that, Larry got to live out his fantasy of flipping her skirt over her head and having his way with her while she was fully dressed. *Turn on!*

He even got her to Nordstrom's on time afterward.

Back in his apartment in a lovely haze, he walked in on a ringing phone and Giselle's crisp Monday morning voice.

"Mel's Drive-In on Geary Boulevard in thirty minutes, Hot Shot. Breakfast is on me."

"Make it forty-five. I need a shower."

The great Yana hunt had begun.

Competing with the clatter of silver and the rattle of plates were a dozen flavors of English from Mel's usual crowd—black, brown, yellow, white, and every shade in between. Larry looked around.

"We're only two blocks from UpScale," he said. "Isn't that a little risky?"

"With UpScale closed down, I figured this would be the safest place in town to meet. Especially in this crowd. I had trouble spotting you myself." She paused. "So where were you this morning, Hot Shot? I've been calling since dawn."

Larry cleared his throat. "Uh . . . I've had a lot to do . . ."

"To whom?" She held up a detaining hand. "Whoever she is, you're going to have to refocus your energies on your old flame Yana for a while. She's missing, and Dan has accepted an assignment from Staley to find her."

Larry laughed. "From Staley? The Great White Father must really want to put me to work. This puts me back in the field with billable time and mileage to cover my salary, and the *Rom* won't want written reports."

"Just don't show up at the office and screw up the court case and get yourself sued personally."

"I won't."

He leaned back, one hand idly turning his teacup.

"So why do they want Yana?"

Giselle looked at her notes. "It's a confused story. The long and the short of it is, she's wanted for the murder of her husband."

"Poteet?"

Giselle nodded.

"That flake," muttered Larry.

"But apparently she had been ostracized by the tribe before this happened." She circled something on the page in front of her. "Something called *marime.*"

"*Marime!* Any idea what for?"

Giselle gave him a wide-eyed look from beneath arched eyebrows.

"Could it be . . . Satan . . . ?"

"Knock it off, Giselle, Yana and I were friends as well as . . . well, friends. I helped teach her to read, for God's sake!"

"Be that as it may, all the evidence points to her in the murder of Ephrem Poteet. His dying statement—legal bedside testimony, by the way—an eyewitness next door."

Larry waved dismissively.

"Eyewitness is the worst kind of evidence. They got her fingerprints? Hair and fiber samples? DNA? They able to put her in L.A. that night?"

"They've got to find her first," conceded Giselle. "But she's slippery. Rosenkrantz and Guildenstern had her in their hands and she waltzed right out from under their noses."

Larry looked at the table for several moments.

"Let me tell you a story that Yana told me," he said. "A true story. There was a big shoot-out down in Mexico City between

two feuding Gypsy families from Puerto Rico and Cuba. A bunch
of people were killed. Each family was tried by a *kris*—"

"A court?"

"Yeah. And each family was given a *marime* sentence. It
was the worst disgrace in the history of the Gypsies on this continent. That was in 1947 and even now, fifty-three years later,
neither extended family has recovered from the disgrace.
They've lost their businesses, other families won't marry their
grandchildren, and they are afloat between two cultures, considered pariahs in both. The way Yana told that story, I could
see how horrified she was, and how much her tribe meant to
her."

"Maybe she doesn't believe in *marime* anymore," Giselle
said gently.

"And murder!" Larry said, as if he hadn't heard her. "There's
something called a *mulo*—the ghost of the victim. I don't believe in ghosts, but Yana was a powerful person, and she did.
None of this makes sense."

"Well, find her." Giselle's voice had an edge of impatience.
"Maybe you can sneak a peek at her crystal ball and get the answers you're looking for."

Larry stood up. "Ask Dan to make Staley point me in the direction of Yana's brother, Ramon Ristik. I'll try to get a line on
what the cops have, too." He looked ruefully at his empty plate.
"I guess I'll have to start with Beverly at Jacques Daniel's. I
swear those guys eat lunch there two-three times a day."

Three of the UpScale classics were still outstanding: a black
1970 Aston Martin Volante; a champagne 1990 Jaguar XJS convertible; and a red 1966 Mustang convertible. So Ken Warren
wanted to check out the rest of the former UpScale salesmen.

Christian Roxborough lived in a gray two-story house at 557
Raymond Avenue in Visitacion Valley. In this mixed
brown/black/yellow neighborhood, nobody would tell Ken
anything. He was white, he was tough-looking, and he talked

funny. And Roxborough was a community pillar: married, family man, Little League coach, wife a churchgoer.

It was a tough stakeout. The houses faced the sharply rising eucalyptus-dotted slope of McLaren Park, so Ken had to park in the turnaround at the street's dead end behind a big powerboat on a six-wheel trailer under a blue tarpaulin cover. He never saw Roxborough; but the wife parked her Dodge van in the double garage under the house. If Roxborough had made Ken, which was likely, he could leave and enter the house in the back of the van where Ken couldn't see him. Of course he might not be hiding one of the classics at all.

But Ken kept right on checking the neighborhood for info on what cars Roxborough drove. Early Saturday morning, he got to Discount Liquors on the old Bayshore just as the owner was unlocking his black steel thief-guard shutters.

"Hnood hnmornin," said Ken to the guy's back.

The big black man whirled around. "Kenny!" he exclaimed in a big booming bass voice, his ebony features aglow with delight.

In pre–Pac Bell Park days, Ken and Clarence Withers had parked cars for the Giants' home games in a cheapo dirt lot across the street from Candlestick's regular lot. They'd had some times together for sure, before Clarence got married and got religion during a single disastrous weekend.

"Hyna nrepomnan neow," said Ken.

"A repoman?" Clarence went into a bout of high hee-hee-hee laughter. "Ain't after my slick, is you, man?"

"Hncritn Gnroxbro."

"Christian Roxborough? He buys his booze here."

They went into the store and Clarence got down behind the counter with an X-Acto knife to open cases of Early Times. He handed the bottles up for Ken to shelve while they talked.

"Hngew hngow nhwha he'n hndrivin?" Ken asked.

"An old Mustang ragtop in beautiful condition. Maybe a sixty-five, sixty-six, in there." He stopped, frowning, and shook his tight-curled head. "Ain't seen it lately, though. Come to think of it, ain't seen *him* lately. That cause of you?"

Ken nodded.

"I heard the man just got a job selling cars, starting last week. Mercedes? Lincolns? Maybe it was Cadillacs."

Cadillacs. After Ken promised to come over to Clarence's home for dinner the next day, he called the office. Even on a Saturday, Giselle had the info within a few minutes.

"Jack Olwen Cadillac on Van Ness Avenue," she told Ken on the phone. Which was great. DKA had picked up a lot of delinquent Caddies for Jack Olwen over the years.

For half an hour Ken cruised the streets around the Jack Olwen Cadillac dealership on the sadly depleted Van Ness Avenue Auto Row. No '66 Mustang. Then he boldly drove into the Olwen service entrance on Washington below Franklin.

Along both sides of the broad open grease-stained concrete floor were work bays, each holding a Cadillac in some stage of undress, like backstage at the ballet. Blue-coveralled mechanics swarmed around the cars like stage-door johnnies around the scantily clad dancers. The place echoed hollowly with the clank of tools and thunk-thunk of compressed air hoses. No Mustang.

So he went down to the ornate Olwen showroom with its lofty fake-marble pillars. Sleek Escalantes, Fleetwoods, Allantes, Eldorados, DeVille DTSs, Broughams, and an Escalade 2000 SUV rested in stately splendor on the gleaming display floor. Each sported its stunning price tag and its new-car smell, like an expensive call girl negotiating her splendid fee while poufing Chanel No. 22 talc in all the old familiar places.

Ken was immune to their charms. No Roxborough, no '66 Mustang. He went down a narrow aisle between glassed-in cubicles to find sales manager Paddy McBain behind his paper-littered desk. Paddy was a thick-bodied man with most of his hair and the crinkly blue eyes and humorous mouth of the professional Irishman who always leads the parade on St. Paddy's Day.

"BeJaysus and it's Ken. And how's the bhoyo?" He stood, reached across the desk to shake hands.

"Hngfyn," said Ken.

It was the first of only four words he spoke. McBain was never able to understand one single damned thing he said, ever, so Ken always wrote out what he wanted. McBain scanned his note.

"Yeah, Chris Roxborough, started last Thursday. He's got a customer out in a demo right now, hell of a salesman. But Chris isn't driving any sixty-six Mustang ragtop—he drives a van. He coaches Little League, you know."

"Hgneys, Hny hknoh," said Ken wearily.

McBain didn't understand that, either.

Ken left almost convinced Roxborough was as squeaky-clean as everyone seemed to believe. But crossing the show-room he was intercepted by a lean, handsome, impeccably dressed African-American with bright eyes and a pencil-thin mustache. The man jabbed an angry forefinger at Ken's chest.

"If I see you around my neighborhood again, dickhead, I'm calling the cops. If you said anything to Paddy just now that makes trouble for me here, I'm calling my attorney. If you have a sister, you sorry piece of shit, go on home and fuck her."

Wrong, all wrong for a guy with his sort of surface charm. He *was* hiding that Mustang, and he was sore because he was afraid Ken was going to find out *where* he was hiding it.

Well, Ken was. Make book on it.

twenty-three

Dan Kearny, behind his desk, got out a cigarette, looked at it, and stuck it back into his pack. "I really gotta get serious about quitting." He lifted his coffee cup, then looked up at Giselle from under raised brows. "Coffee's still okay, right?"

"Decaf," she grinned.

He chuckled. "Okay, shoot. I presume Larry's on Yana's case full-time, and that he thinks she's innocent. Right?"

"Absolutely, until convinced otherwise." She was rummaging in her purse. "Here's a number you might reach him, evenings."

"His latest doxy?"

"She's a really nice girl, actually. Midori Tagawa."

"Little Japanese number lives in the back apartment?"

When she nodded, he crumpled up the paper and threw it in the wastebasket. Midori reminded him of Kathy Onoda, their much-missed office manager who had died of a CVA at age twenty-nine; let 'em have their loving in peace. He shook his head.

"Nice girl like that and she gets mixed up with Ballard, for Chrissake. Okay, where do we stand with Wiley's classics?"

"O'B got the Panoz and Morales knocked off the Acura. And Ken says Roxborough has been driving the sixty-six Mustang."

"So why isn't it in the barn?"

"He's gotta see it first. He'll get it."

"When? Stan wants to auction those cars off."

"Whoa, Dan'l! What about my little red Alfa Quadrifoglio Spider? Give me a chance to get it together. They still haven't brought in the Aston Martin and the Jag convertible."

"Okay, okay. So put O'B and Morales back on their regular cases and divvy up Larry's files between 'em." He picked up his cigarettes, laid them down again. "And tell you what. On the Gypsy case, line Bart up with a new set of wheels, and send him up Poteet's backtrail. Maybe have him start with that Bunco guy, what's his name . . ."

Giselle made a face. "Dirty Harry."

"Yeah. Him. Maybe he knows what Poteet was doing when he was living up here. If he doesn't, send Bart down to L.A. to snoop around. I'll give Staley a toot and ask for information on both Ristik and Poteet."

How's that for delaying an auction?

Lulu was still aghast at the idea of using the *gadje* to look for one of their own even if she was *marime*.

"What's he want all that stuff for?" she demanded crossly.

"Kearny thinks Ramon might know things about his sister that we don't," said Rudolph.

"You know more about Yana than anybody."

"Not since the *kris* declared her *marime*."

Staley sighed. "Looking back, maybe that wasn't such a hot idea, that *marime*." He waved a hand. "Okay, let 'em find Ramon. He don't matter. But Ephrem—why they wanna spend all that money nosin' around him? He's dead, he can't tell 'em nothing about Yana."

" 'Cept that she killed him, and he's already told us that," said Lulu snidely.

"Okay, you guys, as King, I say we hold off giving Kearny the Marine World stuff on Ephrem."

Richard Kinsman Robinson was six-foot-one and 225 pounds and had broad meaty shoulders and big hands with thick fingers that could crack walnuts without effort. Most people found his size intimidating; as a guard in the tough state prison at Walla Walla, Washington, he had gotten his edge from intimidation.

But as head of security at Xanadu, Victor Marr's hilltop sanctuary at the edge of Big Sur's rugged Los Padres National Forest, he was intimidated by his boss. Victor Marr had eyes that could eviscerate you with a glance, bury you with a glare.

At 9:00 A.M., R.K. was on his rounds with Charon and Hecate, the twin Dobermans. Suddenly the dogs came to attention, ears pricked, lean bodies taut with incipient aggression. Then R.K. heard it, too: the unmistakable *whomp-whomp-whomp-whomp* of helicopter blades.

He knew that chopper. Marr rarely showed up at the mountaintop retreat, and called ahead when he did, which suited R.K. just fine. It gave him a chance to get everything dressed down and tightened up before Marr arrived. Until this morning. He broke into a heavy-bodied run across the broad green grounds.

"The bastard!" R.K. exclaimed bitterly to the dogs.

The big sleek Bell 206 JetRanger came up out of the rising sun, over the tops of the dense stands of evergreens flanking the grounds, the anti-collision beacon on its upper tail fin blinking pink in the bright morning light. It came in almost as if it meant to strafe Marr's three-story flat-roofed futuristic building, and settled on the roof landing pad. Marr and his entourage came strolling out of the front door just as R.K., panting, arrived with the dogs at the foot of the broad front stairs. With Marr were his pilot, a military-looking man named Carmody who had served in Desert Storm, and Marko, his personal secretary. Marko looked as if any keyboards he was familiar with would wear ammo belts and magazines rather than computers.

"Sir! Stop right there!" barked R.K.

"What did you say?" demanded Marr in true astonishment.

People didn't order him around. Marko suddenly had a Glock 17 in his right hand without seeming to have moved at all.

R.K. held his ground. "The dogs don't know you, sir."

Hecate and Charon were straining at their leashes, teeth bared, ears laid flat back against their skulls. Marr paused on the third step from the bottom.

"Leicht," said R.K. in a low voice. R.K. did not speak German, but he'd felt it was his duty to learn a few key words. The dogs relaxed. Marr nodded his approval.

"That's very good, R.K." R.K. Not Robinson. Everything was all right. "What is the attack command?"

It was *Angreifen*, attack, but R.K. said, "If I told you that in front of them, sir, they'd take it as an order."

Marr waved a hand at his secretary. The Glock disappeared as easily as it had appeared. R.K. and Marr strolled toward the front gate with the dogs falling into step beside them. At the gate was a uniformed guard with the West Indian oil logo on his military-style cap. He had weasel eyes and a chin going south, but he wore a Sam Browne belt with a holstered pistol on his hip, the holster flap unsnapped. Marr exchanged a few pleasantries with him and walked on, R.K. and the dogs close behind.

"How many men patrolling the grounds?" Marr asked R.K.

"Three at all times besides myself. Our guard complement is twelve men on a rotating basis, each team working eight on, twelve off so nobody gets stuck with night duty all the time. Each team gets four days off the mountain every two weeks."

"Good. Everything looks in order. It seems you've done what I've asked, R.K.—made Xanadu secure. But I've been warned someone may try to breach our defenses here. I have a security consultant coming from Germany to look over our arrangements."

"Hell, sir, me and my men can handle anything that—"

"You are to extend every courtesy, Robinson."

Marr's face did that thing that meant he thought he was

smiling. "When he has made his recommendations, I want your evaluation on how good you think he is at *his* job."

"*Yessir!*" exclaimed R.K. with enthusiasm. He knew already what his evaluation of the security expert would be.

That same afternoon, Larry Ballard got word of Ristik working the Richmond District bars to steer customers to Yana's *ofica* on Geary. As a result, he tramped fifteen, twenty miles of concrete in the cold grey Richmond District streets that night and the next day. He almost had to fight his way out of one joint on Clement Street where Ramon had apparently taken some Russian for $500. Eighty-seven people interviewed, five definite Ramon-sightings—but none since Yana had disappeared.

By 10 P.M. Wednesday, only the thought of Midori was keeping him awake. Leave a blind message on DKA's unlisted number first, in case they could sleep in the next morning.

After one ring it was picked up with a guarded, "Hello?"

"Giselle, what the devil are you doing working so late?"

"Ah . . . Mr. Bush! What are you doing calling in? But I'm glad you did. Rudolph called. Some Gyppo spotted Ristik in North Beach tonight. He has a gig at some private club there."

"Reading the palm of the corpse at a wake? 'You have a short life line' . . ."

"Very funny. It seems our Ramon is—also a knife-juggler."

"A *knife*-juggler?"

"So says the note Mr. K left."

"I'll try to catch up with him, and hope he doesn't throw one at me."

twenty-four

The Golden Gate was a roomy box of a place on Columbus Avenue that hosted weddings, bar mitzvahs, and conventions for under two hundred people. Its main claim to fame was a small, arched, foreshortened, slightly tipsy model of the Golden Gate Bridge that you had to cross upon entering from the street.

For an hour, Eli Nicholas played lively *baya bashilba* on his Gypsy *bosh* in honor of the happy couple. Wearing his bright Gypsy costume, Ramon Ristik, drunk from endless glasses of the newlyweds' Korbel champagne, began his knife-juggling routine. Afterward, Eli clapped him on the back and said he was the best Gypsy knife-juggler on the west coast. High praise indeed from the Bay Area's primo *bosho mengro*—Gypsy violinist.

But it was a melancholy Ramon who wended his way up Taylor toward Vallejo Street, knife case in hand, at 2:00 A.M. Melancholy because the champagne had been domestic and because his fee had been only $200.

Why couldn't Yana have stayed in North Beach? He lifted his head and howled at the moon. *We didn't want you to go, because we needed you. But you didn't listen to us.* Together, they had raked it in. But now she, who once aspired to be Queen of the Muchwaya, was *marime*. And the police were looking for her. *Now you are gone, living but no longer alive.* It was all the fault of that tall filthy *gadjo* pig, Larry Ballard. From their sexual liaison, all evil had flowed. *He* was the thief of Yana's Gypsy wisdom, he had seduced her and destroyed her. *I miss you, Yana my sister . . .*

He imagined Ballard walking into the Golden Gate when Ramon was juggling his gleaming knives. He stopped on the sidewalk to finish the *gadjo* off, a knife in each hand, slashing, stabbing . . .

"Jesus, man, I'll give you the bottle!"

He looked down. A cowering homeless man was holding up a half-empty bottle of muscatel to him with shaking fingers.

Ramon scurried off, the vagrant staring after him bleary-eyed until he was out of sight, then glug-glugging down the wine.

Ballard spent nearly two hours working his North Beach contacts: the drivers at the taxi stand on Columbus; the bartender at Big Al's; the cook at the unnamed family-style Basque café halfway up narrow Romolo Place above Broadway; waiters, parking attendants, street types, hustlers, hookers. Always trying to get news of a Gypsy who might be doing some sort of sword dance. He got his first real lead from muumuu-clad Mama Gina in the Opera Bar on Broadway at Taylor.

Over *Per Pieta Non Dirmi Addio* from the jukebox, she shouted, "A Gyppo violinist is playing at a Bohunk wedding at the Golden Gate; maybe he brought your knife-fighter along with him. It's a private reception, that's why you can't find it, honey."

Ballard gave her a hug, and went striding down Taylor toward Columbus, hoping the reception hadn't already ended.

Full of hostile thoughts about Ballard, Ramon glanced up as he heard approaching footsteps, to stare into Ballard's eyes.

*   *   *

Full of sexual thoughts about Midori, Larry glanced up as he heard approaching footsteps, to stare into Ramon's eyes.

Ramon leaped back as he threw aside his knife case. A huge knife was in each fist. He yelled, *"Gadjo* pig, you sullied my sister's honor! I challenge you to a Gypsy duel!"

"A Gypsy duel? I guess that's where you have two knives and I don't have anything."

A moment's reflection. Ristik handed him one of the knives. Ballard gripped it gingerly in the utterly wrong position for a knife fight—blade pointing down as if for stabbing.

They were at the mouth of a half-block alley, narrow, dim, wet with drifting fog. Water dripped, light gleamed off uneven cobbles. Why didn't he just throw down the knife and run like hell? Practicing unarmed hand-to-hand techniques against an armed assailant in the dojo was one thing, but facing a guy with a real knife in his hand, a guy who *juggled* them for Chrissake . . .

"We don't have to do this, you know, Ramon."

"Yes we do." The recently despised domestic champagne was now singing in Ramon's blood. "Unless you are *daranòok* as well as a *gadjo* pig!" He whipped the red and yellow and green kerchief from around his neck and held it out to Larry. "We each take an end of this *diklo* in our teeth—"

"Are you crazy?"

"You are the crazy one, for dishonoring my sister. We will fight to the death . . ." A wisp of his usual caution drifted through his mind. "Or, ah. . . . until one of us admits defeat."

Larry said instantly, "I admit defeat."

Ramon laughed a great triumphant laugh. Oh *Devèl!*, it felt good to have this cowardly gadjo cringing before him! Brought to Aladdin Terrace by the power of Ramon's killing fantasy of a few minutes before. Maybe he had some of his sister's powers.

"Until we fight, you cannot quit."

"Aw, shit."

Larry took one end of the kerchief between his teeth. Ramon did the same. They began circling each other, two feet apart. The only sounds were sparse traffic on Columbus, the drip of water, their shoes on the wet uneven pavement. He tried one more time, his voice muffled and distorted by the sweaty *diklo* reeking of smoke and champagne clamped between his teeth.

"I just want to ask you a couple of questions, Ramon—"

But Ristik feinted at Larry's face, then slashed at his knife hand. Ballard's left arm automatically blocked Ramon's blade outward, even as his right foot delivered a lightning-fast karate front-kick to Ristik's already-tender balls. Ballard didn't pull it as he did in training. Not totally, anyway.

Ramon doubled over with a great WHOOSH of air and dropped his knife as the *diklo* floated to the ground. He fell on top of the bright silk in a fetal curl, wheezing.

"That's a Larry Ballard duel, asshole."

No response. Larry sighed and kicked the knives away and sat down on the curb. Ramon half-sat up, gingerly.

"You have ruptured me," he moaned.

"Again, I admit defeat, okay? Will that satisfy your fucking Gypsy honor?"

Ramon said, "I feel sick," and proceeded to prove it.

"Wonderful," said Ballard, on his feet to avoid the mess. As Ramon wiped his mouth with the *diklo*, Larry added, "Tell me everything you can about your sister and I'll be on my way."

"Never!" Ramon managed to wheeze out.

"I found you once, and look what's happened. You want me to find you again?"

"I'll die before I betray another *Rom* to the *gadje*."

Larry crouched beside him. "I'm *working* for the Muchwaya."

"I do not believe you."

He punched in a number and held out his cell phone.

"Call Staley, ask him."

"No, no, it's okay." Ramon could not stand the thought of news of his defeat moving through the *Romi* community.

Larry walked the limping Gypsy back to the house of an Italian family who thought he was an illegal immigrant from their grandparents' hometown of San Benedetto del Tronto on the Adriatic Coast north of Bari. Ramon didn't have the slightest notion of where to find his sister.

All he had was a bunch of Presidio message-drops they had never used, and the name of one of Yana's *boojo* clients who lived on Chestnut Street.

It was 5:00 A.M. when Larry fell into bed with the rueful realization that he was older, no wiser, and worst of all, alone.

At 7:00 A.M., a nude, hot-bodied Midori slipped into his bed. She brought him awake in the most amazing manner possible, then kept them both hovering on the edge of orgasm for forty-five minutes before they lost control and came together. He slid down the silken rope of sleep with a big amazed smile on his face, the smell of Midori in his nostrils, Midori's self-satisfied giggle in his ears.

twenty-five

Two hours later, Bart Heslip waited across the desk from Dirty Harry's empty swivel chair in Bunco, looking at the brass plaque Giselle had described: FEEL SAFE TONIGHT—SLEEP WITH A COP. Slimeball Harrigan finally showed up, smelling of Polo aftershave.

"So what's the beef?" he asked in a disinterested voice.

"Bart Heslip with Daniel Kearny Associates. We're trying to trace the movements of a man named Ephrem Poteet."

There was a flash of alarm in his eyes at mention of Poteet. "Gyppo. Fucker's dead. Got scragged down in L.A. by his Gyppo wife. End of story."

He spoke with flat, quick disinterest. Was it too flat, too quick? Why would Bart's innocuous question about a man killed in L.A. push a San Francisco Bunco cop's panic button?

"We have a client who's interested in Mr. Poteet and his contacts here in the Bay Area."

Again, that flash of alarm. "Client got a name?"

"Sorry. Confidential."

"Well, hell, you want me to spill my guts, but you—" He stopped abruptly with a little embarrassed chuckle. "Sorry. I was up all night shovin' my spittin' cobra into this little old gal gets turned on by the uniform—"

"Ephrem Poteet," interrupted Bart coldly.

Harry got a faraway look in his eyes. "Seems to me a cop

pal of mine on the Vallejo Pee-Dee told me Poteet was pickin' pockets at Marine World up there. Guy was a hell of a dip."

Wait a minute! Poteet was living in the Bay Area? "Wouldn't know where he was living then, would you?"

"Sure wouldn't," said Dirty Harry in great disappointment.

"Would your friend on the Vallejo police know?"

"Hell, don't you know, he retired and moved to Oregon."

Bart went back to his new car—a nifty Chevy Caprice Giselle had found for him that was only two years old and even had a tape deck and C/D player—and thought about Dirty Harry. Then he called Giselle at the office.

"You got contacts at SFPD records, right?"

"One, but she's a personal friend," said Giselle.

"Think she could find out whether Dirty Harry ever busted Yana for anything—or Ephrem either, for that matter?"

"I can work on her. I can't promise anything."

As soon as Bart cleared Bunco, Dirty Harry went down the hall to make a panicked phone call. He caught her just as she was leaving for her *gadjo* job.

"There was a private eye around asking questions about your husband's movements for the last month or two . . ."

When he was finished with his sad tale, she said, in the saccharine tone she knew angered him, "God, you're a *kekeno moosh*. All you did was get him suspicious, Mr. Nobody."

"Yeah, well, you weren't there, I was." He went on the offensive. "What about my cut? I told you I wanted—"

"And I told you that you'll get your cut when I feel it's safe to get mine. Then I will be your little *sapengro* again." She gave a dirty laugh. "Your little snake charmer."

Despite this promise of future sexual delight, Harry hung up with panic nibbling at the edges of his mind.

* * *

Josh Croswell fought panic. Mr. Petrick was due back to-morrow. Better remind the silly little nerd Donny that the emer-ald was here in the safe waiting for him.

Josh dialed the 650 area code number on the *faux*-engraved business card Donny had left with him. Three-tone beep.

"The number you have dialed is not in service at this time. Please recheck the number and try again."

"Hello, Josh, how did it go while I was away?"

He dropped the phone as if it were red hot. Burton Petrick, back a day early!

"It was, ah, er . . . quiet, sir."

Petrick was a skinny hollow-chested man just into his 40s, with coal-black hair slicked straight back, piercing dark eyes behind heavy-rimmed glasses, and a prim mouth under a small and rather narrow but bristling black mustache.

"Not too quiet, I hope. I spent a lot of money in Holland. A lot of money. But wisely, Josh. I spent wisely."

He was twirling the knob of the office safe. Trying to fore-stall him, Josh said, "I, ah . . . I sold that fifteen-carat Portuguese step-cut emerald."

A pause. The piercing eyes regarded him. "For how much?"

"Uh—twelve-five."

The thin mouth smiled. "Excellent! Secured funds?"

"Uh—cash."

"Ah, yes, the most secured funds of all. What else?"

By then the safe door was open. Petrick took out the chamois bag that held the emerald Josh had bought from Solly David. He spilled the stone out onto his flattened palm.

"I thought you just told me you sold—"

"That's a, uh, different stone that I bought because—"

"How much?"

"Fif . . . uh, fifty, uh . . ."

"Fifty thousand?" Petrick asked in incredulous tones. "You paid fifty thousand dollars for this stone?"

"It's from a hidden mine in Colombia, where the very best

emeralds come from. They are very high in chromium, which gives them their unique deep green color and—"

"You dummy, *it's the same stone!* You sold it to one con man for twelve-five, and bought it back from another con man for fifty! How did you pay fo—"

Petrick stopped in mid-word. He flipped open the three-tier corporate checkbook, stood looking at it for the longest moment in Josh Croswell's young life. Then he dialed 911.

"I wish to report an employee embezzlement."

Burton Petrick, unlike Josh, had not been born yesterday.

After getting Beverly's call, Larry Ballard strolled into Jacques Daniel's at 9:15 A.M., still yawning. Rosenkrantz and Guildenstern were at the bar telling Beverly a joke.

"So this guy comes home from work and he finds his live-in girlfriend packing her bags," said Rosenkrantz. "The guy says, 'Hey, what are you doing?' She says 'I'm leaving.' The boyfriend says 'Why's that?' And the girlfriend says, 'Because I just found out that you're a pedophile!'"

Guildenstern took it up seamlessly. "'Pedophile?' he says. 'That's a mighty big word for an eight-year-old.'"

"You're both disgusting," said Beverly. She turned to Larry. "Danny had to go down to the union hall."

Larry shrugged and said, "Could I have a liverwurst and Swiss on a French roll with everything on it, Bev?" When she nodded, he turned to the cops. "You two guys ever do anything besides hang around here telling Beverly feelthy jokes?"

"Sure," said Rosenkrantz seriously, "we protect and serve."

Making his sandwich, Beverly said disingenuously, "Larry, they were telling me about some Gypsy girl they're looking for. Didn't you guys have a big Gypsy case a couple of years ago?"

"Thirty-one Cadillacs for Cal-Cit Bank." Ballard nodded solemnly. "Maybe a draft with that sandwich, too, Bev."

"You get all of 'em?" asked Rosenkrantz.

"Of course they did." Beverly set Larry's sandwich down in front of him. "They work lots of Gypsy cases."

"So you know all about the Gyppos." Suddenly, as Larry had hoped, the two cops were working.

"Not all. Not much, even." He took his first big bite of sandwich. "They're as hard to get information out of as the Chinese. All of a sudden nobody speaks English. But sometimes they'll sell each other out if they've been feuding."

Rosenkrantz leaned forward to talk around his partner.

"Harry Bosch, homicide cop down in L.A., does us a favor from time to time, he asked us to try and grab a Gypsy gal gutted her husband down there earlier this month. Name of Yana Poteet. The vic was Ephrem Poteet. Yana ran a mitt-camp on Geary at Twelfth. Ever hear of either one of 'em?"

"I questioned her six, seven years ago at her mother-in-law's fortune-telling joint up in Santa Rosa. She was just a kid then— eighteen, nineteen years old. At the time, the mother-in-law was calling herself Madame Miseria."

"That's the name this Yana's using now," mused Rosenkrantz.

"The husband, what's his name, Ephrem—him I never met."

"You sure as hell won't meet him now," said Guildenstern. "Got some other names to throw at you. Staley and Lulu Zlachi—they both got bunco records—and a slick-looking article calls himself Angelo Grimaldi who isn't in the computer."

"Staley and Lulu—they're the King and Queen of the Muchwaya that we took the Caddies away from." He paused, a bogus thoughtful look on his face. "Grimaldi is an Italian name."

"He figures as a Gyppo, though."

Then they dumped the bag for him. Even walked him out to their car to give him a photo of the dead Ephrem Poteet.

"You don't have one of Yana, do you?"

"She ain't officially a suspect—yet," said Guildenstern.

"We got this one of Ephrem from Harry down in L.A."

Larry went inside to find Beverly shaking her head.

"God, Larry, you're an awful liar." She grinned up at him. "I'm sure glad I'm not involved with you anymore."

"So am I."

"Bastard!" She dug him in the ribs, then got serious. "They're going to be really mad if they find out you were stringing them along just to get information out of them."

"A man's gotta do what a man's gotta do," said Larry sententiously. And did what he had to do. Paid for his sandwich. When he got back to his apartment, Bart was waiting.

twenty-six

"A ll rise," said the bailiff.

It was 10:00 A.M. that same Friday morning, and Judge Anthony Valenti strode into the courtroom with his black robes billowing. He made a very impressive figure. Giselle noted his stern visage with a sinking heart.

At the prosecution table were Ellen Winslett, the marks of her beating still showing plainly; her husband, Garth, in a suit and ill-knotted tie; and a young, very handsome man Giselle took to be the prosecutor. Ellen was hollow-eyed and big as a house, as if ready to go into labor right there in the courtroom.

She visibly started, as if from fear, when Kearny took his place at the defense table with Hec Tranquillini. Giselle was the only other person in court on the side of the angels.

Among the scattered spectators was Big John Wiley and a rather flashy—and fleshy—version of Ellen, also blond. Obviously Wiley's wife, Eloise. Also that creep Deputy Willis Franks of the San Mateo Sheriff's Department. And half a dozen print and TV reporters, obviously tipped off by the prosecution.

Valenti cast stern glances around the courtroom over the top of his rimless glasses.

"This is not a trial. It is a preliminary evidentiary hearing to determine whether, in my view, the prosecution has sufficient evidence to bind the defendant over for trial. Only the prosecution can present evidence, which the defense can challenge only under the usual rules of cross-examination."

Dan and Hec looked, if not relaxed, like men confident of a favorable outcome. But Giselle felt herself getting tense.

"I want no grandstanding by either counsel, and I trust I can count on the members of the press to keep this courtroom decorous. Mr. Scarbrough, are you ready to proceed?"

"I am, Your Honor."

"Mr. Tranquillini?"

"Ready for the defense, Your Honor."

"Mr. Prosecutor, call your first witness."

Scarbrough cast significant glances at the reporters and then was on his feet in his splendidly fitted $2,000 suit. Giselle figured his tie must have cost at least $100. Must have family money. Well, Stanford . . .

"The state calls Mr. John Wiley to the stand."

"John Wiley," intoned the bailiff.

Big John took the stand and was sworn, confirming in Giselle's mind Hec's theory that Big John had created the whole scenario. He had lots to say about the day of the great dealership raid. He made DKA sound like Quantrill's Raiders who, on a lootin' and burnin' and rapin' and pillagin' day in August 1863, sacked Lawrence, Kansas, and left a sole survivor, a boy named David Schamle, hiding in a cornfield.

"Kearny and his goons were very unprofessional, nasty as hell. But no repoman is going to push me around!"

"They only push women around," agreed Scarbrough softly.

"Objection!"

"Sustained."

Scarbrough said, almost indifferently, "Your witness."

"At the time you spoke with Mr. Kearny," said Hec, "didn't you offer him several hundred dollars in cash to let you hold back a number of cars that you said had already been sold—"

"Certainly not!" exclaimed a hugely offended Big John.

Scarbrough was on his feet, screaming. *"I object, I object, I object! This infamous suggestion, these sleazy courtroom tac-*

tics, are just what we can expect from these big-city scavengers who think they can—"

"Objection overruled. You brought up the conversation yourself on direct, Mr. Scarbrough. The question may be impolite but it is proper cross-examination. Proceed, Mr. Tranquillini."

Hec said, "Your Honor, on second thought, I move that the entire testimony of this witness be stricken as incompetent and irrelevant."

"On what grounds?" yelped Scarbrough, caught off guard.

"He wasn't even in Pacifica on the day in question."

"His testimony covers the originating incident and goes to the defendant's character. I'll have to allow it to stand."

Hec shrugged, sighed, and sat down wordlessly.

"Deputy Sheriff Willis Franks to the stand, please."

Franks and his pin-the-tail-on-the-donkey mustache came up to be sworn in. Scarbrough had coached him well: no drama, no half-derogatory adjectives Hec could seize on. And above all, no mention of handcuffs. Mr. Scarbrough had told him, he said, to go to San Francisco, serve an arrest warrant on the defendant, and bring him back to San Mateo County. He had done so. Period.

"Your witness."

"In what way did you bring the defendant to San Mateo from San Francisco?"

"In my squad car."

There was a ripple of laughter in the court. Hec nodded.

"I see. And what happened at the San Mateo County line?"

"I stopped for a red light."

There was a burst of real guffaws this time, quelled only by the judge's fierce glare at the spectators.

"After the light changed and you crossed the San Mateo County line, Sergeant, didn't you stop the car and—"

"Objection, Your Honor!" sang out Scarbrough. "No conversation has been reported here, and nothing about stopping the car was brought out on direct."

"Sustained," said the judge. "The defense cannot elicit evidence not directly referred to in the prosecution's case."

Hec, looking very crestfallen, sighed and sat down.

Giselle was worried. There were other things he could have tried to get into the record—the tight handcuffs, the non-notification of counsel of the arrest. Why didn't he insist?

"The prosecution calls Mr. Garth Winslett to the stand."

Winslett heaved himself to his feet and strode self-righteously forward. He raised his big right hand to be sworn. He had also been coached. He was ready.

"On the day that the assault occur—"

"Objection. Alleged assault."

"On the day of the *alleged* assault, did you have occasion to return home at about two-thirty in the afternoon?"

"Yeah, I'd been buyin' PVC pipe and exterior ply for—"

Scarbrough said piously, "Please limit yourself to answering my questions."

"Oh, uh, yeah. I come home around two-thirty. I saw this pickup coming up Palmetto, didn't think nothing of it. But he had a car on his towbar looked a lot like the '62 'Vette my brother-in-law had asked me to keep in the garage until those creep repossessors—"

"Mr. Scarbrough," snapped the judge, forestalling Hec. "Control your witness or I will."

"I'm sorry, Your Honor. It won't happen again." He turned back to Winslett. "You noted truck and driver very carefully?"

"I sure did." Winslett pointed at Dan Kearny. "It was him, right there, that's who was behind the wheel."

Hec didn't challenge; he was conferring with Kearny as if this testimony had been a heavy blow to them. Giselle felt scared: Dan might go to jail on these trumped-up charges.

Scarbrough milked the moment. "What did you do then?"

"I knew I'd left that car in the garage with the door locked, and I knew my pregnant wife was home alone, so I rushed down the hill. The garage door was split from top to bottom, like he'd took an axe to it. Inside I found my wife laying on the cement floor. She'd been attacked and was all messed up . . ."

Scarbrough turned to the bench.

"Your Honor, at this time we would like to introduce into evidence a series of Polaroid photos of the garage door and have them labeled as Prosecution Exhibit One. At the time of Mrs. Winslett's testimony, we will introduce photos of her condition when her husband found her."

"So ordered."

Back to the witness. "What did you do then, Mr. Winslett?"

"I took the pictures and then me and Ellen drove up to San Francisco to confront Kearny face-to-face. But his office said he wasn't in. He was afraid to look me in the eye—"

This time it was Scarbrough who restrained his own witness.

"Only what you know, Mr. Winslett, not what you believe." He turned to Hec with the hint of a bow. "Your witness."

Hec shambled up to the witness stand.

"When you drove past the Kearny Associates truck with the Corvette on the towbar, how far away from it were you?"

"He was in one lane, I was in the other. Eight, ten feet."

"You have testified that seeing the car on the towbar was what directed your attention to the truck in the first place—"

"Well, yeah, sure, but—"

"So when you tried to see the driver, you were several car-lengths behind the truck. How can you be so sure that—"

"It was him all right! I'll never forget his face."

Hec seemed stymied. He turned elsewhere.

"You have testified that you found your garage door split from top to bottom, and found your wife, badly beaten, lying on the garage floor. What did you do then?"

"I already said. I took pictures of the door and of her."

"You didn't seek medical aid for her?"

"Objection!"

"You brought it up on direct."

"Overruled."

"You found Mrs. Winslett at two-thirty in the afternoon?"

"I've already said I did."

"And you took your Polaroid pictures of the garage door and of your wife, and without seeking any medical aid for her you rushed off to the city, and—"

"Have it your way," Winslett snapped angrily.

"I will. You arrived there, according to the DKA log-in records which I have right here, at five-thirty-seven P.M. Over three hours to drive a dozen miles? During that time, what did you do apart from not take your wife to the hospital? Did you have a meeting with your brother-in-law, John Wiley, and did he suggest—"

"*Objection!*" Scarbrough was on his feet bouncing around as he realized his witness was in trouble. "Defense can't introduce that company log-in sheet as evidence."

After a long considering pause, Valenti said, "Sustained."

Hec blew out a long breath and waved his hand in dismissal.

Judge Valenti said regretfully, "I had hoped to have this matter concluded this morning, but we have run into the hour of the lunch recess. Court will reconvene at two-thirty."

"All rise," said the bailiff.

twenty-seven

In the ring, involved in the ultimate *mano a mano* face-off, Bart Heslip always had to outthink and outmuscle the other guy. As a repoman with DKA, he had to outthink, sometimes outmuscle, and always *outwit* the other guy. Still you against him, still *mano a mano*; but it didn't leave you with raccoon eyes and ringing ears three days later. Not often, anyway. So since repo work depended on luck, intuition, and hunches as well as physical responses, Bart often winged it as an investigator.

Thus, he picked Larry Ballard's brains about the case, got a copy of Ephrem Poteet's photo, and drove up to Six Flags Marine World outside Vallejo in Solano County without phoning ahead. Here, according to Dirty Harry, Poteet had been a dip during the early spring months.

Bart expected to spend the day seeking out anyone who might remember the man who had picked their pockets. Instead, he found the park closed, its swooping futuristic rides silent. Marine World ran on a weekends-only schedule until Memorial Day.

"Isn't there *anyone* around today who could help me?"

The red-faced porcine guard not only knew nothing, but was hostile in his ignorance. "Can't bother nobody 'thout the head of security's okay."

"Where do I find the head of security?"

"He's at lunch. But I got no authority for you to—"

"I'll be back."

*   *   *

Judge Valenti's court reconvened at 2:30 P.M. Looking over Dan's shoulder at the Polaroids of Ellen Winslett, Giselle thought that if it had been anybody but Larry, she might have halfway believed . . .

Judge Valenti's expression as he looked at the photos said he did believe. Even if Hec managed to get Kearny probation rather than actual jail time, Dan's detective license would be gone. The damage award at the civil trial sure to follow would shut DKA down for good. Big John Wiley was getting his revenge.

Ellen spoke with lowered eyes, her hands twisting together like snakes in front of the big rounded tummy under her maternity dress. A sympathetic Valenti had to ask her to speak louder.

While collecting laundry for the washer, she heard noises in the garage and found a man "fooling around with" the Corvette her sister had left there the day before. Surprised, she dropped her laundry. The man, surprised in turn, knocked her down. She came to on the oil-stained floor with her husband standing over her. Her low, halting voice made the assault very vivid. The courtroom was deathly silent.

Scarbrough's voice dripped sympathy. "Mrs. Winslett, I know this is very difficult for you, but could you point out the man who attacked you for the court?"

Ellen slowly extended her right forefinger at Kearny.

"That man sitting there. The one they call Daniel Kearny."

"Thank you, Mrs. Winslett. That is all." He turned to the judge. "Your Honor, that is the prosecution case. I am sure you will agree that—"

"I have a few questions on cross-examination," said Hec.

Didn't this little idiot know when he was beaten? For the press, Scarbrough gave a long-suffering sigh.

"Your Honor, Mrs. Winslett has undergone a terrible ordeal and it seems almost inhuman to subject her to—"

"I sympathize, Mr. Prosecutor, but the law is the law." Judge Valenti looked at Hec Tranquillini with ill-concealed distaste. "Proceed, sir, if you have the stomach for it."

Hec bowed slightly. "I do." He turned to Ellen. "I will be brief, Mrs. Winslett. I just want to take you back to your garage at two-thirty on the afternoon of that fateful day . . ."

Fateful day? Giselle was almost as disgusted with Hec as the judge was. Couldn't he see he was just making it worse?

"Is there any chance, any chance at all, that you are mistaken in your identification of Mr. Kearny as your attacker?"

"There is no chance at all," Ellen Winslett said clearly.

Hec seemed to deflate. He shook his head in apparent sorrow. "Then I have no further questions of the witness."

"*Now,* Your Honor, I'm sure you will agree there is more than enough evidence to bind the defendant over for trial—"

"But, Your Honor, I have a question of the court."

Without waiting, Hec was hauling two sheafs of legal-looking papers from his briefcase. Something in his voice made Valenti's eyes fix on those sheafs of paper with sudden interest.

"You have the right to be heard, counselor, but I can't conceive of anything that could alter this court's opinion."

"I just want to know why, Your Honor, if these two are so totally unshakable in their sworn testimony that Mr. Kearny and only Mr. Kearny was in the garage that afternoon . . ."

He had thrown one sheaf down on the prosecution table in front of Scarbrough, was advancing on the bench with the other.

". . . that these fifty-two people whose sworn and notarized depositions I herewith hand to you . . ."

He was thrusting the second sheaf into Valenti's hands.

". . . are equally sure that they were watching Mr. Kearny deliver the keynote speech to five hundred people at a convention in Chicago, Illinois, at the exact hour and minute these *witnesses* say he was attacking Mrs. Winslett here in Pacifica?"

Scarbrough was on his feet, screaming.

"Your Honor, this is an attempt to present evidence—"

Hec thundered, "This isn't evidence, you fool! These are papers of impeachment proving that the prosecution doesn't have a case. *Never* had a case." He flung a dramatic arm at Kearny. "That man was not in Pacifica that day. Nothing anyone can say or do will make him have been there. He was in Chicago."

The judge looked up at Hec from the affidavits with a very different expression on his face than he'd worn a few moments earlier. He said in subdued tones, "One of these appears to be a sworn statement by the senior United States senator from the state of Illinois. And another is by Mayor Daley of Chicago?"

"Yes, Your Honor. They both enjoyed the speech very much. Mr. Kearny was given a standing ovation."

Scarbrough began, "Your Honor, I demand that—"

"Shut. Up." Valenti spoke without raising his head from the affidavits. But after a few more pages, he did, to stare at Scarbrough with heavy brows drawn down over angry eyes.

"Mr. Prosecutor, subject to verification of these papers, it appears that Mr. Tranquillini is right. You have no case. Your only direct evidence is from eyewitnesses who have sworn repeatedly that the assault was committed by a man who could not possibly have done it. The most charitable view is one of mistaken identification. But I am not a fool, so I strongly suggest that your office look into the very real possibility that perjury for personal gain has been committed."

"But Mrs. Winslett was severely beaten—"

"When? Where? By whom? Did you even ask Mr. Kearny or Mr. Tranquillini if the defendant was in Pacifica that day?"

Scarbrough cleared his throat. "In light of what these witnesses told me, Your Honor, I saw no need to—"

"Case dismissed," said Valenti coldly. "With prejudice. Prosecution will bear all legal costs of the defense. You can only hope Mr. Kearny does not bring suit against this county for false arrest and you personally for criminal persecution."

"I'll appeal," said Scarbrough intensely. "I'll—"

"I also hold you, personally, Mr. Scarbrough, in contempt of this court. During my twenty years on the bench I have never had the court's time wasted in such an egregious manner. Your fine is one thousand dollars cash. And I don't want to hear another word out of you on this subject."

"Your Honor, defense counsel led on my witnesses—"

"Two thousand dollars. If I hear another word out of you on any subject, *any* subject at all, the fine will be five thousand dollars and I will remand you to your own jail until it is paid in cash from your own pocket." He slammed down his gavel. "This court is adjourned."

But it wasn't, not quite. Garth Winslett brayed, "Case dismissed? Court adjourned? We don't get nothing?" He whirled on his wife, face contorted with rage and yelled, "You stupid bitch!" Then he smacked her in the eye with his big right fist.

Dan Kearny was on him from behind, wrestling him to the floor. Big John Wiley was sliding from the courtroom with a terrified look on his face. His wife was down on one knee beside her sister's chair, holding the battered woman in her arms. They both were crying. Tardily, the bailiffs were taking over from Kearny. Giselle stood up, thinking complacently that Larry Ballard could come to the office again like a proper P.I.

But even then it wasn't quite over. Because as Eloise was helping her sister to her feet, Ellen's tear-filled eyes met Giselle's for just one fleeting moment.

And, despite her battered face, she *winked*.

Then it was over.

twenty-eight

A huge *Tyrannosaurus rex,* teeth gleaming, roared at them from thick, ferny-looking foliage approximating the primitive angiosperms of the Cretaceous period. A startled Bart Heslip leaped sideways in his motion-simulator seat like a scalded cat.

"Nice reflexes," said Bruckner.

Bruckner was a medium-size man with very direct eyes in a deceptively placid face, and pale down on the backs of his fingers and sprouting up above the collar of a uniform shirt open at the throat on this day of rest at the theme park.

They exited the 3D DinoSphere TurboRide to walk through a small wooded area to a looming mountain of fake stone. Bruckner stopped. Real-looking lianas hung down in front of a camouflaged door set into the rock wall. He used a key on it.

"We go in here."

He led the way to a room at the end of a brightly lit cream-colored corridor. Inside, he sat down in a wooden swivel chair behind an elderly oak desk that had a brass HEAD OF SECURITY plaque on it. Facing the desk on a swivel above the door was a big-screen monitor, dark and silent now. Bruckner waved Bart to a white plastic armchair.

"Now, Mr. Heslip, what can I do for you?"

Bart told his story straight through. When he was finished, Bruckner said, "And this Poteet character was murdered."

"In Los Angeles. His wife may or may not have made herself a widow, but we want to beat the cops to her if we can."

Bruckner nodded his understanding. "Well, the good news is that you're right, we did have a pickpocket working the park in March and early April. Took us a month to realize what was going on, but we finally got an identification of him. The bad news is, the I.D. did us no good. It won't help you, either."

"Try me."

"He was a gorilla. At least, a guy in a gorilla suit. Great hit with the kids, so it took us two of those weeks just to figure out he wasn't employed by the park. By then he was gone." Bruckner raised his shoulders in resignation. "So if you've got a description of this Poteet, it won't do any good."

"How about the cops? What do they say?"

"Since we could never give them anyone to arrest, we handled it internally to avoid publicity."

"The Vallejo police were never involved at all?"

"Never."

So much for Dirty Harry's supposed buddy on the Vallejo P.D. Bart sighed, but to be thorough he put Larry's photo of Ephrem Poteet on the blotter. Bruckner gave it a cursory glance, then paused, frowning. "Hell, I do know that face! He showed up after the gorilla disappeared. But . . ." The animation left his features. "He can't have been our pickpocket."

"Why not?"

"Family man. He and his wife brought her father to the park a few times because the old gentleman liked all the goings-on. One visit they lost him and got in a panic, we finally found him at the petting zoo for the kids. He was Basque, he liked the goats. The wife told me he had Alzheimer's and it was getting worse, that's why they were so scared when he wandered off."

"When was all of this?"

"Probably Easter. I remember holiday crowds." Bruckner tapped computer keys. "We log in all this stuff . . . Yeah, here it is. Easter Sunday."

"What'd the wife look like?"

"Beautiful woman. Flashing eyes, I remember that. Strong features. Sexy mouth. Very animated face. Black hair almost to her waist. Golden brown skin. Great figure. Long legs."

So Ephrem and Yana were together this spring, running some scam or other with some old guy. Staley Zlachi, maybe?

"The father—can you describe him?"

"Short, frail, white-haired. Handlebar mustache yellowed from chewing tobacco. Name of Eduardo Moneo."

Not Zlachi. "Was he maybe faking the disorientation?"

"How do you fake that lost look in the eyes? They came once more after Easter, and Moneo looked even more frail than before. Just skin and bones." He shrugged. "Why don't you go talk to him yourself, make up your own mind?"

"You have his address?"

"I told you we log all incidents."

Bart was waggling greedy fingers. "Gimme," he said.

After the dismissal of all charges against Kearny, the three of them stopped on their way up to San Francisco for either a very late lunch or a very early dinner. They were in the Porker, a ribs joint in Brisbane, that tough little town leaning back against the eastern slope of San Bruno Mountain with a cigarette in its mouth and a sneer on its unshaven face.

"Looking at it now," Giselle said, "how did they ever think they could get away with it? The husband never saw Larry's face, and Ellen *knew* Dan wasn't the one who'd repo'd the Corvette."

"Who was she going to tell? She couldn't stand up in court and say it *wasn't* Dan. So she did the next best thing—just what they told her to. Only she deliberately did it too well."

"Well, I wouldn't go so far as to say 'deliberately,'" said Kearny.

"Beat up as she was, she winked at me," said Giselle. "I read that as letting me know that she was getting back at her husband."

Hec shrugged and said, "Since Winslett belted her right there in court, they won't even call Ellen to the stand." Then he asked, "So do I file against San Mateo County for false arrest? And against the prosecutor for criminal persecution?"

"We file suit," said Dan, "but then at some point we let them talk us into withdrawing the charges. Leaving them owing DKA a great big favor." He tipped Tranquillini a secret wink. "But we can go after the Winsletts full bore."

"Yeah," said Hec zestfully. "They've got assets. His Cherokee, her new Lexus, that house in Pacifica—"

"Don't you *dare!*" exclaimed Giselle in outrage.

"Why the hell not?" asked Kearny, too overtly astonished.

"Why not? She's got a little baby coming! Where's she supposed to raise the child—in a tent?"

Kearny gestured to Hec. "See what I mean? Women!"

As Giselle realized she'd been had, Kearny's beeper went off. He took it off his belt to check the number.

"Stan Groner at the bank," he said.

Giselle wordlessly handed him her cell phone. After a low-voiced conversation, he flipped it closed and handed it back.

"On Monday they're going to auction off all the classics we've recovered so far. Stan wants me there to discuss something he can't talk about on the phone. And he says he's sure you'll be there, too . . ." He paused. When Giselle was not forthcoming, he asked, "Ah—why's that?"

"If you must know, I'm prepared to bid on my car."

"STATO," said Kearny promptly. "Let's get back to the office so we won't have wasted the *whole* day."

As if he didn't know, she thought. He didn't miss much— and he never forgot a license plate. Especially vanity plates.

twenty-nine

"Like a damned spy novel," muttered Larry Ballard through clenched teeth as he climbed his third tree of the day. He had spent several fruitless hours in the remote wooded and brushy reaches of the Presidio where, Ramon had said, were the secret places he and Yana had set up drops when she became *marime*. In this tree it was a rotted knothole twenty feet from the ground. No message.

Ramon Ristik, he decided, must have just a hell of a lot of time on his hands if he could wander around the Presidio finding places to leave secret messages for his sister. Of course Yana being *marime* meant he couldn't make contact with her openly.

The last drop was below the farthest corner of the cracked and weed-grown blacktop parking lot for the long-abandoned Presidio Language Institute. Spent and panting, Larry had to thrash downhill through dead, broken-limbed eucalyptus trees to hit a jogging trail. Then he had to find a wooden post that held one end of a cable with a NO TRESPASSING sign hanging off it. If you had enough faith to blindly force your fingers into a tiny opening under one corner of the post's concrete base . . .

Larry touched something furry, jerked out his hand with a yelp. Nothing had bitten the ends off any of his fingers, but if Yana had left a message in there, it was safe from him.

Well, all of that had been just a whole lot of fun. And so

productive. Still, he had Ramon's final lead: a certain Meryl Blanchett with an address on Walnut Street.

Bart Heslip took California 37 up over the bridge past closed-down Mare Island Naval Shipyard and out across the flat delta marshes toward the Marin County town of Novato. It was a lovely May day, with a couple of small planes circling overhead and puddle ducks upending themselves in shallow ponds along the road. A raucous V of Canadian geese came up off the wetlands like a living arrow shot from some marsh god's bow.

According to Bruckner at Marine World, Alzheimer-sufferer Eduardo Moneo lived on Yukon Court, a cul-de-sac in a neighborhood of small post–World War Two houses with attached garages, tidy triangles of yard, a fruit tree or two.

Bart parked in the driveway to go up the walk to a white bungalow with green trim. He carried his clipboard. The door was opened by a small round owl-like woman in her seventies who looked at him dubiously from behind big round glasses.

"My name is Heslip. I'm looking for a Mr. Eduardo Moneo."

She didn't quite cross herself. "Mr. Moneo passed away in April. He was such a nice gentleman."

Well, Bruckner had said the guy was old and frail.

"Are you a relative?"

"No. I'm Helen Lee. My daughter and I are renting from Nadja—she's Mr. Moneo's daughter—until the paperwork gets straightened out." Belated caution showed on Helen's face. "Exactly what is your interest, Mr. Heslip?"

"We understood the house was for sale."

"It was. But my daughter and I are buying it, we've already put money down. There's been some difficulty with the title papers, but we hope to close escrow this week."

"Well, I'm glad of that," said Heslip with relief. "I'm from the escrow company and we're concerned about the delay."

Her face wreathed itself in smiles. She stepped back so Bart could enter. "Please, come in."

In the small, neat living room, Helen sat in a wingback chair that faced the big-screen TV beside the fireplace. Bart faced her from the sofa with its back to the picture window. On every flat surface were tiny owl figurines of glass, metal, ceramic, carved wood.

"The Realtor hasn't been very helpful, and frankly, Mrs. Lee, we can't guarantee title without more information."

"This house is the only asset Mr. Moneo left Nadja. She had his power of attorney, and the house is in her name. She didn't want to sell, but she and her husband need the money. Then there was that delay in getting the title papers—"

File that one. "Uh—how did Mr. Moneo die?"

"Nadja said he just sort of wasted away. Her husband's name is Punka Mihai." She leaned forward and dropped her voice. "They sound foreign but they're just as American as you or me."

Heslip made a meaningless note on his clipboard. "Have you known Nadja long?"

"I met her at the 'B' word in March." She gave a hearty laugh. " 'B' as in bingo—at Our Lady of Loretto's on Virginia Avenue. I'm a gambler at heart."

Bart stood. "I'm very grateful for your time, Mrs. Lee. We probably can guarantee title within a few days." He showed her his photo of Ephrem Poteet as he had to Bruckner at Marine World. "Just for my report, is this Mr. Mihai?"

"Yes." Helen's eyes twinkled. "A handsome man, isn't he?"

Bart put the picture away. "Do you have the Mihais' current address? We've had mail returned . . ."

Helen picked up a black-backed address book from the table at her elbow. He guessed she spent a lot of time in that chair.

"Punka looked after Mr. Moneo every day while Nadja was working in the city. They moved down to San Francisco after Mr. Moneo died . . . Here it is."

Good old Punka. Bart copied down a Warren Street address

on his clipboard. He wouldn't let Ballard forget that he found Yana's bolt-hole in a single day of digging, while Larry was still paddling around out in the Richmond District bullrushes.

In fact he'd call Larry right now to rub it in a little.

The call caught Larry in his truck across the street from a graceful ornate Italian Neoclassical apartment house on the corner of Walnut and Washington. Meryl Blanchett, whose name Ramon had given him, had an unlisted phone and wasn't home. No response at the other two flats.

The only person in or out of the building was a handsome mid-30s guy with distinguished-looking touches of grey at his temples. He led a pair of leashed dogs up Walnut from the Presidio Wall and into the apartment house. The hulking black schnauzer with the magnificent walrus mustache pretended not to be with the white miniature poodle barking and circling him.

Ten minutes later, the front window curtains were opened in Meryl Blanchett's second-floor flat. She must have come in the rear entrance. Ballard climbed the stairs to ring the bell. The door was opened by the handsome dude with the dogs.

He would have made a hell of a con man, Larry thought. Broad forehead, wide limpid brown eyes with long lashes, full lips, high cheekbones. As tall as Ballard, and as wide, but obviously a lover, not a fighter. Cashmere cardigan over a T-shirt with IN DOG YEARS I'D BE DEAD BY NOW on it. The black schnauzer leaned against his left thigh, the white poodle against his right ankle.

"Good afternoon," he said in a sonorous voice.

Larry made a slightly confused gesture. "Mr. Blanchett?"

"I'm Meryl's fiancé," he beamed. "Theodore Mumford. And these are our children, Wim and Milli. How can I help you?"

The living room overlooked Walnut Street through rounded turret windows. Photos covered the mantel over a fireplace of whitewashed fire brick. Theodore adjusted one of a pleasant-faced woman of a certain age, with affection bordering on awe.

On a polished antique oak sideboard was a bowl of what Larry thought was the most perfect wax fruit he had ever seen, until he realized it was real fruit, without blemish. Larry crouched to scratch ears and tickle chins.

"I'm Larry Ballard. I hoped Mrs. Blanchett might put me in touch with a mutual friend."

Mumford looked disappointed. "Meryl's getting her hair done. And we're going out this evening . . ."

"Maybe I could catch her at the hairdresser's."

"Excellent!" beamed Theodore, and gave him the address.

JeanneMarie Broussard et cie hairdressing salon was in a converted Victorian on Spruce just below Sacramento. The salon's blue door was up a flight of six red-stone stairs; pots of glowing yellow chrysanthemums graced the corners of the landing.

Unlike other salons Larry had been in, this one was devoid of sharp chemical odors. The five chairs were occupied by women with hair in various stages of disarray. None was young, and none looked like a siren capable of luring a much-younger hunk like Theodore onto the shoals of matrimony. Only one hair dryer in the corner of the room. Blow-dryers were the rule of the day.

Two of the beauticians were young, pretty, slim, chic, and ignored him. The pleasant-faced somewhat overweight girl sweeping gold-highlighted hair from around her chair gave him an almost shy smile. A petite woman in a white smock and a boy-cut left her client to approach Ballard with quick steps. She had level Gallic eyes and a French accent.

"I am JeanneMarie. May I help *monsieur*?"

"Mrs. Blanchett's fiancé said I might find her here."

JeanneMarie beckoned to the heavyset girl, who went over to the woman under the hair dryer, checked the dial on the hood of the machine, and spoke near the woman's ear. The three clients with their hair in different stages of completion looked at Ballard in their mirrors. He couldn't catch a glimpse of the woman under the hair dryer. The girl returned.

"Mrs. Blanchett will be ready in fifteen minutes, sir. Then she is agreeable to taking coffee with you at Beyond Wild Dreams around the corner."

Sir? thought Larry Ballard. Suddenly he felt old.

thirty

Oh, how wonderful! You're a friend of Madame Miseria's!" Meryl Blanchett leaned across the wooden table next to the glass windows to the garden. "I haven't been able to reach her. How is she? *Where* is she?"

Ballard said, "I was hoping maybe you could tell me."

He had been expecting, if not Sophia Loren, at least Rene Russo. Meryl Blanchett had fluffy, gold-highlighted hair and a plain and serious face that lit up at mention of Yana. Now it had darkened with concern.

"I have *such* good news for her, but she just disappeared from her *ofica* and I haven't been able to reach her. You must be a very good friend to be so concerned."

Larry told her a tale of being madly, passionately in love with Madame Miseria. That it had once been true gave the lie weight and substance. A doomed love, of course, star-crossed lovers . . . Which inevitably elicited Meryl's own tale of romantic adventure.

"The day after I . . . the day after the . . . the potion . . . well, on the day after the dark of the moon, Theodore proposed marriage to me." She reached across the table to squeeze Larry's hand. "And we've been deliriously happy together ever since."

Larry noticed that the engagement ring was only one of several pieces of discreet but expensive-looking jewelry she wore. Obviously, the lady was loaded. But the younger and oh-so-handsome Theodore seemed to be truly in love with her, not her money. If Larry didn't know better, he might have thought that Yana's potion actually had done something to make Theodore . . . Nah. Couldn't be. Could it?

"When was the last time you saw Madame Miseria?" he asked.

"Oh, weeks ago. But she called me just before the new moon to ask a favor." Meryl took a forkful of lemon meringue pie. "As if I could ever in my whole life deny Madame Miseria anything she asked."

She told Ballard about the $5,000 check made out to Yasmine Vlanko, Madame Miseria's real name. She told about it being forever uncashed because Madame Miseria wanted Meryl to arrange a job for a young woman as a hairdresser at Jeanne-Marie's salon.

Made sense, thought Ballard. JeanneMarie's would be a perfect place for Yana to hide out from *gadje* and *Romi* alike. But none of the beauticians was Yana, not even in disguise.

"Were you able to do it?"

"Oh, yes. She was the one who told you I would meet you here. Geraldine Tantillo. She's wonderful. She's already getting a following. She reminds me of . . . well, me." She met Larry's eyes across the table. "Pleasant-faced, a bit overweight, and a . . . a sort of ugly duckling among the swans."

"That isn't true of you!" exclaimed Larry, really meaning it. "Look at handsome, distinguished Theodore falling in—"

"That's all Madame Miseria's doing. Of course Theodore doesn't know about the potion. He must never . . ."

Ballard made a zipping motion across his mouth, and Meryl giggled, as if they were schoolchildren with a secret. After paying for her coffee and pie, he walked her to her apartment.

Monday for Geraldine—if necessary. He was glad to have a lead himself, if a tentative one, to match the one Bart had bragged about on the cell phone. If only he hadn't been such a wise-ass about Bart's Woodside misadventures . . .

*   *   *

After a brutal twenty minutes, Bart relented and together they drove to a spotlessly kept-up three-story off-white house in the 100 block of Warren, a leisurely Forest Hill street winding along the foot of Mount Sutro. As they left Bart's Caprice in the spring dusk, streetlights came on. A straight flight of stairs led up the right side of the house to a small square second-floor landing.

From inside, faintly, came television sounds. They rang the bell. The door was opened by a redhead in her late 20s with freckles on her face and a baby cradled in her left arm.

"Oh! I was expecting my little brother with another load of our stuff." She had an open tomboyish face. "But it's okay, HRH here likes to answer the door." She chucked the baby under the chin with her free hand. "Don't you, Poogie?"

The baby gurgled with glee while reaching out exploratory pudgy fingers toward Heslip's dark visage. Apparently Poogie hadn't seen too many of the brothers in his short lifetime.

Stooping to get mauled, Bart couldn't help asking, "HRH?"

"His Royal Highness."

Ballard said, "We understood the Mihais lived here."

"Oh, no, an old man named Brian Glosser had it before . . ." She paused uncertainly. "You'd better talk with my husband. He handles the finances." She raised her voice. "Honey?"

Justin MacGregor also had reddish hair and freckles, but he was nearly seven feet tall. His arms under a short-sleeved striped shirt looked as if they had a heart and lungs of their own. His testosterone rumble sounded like a freight train going through a tunnel. No wonder his wife had answered the door so carelessly at night. Mighty Joe Young was on guard.

"Better take Himself off to bed, sweetie." Watchful blue eyes swung back to Ballard and Heslip. There was challenge in them neither man felt like taking up, not in this lifetime. "You boys look a little old to be working your way through college."

Heslip explained they were trying to find a Nadja Mihai who had given this address to a Novato woman back in April.

"And you are who, exactly?"

They hauled out their P.I. registration cards. The big man looked the I.D.'s over carefully, then gestured them to chairs in the living room and switched off the TV with the remote.

"Who'd you say? Mihai?"

"Punka and Nadja," said Ballard.

"Yeah, well, they're brother and sister, not husband and wife. Nadja was married to old Brian Glosser. He had Alzheimer's and just sort of wasted away. Punka, the brother, took care of the old man while Nadja was at work."

"You know where that was?" asked Ballard.

"She never said."

Bart brought out his photo again. "Is this Punka?"

"That's him, okay," agreed MacGregor.

"And did you have any trouble with your title papers?"

MacGregor gave him a sharp, almost suspicious look.

"Yeah," he finally said. "But just a couple of weeks ago it got straightened out. The Realtor told us we're going to escrow. That's why we're finally moving all our stuff in."

Jacques Daniel's was Friday night jumping. Beverly's partner, Danny—short, quick, muscular, and French—had a sun-browned face and dark piratical eyes. He set bottles of designer beer on their table around behind the jukebox, and laid a hand on Bart's and Larry's shoulders. The three of them had been through some things together.

"On the house tonight, *mes amis*. It is not certain, but Bee-vairly is perhaps *enceinte*. Pregnant." He held up a hand. "It is still a secret, *hein*? Until we are sure."

After Danny had hurried away, Larry said, "Isn't that great? Things are working out for *one* of my ex-ladies."

They poured beer, drank, and their mood darkened.

"Whadda we got here, Larry?" asked Bart. "Ephrem and Yana are husband and wife in Vallejo, brother and sister here.

In both places we got an old man with Alzheimer's who died of a wasting disease and left his worldly goods to Yana."

"We can't be sure that Nadja is Yana," said Larry a little desperately. "You didn't get a positive I.D. of her—"

"Only because I didn't have her picture. Husband—or brother—Punka sure as hell is Ephrem. Positive photo I.D. from three different people. Both deals stalled over a problem with the title papers after Ephrem suddenly disappeared. Two weeks later he turned up in L.A.—stabbed to death. Almost immediately, both buyers got word that the title papers were now available so the sales could go through."

"Goddammit, Bart! Yana just isn't . . . she wouldn't just go around *murdering* people. She was never about just money."

"She seemed to me to be *only* about money."

It was a wake, of sorts, for the Yana Poteet they thought they had known. And in an odd way, for their own innocence.

thirty-one

As Larry and Bart drank beer in solemn memory of the Yana they thought they had known, the real Yana, temporarily taffy-haired and temporarily Becky Thatcher, was still at Brittingham's Funeral Parlor, working Grecian Formula into the hair of a midlife bicyclist run down by an early-morning garbage truck.

Yana usually rode buses to and from Brittingham's, but tonight she felt so good about the job she'd done on her final Beloved of the week that she decided to walk home. Delighting in the sights and sounds, she went down Polk Street through the Friday evening crowds with the long swinging stride she thought a Becky Thatcher from Arkansas's Ouachitas Mountains might have.

Suddenly she felt the cold wind she could never ignore blow through her, emptying her, making her feel hollow and close to death. She turned blindly in at a tiny Greek café called the Parthenon, and saw, reflected in the moving glass as she pulled the door open, Rudolph Marino coming down Polk Street toward her! She slipped into a chair in the dark rear of the room and watched like a cat as he passed, in earnest conversation with a big handsome 60-something *gadjo* with ashy-blond hair and a dark suit of European cut.

That didn't mean a thing. Yana slupped thick black Greek coffee and wolfed a wedge of honey-dripping baklava while thinking things through. Her one break was in being an outcast:

any contact with one who was *marime* was forbidden. That should stop Rudolph from ridding himself of the *gadjo* and coming after her himself, unassisted.

Yellow hair and slanty glasses and a toed-in walk, she decided, would not deceive Rudolph's keen eyes. So the only question was: had Rudolph seen her? The cold wind blowing through her body had already told her the answer.

Just a glimpse of a taffy-haired *gadja* going into a Greek greasy spoon. But that *gadja* moved like Yana. Had *been* Yana? Willem was saying, "Next week we will set it in motion and soon will have—" when Rudolph interrupted him in *Romani*.

"A woman with pale brown hair who moves like a cat . . ."

"Yes. I saw her enter the Greek café."

"I think she is the murderous Yana—the one Staley told you about. She does not know you. If she comes out, follow her. I will do the same if she tries to leave by the rear exit."

No rear exit. Only an alley fire door that would sound an alarm if opened. But over the sink in the filthy, cramped, and stinking ladies' room was an opaque window with chicken wire embedded in the glass. Though her hands were strong from shampooing the hair of dead people, Yana could not open the window's dirt-encrusted latch. She tried the buckle from her purse strap. The buckle bent, skinning her knuckles.

How could she have gotten so careless? Because in handling corpses she had broken so many Gypsy taboos that she had a feeling of false security in her freedom from the *Romi* code? Would any *Rom* believe she would do such things?

The window went up with a squawk like a garroted parrot. Someone tried the locked door. A guttural male voice called out.

"Hey, whatta hell you do in there?"

Stavros the Greek. As she climbed up on the sink, Yana made loud vile retching noises in her throat.

"I am very sick," she yelled, "from the street sweepings you serve as baklava. Go away. If you make me come out, I will vomit on the floor in front of your customers."

There was thunderous frustrated pounding on the door, then muttered Greek curses retreating down the hallway.

She already had her hips and legs out through the window, was squirming around facing into the room. Her skirt rode up to her waist as she slid down the rough exterior wall. From the lid of a garbage pail a scarred old coal-black feral alley cat examined this intruder into his domain with his surviving eye. He was huge and lithe and scruffy and obviously had owned the two short blocks of Olive Alley for a very long time.

"*Ač tu, ač tu, čá mánge; ăč tu, ăč tu, ăč káthe!*" exclaimed Yana. "Be thou, be thou, only mine, stay thou, stay thou, stay here!" The tomcat meowed. She scratched him behind a shredded ear, added, grinning, "Stay here and keep watch. If Rudolph comes, delay him. *Ahayàvà?*"

The cat purred. Sternly.

Rudolph slipped the ladies' room lock, then went through the open window in a gymnast's dive learned during two boyhood years with one of the Midwest's last traveling tent shows. He landed in a shoulder roll that brought him to his feet just short of the far side of the narrow blacktop alley.

To be struck in the face by eighteen pounds of clawing, snarling fury. A one-eyed black tomcat almost took his eye, shredded his ear, then disappeared into the shadows with a shriek of triumph.

Rudolph leaned against the brick wall, bleeding, panting. Now he was *sure* the woman was Yana. His lacerations were real even though the black cat that had made them was not, only some malevolent spirit set there by Yana to guard her backtrail. Rudolph would make no further attempt to find her in person. Let the *gadje* detectives of DKA feel the weight of her occult powers.

*   *   *

She was only five blocks from the women's residence, but Yana told the old black cabbie who picked her up on Van Ness to take her to the Exploratorium, two miles in the opposite direction. She would take no chances on being followed home.

The driver had kinky white hair and melting chocolate eyes that held hers in the rearview mirror.

"Exploratorium's closed this time of night, missy."

She gave him a dazzling smile, said, "I'm meeting my friend there," and paid him off with too much money. Then she rode a bus up to Lombard Street and caught another cab to City Hall, two blocks from Columbine House.

During the cab ride she realized she knew the big handsome 60-something *gadjo* with the ashy-blond hair. He had been raised in a *vitsa* in Holland and was married to Lulu's Italian *Romni* niece and had some high-powered *gadjo* job. Where was it—Georgia? Florida?—maybe fifteen years ago, when she was twelve, he and his wife came to visit Lulu. Yana had a secret crush on him for a long month after he'd left.

Now it all made sense. Rudolph was after the money and the valuable papers taken from Ephrem's light fixture the night he'd . . . departed. To say nothing of the proceeds from his big Universal Tour score that day. Once Rudolph had the money, he'd turn her in to the police because Rudolph was a man and she was a woman and, after all, *marime.*

No, *Devèl!* Never! She would bide her time until she saw a way to safety.

At 9:30 P.M., Ken Warren left his truck in his usual spot at the end of Raymond Street behind the all-too-familiar boat and trailer, and walked down to 557. He was just going to ask where the Mustang was and demand the keys. He laid one big forefinger against the doorbell and left it there. After thirty seconds, the door opened on the chain to let the dark face of Christian Roxborough's wife peer out at him. He took his finger off the bell. Recognition entered her eyes. The door slammed.

Ken laid his finger against the bell. Left it there.

Rattle of security chain. The door was suddenly flung wide by an enraged Christian Roxborough, dressed in designer running shoes and designer jeans and holding a pump shotgun at port arms across his body. He pumped it once, loudly. He didn't sound like any leader of the community to Ken.

"Warned you gonna blow your shit away motherfucker!"

Ken snatched the shotgun out of his hands with a movement almost too quick to follow. He twirled it like a marine at dress-parade, slammed it stock-down against the wall beside the door frame even as his forefinger found the safety and pushed it in. Then he waggled a monitory finger in Roxborough's face, turned, and walked back down the stairs. His massive moral indignation kept him from even glancing back to see whether Roxborough had snatched up the shotgun again. At the end of the street, he got back into his truck.

He had barely settled in before red and blue revolving lights approached, fast. From his inner jacket pocket, Ken removed a folded piece of paper. The silhouetted shape of Roxborough capered around in the street, waving the forgotten shotgun as a patrol car slewed sideways to a stop. A bullhorned voice bellowed.

"Drop the shotgun!"

"It's okay! It's okay! I'm the one who—"

"DROP THE SHOTGUN!"

Roxborough threw the weapon away in sudden panic as the cops emerged with drawn guns. He pointed up the street at Ken's truck, the words tumbling out of him.

"I'm the one who called you. *Him*, right up there at the end of the street in his truck, he's the one you want! He came to my door and threatened my wife, and—"

"With the shotgun?"

"No, that's mine, but—"

"What did he threaten her with?"

"Well, nothing, but—"

"What did he say to her?"

"He never says *anything*, that's the trouble. He just keeps harassing us. I've filed complaints with the precinct . . ."

"We've read them," said the tall one without enthusiasm.

The shorter, wider one added in neutral tones, "Seems you allege he spends a lot of time sitting in his truck at the end of the street." By this time they were within a dozen feet of Ken's truck, their weapons still in their hands. Short-and-Squat pointed a powerful flashlight at the windshield, dazzling him. "Out of the car, pal, and keep those hands in plain sight."

Instead of getting out, Ken, with no sudden moves, pressed his sheet of paper, face-out, up against the window with a splayed hand. The light shifted to the paper. Hard cop's eyes in a round red cop's face under a blue cop's hat stared at the paper, turned away to Roxborough.

"Shit, pal, he's legal, he's got a repo order on your car."

Roxborough was jumping up and down again.

"But that's what I'm telling you! He's harassing me for a nineteen sixty-six Mustang convertible that I don't have!"

"California-Citizens Bank says you do." The flashlight went out, the guns disappeared. The tall cop said, "Guy's sittin' in his truck on a public street, you're runnin' around wavin' a shotgun. Argue it out with the bank." He shook his head. "Saturday night fever in Visitacion Valley."

Ken started his truck as the cops, chuckling, walked back to their cruiser through the crowd of gawkers. He knew now where the Mustang had to be hidden.

thirty-two

Cruising, Trin Morales spotted the '99 Honda off the constantly updated hotsheet fastened to his visor in hope of that rarest of scores, a drive-by repo. He stopped in a fire hydrant red zone to dig out the file on the red Civic. *Sí!* REPO ON SIGHT. Client, Earl Watters Motors at the top of the hill in Daly City; Subject, Gustave Dumont; three payments down, dead skip from the given address.

A Ballard account, reassigned to Trin while Ballard was off dicking around on some hotshot special assignment. Might have known. That *cabrón* couldn't find his butt with both hands.

But the Cisco Kid could. He'd take care of Gustave Dumont.

Except the last thing he needed was a big crowd of gawkers at ten o'clock on a Friday night in the Castro. When Trin got back to the Civic, the Castro Theatre two blocks away was just letting out and 18th Street was crowded with people strolling through the usually quiet neighborhood. Two nuns, cowled and wimpled and wearing long black habits, stopped to watch him.

"What do you think you're doing, young man?"

She had a rather deep voice. Trin gave her a sickly smile that flashed his gold tooth in the streetlight.

"Well you see, sister, I lost my keys and . . ."

He trailed off in mid-sentence. Both nuns had beards. Not nuns at all. Fruiters, practicing up for Memorial Day.

"Are you sure that's your car, young man?" asked the other.

"It sure as hell ain't yours," grunted Morales, and made a nifty move with his slim jim down the outside of the window to hook the locking arm for the doorlatch. The knob popped up.

As he slid into the driver's seat, a different voice spoke up behind him. "Show the sisters some respect."

Shit. He'd have to wire it under the dash, but he didn't want to stick his head under there with some guy egging on the crowd. He leaned back out of the car and spoke to the big black-bearded guy who had his arm around a wispy blond guy.

"They ain't sisters, they're—" He stopped. The crowd was so gay it was giddy, and had grown exponentially. "They're in costume," he finished lamely.

Few years ago, this wouldn't of happened. The gays had been in the closet where they belonged, you could grab a car off the street in the Castro any freakin' time you wanted, nobody would of dared lift a finger. Now everything had changed. Gay rights. Gay pride. Hell, the Chairman of the Board of Supes was gay, for Chrissake, and had run for mayor last year!

Trin fought an urge to jump into the car and slam the door. He'd be safe, but he wouldn't be able to drive away. The bearded guy put hairy-backed fingers on the edge of the open door.

"Maybe you're a gay-bashing car thief working here in the Castro because you figured we'd be easy pickings."

The crowd gave an approving rumble. Trin stepped back out of the Honda, thinking: if they come after me, the slim jim'll make a good weapon. He hadn't thought that way in months. *Caramba,* such thoughts felt good. Real good.

Just then a handsome dude with bright dark eyes and high cheekbones and some sort of soft flat cap down over one ear turned to face the crowd with his arms spread wide.

"This man is a member of a minority, just like us," he said in some sort of continental cadence. "He didn't have any choice about being Latino." He turned to Trin with his hand out. "Besides, I know him. How's it been, *amigo*?"

"Uh—fine," said Trin. They shook hands. "Haven't seen you around lately." He'd never laid eyes on the guy before.

"I've been out of the country on vacation. In Paris."

The crowd was losing its cohesion. The surface tension had been broken, like water flowing down the sides of an overfull glass if a finger touches the surface. The man winked at Trin.

"I'll drop around to the bank on Monday for a chat."

"Yeah, you do that."

The guy melted into the quickly dispersing crowd. Trin got into the Civic, pulled the door shut, locked it, and opened his right hand. On his palm rested the ignition key Gustave Dumont had slipped him. He started the motor. Clever dude. Hoped he wouldn't have too far to walk.

The town-house complex at Townsend and the Embarcadero had an under-the-building parking garage where entry was by electronic door-opener only. Ken Warren knew the '66 Mustang would be stashed behind those formidable overhead steel doors because he remembered what Larry and O'B said when he brought in Benny Lutheran's 280Z on the day of the classic-car raid.

"That's one guy we won't have to check out."

"Sure we will. They might play liar's dice with those cars, maybe hide another one in his garage just to finesse us."

Ken trudged stolidly up the front steps of the gleaming high-rise condo building just as a skinny guy came out wearing a psychiatrist's beard and a Shetland wool tweed coat with elbow patches. With him was a slim blonde with an improbable bosom under a bright red woolly sweater.

Before it could close and without checking his stride, Ken was through the door the psychiatrist hadn't bothered to hold for him. The blonde looked after him with an expression seldom seen outside the boudoir. The bearded man took her arm with some asperity to lead her away from temptation.

When the hall buzzer sounded, Benny Lutheran was taking a drag on his cigarette and staring through the living room picture window at his fabulous view of the Bay Bridge. She was early. Probably some chivalrous gent had opened the door for her. Who wouldn't? Ever since the black-haired pixie-faced girl in the red warm-up jacket gave him an exuberant finger outside USF's Lone Mountain campus, Benny Lutheran knew he wanted her. Nineteen years old! Tonight he was going to have her.

A little clear liquid GHB (*gamma hydroxybutyrate acid*) in her Pepsi, along with a shot of tasteless vodka she would know nothing about, and he would feast on her for the rest of the night. She would wake up in the A.M. on her folks' front porch with a headache and chafed thighs and a bad taste in her mouth, and she wouldn't be able to remember a thing about any of it.

Benny admired himself for a final second in the bathroom mirror, spritzed breath-freshener into his mouth, and went down the hall and across the living room to swing the front door wide with welcome.

His eyes bulged. "You!" He tried to slam the door.

Ken Warren, the original immovable object, was in the way. Benny fisted his big right hand. His broken nose had a Pavlovian flashback. His hand unfisted. Ken's even bigger right hand was extended, palm up.

"Hgna Hmuhntang," he said. "Hgna hknees."

This time, Benny Lutheran had no difficulty at all in understanding him. The Mustang. The keys. He didn't own a gun. If he tried to defend himself with a knife, the blade would shatter when it struck the big retard's flesh.

"I . . ." He held up a finger. "Just a second . . ."

He dashed madly back to his bedroom to rummage through drawers and briefly considered calling the cops. No. Bad move.

After cringing when he dropped the keys into the outstretched hand, he tried to reupholster his self-esteem with bluster.

"You got your keys, asshole, you got your car, now get to fuck outta here. I don't ever wanna see you again."

But all was not lost. Even as the retard turned away, Colleen was coming up the hall, all bright eyes and saucy black ringlets and a tight skirt that ended a foot above her knees. *Great* cheerleader legs! Innocence aching to be defiled. And Benny was just the boy to defile it.

But Ken Warren stopped in front of the girl, once again the immovable object. He held up his hand.

"Hgno!" he told her.

She gazed up at him, wide-eyed; she came only to his chest.

"Okay," she said, and turned around and went back down the hall with him. Benny slammed the door so hard it resonated until they reached the elevator.

Colleen thought the Mustang was so, like, awesome, that Ken let her drive it back to DKA for him, gave her $25 as a driver's fee, and drove her safely to her folks' place. He even got her home before midnight.

Trin Morales stopped on Mission Street for the pizza he hadn't gotten last time around. Yeah, that pizza joint. Where Milagrita worked. But he'd been a scared rabbit then; now, the Cisco Kid rode again. Besides, she worked weekdays and this was midnight on a Saturday night. He just wanted a pizza, right?

But when he went in, his eyes instinctively sought out and, amazingly, were rewarded by her slim and graceful person. She was there, waiting tables! Pulling a split shift? Filling in for someone out sick? Maybe she had switched to nights. He slid into an empty booth so when she came over to take his order he could flash his biggest gold-tooth grin at her.

"I just made an *estraño* repo," he said, "an' I wanna—"

"*No!*" She thrust out both hands, palms-forward, as if to ward off *el diablo* himself. "Go! Get out! Esteban . . ."

If Esteban hears you were in here, he will kill you.

Too late, survival instincts revived. In a window booth were four young Latino bucks with beers and cigarettes in their hands—who had the balls to bring up no-smoking laws to *them?* They were galvanized to action by Milagrita's cry of warning.

Trin's choice was simple: flight or fight.

If he fled, they would own him forever.

If he fought, he would be smashed up again. Maybe killed.

Nine months ago, fuck 'em, he would have fought.

But now . . . Now, he ran for his life in blind panic, away from his car—they would drag him down on busy Mission Street before he could even get the door open. Instead, he sprinted left and around the corner and three doors down to the fleabag hotel where he'd been a bellhop when he was 18. He remembered that in recent years it had become a sort of residence hotel for old geezers on Social Security.

He jammed an elbow through the glass of the door, twisted the knob to open it, and flung himself into the dust-shrouded and night-deserted lobby. The shoes of his pursuers thudded on the sidewalk. He skittered around the corner beside the deserted check-in desk. If the utility room was unlocked as it used to be . . . Yes!

Trin slammed shut the heavy old hardwood door, rammed home the deadbolt. That would hold them only until they realized the hinges were on the outside of the door.

Each breath was like a razor blade in his chest, not from exertion but from terror. Sweat stung his eyes. During his bellhop days, the room was crammed with maids' carts, the shelves stacked with linens and towels. Now, crammed with old suitcases, dusty boxes of abandoned belongings, broken TV sets, three-legged chairs, bureaus without drawers, cracked mirrors . . .

He fought his way around, through, under, over, and between the obstacles to the back wall. Behind him were excited hunting cries, the thud of shoulders against the door.

Then a shout, "*Los goznes!* The hinges! Get out the pins!"

At eighteen, Trin often escaped the house dick's wrath by throwing himself headfirst down the laundry chute to land in the dirty sheets piled in the basement laundry room below. Twenty years later, he gingerly levered himself into the chute feet-first—if he got stuck, they would carve him out of it like corned beef from the tin. Hell with it. He let go, slid down into darkness. The lost forty pounds was just enough. He landed on water-puddled concrete, somehow retained his footing. From the storage room above came the crashing of boxes being hurled aside.

Trin dragged a wooden crate under one of the high narrow windows, smashed loose the wire mesh with the butt of his hand. Seeing blood on his knuckles, feeling nothing, he rolled out into the alley that would take him around the block to his car.

Couldn't go back to his apartment. Not now, not in any future he could foresee. His desperate mind leaped to DKA.

That was it. Hide his car in the fenced storage area they couldn't get into, sleep in the personal property storage room on the second floor with a lot of locked and burglar-alarmed doors between him and them. Let nobody at DKA know he was sleeping there. Safety. For the moment.

To a despairing, self-adjudged coward like Trin Morales, safety for the moment was enough.

thirty-three

It was a bright, cool May Monday. At California-Citizens Bank's outdoor lot below Telegraph Hill, gulls swooped and squawked, unseen traffic rumbled on the nearby Embarcadero. Stan Groner, president of the bank's Consumer Loan Division, was holding the classic-car auction now, at the beginning of the week, because on a weekend the place would be jammed with the kind of old-car buffs who kicked tires and never tired of telling each other about the beauty they'd picked up for a bag of peanuts—and never bid on anything.

Today it was serious classic-car dealers, with a sprinkling of 20-something execs from Silicon Valley, kids with money to spend and nostalgia for a past they'd never known.

Dan Kearny watched as Groner, a pleasant-faced man of 42 with warm brown eyes, wearing a three-piece banker-conservative suit, worked the crowd before the auction started. The banker had learned some tricks a few months back, during the day they'd spent playing private eye together. For one thing, just how damned tough it was to get information out of people who didn't want to give it to you. Obviously wanting something from DKA, he was trying to not be too obvious about it.

"Mr. K!" Stan exclaimed, pumping Dan's hand with half-real, half-synthetic enthusiasm. "Lots of Wiley's competitors here today looking for bargains."

"Ex-competitors," said Kearny. "Wiley's out of business."

Stan chuckled. "Giselle was around at the crack of dawn to grab that little red Alfa for herself."

"I hope you gave her a good deal on it." Then, since Giselle's love affair with the red Alfa obviously wasn't why Stan had asked him to come around today, he got his face close to Stan's ear and spoke in his best *sotto voce* tough guy growl. "Who you want bumped off?"

"Bumped off?" exclaimed Stan in alarm. Then he got it, and actually started to blush. "Okay, so I . . . well, I want you to meet one of the bank's overseas customers who has a problem I thought you could help with. He's a baron. You'll find out all about it at lunch."

Ladies who lunch, thought Giselle rather giddily. She slid the gleaming red low-slung Alfa Quadrifoglio Spider to the curb in front of the Hall of Justice on Bryant Street, just as Sofia Ciccone came trotting down the broad front steps. Sofia was out of her SFPD uniform and into civvies for the occasion. Oh, let the printouts be in that white handbag slung over her shoulder!

Sofia stopped amid the river of fellow cops, lawyers, civilians, accused felons, and weepy relatives that flowed up and down the wide steps. Giselle touched the Alfa's horn. Sofia's mouth fell open in surprise at the sight of the sleek red car.

She got in with fluid grace, glittery earrings swinging, essentially unchanged by the years since they'd been dormmates at S.F. State. Her dark Italian eyes were round with wonder.

"I thought Kearny never let you guys drive repos."

"No repo, Sofia. It's *mine!*" Giselle checked her rearview and zipped the Alfa away from the curb with a throaty chuckle of engine, adding the classic, "And the bank's."

"How much?"

"Five thousand dollars."

"No way!"

"Way. So today it's the Bocce Café to celebrate."

Sofia squirmed her tidy bottom around in the pale leather bucket seat, sighed luxuriously, then looked over at Giselle with sudden suspicion. "Is it still the Bocce even if I wasn't able to Xerox those records you wanted?"

"Hey, we're celebrating my new car, remember?"

"Just testing," Sofia grinned. "I got what you asked for."

"But did you get what I need?"

"I don't know what you need."

Giselle stopped for the light at Sixth and Howard. A short dumpy Asian woman in cast-off clothes was taking a long, oblivious time to cross while deep in discussion with a tall thin black man.

"Some of those MamaSans make ten thousand dollars a day at the illegal food stamp trade," Giselle observed. "The guy with her is obviously one of her runners. Where's a cop when you need one?"

Sofia tossed her dark, shoulder-length hair back out of her eyes. "Be polite or I won't tell you what I found."

"Oh come on! Did you get anything salient?"

"After lunch," said Sofia firmly. "If I lose my civil service pension 'cause I stole worthless records for you, I want to go down full of good Italian cooking."

The three men were having lunch at the shining chromium-and-glass Fog City Diner on the waterfront. Baron Herbert Von Knottnerus-Meyer had thinning too-black hair combed across his scalp, muttonchop whiskers, a Kaiser Wilhelm mustache, and a monocle on a black woven silk cord strung through his lapel buttonhole, a monocle that kept falling out of his right eye as he talked. He kept replacing it as he held forth, in a Prussian accent, about a certain class of animals descended from arboreal phalanger stock.

"All thirty species uff dot kangaroo, best known uff de marsupials, are found only in Australia unt New Guinea. Since de-

velopment uff de young marsupial takes place partly in dot
mother's uterus unt partly in dot pouch, dere iss perhaps even
something Freudian in deir reproductive strategy. Vould you
not agree, Herr Kearny?"

"I have no opinion about it, Baron," said Dan blandly.

"You *do* know vut a marsupial is, don't you, Herr Kearny?"

"Pogo the Possum," said Dan sagely, to Stan's shocked expression and the Baron's bewildered one.

"Possum? Dis I do not unterstand," muttered the Baron.

"Little rat-tailed guy about as big as a cat." Dan drew a
quick sketch on his cocktail napkin. "Good eating where I
come from. Got the stomach pouch for the kits and everything."

"I vould like to see one," said the Baron solemnly.

Groner said quickly, "The Baron is an amateur naturalist in
the true sense of the word—he is devoted to animals . . ."

"Animals haff naturally goot manners," agreed the Baron.
"People dogs do not trust, vor instance, are chenerally un-
trustvorthy. How do dogs feel about you, Herr Kearny?"

"We get along all right. A little kick here, a little—"

"Goot. A joke." He stood up, made the slightest of bows.
"Iff you vill excuse me . . ."

The two men stared after the Baron's stiff retreating back.
He was heavy without being fat, his erect military posture
causing rolls of flesh to form above the back of his tight shirt
collar. Dan turned to look at Stan unbelievingly.

"People who dogs don't trust are untrustworthy?"

"You gotta go along with me on this, Dan! He's a major
stockholder in one of the bank's biggest international clients.
Their deposits in our Berlin affiliate would make you weep."

"What's this company do?"

"Consults. The Baron is here on a security consultation for
an American, a real heavy hitter in financial circles in L.A.,
who's worried about his private art collection in the mountains
behind Big Sur. The firm was recommended to him by a man

in Hong Kong; they need to liase with someone local who can keep his mouth shut."

"We're private eyes, Stan, not security guys."

"But you know a lot about security systems and alarms from getting in and out of places on the sly. I've watched you operate, remember? And you're smart and a quick learner."

"I'm the only guy you could think of on short notice?"

Stan cast a quick look down the long narrow diner toward the rest rooms. "His people came to *me*, personally, for an expert, so I vouched for you, *personally*, with the bank."

"Who pays us, and how much?"

"The client pays the Baron's people, they pay you—lots."

"With Cal-Cit Bank guaranteeing our payment," said Dan.

"That goes without saying," Stan agreed airily.

Giselle asked, "You think Dirty Harry is really dirty?"

"He sure lies a lot." Bart Heslip was sorting through the arrest records on Giselle's desk. "He said it was a cop friend in Vallejo who told him Ephrem was a dip at Marine World."

"Ephrem *was* a dip at Marine World."

"Marine World's security never notified the Vallejo cops about him. They didn't know, so how'd Harry find out? He claims he didn't know either Ephrem or Yana personally, but . . ."

Giselle scaled a file folder across the desk at him.

"He arrested Ephrem twice for reading palms without a license, Yana once for illegal fortune-telling."

Bart, scanning the records, said, "Dirty Harry never showed up to give evidence, so both cases were dismissed."

"Small potatoes if they slipped him a few bucks for the no-show," she said.

"Yeah, but dammit, Giselle, there's a lot of death going around in this one all of a sudden. Two old men are dead, Ephrem Poteet is dead—Yana's the only one left standing."

"Except for Dirty Harry," said Giselle. "Get down to L.A.,

Bart, and find out what Ephrem was doing on the day he died."

"Damn!" Bart exclaimed. "We should have asked your buddy Sofia for a mug shot of Yana."

"I did. She said it was really hard for her to access closed files and get the mug shots out of them to copy."

"I bet I'm gonna wish I had one to show around," said Bart.

thirty-four

Waiting to take Midori to a late lunch in the Stonestown Mall before going to talk to Geraldine Tantillo, Larry saw a familiar face. Whit Stabler, who reminded him of his grandpa less than before because of his costly but too-youthful duds. Larry went over to shake the old gentleman's hand.

"I'm sorry," stammered Whit. "I don't . . . do I know you?"

"No reason to remember me, sir. We met just the one time through Luminitsa."

The rather vague blue eyes sharpened. "That Luminitsa! She's some babe, eh? She's real good to me." He dug an elbow into Larry's ribs. "Magic salt in the soup. Better'n Viagra."

"Magic salt," agreed Ballard. Poor old guy was losing it.

He looked around for Midori, but it was Luminitsa who came up to hook her arm possessively through Whit's.

"What lies have you been telling my beautiful Larry?"

"He told me you were some babe," said Ballard.

"Well, *that's* no lie!" she said with a laugh so wide it showed her back teeth. She gave Whit a little tug. "Come on, you, let's get you home for your nap." She winked bawdily at Larry over her shoulder as they went off.

Over fresh Mex at Chevy's, Midori said, "Luminitsa say she been taking poor Mr. Stabler to see the doctor, but she no ought to sleep with him. He pretty sick, she maybe hurt him?"

"Sick how?" asked Ballard around a big bite of burrito.

"Something called leukemia, maybe?"

"That's sick, all right," agreed Larry sorrowfully. He liked the old banty rooster who wasn't giving up without a fight.

"Luminitsa say she gonna maybe have to take leave of absence to take care of him if he keep on getting worse sick."

Geraldine Tantillo had called in sick—the first day of work she had missed since starting her job at JeanneMarie's beauty salon. She sat in front of the window of her one-room walk-up under the eaves of this old five-story Victorian in Dolores Heights, bawling her eyes out.

Last night, as she was getting ready for the workweek, someone knocked on her door. She opened it and perfidious Ariane, beautiful of face, beautiful of hair, tall and willowy but with a luscious bosom, peach-soft skin, and lo-o-o-o-ong legs, fell into her arms.

"I'm back!" cried Ariane, covering her face with kisses.

Geraldine somehow extracted herself from the embrace, and somehow found the strength to say coolly, "Where's my seven thousand dollars?"

Ariane collapsed loosely into Geraldine's woven wicker chair. "It's all gone. Every penny." She made a wan gesture. "I barely had enough left for the flight back from Cabo." She brightened. "But now the two of us are together again!"

"There is no 'us,'" said Geraldine coldly. "I've rebuilt my life, I can't let you take it away again. Just . . . go."

Ariane sneered, "I *will* go. I always *hated* this place. Back in Iowa there are real people who *care* about a person!"

And ten minutes later she was gone—with a check for $400 to cover plane fare to Dubuque she probably would use on clothes. It cleaned out Geraldine's account, and here she sat on the edge of her lonely bed, crying with great abandon. She knew, deep down inside, that Ariane was manipulative and destructive, but . . .

There was a knock on the door.

Geraldine went to the door steeling herself for another confrontation. But it was a man, big and blond and handsome. She remembered him from JeanneMarie's salon.

"My name is Larry Ballard," he said.

"My name is Milagrita," said a quiet little voice at Giselle's elbow. "The nice English girl in the front office said I should come talk to you."

A pretty girl, eighteen or nineteen, Latina, probably Mexican. Long black gleaming hair and big eyes brimming with intelligence. A summery blouse with a ruffled neckline and a swirly skirt. Giselle reached for the application forms.

"We don't have any openings right now, but . . ."

"It is nothing like that." She sat down unbidden in the chair across the desk. She had a great deal of natural dignity. "I must find Trinidad Morales."

The usual sad little boy-girl story? This girl somehow didn't seem the type to get into trouble, but Giselle spoke as if she had never heard the name before.

"Trinidad Morales? I'm afraid I don't—"

"He works here. He is a repoman. I was his driver on the night of the repossessed Acura. Some men want to kill him."

"*Kill* him?"

"They are led by my brother."

It suddenly made sense. The gang that had beaten Morales almost to death had been led by a Latino bent on vengeance for a wronged sister.

"Last Saturday night he came into the pizza place where I work. He did not know I would be there. My brother and his *compadres* were there and chased him, but he escaped."

Giselle hadn't seen Morales all day. "Are you sure?"

"*Sí.* They came back afterward, very angry because he got away. They do not know he works here, so you must tell him— do not go home. Be careful. They truly plan to kill him."

Giselle leaned back in her swivel chair.

"I think you'd better tell me *everything,*" she said.

"I would be honored," said Milagrita with a suddenly dazzling smile.

Afterward, Giselle pointed to the private phone on her desk, the one that didn't go through the switchboard.

"Milagrita, you ever need me, you call this number, okay?"

They were having tea. And even in that postage stamp of an apartment, pouring from an old ceramic teapot with a tannin-browned crack running down its bulbous side, Geraldine was doing a splendid job of it. She might cry again when she was alone, Larry knew, but meanwhile she was the perfect hostess.

He began, "So you were working at a mortuary . . ."

"The chic San Francisco beauty salons wouldn't hire me." She gestured down at her ample self. "The mortuary was all I could get. I hated it, all those poor dead people . . ."

Ballard drank tea and ate butter cookies while she told him how she had met Yasmine Vlanko at Sappho's Knickers—Yana, obviously, the recognizable rose by any other name. Yasmine had promised a great change in Geraldine's life if she quit her job. She did, and lo and behold, here came the job at Jeanne-Marie's—where Geraldine had been turned down flat the previous year.

"This Yasmine Vlanko, where might I find her?"

"I don't know how to reach her." She was blushing; true love was rearing its beautiful head. "Oh, how I wish I did!"

So did Ballard. Yana had wanted *something* this girl had, and for damn sure it wasn't lesbian love.

Yana emerged into Sutter Street from Brittingham's Funeral Parlor with Becky Thatcher's long strides, and the caution made necessary by last Friday night's glimpse of Rudolph Marino. Tonight, this very minute, he might be waiting around the corner on Polk Street. But she had a debt to pay.

She stopped at a mom-and-pop grocery store for a purchase, asking the Punjabi proprietor to open the can for her and put on it one of the pink plastic covers displayed by the cash register. In Olive Alley behind the Greek café, she removed the taffy-colored wig and put it in her bag.

"Me sem athè," she said in low-voiced *Romani*. "I am here."

The big feral tomcat leaped up lightly from a garbage pail to balance on the windowsill with his broad whiskered face a foot from Yana's. He stared at her with his one golden eye.

"What have you to tell me?" she asked, still in *Romani*.

The cat seemed to purr and meow at the same time. Yana shut her eyes to let the images pass behind her lids. Yes. Somehow she knew positively that Rudolph had seen her. Then why hadn't he . . . She opened her eyes. Even from here she could see a reddish brown smear on the far wall, some sprinkles on the alley floor. Dried blood. A meeting. Rudolph. The cat.

She straightened up and ran her hands through her long black hair, untangling it where it had been stuffed up under the wig. She dragged the heavy black mane across the cat's back.

"Čin tu jid', cin ádá bálá jidin," she said to him. "So long live thou, long as this hair shall live."

She removed the pink plastic top from the big can of tunafish, set it on the lid of one of the garbage pails, returned the wig to her head, and left the alley, her obligation discharged.

Larry Ballard was halfway through a light karate workout at the Ninth Avenue dojo when the answer struck him. Geraldine told him more than she realized over tea two hours earlier. He hurried through his shower, jumped into his clothes, perfunctorily bowed to his *sensei,* and trotted the three blocks to his car.

Yana's meeting with Geraldine at the lesbian bar had not been just a chance encounter. She knew just what sort of mumbo-jumbo would get Geraldine to quit her job, so, after finding Geraldine a better job with JeanneMarie, Yana could take the mortuary job. A great place to hide out, disguised and under a phony name. Okay, so his logical construct only suggested that she *might* be working at Brittingham's, but he was sure he was right.

Thirty seconds after Yana disappeared into Polk Street, Ballard parked in the lot for Brittingham's Funeral Parlor on Sutter. He paid his respects to the remains of a Mrs. Henrietta Henderson, whom he had never seen before, dead or alive. Lugubrious Carter Brittingham IV was waiting to shake the mourners' hands as they emerged from the viewing room. Larry contrived to be the last one out.

Brittingham said unctuously, "She has gone to a better place."

Ballard nodded, a dumb show of grief, then brightened.

"Auntie Henrietta sure looks natural, doesn't she? Whoever did her hair and makeup is a true artist. I'd really like to thank her for making Auntie look so good."

"Our cosmetician? Sorry to say, she's gone for the night." Then Brittingham was moved to an incautious moment of genuine emotion. "Yes, she's a jewel, isn't she? A, um, er, hillbilly girl from Arkansas named Becky Thatcher . . ."

Ballard felt an unexpected emotional wrench. Becky Thatcher. The heroine of *Tom Sawyer*. When he first met Yana at her mother-in-law's *boojo* room in Santa Rosa almost eight years ago, Yana was teaching herself to read. She was doing it with a dictionary and a simplified grammar-school edition of *Tom Sawyer*.

thirty-five

Dan Kearny and Knottnerus-Meyer flew into Monterey in a high-winged ARV Super2 with a tricycle landing gear suitable for the small wind-blown airport. If security conditions at Xanadu were satisfactory, the Baron would jet back to Germany over the Pole in the morning. If not, then . . . Well, he hadn't confided what his next step would be if his findings were negative.

The Baron seemed happy to let Dan Kearny do the driving of the rented Nissan Xterra SUV that awaited them at the airport.

"I haff an international driver's license, but I'm used to dot Autobahn. I haff heard dis Big Sur iss very . . . rustic."

"Where we're going sure as hell is," agreed Kearny.

He was dressed for the backcountry; hanging from his neck were the binoculars he used at the racetrack. One of his lace-up hiking boots had a survival knife scabbard stitched to the outside. The scabbard was empty: Kearny had burned a hole right through the knife's blade trying to jump-start a repo with a bum solenoid one stormy night on the north coast above San Francisco.

The Baron was dressed as if he were going grouse-hunting, right down to one of the plaid deerstalker caps made famous by Sherlock Holmes. All he lacked was a shooting stick.

Kearny began, "Should we call ahead to let them know—"

"Our arrival must be a surprise," stated the Baron coldly. "Vut sort uff security expert are you?"

Not much of one, thought Dan, but he said, "They already know we're coming, right?"

"Not de day uff our arrival." Knottnerus-Meyer paused dramatically. "Today iss dot day."

Dan drove out the Carmel Valley through rolling horse country with rambling houses perched on the hillsides. Some thirty miles south, well into the rugged pine-covered terrain flanking the eastern slope of the Los Padres National Forest, he pulled off to consult the map.

"Our road turns west into the Coast Range at a T-junction just short of a little burg called Sycamore Flat. Exactly two point three miles from the junction our gravel track goes off to the north."

It did. Immediately, it began climbing and twisting through a stately mixture of hemlock, fir, and blue spruce. Kearny put the SUV into four-wheel. Knottnerus-Meyer screwed his monocle into his eye, took a deep breath of the bracing air.

"De Black Forest iss more orderly," he observed.

Kearny took the Xterra around yet another hairpin turn to yet another switchback and mashed the brakes. They skidded to a stop in a cloud of grey-white dust two feet from a partial road cave-in. He backed and filled, turned, went on.

Knottnerus-Meyer, who had been hanging on with whitened knuckles, said abruptly, "Brachiation proved to be de key to de survival uff de great apes."

"Brachiation?" asked Dan.

The Baron unclawed his right hand from the crash bar to wiggle his fingers in illustration.

"Using deir hands. Swinging below de branch rather dan running along de top uff it. De apes dat made de adaptation survived, dose dot did not vent extinct. At least twenty-two pithecoids disappeared, thirteen species in Africa alone."

"I'm really glad to hear that," said Dan.

"Goot! You make another joke!"

Another rise put them at the top of the world. Dan stopped the Xterra. To the east was spread out California's great central valley, robbed of detail by distance. Far beyond was the Sierra, a long dark uneven band running along the horizon.

To the west, the Pacific. The horizon was ruler straight, two blues meeting without mingling, so distant the surface looked like glass. Closer in, Kearny knew, breakers would be smashing on black rocks, spume would be flying, gnarled black Monterey cypresses would be twisted into frozen agony by the never-ending wind, gulls would be swooping and skirling like bagpipes against the clamor of the sea. Up here all was stillness and serenity.

"Looks like we made it," said Kearny.

"Magnificent!" breathed Knottnerus-Meyer. The monocle had fallen from his eye to dangle forgotten on his chest.

They were at one end of a vast mountain meadow. Close-packed sedges and grasses waved in the cool high-country air. At the far end stretched ten acres of achingly green grounds dotted with artfully planted shrubs, bushes, and hardwoods, crowded on three sides by pine forest. All of it enclosed by a formidable cyclone fence.

Dan raised his binoculars, adjusted them. Around the inside of the fence ran a single-lane dirt vehicle track. No petunia borders for Victor Marr. Their gravel road wended its way across the mountain meadow to stop abruptly at an electrified gate topped with barbed wire. The glaring white three-storied flat-roofed futuristic building in the center of the compound could have been a mortuary.

A guard was strolling a pair of leashed Dobermans along the crushed-gravel walk between the building and the gate. Kearny lowered his glasses. "You'd need an army to bust in there."

"Indeed." Knottnerus-Meyer abandoned his monocle for a

pair of miniature opera glasses from his jacket pocket. After a moment, he lowered them. "Indeed," he said again.

Larry Ballard's props were few: a blue windbreaker hanging open over a tieless white shirt; dark glasses; a billed delivery-man's cap from the DKA personal effects storage room; and a bouquet of long-stemmed calla lilies from a Sutter Street florist.

He waited in his car until Carter Brittingham IV went to lunch. Wouldn't do for Brittingham to run into the grief-stricken nephew of poor old Mrs. Henderson so soon again.

Ballard picked a name off the list inside the mortuary door, poked his flowers and capped head into the reception room. A somberly dressed woman in her 30s was using her handbag mirror to put on cherry-red lipstick. Mirror and lipstick were whisked from view when Larry spoke.

"Paul Weissman?"

She consulted her own list. Her half-made-up mouth made him think of Sondheim's "Send in the Clowns." "Viewing room six at seven-thirty this evening. I can take those flowers—"

"No can do. I gotta personally deliver 'em to a Ms. . . . . ah, Becky Thatcher. For inclusion in Mr. Weissman's casket."

"With the Beloved?" She looked mildly surprised, then shrugged, losing interest. "The stairs at the end of the hall, past the NO ADMITTANCE sign. She'll be down there somewhere."

Larry tipped his cap to her—a nice touch, he thought—and turned away. She was already bringing the lipstick and mirror up from below her desktop. She wouldn't remember him past the Kleenex blot of the lips. Good. A short attention span was one of the great boons to private detectives.

At the foot of the stairs was a door that, when opened, led into the embalming room. The cold white sterile blare of over-head fluorescents wiped out every shadow. Ballard squinted his eyes against instant headache and crinkled his nose against the acrid chemical odors of old-fashioned embalming.

A husky kid with a shaved head and a ring in his ear was

bending over a cadaver on a stainless steel table, scalpel in hand. He whirled at Larry's entrance, advanced with menace.

"You can't come in here!"

"Mind the scalpel, I'm not dead yet." Hell, hadn't he won a fight with a Gypsy knife-juggler? "I'm supposed to get these flowers to a Becky Thatcher. You don't look like her."

After a moment, the man shrugged and pointed with the scalpel. "She's prettying up a stiff in the next room."

The tiled floor had a large circular meshed drain in the middle of it. Larry eased an eye around the edge of the window in the door the embalmer had indicated. If she saw him she would split. In the next room a white-smocked, taffy-haired woman was applying eyeliner to a dead woman wearing a green taffeta dress. Taffy-Hair stepped back to get the effect of her ministrations, and was Yana.

Larry turned away, flowers still in hand, the harsh light behind him casting his shadow through the window onto a pastel wall. Upstairs, he put the calla lilies on a casket in a viewing room, and departed. The great Yana hunt was over.

Yana had glanced toward the door to the embalming room just as some deliveryman with an armful of flowers was turning away from the observation window. The silhouette of his exaggerated profile on the wall gave her Larry Ballard's nose and chin despite his peaked cap and sunglasses.

She was already taking off her crisp white medical coat and surgeon's gloves. A year or two ago, when DKA took thirty-one Cadillacs away from the Gypsies when nobody else could even find them, she had been impressed. Especially with Larry. Now, when the Gypsies had to find Yana in the *gadjo* world, who would they turn to? DKA, of course.

Devèl, Ballard was good at what he did! But it didn't matter how he'd found her. She had to be gone from here and from her room at the Columbine within the hour. She was so fast out of Brittingham's that she saw Ballard's broad, tapered back as he walked up Sutter toward his car. She turned the other way, toward Polk Street. To go where? No enchanted alley cat to help her out this time. But maybe . . . just maybe . . .

The uniformed guard was waiting for Dan and the Baron with the two Dobermans outside the closed gate. He had his holster flap unbuttoned and his hand on his pistol butt. The guard dogs strained at their leashes with delighted fury. An open Jeep raced from behind the building on the dirt track inside the perimeter fence.

The Baron said, "Ve shall please to get out now."

Kearny opened his door, the guard released the dogs. Dan jerked his leg back in and slammed the door just as the Dobermans smashed against it. But damned if Knottnerus-Meyer hadn't already opened his door and was stepping out.

"Dogs are genuine optimists," he said. "Alvays cheerful."

The dogs flew around the front of the SUV to attack. Dan had to admit some slight hope the man would get mauled. He was so damned smug, so sure of himself, so damned . . . *Teutonic.*

But the Baron said in a low voice, "Are ve so ill-behaved?"

Hecate and Charon skidded to a stop. Hecate rolled over onto her back, legs in the air. Knottnerus-Meyer leaned down and scratched the proffered tummy. Kearny got out of the SUV gingerly. The guard pressed forward, angry and astounded. The Baron straightened. The mild look was gone. He screwed in his monocle, suddenly extremely Prussian.

"Your top shirt button iss open," he said coldly. "Your boots do not haff a sufficient shine. Your uniform does not haff a sufficient press." He gestured at the fawning Dobermans. "Choke collars on guard dogs are not permitted at dis facility."

Just then the Jeep came tearing up the dirt track to skid to a stop, spilling out a burly uniformed figure. He had a gun at his belt and a swagger stick in his hand.

"YOU SON OF A BITCH!" he yelled.

thirty-six

R.K. Robinson, the veins standing out at his temples and his big jaw muscles knotted, was not looking at the surprised Knottnerus-Meyer. He was glaring at Dan Kearny.

"R.K.," said Dan affably, "long time no see."

"Not long enough, you fuck," snarled R.K.

The gate guard was relaxed now, the dogs along with him. The Dobermans sat on their haunches watching the proceedings with interested eyes and their tongues hanging out.

A few years back, following his stint as a Walla Walla state prison guard, R.K. had drifted south to San Francisco and Dan had hired him as a repoman with DKA. He was big enough, and tough enough, and had to have some moderately hairy balls to have been a screw at Walla Walla. But he didn't work out. R.K. needed structure in the workplace. Rules and regulations posted on the wall, on-shift at eight, off at five, chicken on Sunday, a gun on his belt and a nightstick to slap against his palm.

A repoman out there in the field all by his lonesome had to make his own decisions. E.T. couldn't phone home. R.K. couldn't handle that. Kearny let him go.

R.K. belatedly turned on Knottnerus-Meyer.

"And just who the hell are *you* supposed to be?"

The Baron drew himself up to his full impressive height that equaled R.K.'s, monocle and sneer firmly in place.

"I am de expert brought from Chermany to examine de

Xanadu security. Herr Marr hass informed you uff my coming. Vhy haff you not demanded to see my credentials?"

"I, ah, oh, er . . . Mr. Marr briefed me on your description."

"How could he? Herr Marr hass not yet met me. My contact iss wit California-Citizens Bank." He turned to snap at the guard, "You—vut are you gawking at? Return to your post. Ven your relief arrives, drife de vehicle back to de compound." To R.K. he said, "Ve shall valk de grounds."

The trio walked across the tightly mown lawn toward the facility. R.K. was slapping his swagger stick across the palm of his left hand with exaggerated precision, rebuilding self-esteem.

Kearny saw that the shrubbery had been planted well back from the wall, creating a six-yard-wide dead zone. He began looking for concealed sensors. Yep. He pointed out one of them as they passed beneath it. Knottnerus-Meyer followed his gaze.

"Vut iss it?"

"Infrared sensing devices in the trees with interlocking arc sweeps of the cleared areas. The sensors pick up the body heat and movement of even a squirrel and sound the alarms."

The Baron turned to R.K. "You shall please to demonstrate de vorkings uff dese infrared sensors."

"Yeah, sure, Baron—it'll be my pleasure."

R.K. spun and threw a sudden right-hand uppercut at Kearny's jaw. Dan slipped it. The momentum of R.K.'s missed punch carried him forward. Dan stuck out a foot. R.K. tripped over it and, arms semaphoring for balance, went down face-first.

Sirens screamed. Whistles blew. There were startled shouts from inside the building.

Even before he got up, R.K. was scrabbling at his belt. He got his cell phone up to his face, shouted into it, "FALSE ALARM! FALSE ALARM! THIS IS FADED ROSE PETAL! FALSE ALARM, GODDAMMIT!"

"Faded Rose Petal?" asked Dan.

R.K. scrambled to his feet. "Fuck you, you sack of shit!"

"A most zatisfactory demonstration," said Knottnerus-Meyer in an impeccably neutral voice. But Dan saw, or imagined he saw, a twinkle in his eye. At that moment Dan Kearny started to like the Baron. Who said, "Ve shall continue our tour."

Larry's phone call caught Giselle once more at Kearny's desk. He said, "Listen, I think somebody's sleeping in the personal property room. I was up there this morning early to get a cap and the cot was messed up. When I came back, it had been made up."

Trin Morales, she thought. Had to be. Sacking out at DKA to avoid the pack of vengeful Latinos on his trail. She still hadn't laid eyes on him, but she knew he was around. He was turning in field reports and had made a dandy dead-skip repo in the Castro over the weekend. But Larry didn't need to know any of that, not the way he felt about Morales.

"I've been trying to reach you," she said. "Last Friday night Rudolph spotted Yana on Polk Street!"

"Not surprising," said Ballard. "Yana's setting hair and painting faces on corpses at Brittingham's Funeral Parlor in Sutter Street. I'm staked out here now to follow her home when she gets off work. I just got the lead yesterday."

"Lead from whom?"

"Not our clients, that's for sure. If Rudolph spotted her in Polk Street, why wasn't the place flooded with *Rom* within fifteen minutes? There aren't enough Gypsies in this thing, Giselle."

"Maybe because they think working in a funeral parlor is not a right livelihood for a Gypsy woman?"

"We know damn well they think that. But Yana's already *marime*. It's about what they'd expect from her." He paused. "I wonder if the rest of the Gypsies know Staley, Lulu, and Rudolph are looking for Yana?"

"You mean like perhaps what they are really after is the money and stuff Poteet hid in the light fixture?"

"Something like that. Looking for Yana on the sly. I'd sure as hell hate to turn her up for them and find out they plan to sell her to the cops for money or something."

"They wouldn't..." Giselle ran down. She said slowly, "They didn't tell us about Ephrem picking pockets at Marine World, did they?"

Art Gallery A was on Xanadu's first floor. Kearny was no connoisseur, but even from the doorway he recognized the quality of the tapestries that covered the temperature-controlled walls. Knottnerus-Meyer was staring at one depicting the Christ child in his mother's arms, holding a chalice made of gold thread crusted with woven jewels. In the background a covey of winged angels strummed away on harps and mandolins.

"De *real* Flemish *Mystic Vine* tapestry. Priceless. Dere iss an inferior copy in vun uff de Apostolic Palaces in Rome." The Baron checked the edges of the tapestries and around the bases of the sculptures carefully displayed on their pedestals. "Bernini's terra-cotta *Charity mit Four Children*, Algardi's *Baptism uff Christ*." He turned to snap at R.K. Robinson, "Dere iss no individual security on any uff dese treasures."

"None needed," said R.K. with a smirk. He gestured them out, then passed his hand up and down in the open doorway. "Nothing, see?" He took his cell phone off his belt, told it, "Activate Security Circuit One for Art Gallery A." He turned to the Baron. "Now you try it."

Knottnerus-Meyer passed his hand up and down in the open doorway. Immediately the alarm bells sounded.

State-of-the-art, thought Kearny. Invisible light beams from sensors in the door frame, three across and two vertical. Nobody could slip through them.

Knottnerus-Meyer nodded thoughtfully. *"Goot,"* he said.

The works in Art Gallery B were much more ancient than in the first one. Kearny stopped, caught by a frieze of a woman's head and a bull's head displayed side by side.

"A double herm uff de goddess Isis unt her offspring de Apis Bull," said the Baron. "Early Dynasty Egyptian. Unt *dese* . . ." He indicated display cases of pitchers and urns and vases with ears. *"Oinochoe, olpe, krater, amphora, kylix, hydria.* Greek. Classical Period. Again, priceless."

As they started out, R.K. said, "Here's what I didn't show you in Art Gallery A." He told his cell phone, "Activate Security Circuit Two for Art Gallery B," then said to the Baron, "You got a ballpoint pen?"

The Baron removed a pen from one of the pockets of his shooting jacket. "Uff course. But vut—"

"Just toss it into the room, Baron, if you would."

When the pen hit the floor, an alarm sounded raucously.

"Deactivate," said R.K. to his cell phone. The alarm fell silent. He said to the Baron, "The same in every room. Pressure-sensitive floor-plates. A mouse would set 'em off."

Knottnerus-Meyer reacted predictably.

"But vut if vermin vere to get into dis facility?"

Bart Heslip picked up a rental car at the Burbank airport, then called Giselle up in San Francisco.

"I just remembered—when Dan braced Poteet for information down here during the Cadillac caper, he was picking pockets at Universal Studios."

"In a series of disguises," exclaimed Giselle with sudden excitement. "A cowboy, a country singer, a southern colonel . . . No gorilla, but . . ."

It took Bart nearly an hour just to get through Universal's maze of interlocking bureaucracies to the head of security in a third-floor office overlooking the wet and wild Jurassic Park ride. His name was Jonathan James and he was almost as black as Bart, tall and lanky and wearing horn-rims. Unlike Bruckner at Marine World, he was curt, on the edge of hostility.

"My kid has soccer practice in forty minutes," he said.

"I'll only take ten," promised Bart.

James looked over Bart's I.D. "Private eye, huh?" He gave a thin-lipped chuckle. "We're fresh out of Maltese falcons."

"How about a gorilla who's also a dip?" asked Bart. "This guy always dresses up as somebody else—a cowboy in a ten-gallon hat, a sort of rockabilly character with a guitar—"

"Son of a bitch!" James came forward in his chair. "South-ern colonel, too! I remember all of them! But—"

"They were all our boy," said Bart. "And we think he's back down here again from the Bay Area." He figured James wouldn't waste his time on Poteet if he knew the man was dead and no longer a threat to Universal. "You have a lot of pockets picked about a month ago?"

"Jesus, yeah, we did. But no gorilla. We thought it was an organized gang that hit us hard and then moved on. Had no idea it was just one guy." As James worked his computer, he added, "We had a Smokey the Bear on staff, entertaining the kids in the tram lines . . . Hey! No employment records for Smokey . . ."

"That would have been him, all right," said Bart.

James forgot all about his son's soccer practice. He even scanned Ephrem Poteet's picture into their security system for future reference. Bart pressed him further.

"We think he's been living somewhere in the Silver Lake district and probably handed everything off to someone be-tween here and there. You got any ideas?"

James drummed thoughtful fingers on his computer table.

"Some of the unmarried grips and P.A.'s like to drink at a raunchy bar called the Hurly Burly on North Whitley in Holly-wood. A guy looking to score at Universal might get a lot of hot tips there just by hanging around and listening to them gossip. And the bartender looks like a Gypsy to me." He suddenly laughed. "Yeah, I know—racial stereotyping."

"Don't we all?" said Bart.

He shook James's hand and departed. Later for the Hurly Burly. First, Etty Mae Walston, Ephrem's snoopy ex-neighbor.

thirty-seven

Knottnerus-Meyer insisted on examining every room, even though security was the same in each. Finally, R.K. led them to the second-floor stairs past strategically placed hallway-scanning cameras.

"Live feed twenty-four/seven to Security Control Center."

On the second floor, he stopped in front of a solid steel door without a knob. There was an I.D. card-reader slot in a shiny stainless-steel panel beside it.

"Security Control Center," said R.K. in hushed tones.

Getting into the spirit of the thing, Dan asked innocently, "No fingerprint match? No retinal scan?"

R.K. slid a stiff plastic I.D. card into the reader slot.

"No need for either one of 'em. The operator freezes the door if he sees anyone suspicious trying to come at him."

The door popped open a scant two inches, shut itself behind them with a slight POOF of air.

It was the damnedest security setup Kearny had ever seen. More complex than the skyrooms above the Vegas casinos, if not quite so state-of-the-art. Banks of monitors, rows of lights, buttons and switches for each of the pressure pads and interlocking invisible laser beams inside the various galleries, and for the infrared heat and motion detectors outside.

Seated at the control module was the duty officer, a uniformed cipher with a rice-pudding face and raisin eyes. He demonstrated with his joystick, zooming in on a monitor screen, slowing down, speeding up, and freezing the action. Dan Kearny turned to R.K.

"No heat and motion detectors inside the building?"

"Not necessary with the outside perimeter sensors."

The Baron's attention had been caught by a panel set slightly to one side which had on it only a big red knob and a small black button.

"Most uff de equipment iss self-evident, but vut iss dis?"

"Pull that red knob, and steel shutters drop down over all the doors and windows except for the front door and a stairway from the third-floor barracks. The off-duty guards live and sleep up there." R.K. pushed the inconspicuous black button. A piece of wall slid up to reveal a steep narrow stairway going through the ceiling. "From there they have access to the helicopter landing pad on the roof."

"Let's take a look," said Kearny.

They found a military-style barracks with six single cots down each side of the room, green-metal floor lockers between them, the usual pinups and photos on the walls above them.

One end of the room was a lounge area with a pool table, a couple of armchairs, and a home entertainment center with a stereo system and a flat-screen TV for viewing videos and DVDs. There was even a shelf of paperback books. Nobody was there. R.K. waved a hand around.

"Off-duty personnel are at the mess hall at this hour."

At the other end was a spacious enclosed cubicle with a regular closet and its own shower and sink and toilet.

"My quarters," said R.K. stiffly.

No pinups here. No books, either, although Dan half-expected to see a copy of the Universal Code of Military Justice on the night table. But there was none.

Beside the cubicle was a rough staircase of two-by-fours with one-by-eight stair treads to a heavy door in the roof.

"To the helipad," said R.K. "It cannot be unlocked from in

here, only from the roof or from the Security Control Center."
He took his cell phone off his belt. "Baron, if you wanna—"

"Dot iss not necessary," said the Baron. "Ve vill go down unt
you can introduce Herr Kearny to Freddie vhile I question your
man on de control panel."

Freddie. A nickname for a sculpture? A painting? Some hu-
mongous gemstone? Dan was about to find out why he was
here.

"You're the boss," R.K. said sourly. He paused at the head
of the stairs beside a black button similar to the one on the control panel. "They can use this to get down and defend the Control Center if the door is somehow blown open."

Both men nodded. It was a good system. They went down.
As R.K. led Dan to a door across the Security Control Center,
the Baron said to the duty officer, "You vill please to show me
de Surveillance Room from vhich Freddie iss monitored."

It was a box of a room, sterile and modern, with only one
door and no windows and nobody in it. Above the door was a
scanning camera. An empty cage of black iron bars took up
most of it, with a wooden partition across the back forming a
small room they couldn't see into. A mirror of one-way glass in
a side wall let anyone in the Observation Room monitor this
room without being seen himself unless he wanted to fade out
the mirror effect so the window would be two-way.

R.K. said to Kearny, "Meet Freddie," and began making an
unearthly racket by running his swagger stick rapidly back and
forth across the bars of the cage. He probably had done the
same with his nightstick across cage bars in Walla Walla.

Dan didn't know what response this might have brought
from the prisoners, but here the result was instant and dramatic.
A full-grown male orangutan bounded out from behind the partition to hurl himself against the bars, trying unsuccessfully to
get at R.K. with a hairy, muscle-banded arm. Orangutan. Freddie. Now the Baron's monologue about apes made sense.

R.K. was acting very much like Freddie, leaping around, poking at the orangutan with his swagger stick.

"Yeah, c'mon, c'mon, you lousy ape, try an' get me!"

Freddie tried, he really did, but R.K. stayed just inches from his grasp. He went to a ring of keys hanging from a peg on the wall. He jangled them, grinning.

"C'mon, don't you want the keys? C'mon, try an' get 'em!"

Kearny, fed up, grabbed him by the collar and threw him back against the wall. R.K. fumbled at his holster, but Knottnerus-Meyer's icy tones came over some hidden loudspeaker.

"Dot iss quite enough uff dis disgraceful display."

R.K. froze with his pistol halfway out, then guiltily thrust it back. Freddie was leaping up and down and crowing for joy. He began manipulating his hands at Dan in what almost looked like sign language.

"Is he trying to say something to me?"

"Are you nuts? He's a friggin' ape, for Chrissake."

Knottnerus-Meyer's disembodied voice came again, his guttural German accent heightened by the speakers.

"You vill immediately come out uff dere, both uff you. You haff disturbed Freddie quite enough."

"I'm not gonna forget this, shithead," whispered R.K.

"Don't," said Dan Kearny.

Knottnerus-Meyer was waiting. "Herr Kearny, come in here."

He drew Dan into the Observation Room. The one-way window showed the partitioned area. Beside a cot in one corner were a few large rubber toys. Beyond that was a chair and a computer desk with a terminal, keyboard, screen, and printer. The keyboard was equipped with a bewildering array of outsize lights and buttons and symbols rather than letters.

Freddie was tearing around the enclosed area, still highly agitated. He picked up a big red rubber ball, squashed it several times between his long-fingered hands, then threw it against the wall. He threw himself down on his bunk on his back. Milled the air with his arms and legs. Gradually, he quieted. Finally, he got off the bunk and went over to his work station and seated himself at the console. He began punching in data with great confidence. Each time he hit a button, a tone sounded. Symbols appeared on his screen.

"Before Freddie," said Knottnerus-Meyer, "dere vere language experiments mit chimpanzees unt Koko, dot female gorilla vut chooses certain keys on a computer's auditory keyboard."

"Something like what Freddie's doing in there?"

"*Nein.* It iss clear Freddie hass gone beyond dot. I haff been told dot his trainer in Hong Kong hass taught him whole sentences. Dot iss vhy Herr Marr bought dot ape; he iss unique." He paused. "But now a man in Rome plans to steal him."

"Why?" said Kearny bluntly.

Knottnerus-Meyer gave a heavy Germanic shrug. "Vut does it matter? Maybe a dispute in ownership. Dot man in Hong Kong alerted Herr Marr to de thief. Dot iss vhy ve are here."

When she saw his black face, Etty Mae Walston started to give Bart Heslip a noseful of door; then she saw his detective license. It developed Etty Mae had been a fan of some mid-50s NBC TV series called *Meet McGraw* that featured a lantern-jawed actor named Frank Lovejoy as a sort of P.I.

Standing in her open doorway, Etty Mae even sang, in a cracked contralto, about it being a quarter to three without anyone in the place except you and me . . .

Then, for a solid hour, Bart sat in an antimacassar-covered easy chair that Etty Mae said had been her husband's favorite, while she poured iced tea into him and regaled him with everything that had happened in her life and on television for the past twenty years.

Bart finally got her on to the murder next door, and she was equally voluble. This time he egged her on.

"So you saw this woman go up on Poteet's porch and lost sight of her, and then she came out and you—"

"The first night I never did see her come out."

"Wait a minute. You're telling me you saw her *twice?*"

Etty Mae nodded. "The night before the murder she stopped right under the streetlight and went up on his porch, just like the next night when she killed him. More iced tea, Mr. Heslip?"

"No thank you, ma'am," he said hurriedly. "Did you tell the cops about her being here two nights in a row?"

For the first time, Etty Mae looked uncomfortable.

"To tell the truth, Mr. Heslip, I can't rightly say that I did. With all the excitement, it just sort of slipped my mind."

He had been right. He really needed a mug shot of Yana Poteet. "And you could pick her out of a lineup if you had to?"

"Absolutely. I watched her twice with my binoculars."

Bart used the pay phone next to the restrooms at the Jack in the Box three blocks from Etty Mae's house to call Giselle.

"Yana was down here the night before."

"Are you sure it was Yana? If she can prove she was *up* here on either of those two nights, she'll have a murder alibi!"

"How's she gonna do that? The cops won't listen, they're convinced she's guilty. And we don't know where she is."

"Yes we do! Larry's got her staked out. We'll get a chance to talk to her before the cops do."

The receptionist, and Harvey Parsons, the hostile embalmer, came out of Brittingham's Funeral Parlor at 5:00 P.M. But no Yana. By five-thirty Larry was starting to sweat it. At six, he went in to find Brittingham in his private office.

Larry said, "We spoke last night. I—"

"Of course. Mrs. Henderson's nephew. You wanted to meet Ms. Thatcher." His prim features tightened in anger. "She just walked off this afternoon and left Mrs. Hennessey's face half-made-up." He glared at Ballard. "I won't take her back."

"Sure not," agreed Larry. "But if you have her residence address maybe I can reach her there."

"The Columbine Residence for Women." As Ballard headed out the door, Brittingham stood up to almost shout after him, "I won't take her back. You tell her that!"

She wasn't there to tell. Stern-faced Mrs. Newman rang Miss Thatcher's room, but there was no response. A chunky Latina maid in a blue uniform coming by with a blue plastic bucket full of cleaning materials stopped beside them.

"She is no here." She made a zooming motion with one hand. "Her mother die, she fly away."

Stern-faced Mrs. Newman become sterner of face.

"I think that answers your question, young man."

She pointed to the door and Larry left. Yana must have seen him at Brittingham's after all, and just walked out while he was getting back to his truck to stake the place out. His only consolation was that he was getting less and less sure he wanted to find her for the other Gypsies.

Halfway down the mountain, Dan took a stab at it.

"So this whole thing is about that orangutan?"

"Dat orangutan, or Old Man uff de Forest, iss now very rare in de vild. If vun vanted one in its true, native, totally unspoiled state—"

"One wouldn't want Freddie," said Dan. "Freddie uses a computer. And I swear he tried to sign something to me."

"You know dot American Sign Language?" demanded the Baron.

"A deaf girl worked for DKA after school for a couple of summers. The hand movements looked familiar, that's all."

Knottnerus-Meyer considered him carefully.

"I vas vatching through dot observation vindow. Unt I know some sign language . . ." He paused, then added with an entirely straight face, "I belief dot ape signed, 'HELP. I AM BEING HELD PRISONER.'"

thirty-eight

O'B finally admitted it: he was having a dry spell in more ways than one. He was off the booze, *and* he hadn't repo'd one single car since the Panoz up in Sonoma. At almost the end of May, he was dead last on the repo board in the upstairs office. That had never happened before. Drastic measures were needed, so he was at the DKA office primed for shameful work. It was that or go have a drink, and he wasn't going to do that.

Long before Jane Goldson arrived at 7:30 A.M. to open locks, switch off alarms, and check the fax and e-mail for overnight assignments, he planned to poach new REPO ON SIGHT assignment sheets from the other guys' In boxes on her desk. Go grab the cars, up his monthly average, and blandly say they must have been given to him by mistake.

He reached greedy fingers for a juicy new Integra in Trin's In box, and an angry voice yelled at him from the stairs that led down from the second floor above Jane's desk.

"Hey, what the hell you think you're doing there, man?"

Morales vaulted over the railing to grab the repo order out of his hands. Trin grubbed in his box for his other assignments, memos, close-outs, gold-colored copies of the skip-tracers' work on his various cases, and stormed out. O'B drank six Dixie cups of cold water from the cooler, then meekly followed.

"He's not a bad man," said a woman's determined voice.

She was standing on the sidewalk outside, a little thing in her early 40s, not over five-three, wearing a cloth coat against the morning chill. Her sharp nose had a red tip, her hair was stringy, her eyes close-set, her thin lips determined.

"Of course he's not," said O'B heartily, knowing she sure didn't mean Morales. "What's the old devil up to these days?"

"As if you didn't know," she said almost coyly. Then she was serious again. "The temptation was just too much for Joel, you see. He figured that after a while the big man would stop looking. But he never did. He never said anything, he was just there, waiting, watching, leaving those cards with DKA on them."

The big man had to be Ken Warren, and this had to be Meg Doman, wife of Joel Doman, ex-UpScale salesman. Meg Doman was rummaging in her purse, still talking.

"You'd think, him being a used-car salesman and all, that wouldn't bother Joel. But he's sensitive to pressure. He was going to pieces. So this morning I just did it."

Her fisted hand came out of her purse convulsively—to press a set of keys into O'B's open palm. Now that he looked, the car was squatting right in front of the closed sliding doors to DKA's storage lot: 1990 Jag XJS convertible, champagne over black, just 75,000 miles on the clock, listed retail at $17,995.

"Faith and BeJaysus," breathed O'B. His long drought was finally broken. He even drove Meg Doman home.

Larry's descriptions—big and tough—had been apt. When Rosenkrantz and Guildenstern stormed up to Giselle at ten-thirty and badged her, she unobtrusively flicked open the intercom key, hoping Kearny was back from the bank to listen in. Rosenkrantz sat down on the corner of her desk, started idly swinging his leg.

Guildenstern snapped, "Where's that fucking Larry Ballard?"

"Don't use foul language in front of me," Giselle said, hoping to upset their interrogation rhythm.

"Few days ago, Ballard worked us for everything we had on Ephrem Poteet," said Rosenkrantz indifferently. "Said he hadn't seen the wife, Yana, for something like six or seven years."

"Why would he lie?"

Guildenstern leaned across the desk. "Larry lies when he says 'Hello.' We start going up Yana's backtrail, and whadda we find? We find his footprints all over our case."

Sure enough, it was time for the first joke. Rosenkrantz asked, "How did Pinocchio find out he was made of wood?"

"Don't," Giselle warned. "You're treading on thin ice."

Rosenkrantz was undeterred. "His hand caught fire."

"That's the first time," she said icily.

"Next," said Guildenstern, "we find out at Marine World in Vallejo that Heslip was asking a lot of questions about Poteet. So we call Harry Bosch down in L.A., and guess what? There's *Heslip's* big number nines all over *Harry's* case. Cops don't like P.I.'s mixing in murder, so we—"

"Has Yana been charged with murder?" she interrupted.

"That's police business," snapped Guildenstern. "This outfit is in a lot of trouble for obstructing our investigation."

Rosenkrantz asked, "Why are blondes like dog turds?"

Giselle was suddenly as formidable as El Capitan. "I told you not to do that. That's twice."

"The older they are, the easier they are to pick up."

"That's the third time," she said, and threw her cup of cold coffee in his face. He jumped off the desk, bellowing. Guildenstern got out his handcuffs.

"You're going down for assaulting an officer, sister."

"And you're going down for sexual harassment, brother."

Sexual harassment. The magic words. The two cops' eyes met. Rosenkrantz stopped wiping his face with a wad of Kleenex from the box on her desk. His partner's handcuffs disappeared as Dan Kearny appeared in the doorway.

"You're supposed to drink that stuff, not swim in it." He turned away, gesturing. "You can clean up in the bathroom."

Giselle punched out Larry's cell phone number as she flipped the intercom switch to listen.

Sitting beside Dan's desk, a dried-off Rosenkrantz jerked his head at the back room. "What's biting her? PMS?"

Guildenstern asked, "What do you get when you cross a pit bull with a woman who's having PMS?"

"You're treading on thin ice," said Kearny. "What I want out of you guys is why you're harassing the help on a referral out of L.A. All you've got on Yana is a very shaky eyewitness."

"You're wrong. We got a hell of a lot more than that," said Guildenstern, peeved at not getting to tell his joke.

"Knowing you guys ain't exactly dummies," said Rosenkrantz, "we wondered why you was all of a sudden so interested in two old guys up and died of natural causes—Eduardo Moneo in Vallejo and Brian Glosser here in the City. So we got secret exhumation orders on 'em. Purple foxglove poisoning, both of 'em—*Digitalis purpurea*. That spells a Murder One warrant for Yana."

Kearny's private phone rang. He snatched it up. Ballard.

"I'm at Ray Chong Fat's. Giselle just clued me in on the phone. Should I wait or run?"

"Take your time," said Kearny. He hung up. "Ballard, checking in. He's at the Chinese store down the street, drinking soda pop." He shook his head piously. "I like to protect my men, but Murder One is something else. I guess he's all yours."

Rosenkrantz sighed. "We better go piss in his Pepsi."

They went out the door behind Kearny's desk. Giselle appeared from the back room to flop down in his client's chair.

"Why are you throwing Larry to the wolves?"

"Who's the wolf and who's getting tossed to who?" said Dan.

Giselle suddenly grinned. "Tossed to *whom*," she said.

*   *   *

English letters and Chinese characters spelled out PEKING GROCERY STORE—CHINESE DELICACIES above the door of the narrow storefront. An apparently carefree Larry Ballard emerged eating an egg roll and slupping a soft drink from its aluminum can.

"Hold it right there!" bellowed a heavy voice.

Rosenkrantz, playing good cop, said, "How do you know you've met the woman who gives the best head in the world?"

"You're treading on thin ice," Larry said.

"Knock off the shit, Ballard!" Guildenstern roared. "You conned us at Beverly's bar, how you hardly knew Yana Poteet—"

"I told you I hadn't seen her for years. I hadn't, and anyway, DKA didn't want her yet. Then the Gyppos hired us to look for her, sure, but the only one had any suggestions at all was her brother, Ramon." Larry stuffed the rest of his egg roll into his mouth, said contemptuously, "A few worthless mail drops in the Presidio." He finished his Pepsi in one long swig, belched, wiped his mouth with the back of his hand. "Then I got lucky. I maybe spotted Yana in Sutter Street."

"You spotted her or you didn't," sneered Guildenstern.

"I wasn't sure, she was disguised. Brown wig, glasses . . ." He was gesturing, intense, selling it. "I lost her in the crowd. I started canvassing the businesses along Sutter, and finally found out she was doing makeup and hair on corpses at Brittingham's Funeral Home under the name of Becky Thatcher."

Guildenstern was ominous. *"Was* working there?"

"Yeah, past tense—and don't blame me she's gone. Brittingham told me she was living at the Columbine on—"

"We know it," said Rosenkrantz.

"Gone from there, too. No forwarding. End of story for the moment, but I still think I'm going to find her and—"

"No you aren't." Guildenstern's voice was flat. "DKA is out of it, O-U-T. We got a Murder One warrant out on her now."

Larry was genuinely shocked. "You mean L.A.'s got a—"

"No. *We* do. Find out from your boss why."

As they strutted away, Rosenkrantz asked his partner, "What do you think of that shit?"

"I think we got an expert snow job. I think they maybe even know where she is and are helping her hide from us." He paused. "Why is it so hard to pronounce 'fellatio'?"

Rosenkrantz opened his mouth, then shut it again.

"You're treading on thin ice," he warned.

thirty-nine

Each morning, Geraldine Tantillo put a paper bag containing an apple and an orange and a small carton of Nancy's Organic Non-Fat Yogurt into the fridge at JeanneMarie's salon. Each noon she got it out and walked down to the end of Spruce Street to sit on the Presidio Wall under a tree to eat as slowly as she could. She had read somewhere that after twenty minutes the stomach feels full with only a little food in it.

Today her good resolves were nullified when tall, blond, handsome Larry Ballard fell into step beside her.

"Geraldine, how does the Cliff House sound for lunch?"

The Cliff House! It sounded incredible.

They ate crab sandwiches in the upstairs bar overlooking Ocean Beach, a broad swatch of pale sand with long wide white lines of breakers marching in to smash and smoke below them. Black-clad surfers, miniaturized by distance, rode the foaming waves on their boards. Beach and breakers stretched away to the south until they merged with hazy blue sky at the horizon.

"Ah—have you heard anything from Yasmine Vlanko?"

"No." Excitement made her almost breathless. "Have you?"

His question was the reason for the lunch, a long shot at best, but he'd had to try. Larry sighed and shook his head.

"No. But if you run into her, Geraldine, please tell her DKA has some information she'll really want to have."

*   *   *

The three of them sat in the closed electronics shop, drinking Turkish coffee from small brass handleless cups.

Rudolph Marino looked very *Rom* in a bright red shirt with full sleeves and a kerchief around his neck. He seldom had the luxury of this preferred style of dress anymore; lately, his Angelo Grimaldi persona had almost taken him over. Staley was dressed as a shopkeeper in flannel shirt and polyester pants and his comfortable bedroom slippers. Willem was dressed, as always, like a European businessman. His only concessions to American informality were his loosened necktie and the suit jacket hung over the back of his chair. Staley was telling them about Ballard's finding and losing Yana.

"She must of got out before he even got to his truck."

Willem was the first to react.

"Working at a mortuary, handling corpses? You were right to make her *marime*. She has no respect for traditional values."

But Rudolph was impressed. "She sure knows where to hide."

"DKA can't look for her anymore. The San Francisco cops issued a Murder One warrant for her," said Staley. "Turns out she murdered two old men up here besides Ephrem down in L.A."

All three men crossed themselves. Willem recovered first.

"Well, DKA has served its purpose. And I have important news. Robin Brantley in Hong Kong betrayed me—he told Marr that I am planning an assault on Xanadu. Marr hired a German expert for advice on further security measures." An expression that could almost have been a smile played around Willem's lips. "I have it on good authority that this German told Marr his security at Xanadu was deplorable, and that Marr rejected that conclusion."

They drank coffee and looked at one another with veiled, knowing Gypsy eyes. Staley said, "So you will be busy."

Lulu burst through the door from the kitchen.

"What is this I heard you say? That Yana has killed two old men besides poor Ephrem? What if she—"

Staley chuckled. "I got you to protect me, Lulu."

"This is no joke! You got her declared *marime*, she's got the second sight—that *jookli* is dangerous in every way!"

Staley heaved himself to his feet to go help his wife put away the groceries.

"She's on the run, she ain't got time to worry about us."

At seven that evening Geraldine puffed her way up the long climb to her tiny apartment. After losing nearly twenty pounds to her five flights of stairs, she was almost getting a waist.

A thick savory stew bubbled in her only saucepan on the single-burner hotplate. The table was set with two plates, both soup bowls, and both sets of her Kmart cutlery.

"I'm home," Geraldine called softly. "Alone." Yasmine Vlanko came out from behind the curtain hung at an angle across one corner of the room to form a tiny closet. Geraldine added, "Just as you said, Larry Ballard took me to lunch!"

The stew was subtly flavored with herbs unknown in Dubuque. As Geraldine talked with her soup spoon, Yasmine hung on every word, interjecting little exclamations and clicks of the tongue. Geraldine felt more important than she had ever felt in her life.

"And he gave you no hint of what his information might be?"

Yasmine asked it urgently. Geraldine felt a twinge of quickly suppressed jealousy. Yasmine was so darkly beautiful and Ballard was so blondly handsome: they would make a striking couple. It was comforting to remember that Yasmine, to preserve her powers, slept with no one on earth.

"He just said it was really important."

"The forces of darkness are closing in," Yasmine said almost to herself. She chanted in a low voice:

"Miseç', yakhá tut dikhen,
Te yon káthe mudáren!
Te átunci eftá coká
Te çaven miseçe yakhá!"

Geraldine trembled at Yasmine's unknown words. "What does it mean?" she asked timidly.

"Evil eyes look on thee,
May they here extinguished be!
And then seven ravens
Pluck out the evil eyes!"

Geraldine squealed her chair back, terrified. Yasmine put a quickly comforting hand on her arm.

"Not you, Geraldine! And not Larry Ballard, either. He is not evil. He does what a man must do. The curse is for those who accuse me of evil."

"What must I do?" asked Geraldine.

"You must carry a very special message to a certain person. She must know nothing of where I am or who you are."

"You want me to ask her what Ballard was talking about?"

"You have much to learn, Geraldine. Ask, and you learn nothing. You must make *them* eager to tell *you.*"

"I . . . I'm not very good at lying or fooling people," said Geraldine miserably, her mission a failure before it had begun.

Yasmine made a dismissive gesture. "I will prepare you."

It was just past midnight, black and still and, up here in the mountains, clear and brisk with a billion stars. No moon. The Xanadu gate was safely closed and locked and the uniformed guard was bored and half-asleep. He yawned. Charon and Hecate, lying beside him on their leashes, yawned also.

Far away behind the building was the soft loamy sound of a trenching tool sinking into rich soil. The hole under the electrified perimeter fence got just big enough for a man to crawl through. Dragging a curiously lively stuff-bag behind him, the digger slithered on his back under the high-voltage wire.

Bushes moved on the edge of the cleared perimeter area at the right rear corner of the building. Big gloved hands took a squirming grey squirrel out of the stuff-bag to toss it into the no-man's-land covered by the movement and heat sensors.

Lights flashed, sirens screamed, whistles shrilled.

The black-clad intruder jogged back past his entry point toward the left rear corner of the building. Here he stooped to release a second squirrel, then melted again into the bushes.

More lights flashed, sirens screamed, whistles shrilled.

A quartet of armed guards led by R.K. Robinson rushed down the front steps and turned right toward the first set of alarms. A few moments later, five more guards burst forth to turn left toward the second set of alarms.

The intruder, dressed all in black and wearing a black ski mask, raced up the deserted front steps and into the building. He took the stairs to the second floor two at a time, ignoring the glaring eyes of the security cameras.

A dozen feet beyond the locked-down solid steel door of the Security Control Center, the door to the Observation Room was invitingly ajar. The intruder plunged through the interlocking invisible light beams, crossed the pressure-sensitive floor plates to the observation window. Sirens. Whistles.

Inside the Security Control Center one of a pair of side-by-side monitor screens showed Freddie's room. The other showed the adjacent Observation Room.

Freddie was sitting on the floor of his partitioned-off living area, playing rather disconsolately with one of his toys. His computer was dark and silent. In the Observation Room, a black-clad figure rapped sharply on the window glass.

The duty officer spoke into his mike in an excited voice.

"This is Rose Bush. Intruder in Observation Room, signaling to Freddie. Repeat, this is Rose Bush—"

Through his earphones came R.K. Robinson's bull-like voice.

"This is Faded Rose Petal. On my way, over."

Freddie, leaping up and down with excitement, paused to assimilate the words being signed by the man in the Observation Room: COME BACK FOR FREDDIE SOON.

The hallway door burst open and R.K. Robinson sprang into the room with a loud cry of triumph. He was jerking his gun from its holster as he came. The intruder hurled himself backward right through the pane of the outside window. R.K. Robinson fired at the same moment. The upper edge of the window frame splintered as his shot went high.

R.K. rushed to the window and leaned out. Nothing.

What in Christ's name was Victor Marr going to say when he learned of this night's fiasco?

forty

Very little, to R.K. Robinson's relief the next morning. Marr spoke on the secure line with a shrug in his voice.

"Freddie was unharmed?"

"Oh, yeah, sure, Mr. Marr. The guy only got into the Observation Room. He never laid a glove on the ape."

"Line the bottom of the perimeter fence with steel baffles so no one can dig under it again," said Marr.

"We caught the squirrels," said R.K. proudly. "They made great target practice. Blew 'em all to hell with our AK-47s."

Marr sighed. No way now to learn where the squirrels had been purchased. Was the man a moron?

"Carry on, Robinson. I will be back in touch soon."

Oh Jesus, *Robinson!* And it had been going so well. Why was the old man all of a sudden pissed, for Chrissake?

How much to tell Knottnerus-Meyer of last night's probe into Xanadu's security? Nothing, Marr decided. Never let the right hand know what the left hand was doing. He called the Baron's suite at the St. Francis Hotel in San Francisco.

"Prepare your plan to test the Xanadu defenses, Baron."

Over the phone, heels clicked. "*Ja,* Herr Marr."

Stan Groner was learning. He didn't say it in so many words, but his guarded phone call conveyed the essential message that he wanted a meet where nobody could listen in. It

was a nice afternoon, cool breeze but no fog, so Kearny suggested the trail along the sea bluffs that flanked Lincoln Park
Golf Course.

As they strolled along far above the smashing breakers, Stan
the Man blurted out, "Marr has changed his mind. Now he
wants Xanadu's defenses tested. So the Baron wants you to—"

"Uh-uh. The Baron hasn't paid my consultant's fee yet."

"Cal-Cit guarantees payment." Stan slid a sideways glance at
Kearny's impassive profile. "The Baron let slip that secret
merger talks are going on between his firm and the bank. I
want to be one of those still standing when the smoke clears."

"I just bet you do—but what's in it for me?"

"DKA gets all of Cal-Cit's repo work in perpetuity."

Kearny stopped dead. Crisp spring breeze coming up the
cliff face ruffled his greying hair. His eyes had sharpened.

"Over the whole state? Forever?"

Stan's mild features took on a half-crafty look. He was getting good at this stuff. He nodded. "The bank really wants to
get into bed with these guys in Berlin."

Kearny knew "forever" was a very elastic term, but he said,
"Set up a meeting so I can find out what it is the Baron wants."

Johanna Knudsen was a pretty blonde with a warm face and
big blue eyes dancing with laughter. Last year, she and Edna
Jacob had become partners as Travel Associates of Richmond.
Their office on Park Place in Point Richmond was in a two-story
red-brick converted firehouse and jail originally built in 1910.

It was noon, Edna was out to lunch, and Johanna was making out a South Seas cruise itinerary that two elderly couples
would be in for that afternoon, when the door's spring bell jangled. A stunningly handsome, deeply tanned man in his mid-
30s came gliding down the aisle of the long, narrow office.
Beautifully groomed black hair, zestful eyes, strong features, a
sensual mouth. His suit was exquisite. He stopped at Johanna's
brochure-strewn desk.

"Ms. Knudsen, my name is Alberto Angelini."

Johanna gave him her best smile. "What can I do for you?"

"If I may . . ." Angelini leaned forward with European *élan* to lay a business card on her desk, then sat down across from her. He crossed his legs. His pants had absolutely knife-edge creases. "I wish to charter a plane to take fifty people to Europe." Johanna reached casually for her notepad and drew it toward her. The commission on this might pay off the last of their start-up costs.

"The smallest plane you could get would be a 767," she said, "and that carries two hundred people. We could probably find another charter group to split the cost." She glanced at him with interest. "It sounds as though you have a wedding or a baptism coming up."

"Both perhaps. It will definitely be a pleasure trip." He gave a rich, mellow laugh that Johanna felt right down to her toes. "I am taking my employees and their families to Roma in the middle of the Jubilee year when the festivities will be at their zenith." He pronounced it the British way.

"Lucky employees!" she exclaimed with a smile.

He tapped the card he had put on her desk. "I'm the lucky one. My people have made it all possible. The Millennium of the Church is an historical occasion; it will not recur for a thousand years. Heaven's Helpers supplies vestments, chalices, and candlesticks to churches across the country, books of devotion to Catholic bookstores, and religious items to the gift shops of the California missions. This has been an unusually profitable year for us, and I resolved that the hard work of my staff should be rewarded. Recently holy relics have surfaced from ancient monasteries throughout the Holy Roman Empire, such as have never been seen on this continent. Sacred mementos, carrying the blessings of beatified popes, powerful indulgences. . . ."

Johanna smiled wistfully. Although it sounded a bit exotic, pagan even, it was also, well, in a word, romantic.

Her fingers danced lightly on the computer keys. "I should

think . . . yes . . . I can probably find you something for late August or early—"

"But no!" he cried passionately. "It must be next week. There are time-sensitive considerations that cannot be deferred."

Her face fell. "Next week just isn't possible, Mr. Angelini. We're entering the peak summer travel season—"

"Please—Alberto." He checked his watch, was on his feet. *"Devo scappare.* Lunch, Thursday noon, the Hotel Mac. I leave it all in your hands." His glance at her was a caress. "By then you will tell me how we can manage this."

Ballard was blazing. "Why did you tell the Gypsies we're off Yana's case?" he demanded of Kearny.

Giselle answered for Dan. "The cops told us to butt out."

"Rosenkrantz and Guildenstern got a warrant," said Kearny. "*They* think they've got proof she did the two old men here in the Bay Area. Where you gonna run to, cowboy, if they catch you still looking for her?"

"They won't catch him," said Bart.

"When you find her, what then?" asked Giselle.

"I tell her about the Murder One warrant." Larry suddenly grinned. "Then I ask her if she did it."

Fifteen minutes later, as she keyed the door of her little red Alfa in DKA's repo storage lot, there was a jangling noise behind Giselle. A soft voice asked, "Giselle Marc?"

She whirled, heart thumping. But it was only a buxom tight-waisted woman she had never seen before, peering almost diffidently at her from the shadows beside a repo'd SUV.

Obviously, the woman had dressed for maximum impact. She wore a white off-the-shoulder blouse displaying deep cleavage, and a blue and white full skirt of crinkly material. Gold glittered at her ears, her throat, her wrists, her fingers. She carried a small pink purse at odds with her dress. Her hair was a black cloud around her full, round face. Too much vivid red lipstick; too much mascara, too much musky perfume.

"I have a message for you from Yasmine Vlanko."

Yasmine Vlanko, aka Yana Poteet! Obviously, not all of the Gypsies were honoring Yana's *marime* interdiction.

"What's the message?"

"The forces of darkness pursue her. It is very dangerous for her. All is not what it seems. You must wait for my call with a date, a time, and a place for a meeting. No names will be given. This cannot be shared with anyone."

"If no names are given, how will I know—"

The woman shimmied her hips to jangle her golden coins. Clever. She didn't have to give a name, not even a phony one.

Excitement constricted Giselle's throat. "I'll be ready."

The cab, an extravagance Yasmine had paid for, dropped Geraldine Tantillo on the steeply slanting street in front of her apartment house. She almost ran up the five flights of stairs with equal feelings of excitement and near-pain. She was dying to get at the corset that had tightened her waist from its usual comfortable 35 to a compressed 28, but she felt wonderful. She was a star! Not one of the chorus, not one of the crowd.

Yasmine shut and bolted the door behind her as Geraldine whipped off the great wig of shining black hair.

"I . . . did . . . it . . . just as . . . you told me to . . ."

"We shall drink some wine," Yasmine beamed, "and you will tell it all to me from hello-hello to goodbye-goodbye."

At ten-thirty the next morning, Dan Kearny said in disbelief, "You want DKA to prepare a plan to do *what?*"

They were in a dark-paneled corner office at the Cal-Cit Bank headquarters in One Embarcadero Center's glittering marble-and-glass tower. On the walls were sporting prints; through the windows were fine sun-drenched views of Market Street far below. Ornate gold leaf on the outside of the old-fashioned pebbled glass door, backward from inside the room, spelled out:

STANLEY GRONER
PRESIDENT
CONSUMER LOAN DIVISION

They were all wearing their power suits. Kearny wore his from Chicago, along with the tie Giselle admired. Stan Groner wore Brooks Brothers blue, Baron Herbert Von Knottnerus-Meyer a lightweight pearl-grey wool number.

"It is very simple," Stan said. "Now Marr wants Xanadu's defenses tested in real time. You have to come up with a plan."

"I don't know about real time, but I know those defenses."

"I assure you, de fee vill be more den adequate," said Knottnerus-Meyer. "Vere iss der problem?"

"Stan, tell him where the problem is."

"Uh . . . I'm with the Baron on this one. Hell, Dan, you should welcome the challenge."

Kearny shot Groner an angry glare. It slid right off him. Ah, where was the staid banker of yesteryear? Mired in greed. As was Kearny, of course. Besotted but cautious.

"Hell, Stan, you should be part of the challenge."

"No way!" Stan was aghast. "I'm a *banker*, for God sake!"

Kearny felt he had scored his point. He said, "Okay, I've got a couple of ideas."

Which, he knew, meant a heads-together with devious O'B.

He and O'B met at the Corner Bar, up the street from DKA, happily still a bucket of blood full of rummies despite the on-going dot-com gentrification South of Market. After they'd been served by a squat, swarthy, foul-mouthed bartender in a dirty apron, Dan laid out the specs of the Baron's Xanadu needs.

He finished with, "Our strategy is very simple—"

"Simple?" O'B drained his second O'Doul's. "We gotta get

through the electrified outer fence without getting fried; take out the perimeter sensors; get into the building and bypass the scanning video cameras; deactive the invisible light beams; avoid the pressure plates in the floors; neutralize the security control systems operator; release this ape from his cage and remove him from the building, put him back, and get away ourselves without being spotted or getting our butts chewed off by the dogs or shot off by a head of security who hates your guts. *Simple?"*

Kearny nodded. "Strategy is *what* has to be done. It's always simple. Strategy is my concern. *How* to carry out strategy is tactics. Tactics, O'B—they're *your* concern."

forty-one

Milagrita hadn't seen her brother Esteban and his *amigos* since they chased Trin out of the Mission Street pizza joint. The less she saw of them, the more she worried. What if they, like she, had ferreted out his spare apartment key? What if his paycheck stubs were in the apartment? It preyed on her mind.

So after work that night, she worked her way through back alleys to come out behind Trin's place in the 900 block of Florida Street. She climbed a tree to get over the fence and wormed her way through the concrete runoff to find the rock with the key under it. And came nose-to-nose with the big tortoise who had lived there for fifty years and more.

"Wish me luck, turtle," Milagrita whispered to him.

The tortoise half-pulled in his head and feet to opt out.

She climbed the creaky wooden stairs to Trin's back door, unlocked it, slipped in, stood in the darkened kitchen with her heart pounding wildly. She had never done anything like this before. As she passed through the connecting door to the living room fronting Florida Street, she was seized from behind, run right across the room, and rammed face-down onto the couch.

"I tell your brother I wait long enough, he will come back," sneered Jorge's hate-filled voice from above and behind her. "Instead, you come to meet your lover. Even better! I'll tell Esteban I see you through the window getting undressed."

She squirmed around to look up at him in the semidarkness. Jorge was handsome in the Ricky Martin mode, and vain about it. Curly black hair, dark expressive eyes, a shapely nose, a full-lipped, vulnerable mouth. He made her sick.

"Esteban will not believe you."

But she knew her brother would. Thank the Virgin, it didn't sound as though Jorge had thought of looking for something that would tell him where Trin worked. She stood up gingerly. She had never been so terrified, but she must not let it show.

"I shall leave now," she said formally in Spanish.

But Jorge seized her and smeared his sneering face against hers, mouth open and tongue darting. Instinctively, she brought her knee up between his legs. It was mostly ineffectual, but he grunted, loosened his grip; she ran for the kitchen. He was on her from behind, spun her around, his fist broke her nose and chipped two of her front teeth. He hit her again, in the belly.

She felt darkness engulfing her. She had no breath, no strength, no will to resist. For a long time there was only him on top of her, thrusting and grunting his harsh triumph.

She was sprawled face-down on the couch. Blood from her mouth stained the fabric. She knew only pain. Jorge grabbed her long black hair to jerk her head back.

"You ain't ever gonna tell your brother what you made me do to you tonight, little whore." He held up his cell phone. "You just gonna call Morales and tell him you waiting for him with your legs spread. After I call Esteban and tell him Morales is coming here, you gonna leave right away, *comprende*?"

"But Esteban will kill him!" she whimpered.

"No, I gonna do that. Then, any time I say, you will come crawling." He thrust the phone into her hands. "I know a little whore like you has got a secret number you can call your lover."

She didn't, but she knew he wouldn't believe her. She had only one little forlorn hope. "I . . . all right. I . . . I'll call."

*   *   *

Giselle, working late, was just leaving her desk when her private phone rang. A small, pain-filled, Spanish-accented voice exclaimed weakly in her ear, "Trin! I'm so glad I caught you."

Milagrita! In trouble! Thank God she had given the girl her private number. Giselle sat back down, grabbed a memo pad.

"Keep talking to Morales," she said. "Where are you?"

"At your place," Milagrita said in a sad parody of banter.

"Is someone there with you?"

"Of course. And waiting for you."

"Jorge?" Milagrita's silence was confirmation. "Are you hurt?" Silence. "Raped?" More silence. Giselle thought of calling an ambulance, then realized the first priority had to be getting her away from Jorge. "Can you leave there?"

"Soon as you can, *querido*," she said with a ghastly giggle.

"Bryant and Twenty-second? In ten minutes?" That was two blocks from Morales's apartment, only three blocks from S.F. General Hospital's Emergency and Trauma Center.

"I can hardly wait," said Milagrita faintly.

Where was Morales? If he was out in the field, and went home to his apartment, he'd run right into the ambush. If he was here, it would be all right.

Morales was lying on the cot in the personal property room in his underwear, reading a Spanish language newspaper. When Giselle stuck her head in, he started up in alarm. She waved him back to his place.

"I know you've been sleeping here, it's okay. I was just looking for Mr. K—"

"Like hell." Morales swung his stockinged feet to the floor. "I heard you tell him good night half an hour ago." He grabbed her arm with shocking speed and strength at odds with his almost feminine intuition of her distress. "What's wrong? Has something happened to Milagrita?"

She shook him off. "Never mind that. Just don't go home, all right? They're waiting there for you."

"Jorge done something to her," Trin said with certainty.

She didn't reply, just ran out, leaving him fumbling under the cot for his shoes. She clattered down the stairs. Ballard, coming in the back door, stopped dead at sight of her face.

"What's wrong?"

"A little Spanish girl has been raped. I've got to—"

"Need help?"

"No." She paused. "Yes. She's the sister of the guy who beat up Morales." She jerked her head at the stairs. "Keep him here, Larry. He wants to face those thugs all alone."

Ballard's face went dead. "He can fight his own fights."

She ran out the door for her Alfa. Too many minutes had passed already. As she left the garage, Ballard was unconcernedly strolling back across the street to his truck.

She yelled out of her window, "You're a real turd, Larry!"

Ballard watched her roar away down Eleventh Street. She was wrong, dammit. Fucker deserved all things bad. Didn't he?

He got into his truck, turned on his C/B radio.

Jorge waited just inside Trin's front door, watching the street through the filmy curtain. Esteban was parked in front of the apartment, Manuel was hidden in a recessed entry a few houses to the south, Pedro hidden in a similar recess to the north. No car passed. No window curtain twitched. No one walked the street. These four were known and dreaded in the neighborhood.

And here came stupid Morales, parking and walking across Florida Street right into the trap. Jorge swaggered down the steps of the apartment, baseball bat in hand. Morales stopped, looking up. Esteban, unseen, silently got out of his car right behind Morales. Like last time—only now Esteban had a knife.

Morales told Jorge, "Your mother gives blow-jobs to dogs."

Esteban, grinning, knife in hand, said to Trin's back, "And you are a pig to be butchered, *maricón.*"

Trin whirled around. Manuel and Pedro were moving in

from the sides. Morales was boxed in and all alone. He put his
back to a wrought-iron railing flanking the sidewalk.

"Come and get it," he said to them all, fists clenched.

They came. They got it.

Because three other men materialized out of the night behind them as Trin gaped in surprise. One was tall and blond
and muscular. One was shorter and black and wide as a door.
One was huge and quick and hard-faced. None of them was
shy.

Ken Warren grabbed Manuel by the scruff of the neck and
the seat of the pants, ran him out into the middle of Florida
Street, and spun like a shot-putter to hurl him bodily against the
side of a parked car. Manuel's face broke the car's window. The
car's window returned the favor.

Bart Heslip had already driven a tremendous kidney punch
into Esteban's unprotected back. Esteban screamed and
dropped his knife and would have fallen down except Heslip
slapped him up against his own car and began pumping com-
binations into him.

Meanwhile, Larry Ballard's *yawara* stick, the medieval Buddhist monks' lightning bolt of Siva, flicked the bat out of Jorge's
hand. "Take him, Morales!" Larry shouted, and sent the *yawara*
stick spinning after Pedro. It swept the fleeing man's legs out
from under him. Then Ballard was on him.

No science, no finesse to Trin's attack on Jorge: head-butts,
elbow smashes, steel-toed work boots. Jorge's nose went from
shapely to mushroom in one awful instant. Blood and teeth
flew in several directions at once. Trin only stopped kicking the
inert mass on the sidewalk so he could crouch down and bring
his face close to what had been Jorge's face. It was crying.

"You ever touch Milagrita, you will eat your own *cojones*,"
said Morales. "You believe what I say to you, man?"

The crying mess somehow was able to mouth, *"Sí."*

Trin stood up. He met Ballard's gaze. Ballard must have

called the others on the C/B radio from his truck. And they had come. The two men nodded almost formally to each other.

Manuel was unconscious in the middle of the street.

Pedro was unconscious in the middle of the sidewalk.

Esteban was erect against the side of his own car, but only because Bart was holding him up so he could deliver his line.

"We know where you live, pal," he said in soft menace.

And let go. Esteban could finally fall down. He did.

For the first time in his life, Trinidad Morales had his own band of *amigos*, his own posse. From somewhere not too far off came the sound of police sirens. Ken Warren spoke.

"Hngleth nyetta hehl hnougtta hneer!"

So they got to hell out of there.

Just before the sedatives put her under, Milagrita managed to mumble to the S.F. General Emergency Room doctor that she didn't know who had done it. Just . . . someone in an alley . . .

Giselle was equally vague. Never saw her before in my life. Good Samaritan, that's all. Found her, brought her in.

forty-two

The Colonial Hotel, a three-story mellow red-brick building at 550 Washington Street, was built in 1911 to furnish rooms and meals for workers at the nearby Standard Oil facility. After declining for decades and finally being gutted by fire, in 1978 it was renamed, restored, renovated, and reborn along with the rest of Point Richmond.

Now it had a huge sign on top spelling out HOTEL MAC. The double front doors had a canopy over them bearing the same name in bold white letters. Through big flanking leaded windows that looked out on Washington Street could be seen drinkers at the bar on one side, loungers in the lounge on the other.

Johanna Knudsen and Alberto Angelini went up to the second-floor dining room. A burly maître d' in a flowery sport shirt seated them at a choice table under one of the carefully restored stained glass windows. By that time, Johanna had waved or exchanged a word with no fewer than seven of her clients.

She was pleased to be lunching with such a remarkably handsome man. Who insisted she throw her diet to the winds and order the most expensive dishes on the menu—with dessert.

She groaned, "You're going to ruin my figure."

"It will take a great deal more than honey garlic lamb chops to do that, *cara mia,*" grinned Angelini. What an utterly charming man he was! "And the salmon is from your native Norway, it must be good for you, no?" It wasn't until they were drinking coffee and feasting on rich gooey slices of Snickers pie that he laid a hand on his chest and said, "Johanna, in my heart I have every belief that you have solved my travel problems."

So did she: Johanna loved being ingenious for the rare client who appreciated how clever she could be.

"I can schedule your people separately on a scheduled airline. There aren't enough individual seats next week to Rome, but Alitalia has daily eleven-and-a-half-hour nonstops to Milan that do have room."

"That is even better than Rome!" he told her. Which was true. "I have relatives in Milan." Which was a lie.

"Great! Your people can be spread out over three or four days and half a dozen flights. All I need are their names and credit card information. They all have their passports?"

"But of course."

"And they don't need visas for Italy." She grinned. "The best news is that each fare is only nine hundred twenty-two dollars plus tax, round-trip. That's really good for last-minute reservations at this time of year!"

"It is indeed."

Angelini took an envelope from the inside pocket of his suit and laid it on the table. "Here are the names. I shall give you my credit card later."

"I'll get busy then. You are all going to Italy, Alberto."

"*Benissimo!* You are extraordinary, *cara mia!*"

Dan Kearny looked at the handpicked troops assembled after-hours in DKA's big back office. O'Bannon and Giselle were listening to an intent Bart Heslip. Ballard and Morales stood in front of the mainframe computer, beers in hand, chatting as if they were pals. "Sorry to hear about your lady, Trin."

". . . just came from the hospital," Morales said. "She's doing better, man. Takin' her home to her mother's on Tuesday."

"Glad to hear it."

Of the DKA regulars, only Ken Warren was not there. He had located the last outstanding classic car, the $95,000 1970 Aston Martin Volante; it had been legitimately sold by UpScale Motors to a man named Adam Zeccola the day before DKA's raid, but no payments had been made to the bank. Ken had dug up a lead on him in Medford, Oregon, and was driving up to drop a rock on the car before Zeccola could move somewhere else.

Kearny walked to the middle of the room. "Okay, guys, let's get to it." He looked at Morales. "Trin. The truck?"

"It'll get there. Maybe not back, but—"

"It doesn't have to get back. Clean?"

"Yeah. Outfit back in Jersey we repo'd it for is gone—they got firebombed in a mob dispute last month. No way to trace it back to us."

He swung his gaze to Heslip. "Bart. The dental mirrors?"

"Ten of them. Adhesive putty fixed to the handles."

"And the crossbow and the expanding-head quarrel?"

"Yassuh, boss."

"Clown around." Dan turned to Giselle. "The skyrockets?"

"With a fuse to lead to the cab of the truck. Got 'em out in the Sunset from an illicit fireworks guy on Nineteenth Ave."

"I thought he blew himself up last year."

"Same part of town, different guy."

Kearny nodded. "O'B. The firecrackers?"

"A hundred strings. Same guy Giselle dealt with."

"Okay," said Kearny, "I've got the talcum powder, and the fishhooks strung every ten feet on the Primacord." He looked at Ballard. "Larry. The steel ball bearings?"

Kearny was wired. They all were. Ballard suddenly thought, We're in a caper movie here. Flat delivery, keen glances, tight clipped sentences. In his mind played the faint far strains of the *Mission: Impossible* theme. Of course, he was a little old to be

Tom Cruise. But then, Tom Cruise was a little old to be Tom Cruise.

"Eight dozen, like you said. And I found two of those dart pistols that shoot little sticks with rubber suction cups on the ends in that magic and trick shop in the Marina. They're almost collectibles now, but they'll work great."

"The Baron is furnishing the tranquilizer darts," said Kearny. "He tells me the dosage is tricky. And I've got the grappling hooks. Anything I'm missing?"

"The shaving cream," said Giselle. "I've got that—two cans. What about the uniforms?"

"The Baron's dropping them by tomorrow morning."

Giselle's private phone rang. Sitting on the edge of her desk, she turned to pick up and heard the jangle of gold coins. The Gypsy messenger from Yana Poteet! She looked quickly around, then hunched over the phone with the woman's voice in her ear.

"Two nights from now, midnight, Jackson Playground on—"

"On Mariposa?" Giselle clapped a hand over her careless mouth: she wanted to beat Larry to Yana. She wanted to beat *everyone* to Yana. Probably because Yana had chosen to communicate with her, not Larry or anyone else.

"Yes. Wait for the Gypsy outside the park," the gentle voice was going on. "She will take you to the Undertaker."

The Gypsy had to be this woman, the Undertaker had to be Yana. "Fine," said Giselle, afraid to slip again. But she needn't have worried. When she hung up, Kearny was still talking and everybody was still listening.

"The Baron has already learned that three guards will be taking off for Memorial Day on Monday. That makes our—"

"Zloppy zecurity!" barked Ballard in his best S.S. Storm Trooper voice. "Unt zeir ties are crooked!"

Kearny plowed on, ignoring him. "Questions? Comments?

Objections?" Nobody spoke. "Okay. It goes down two nights from now. Sunday night."

No! screamed Giselle.

But the scream was silent, inside her head only. At last she was getting her chance to get out into the field again on the greatest, most exciting caper that DKA had ever planned—and it was on the night she had just committed to meet with Yana. She couldn't change her mind now. For some reason, she really needed to hear what Yana had to say.

"This Sunday?" she managed to get out, tight-lipped. "My parents are coming up from San Diego for the holiday. I can't let them down again."

"It's okay," Dan said quickly, relief hidden in his voice.

I just bet it is, thought Giselle. The old male bonding thing yet again. All the boys eager to go out and play with their toys with no woman along to lend some sanity to the proceedings. Well, she had her own P.I. license, didn't she? Sunday night she was going to go out and use it and act like a private eye all on her own.

forty-three

Sunday night, a few minutes before midnight, Giselle parked behind a Porsche and in front of a Mercedes on Mariposa Street across from Jackson Playground. Scattered up and down the street were other expensive cars. When she got out of the Alfa, the streetlight on the corner showed her the buxom Gypsy woman who had approached her in the DKA lot a few nights before.

"We are going to the House of Pain," she told Giselle. "Stay close to me."

They fell in behind two stylish mid-40s women who went down the street and turned in at a ramshackle faded-yellow warehouse wearing a broker's FOR SALE sign with a big red vertical SOLD slapped across it. Another Silicon Valley buyout. The inevitable aluminum-framing and double-glazing could not be far behind.

One of the women tugged at the old wooden door, which slid wide on well-greased runners. The place was cavernous, stretching into obscurity, echoing with a murmur of voices—all feminine—and slapping sounds she couldn't identify.

A woman in black leather shone a flashlight into the well-dressed women's faces, passed them through. Giselle and her guide next. Giselle blinked against the light as they went in.

Overriding all else was a rich, dusky incense; underlying this, subtly emphasizing it, a bewildering *mélange* of perfumes, sweat, and smells Giselle could only think of as . . . emotions.

Fear, perhaps? Even pain, physical or emotional? Or was she pro-jecting because of the muffled cries from the dark interior?

The women ahead of them simultaneously reached up and swung their arms. There was a sharp cry of real pain. Giselle looked up and saw a nude woman in her 30s lying above them face-down in a hammock of woven hemp. The openings be-tween the strands were a foot square; her huge, famished eyes stared down at them through one of them. Her bared breasts hung down through two others; it was those breasts that these other women had struck. She was staring at Giselle.

"Now you do it! Please! Do it! Do it!"

Giselle said coldly, "Pass," and pushed on by.

Her guide led her down a central aisle past partitioned cubi-cles some fifteen feet square with floor-length red velvet drapes hanging from brass rings on ordinary curtain rods. From behind the drapes came the strange paddling and slapping noises she was hearing, along with the murmurs and low-voiced cries.

One of the curtains was not drawn completely shut and in-side Giselle could just see, by a flashlight's dim glow, a masked woman in a Gestapo uniform. She was whipping another woman with a riding crop. The victim's hands were shackled; angry red welts crisscrossed the pale skin that could be seen through rents in her rags. There was blood on the edges of the torn cloth.

The victim cried out, "Auschwitz!"

The Nazi kept right on beating her.

"Auschwitz!" She screamed it this time.

Two husky women in slacks and T-shirts jostled by Giselle and the Gypsy and into the cubicle to grapple with the out-of-control dominatrix. One tossed Giselle a flashlight.

"Hold it steady so we can see what we're doing!"

They subdued the dominatrix and removed her from the cu-bicle. They took back their flashlight. Another woman unshack-led the sobbing victim.

"We must find the Undertaker," said the Gypsy.

*   *   *

The large open area at the back of the building was softly lit by strings of small pastel lights. Gen-X music dripped from the speakers. Behind a couple of planks laid across two wine casks, a pair of women dressed only in black aprons served beer and wine. On a corner of the makeshift bar were a big coffee urn, cups, spoons, sugar, non-dairy creamer.

The women crowding the room were dressed in everything from outlandish costumes to wispy bras and panties. Some were masked. Others were nude. Because those around them were fully clothed, the nude women had a vulnerability that Giselle knew full well was deliberate.

Standing in one of the groups, dressed in skintight black leather, was Yana, masked but unmistakable. The women crowding around her were animated, competing for her attention. They all looked like potential victims. What was Yana doing in a place like this? Some of her family surely had died in concentration camps. Forget *marime*. For the first time, Giselle was struck by just how far Poteet's wife had journeyed to the dark side. From crystal ball to the palace of evil.

Yana glanced toward them and turned away without the slightest flicker of recognition.

"The Undertaker will come to us. Follow me."

When Yana saw Giselle's vivid intent face she turned quickly away; was there still enmity between them? During the great Cadillac caper, they had been foes, outwitting each other turn and turn about. In a Gypsy encampment in Ohio she saved Giselle from a beating, perhaps worse; Giselle owed her for that. But *Devla!* What had she come to? When she needed an ally, she could trust only a *gadja*, and a former enemy at that.

Voices floated around her like detritus around a pier.

"Even *I* don't want a baby *that* much."

Laughter. "Maybe you can get Clinton to donate his sperm."

"It would be better than the old turkey baster."

More general laughter. One of the women touched Yana's arm and said, "Please, take me into a cubicle. I *need*..."

"You do not need the level of pain I invariably inflict."

Yana spoke in a guttural, indifferent voice, letting her contempt for this poor creature show through her words. *Akoosh* her! It was what she wanted, anyway. Abuse. Degradation.

The curtain's brass rings made a bright metallic sliding sound on the rod. The Gypsy switched on a flashlight to show rugs, throw-pillows, even a couch. In this enclosed space, the incense and mingled perfumes were insistent, almost cloying.

"Can I get you something to drink? There is herb tea."

Giselle studied the face beneath the makeup and bangles: this was no Gypsy. She saw a round pleasant Mediterranean face and warm brown eyes concealing a lot of pain.

"Italian, right?" asked Giselle.

She might have blushed. "Geraldine. Geraldine Tantillo."

"You are Yasmine's contact person?" Geraldine nodded. "Give me your phone number. I might need to call you in the days ahead."

After a moment's hesitation, Geraldine did. They waited in silence. Yana did not come.

" 'Auschwitz' was supposed to stop the beating, right?"

"Yes. The house rule is that you must have a word you can use when you've had enough—the most sacred word you know."

"Why 'Auschwitz' for that woman?"

"Her grandfather was a guard there, so she wears prisoner's rags and is beaten by a Jewish dominatrix in a Gestapo uniform. But most of the women who come here were abused as kids—maybe by a father, an uncle, sometimes with their mother's tacit consent."

"Shouldn't it be the opposite? Wouldn't you want to beat the crap out of somebody looks like the person who abused you?"

"No," said Geraldine. "Deep down kids trust grown-ups

even if they are abused. Even grown up, they feel they deserved the abuse. Being punished makes them feel less guilty—
at least for a while."

A new voice said, "You sound as if you have pity for these
sick creatures." And Yana was there, removing her domino
mask.

"Yes," said Giselle crisply, surprised to realize that she did
feel pity, and at the same time finding herself miffed that Yana
didn't. "There's a lot of pain here. Psychic pain."

"*Pah!* What do they know of pain?" In the gloom, Yana's
eyes flashed sudden fire. "I spit on their pain! If they had to live
even one day as a *Romni* . . . But *epesèl*, time is short."

And she was suddenly loud and strident, her voice that of
a dominatrix, vicious, cutting, full of contempt.

"You slut! You bitch! Did you think you would not be punished for your disgusting practices? Off with your clothes, you
unspeakable whore, and down on your knees . . ."

By the flashlight's glow, Geraldine grabbed up a Ping-Pong
paddle and began beating the arm of the sofa with loud slapping sounds that covered Yana's lowered voice.

"Thank you for coming. Only here could we meet safely. I
know you have information for me."

Geraldine interrupted with a little shriek, began panting
very quickly like someone in pain. White noise, Giselle
thought, like that thrown up against electronic surveillance.

"The San Francisco police have issued a Murder One warrant for your arrest," she said.

"But . . . Ephrem died in Los Angeles."

"This warrant is not for your husband's murder. It is for the
murders of two old men here in the Bay Area." Giselle studied
her, but saw only amazement in Yana's face. "They believe
Ephrem, calling himself Punka Mihai, and you, under the name
of Nadja Mihai, were working together."

Giselle thought she saw Yana stagger slightly, as if from an
unexpected blow.

"I have no knowledge of a woman named Nadja Mihai," Yana said almost formally. "Ephrem conned people, yes. Picked pockets, yes. Christ on the cross gave the *Rom* permission to scam the *gadje*. But murder? He would be in terror of the *mulos*. He would never—"

"Be straight with me, Yana. Did you kill your husband?"

"No." She paused as Geraldine beat the sofa vigorously and wailed. "I did not even know he was dead until my brother got word to me. I still don't know the day of his death."

"Easter Monday," said Giselle, then added, "Nadja Mihai's description from the police files matches yours exactly. So where were you Easter and Easter Monday?"

"Why Easter?"

"They have an eyewitness who saw the same woman at Ephrem's house both nights."

Yana met her eyes with a surprising directness. "On Easter I went to mass. That evening I was in my *ofica*, giving readings. It is like that on every religious holiday. People off the street, I don't know who they are. I have no names. It would be impossible to find them now. I have killed no one, but without proof, I must flee." She sighed deeply. "There is no rest for me."

forty-four

Trin Morales let the truck glide to a stop a quarter of a mile from Xanadu, not too far from the place where Dan Kearny and the Baron had stopped when they had come here. The lights were off, the engine throbbed too quietly to be heard at this distance by the guards on the gate.

The other three DKA men swarmed silently out of the truck. All of them wore Xanadu guard uniforms. All carried bulging stuff-bags. None was armed. None spoke a word.

By pale blue moonlight, O'B tapped the face of his watch. It read 12:33 A.M. They had synchronized before starting up the mountain. Thirty minutes to wait. Trin nodded.

Morales switched off the engine and settled back against his seat. The sounds of the night started up again, cautiously. Animals, birds, killing each other, who the hell knew what they were? Nature wasn't his strong suit. But he realized that he was identifying with the predators again, after all those months of being only able to think like prey. Because of Milagrita.

Well, shit, what good had it done her?

He checked his watch. Twenty minutes to go.

By the dime-size disk of light from his tiny pencil flash, O'B worked his way up close as he dared to the brightly lit gate where two guards yawned and smoked their way through their graveyard shift. O'B moved away outside the electrified fence toward the left corner of the compound, unspooling a roll of

Primacord festooned with strings of firecrackers. He hooked the fishhooks tied at intervals to the fuse over branches and bushes, and ran out of Primacord halfway down the left side of the compound. He checked his watch. Seven minutes to go.

Ballard and Heslip moved so quickly by the light of the failing moon that they came to near-disaster. They smelled the guards' cigarette smoke just in time, veered off to the right. Just as the Baron had promised, no dogs. They'd have to be dealt with, but not now. Bart winked at Larry and preceded him down the right side of the perimeter fence away from the gate. Larry went more slowly, festooning the undergrowth with firecrackers. He ran out of Primacord halfway down the right side of the compound. He checked his watch. Five minutes to go.

The Baron had said the best place to go over the fence was at the back of the compound. Bart laid down his set of grappling hooks and coil of Gold Line nylon rope. From his stuffsack he took the two toy guns and two darts. He very carefully inserted the darts' shafts into the guns' muzzles until they engaged the projectile springs with little audible clicks. No need to check his watch. The action would be loud enough to wake the dead.

O'B stared at the luminous dial of the watch on his left wrist. His right hand held an open cigarette lighter. The digital readout hit the mark. He flicked the lighter.

Larry stared at the luminous dial of the watch on his left wrist. His right hand held an open cigarette lighter, *Mission: Impossible* playing in his mind. The digital readout hit the mark. He flicked the lighter.

Sitting behind the wheel of the truck, Trin stared at the luminous dial of the watch on his left wrist. His right hand held an open cigarette lighter. The digital readout hit the mark. He flicked the lighter. He laid it against the end of the Primacord that led out of the window to the big box of fireworks in the bed of the truck. Flame ran along the fuse.

He floored it. The engine bellowed, his blazing high beams showed DANGER—HIGH VOLTAGE rushing toward him at warp speed.

Unseen by the guards, twin balls of sizzling flame raced along the Primacord fuses from both the left and the right sides of the perimeter fence. Unseen because the guards were leaping for their lives as the truck smashed into the gate at full throttle. They infiltrated toward the main building, running from tree to tree and bush to bush in evasive action as the strings of firecrackers around the perimeter began exploding with loud POPS! and spit flame toward Xanadu as if an encircling force was firing through the fence at the compound.

Trin rolled out of the open door and kept rolling right into the undergrowth flanking the track to a great BURST! of flashing electricity and ROAR! of destruction. The gates spronged wide open. The truck, going through, took out the circuit box for the electrified gate and perimeter fence with a huge burst of eye-searing sparks.

That should short out the fence, Bart thought. He let the grappling hooks fly. They arced up to tangle themselves in the barbed-wire rolls topping the fence. No sizzle. No sparks. No electricity. But he made no move to clamber up the Gold Line.

R.K. Robinson rushed to the window of the Security Control Center when he heard the crash. Electric starbursts showed him a truck rammed into *his* compound. As he stared, it erupted with a massive outburst of skyrockets, sizzlers, and Roman candles that looked like detonating explosives. Massed flashes and pops of gunfire came from both sides of the perimeter fence.

"Hit the alarm!" he yelled, whirling from the window. "Get out the guards! We're under attack!"

He unleashed the dogs, yelled *"Angreifen!"* With a frantic scrabble of paws on the tiles, they sprang down the hall toward the stairs, R.K. hot behind. At the front door, he swung his arm in a circle. The dogs streaked off around the building.

Rose Bush, the duty officer, gleefully punched the red button he'd never had a chance to use before. The wall panel slid open. Guards tumbled pell-mell down the stairs from the third-floor barracks, still pulling on their uniforms. Rose Bush watched with satisfaction as the door swung shut behind them and the deadbolt shot home. His orders in attack mode were to not leave or open the door until the attack ended. Nobody could get at him in here. He studied the monitors avidly.

Bart Heslip waited with a toy pistol in each hand. The Dobermans came running in silent ferocity around the corner of the building. From six feet away they hurled their lean muscular bodies at the fence trying to get at him, deadly teeth actually *biting* at the steel diamonds of cyclone fence. Pfft! Pfft! Easy shots with the tranquilizing darts into their underbellies. The dogs spun away, puzzled and whimpering, then sprang again, but with less force. The powerful drug was taking effect.

Bart blew imaginary smoke from the barrels, thrust the toy guns into the pockets of his guard jacket as if into holsters at his hips. Inside the fence, the dogs had lain down and gone to sleep. Bart started climbing the Gold Line.

R.K. Robinson and his heavily armed guards fanned out across the grass, rushing from tree to bush to tree, dropping behind each bit of cover to fire at the muzzle flashes coming from the horde of attackers lining the perimeter fence.

Bart cut through the rolls of barbed wire topping the fence beside him so it sprung back, leaving an opening. Larry went over first, then O'B, panting heavily. They reversed and dropped down inside the fence. Bart followed, leaving the grappling hooks and the Gold Line in place for Trin. He dropped to the ground beside the gently snoring Dobermans, patted each dog on the head, then ran after the others, stuff-bag in hand. All three men were dressed like Xanadu security guards.

As the three DKA men got to the front steps of Xanadu, the two gate guards came panting toward them. When they were still too far away to see faces in the flickering light, O'B swung his arms at them.

"I'm the new Deputy Security Chief, Sergeant Ryan. Captain Robinson wants you to take a long, slow turn around this building and see everything is secure. We're in control here!"

They split up to trot away around the building. The three DKA men ran up the front steps of Xanadu, and ducked into an open doorway a few yards inside the entrance. In like Flynn!

As Trin crawled inexpertly through the frigging woods, tearing his clothes, getting slapped in the face with branches, buzzed by a slug a foot from his head, he felt like a Green Beret, for Chrissake. Those guys shooting out into the darkness at the firecrackers were using live rounds.

The grappling hook with the line dangling down on his side of the fence was there, all right. The frigging dogs were out cold. He'd be up and over before they . . .

Voices! He leaped back into the bushes. Two guards came trotting right up to the fence and stared at the grappling hooks.

"Jesus, some of them came in this way, too."

"Do we report this to Ryan or to Captain Robinson?"

"Whichever one we find first."

The bastards took away the hooks and the Gold Line. Trin looked longingly at the Jeep parked behind the building on the other side of the fence. So near and yet so far. But hey, the new Morales, forty pounds lighter, could probably jump up, grab the top of the fence, scramble over without the line.

And then the dogs started stirring.

To hell with it. He had to do it now, before they were awake, or not at all. Trin crouched—and sprang.

forty-five

R.K. Robinson was in the prone position behind a sturdy elm halfway to the front perimeter fence, peering through drifting smoke and popping gunfire. Their situation was precarious. They were taking heavy fire, and he could see by the attackers' muzzle flashes that they were closing in on the bridged front gate. One of the gate guards dropped, panting, to the ground at his elbow. Good! He had made it! The guard held a set of grappling hooks.

"This was tangled up in the barbed wire on top of the perimeter fence at the rear of the facility, sir."

Grim-faced, R.K. auto-buzzed Security Control.

"Faded Rose Petal to Rose Bush. We believe the defenses at the back of Xanadu have been breached."

Rose Bush's voice said, "Perimeter fence power is knocked out, sir, but all other scanners and alarms are condition green."

"Roger that. Keep me informed."

The three DKA men were crowded into the janitor's closet inside Xanadu's front entrance. When O'B stuck an eye around the edge of the door frame, the surveillance camera was just swinging its baleful eye away from the closet.

"Now!" he said.

Larry Ballard thrust a can of shaving cream out and up to send a thick stream splatting against the lens of the camera. He and Bart burst from the janitor's closet and raced down the hall with their stuff-bags over their shoulders. At the corner, Larry stuck his can of shaving cream around the edge. PHHHHHT!

Bart raced by him and up the stairs two at a time to just below the first landing. He stepped around the corner. PHHH-HHT! Larry was already running by him to race up the next flight.

R.K. was heartened by the attackers' slackening fire. None of his men had been hit. The invaders were lousy shots. He sprang to his feet to finally lead a concerted charge down the sloping lawn to the front gate—and his cell phone buzzed.

"Rose Bush to Faded Rose Petal. Scanners one and two are disabled, sir. And scanner three. And scanner four, sir."

R.K. cupped his hands to shout at his men.

"*All personnel fall in on me. Internal security of Xanadu has been compromised. Repeat. Xanadu security compromised!*"

O'B walked along the first-floor hallway past the disabled overhead scanners, breaking the invisible infrared light beams crisscrossing the open doorways by throwing handfuls of steel ball bearings into each room that he passed.

"Rose Bush to Faded Rose Petal! Door light beams and floor pressure plates have been activated in Art Gallery A . . . Art Gallery B . . . There goes Computer Room One, and now, yes, Computer Room Two! The entire ground floor has been taken over by hostile personnel, sir!"

R.K. told his troopers, "They've occupied the entire ground floor, men. We gotta flush 'em out room by room!"

The second-floor hallway's single scanning camera stared only at the locked-down steel door of the Security Control Center. On the floor in front of the Observation Room, Larry and Bart laid out the ten dental mirrors in two rows, each with a blob of adhesive putty on the handle. Larry sprinkled talcum powder generously on his palm, blew it into the open doorway.

The invisible light beams became thin red visible lines. Bart positioned himself by one side of the door frame with a dental mirror. Larry did the same thing on the other side.

"One . . . two . . . *three!*"

In unison, they moved their mirrors down to exactly face one of two paired photoelectric cells. The light emitted by that cell was reflected back into itself. No alarms sounded.

They pressed the adhesive putty against the doorjamb to hold the mirrors in place. O'B came down the hallway behind them and rummaged in his stuff-bag for the crossbow as they disabled the next set of sensors. O'B cranked the bow down, arming it.

R.K. Robinson stood tensely off to the side of Art Gallery A so as not to be hit by possible fire coming from the room. He spoke into his cell phone in low, guarded tones.

"Rose Bush, cut the security for Art Gallery A. Then cut the first-floor hallway lights."

When the hallway lights went off, R.K. spun off the wall and into the doorway, Colt .45 in his right hand, flashlight in his left. The light gave him a quick glimpse of figures massed in the darkness. He emptied the .45's clip at them.

Oh Jesus! He heard the sound of smashing terra-cotta over the slam of the .45. Taking his lead, the other men were firing.

"CEASE FIRE!" he bellowed. "Hold your fire, goddammit!"

The gallery was deserted except for the maimed art. He realized, all too late, that the enemy merely recced the room and moved on—no place to hide in here. No, they would be in the computer rooms where the machines would give them cover.

They converged on Computer Room One. R.K. gave the signal. Yelling, they charged in. And went into wild tarantellas as their feet came down on the ball bearings strewn across the floor. They crashed down like bowling pins. A perfect strike.

*   *   *

O'B heard the first far faint *whup-whup-whup* he'd been half-listening for. They would have maybe three minutes. He fitted the quarrel with the expanding-bolt head into the cranked-down crossbow. Fastened to a ring behind the fletching of the arrow was a coil of light, strong nylon rope. He raised the bow, sighted, pulled the trigger. *SPRONG!*

The arrow buried its heavy steel head deep in the center of the ceiling. The flanges popped open to anchor it securely. The thin nylon rope angled down from it to the coil in the hallway.

Ballard grabbed the end of the rope and swung, legs out straight ahead of him like Tarzan going through the jungle, his butt clearing the floor by inches. At the far end of his swing, he jammed his feet down on the floor just in front of the observation window where there were no pressure plates. He grabbed the sill to keep from stepping back and causing the alarm to sound. Seconds were precious.

He faded the mirroring, tapped on the glass. In the next room, Freddie swung himself off his cot. The Baron had assured them that the orangutan knew this trick from Hong Kong. Ballard very slowly spelled out the unfamiliar signs for USE STICK TO GET KEY.

Freddie signed something, Larry didn't know what, picked up his play stick and thrust it through the bars toward the ring of keys hanging on the wall flanking the cage.

R.K. got gingerly to his feet and held several ball bearings in one hand while rubbing his hip with the other. It had all been a feint! He hurled the ball bearings across the room and yelled into his cell phone.

"Check the ape."

Rose Bush brought up Freddie's room on the monitor. He gaped in astonishment. "The ape is *gone!*"

Rose Bush leaped to his feet, ripping off his headpiece. When he did, he heard the unmistakable *whup-whup-whup* of helicopter blades! He dithered for a moment, flung open the door and rushed into Freddie's room. The empty cage's door gaped.

Freddie waddled out from his hiding place behind the opened Security Center door and beneath the scanning camera. He shoved. The duty officer stumbled forward. Freddie, playing the game as he played it so often in Hong Kong, slammed the cage door shut.

On the floor below, in Computer Room One, R.K. yelled into his cell phone, *"Rose Bush, Rose Bush, this is Faded Rose Petal. Come in, Rose Bush."* No response. *"Come in, goddam you!"*

Still no response. He hurled the cell phone to the floor, jerked out his .45 and rushed from the room.

Freddie lumbered into the Security Control Center to stare at the glowing lights, pushed the black button. The panel slid back, Kearny and Knottnerus-Meyer came clattering down the stairs from the third-floor barracks as Ballard, Heslip, and O'B burst in from the Observation Room. Freddie grabbed the Baron's hand.

"Everybody here?" demanded Kearny.

"We haven't seen Trin since he took out the gate."

"Ve can't vait," said the Baron. "Ve must get Freddie to der roof and into der chopper."

The hall door burst open and R.K. Robinson came through in a headfirst dive. He tucked and rolled, came up to his feet with the only gun in the room in his right hand.

"Hold it right there, wiseguys!" he yelled.

"Dis exercise iss finished," said the Baron frostily.

R.K.'s .45 didn't waver. And then Freddie punched him in the chops. His eyes went vague, his legs went rubbery, his gun sagged. They all ran for the stairs as R.K.'s troopers came charging up the hall, too late as usual.

*   .   *   *

The DKA men were already in the big chopper. Knottnerus-Meyer shoehorned Freddie into one of the rear seats and got in beside him. Everyone was excited and talking at once.

"Take it up, Jacques. Vunce around der meadow, den ve bring Herr Freddie back home again safe and sound."

The rotors roared as the chopper lifted off. Xanadu fell away below them. The open meadow below was a pale blue by soft moonlight, pretty and peaceful. But then the pilot tapped the instrument panel, switched on his glaring landing lights, and started down.

"Vut iss der matter?" shouted the Baron.

The pilot yelled back over his shoulder, "Oil gauge acting up. I'll have to do a manual check."

He set it down just at the far edge of the meadow, opened his door, and yelled over the diminished noise of the rotors.

"Everybody out except the ape."

They trotted well away from the chopper in that peculiar bent-over primate stance almost everyone adopts even though it is seldom necessary. Knottnerus-Meyer was last out. None of them noticed him turn around and climb back in after the pilot.

The engine roared, the rotors screamed, the chopper leaped into the air as if shot from a cannon. The four DKA men turned and ran after it instinctively. There was a very long, astounded, chagrined silence.

Dan Kearny started for the top of the road down the mountain without a word, too enraged to speak to anyone.

"Twenty miles down to Sycamore Flats," said O'B hollowly.

"Ve haff vays uff making you valk," said Larry.

"Vehicle coming," warned Bart.

Headlights were rushing toward them along the uneven dirt track. The driver was pushing it hard; the vehicle was leaping into the air and crashing down, its lights jumping around crazily. They stood there, dispirited, as R.K. Robinson's open Jeep skidded to a stop in their midst.

Beaming out at them from behind the windshield was the round moon face of Trin Morales.

"Need a lift, gents?" he asked.

forty-six

Staley's whole *kumpania*, all fifty of them, was shoehorned cheek by jowl into the spacious front room of Rudolph's purloined Point Richmond house. The janitor from the Masquers Theatre down in the flats arrived with a truckload of folding chairs liberated from the playhouse. Kids with brown faces and shoe-button eyes ran from room to room, in and out between the adults' legs, loud and noisy and joyous underfoot. The Gypsy flag was on one wall to make them feel proud of the occasion. At its center was a red sixteen-spoke *chakra*; the flag was halved horizontally, the blue above representing the sky, the green below representing the earth.

Staley was in fine form. Tonight he would distribute the tickets and tomorrow groups would begin to depart for Milan, then on to Rome. And he had a surprise visitor for his people that made his mustaches bristle and his eyes shine.

Voices rose and fell in English and *Romani* and several Eastern European tongues; there were laughter, jokes, and snatches of song. Musicians were setting up their *tombouritsa*, their *bosh* and *bugaija*, their *prim* and their *tamboura*. Three of them, dressed in bright colors, played Gypsy music at an Andalusian restaurant in the Sunset District. Others, who could have been Latino or *gadje*, day laborers or salesmen, had brought their own instruments and would drop in and out during the night.

Josef Adamo, just returned from a night in jail for intoxication, stepped into their midst to toast them with a tall glass of ouzo. The musicians struck up the lively *Grastoro*, and Adamo, keeping time to the music with his glass, sang in a fine comic vein:

> *"My little white horse, you saved my head!*
> *You brought me home from the jail in the village,*
> *My little grey horse!"*

The aroma from Lulu's *sastra* dominated the kitchen. Six rabbits (snared by Nanoosh Tsatshimo and his sons atop Mount Bruno), carrots, onions, potatoes, and field herbs simmered on the back burner of Rudolph's stove in the big iron pot. Thank the God-Bearer, the heavy *sastra* didn't need to be suspended on a tripod over a wood fire this festive night.

Immaculata Bimbai, looking more Gypsy than countess tonight, carved holes out of the centers of half-baked potatoes and passed them on to her brother. Lazlo filled the holes with jam and replugged them, with as much attention as he had given to playing Donny, the computer nerd, in the jewelry-store scam.

Immaculata leaned close to Bessie Adamo and asked in a low voice, "Would you recognize the guest of honor?"

"The nephew of the King?" Bessie checked the oatmeal spread out to dry on the table to see if it was dry yet. "No, I never met him. But it's still early, he wouldn't be here yet."

"I think he's actually Lulu's kin," said Immaculata.

In the front room, Adamo concluded his song with the head-tossing whinny of a horse. Bessie laughed delightedly, as she did at her husband's jokes, while mixing the dried oatmeal with honey, pounded nuts, and butter. She began forming the little *buni-manricli* cakes to pan-roast on top of the stove.

"It's easier than doing them over a fire at the side of the road," she said. "But there's always something missing some- how."

"Yeah, they don't get burned this way," said Pearsa the quick-tongued teenager in passing.

Lil Tomeshti was stuffing chestnuts and herbs into the four possums caught by her husband, Wasso, in Golden Gate Park over the weekend. He came in, bent over her to make sure justice was being done to the game he had brought. Lil and Lulu sent him packing. The two women carefully rolled the possums into clay cylinders, sealed them, and put them into the larger of the two ovens in Rudolph's kitchen. Lulu bustled away to other tasks.

"In Europe I always made my *hotchi-witchi* with hedgehogs," said Lil dubiously.

"You'll like possum even better than *kanzavouri*," Dina Tsatshimo assured her. Then she confided, "I met the Queen's nephew many years ago in the south of Spain. He is from Holland, not one of us by blood. His wife is Muchwaya, of course."

"What does he look like?" asked Lil breathlessly.

"A Dutchman!" laughed Dina. She slipped a tall-sided pan of cornbread into an equally tall pot of boiling water. "Big square head. Big shoulders. Very strong. I would never forget such a man!"

"Did you put yeast in that bread?" demanded Lulu, appearing at her elbow.

"Of course not," said Dina a bit flatly.

She knew the Queen had not bustled up to ask about yeast in the cornbread. There was none. Traditionally, Gypsies made no bread that had to rise, because yeasted breads needed an oven in which to bake, not an open fire. No, Lulu had heard them gossiping about her nephew. She could not stop them from speculating, but she could make her formidable presence felt.

The possums baked in the top oven, the potatoes below. The *sastra* bubbled and the *horta* and other vegetables rested on the range in their pans, ready to be transferred to the serving platters. But the guest of honor still had not arrived.

Lulu, seeking to make work while they waited, demanded, "Is the tea and coffee prepared?"

"The nettles are steeping for the tea right now," said Pearsa cheerfully.

"And I am brewing the dandelion roots for the coffee," said Sonia Lovari. Dandelion coffee was made, not from the flowers, but from the roots, sun-dried, chopped, pan-roasted, and pounded into particles, then brewed like coffee.

The teenage girls were laying out the sweets they had made at home for the occasion: *loukomi* flavored with mastic, and rich spherical cookies made with butter and chopped nuts and rolled in powdered sugar, each topped with a currant.

"You'd better move the desserts to the sideboard in the dining room," said Lulu.

Yula Marks, only twelve years old and eager to be useful, lifted a tray and wheeled out of the kitchen, moving gracefully as if to some inner music.

"Careful!" yelled Pearsa.

In one lightning movement, Yula balanced the tray on her right hand while using her left to snatch up her skirt. She just avoided contact with Kore Kronitos, who was seated just beyond the open doorway to the living room. If even the hem of Yula's skirt had brushed him, Kore would have been made unclean, requiring ritual purification before he could rejoin his comrades.

In the front room, the band was taking its third break. In the kitchen, the women had brought out their own wine from underneath the sink, and were joking salaciously and dancing suggestively as they moved around the crowded kitchen in time to Latino music from the radio. Lulu deliberated. What was delaying her nephew? They would have so little time with him before he flew home. But she would have to serve the feast.

Staley appeared in the doorway, caught her eye, and nodded. He had obviously come to the same conclusion. He disappeared, Lulu and Lil put the possums on platters and carefully broke open their clay cylinders. The fur and skin came off with the baked clay, leaving only the stuffed, steaming meat. Tureens and platters were carried out into the front room where Staley was seated in the middle of the head table, more sober than he had been earlier but still in a jovial mood.

With a few minor pecking-order spats between children and adults alike, everyone was gradually seated and ready to feast on rabbit stew and baked possum and innumerable vegetables and boiled cornbread.

Staley, in the seat of power at this last supper of the Muchwaya in the Bay Area, was watchful, his eye on the door. The seat of honor on his right was still empty. Everyone was just about to start feasting when the front door banged open to bounce loudly off the wall beside it. Every eye leaped to the monocled intruder in some sort of guard's uniform who strode into their midst, clicked his heels with Prussian precision, and glared at them. Dina jumped in surprise.

"That's not the Dutchman!" she whispered to Lil.

"Shhhh!" said Lil. "There's two of them!"

At the same time the interloper roared at them, "A fine gang of thieves!"

Ramon Ristik leaped to his feet and snatched up the huge carving knife from the *hotchi-witchi* platter. But before he could move from his place, a hulking figure of sheer power, the second one that Lil had marked, sent a shock wave around the room by bounding by the first man. He too was dressed in a guard's outfit. He stopped and surveyed the astounded *Romi*, then made his way to the empty chair of honor at Staley's side, and sat down.

"He's not . . ." Lil stammered. "That's not . . . not . . ."

But the Prussian was mussing his own carefully thinned hair, was removing his muttonchop whiskers, and dropping them with his monocle on the floor. Suddenly he was Lulu's strapping nephew from Europe, known to many of them in the room.

"I said I would never forget such a man!" exclaimed Dina.

"Welcome, kinsman!" shouted Staley.

The erstwhile Baron gestured grandly with his left arm.

"I am proud to introduce you to my magnificent friend, Freddie, who was lost and now is found."

"Sit, sit!" went up the cry. Freddie was already being accepted by the company, responding to their almost mystical connections to animals. Chairs were shifted, and the Baron found space next to the orangutan.

"We cannot stay long," he said. "There still is danger to Freddie. This very night we fly from Oakland in a private jet arranged by certain highly placed friends."

"But you must eat something, and Freddie . . ." Lulu trailed off as she stared at the ape sitting next to her husband.

"There is always time for *hab-naske*," agreed the Baron. "As for Freddie, he is easy, my aunt. Some fruit—an apple, an orange, a banana. Some nuts, some seeds . . ."

As they all feasted, the Baron and Staley took turns describing the people and events that had shaped their plan of grand Gypsy tricks, called *bengipe*. And they told how gradually it had grown into the most audacious Gypsy con game ever played on the *gadje* by any tribe in the long history of the *Romanipe*. The children especially listened with rapt attention, intelligence moving like wild animals in their black Gypsy eyes as they absorbed every detail, delighted in every triumph over the *gadje*.

"Why do you have need of him?" asked Dina's little son. He had been stroking Freddie's massive forearm and hand-feeding him bits of cornbread.

The Baron quickly spooned the last of the cornbread onto his own empty plate.

"Because Freddie is not an ordinary ape, oh no," he said. "He is master of many tricks, he can even use a computer. The man who taught him in Hong Kong will soon join us to continue his education . . ."

Tucon, twelve years old, twinkling of eyes, already a trainer of racehorses at Golden Gate Field, broke in.

"And the *gadje* of DKA? What of them?"

"The last I saw of them—from the air, mind you—they were standing on the rooftop of the world twenty miles from the nearest town!"

Then it was *achsòv devlèsa* to the Baron and Freddie. The Baron embraced many of them, both he and Freddie shook hands all around, then were out the door with cries of *lacshès kusmètsi* ringing in their ears.

Later that same holiday morning, Victor Marr helicoptered into Xanadu with his pilot, Carmody, at the controls, and his bodyguard, Marko, carried on the books for tax purposes as his personal assistant, at his side. Marr was boiling but was so disciplined he would never show his rage to a pair of mere employees. Freddie, the totally unique possession unmatched anywhere in the world, had been his. And was now another man's.

"There never was any Baron Knottnerus-Meyer," he told Marko. "This morning I spoke with the head of the firm in Berlin. They never had such an employee. He is probably the agent of the man who bought the beast in the first place—sent to retrieve him. Whoever he was, he went into Xanadu, cased the place, then conned Cal-Cit Bank into hiring a gang of repomen to steal *my ape!*"

"So first we go after the repomen, then—"

He stilled Marko with a gesture. "Until the very last moment, they thought they were testing Xanadu's defenses. When they realized what was going on, it was too late."

"I'll leave for Europe tomorrow," said Marko. "After I kill this man and get Freddie back—"

"We . . . don't know who he is." Marr sounded uncomfortable. Money and power had always worked for him before; but now he was faced with a slyness he could not comprehend. No organization he had ever dealt with had moved so swiftly and so secretly. "There is no record of him leaving California with

Freddie, no record of him arriving with him at any major airport in Europe."

Marko audibly ground his teeth. Marr was reminded of the
Dobermans at Xanadu. Marko said, "I'll fly to Hong Kong—"

"I talked with Kahawa this morning," said Marr. "Brantley
has disappeared. Again, no record of his departure."

"Five minutes," said Carmody over the intercom.

Once on the ground, Marr started for the perimeter fence
with R.K. at his elbow.

"A con game," said Marr thoughtfully. It all *had* been a con
game. Hitting Xanadu. Grabbing Freddie. Disappearing Brantley from Hong Kong. Smoke and mirrors. He had never faced
anything like it before.

They stopped at the fence. "Firecrackers," he said, shaking
his head. "An old trick."

"In the dark, we could only figure we were taking fire."

"And they kept you occupied downstairs with a few ball
bearings tossed on the floor, while the *helicopter . . .*" He got
his rising voice under control. "The helicopter was landing on
the roof to take away Freddie. Where was the duty officer?"

"He was, ah, locked up in the ape's cage."

"By the ape, no doubt," said Marr in dry sarcasm.

"Ah—as a matter of fact, yeah."

Marr found himself nodding approval of the mirrors affixed
to the light beams on the Observation Room door frame. He
stared up at the crossbow-driven arrow with the expanding
head in the ceiling of the Observation Room.

"And the white powder scattered on the floor?"

"Just seems to be talcum. I can't figure out why they—"

"To make the light beams visible," sighed Marr.

He looked over at the glowering R.K.

"You've got one hour to be out of Xanadu," he said. What
else could he do? If R.K. was not an incompetent, then Victor
Marr himself was at fault. Victor Marr was never at fault. "I will
see you never hold any sort of security job again."

"That isn't fair! And the Jeep's gone. I got no way—"

"Walk," said Marko.

R.K. walked. Vowing, with every step of those twenty miles down off the mountain, vengeance against Dan Kearny some day.

forty-seven

At nine on Tuesday morning, the day after Memorial Day, a grim-faced Dan Kearny stormed into Stan Groner's office. Groner's assistant jumped to her feet behind her desk.

"You can't go in there, Mr. Kearny, he's not—"

Kearny flung the private door open and started across the carpet, then slowed to a stop. Stan was not alone. Jackson B. Gideon, president of Cal-Cit Bank, was beating the desktop with a sheaf of rolled-up papers and yelling.

"The bank's image, Groner!" Thunk, thunk, thunk. "You have compromised this bank's image!"

Gideon, a man with a beaked fleshy nose and pig eyes under eyebrows like bleached fuzzy caterpillars, wore a dove-grey wool suit that wished it was two sizes larger. His mouth was twisted with the same rage that had turned his fleshy face red.

Stan began, "But, sir, you were the one who told me not to do anything to upset—"

"None of your whining excuses, Groner." Catching a glimpse of Dan Kearny, he pointed a finger at him. *"Kearny!* DKA will rot in hell before you get any more auto contract recovery assignments out of us." He stormed toward the door, throwing over his shoulder, "Explain it to him, Groner!" and waddled out.

"Yeah, Groner, explain it to me," said Dan ominously.

Stan was behind his desk, head in hands. "So sue me."

Dan sat down. The disaster was not DKA's alone, obviously. Stan's feet were also in the fire. It just went on and on.

"Why don't you take it from the very top," he said.

"The Baron is no baron. The company in Berlin never heard of him. He conned Cal-Cit corporately, and me personally. The bank—on my assurances—paid him an advance and got stuck with the cost of his hotel suite, the chopper, everything. Marr is of course refusing to honor any commitments we made." Groner was on his feet, pacing. "And we were made to look like fools with the company in Berlin in the bargain. There never were any merger talks. That bastard Baron just made them up. I'm hanging on to my job by a whisker, Cal-Cit sure as hell isn't going to pay DKA anything or assign you any repo work. Not now, anyway."

"If he isn't Knottnerus-Meyer, who is he?"

"We don't know. Robin Brantley, the guy in Hong Kong who recommended him in the first place, has disappeared. Gideon is blaming me, but he's the one who told me to handle the Baron with care and never checked on him with Berlin. So I take the fall."

"So do I," said Kearny. "So does DKA. Thanks just a hell of a lot for getting me into this, Groner."

"I didn't. Actually, the Baron asked for you by name."

"I've never heard of Brantley. What'd he do for Marr?"

"Purchasing agent for him in the Orient, I assume."

Kearny paced, blue-grey eyes computing. "And the Baron was the agent for the man in Rome who wanted Freddie."

Groner was on his feet, too. "Whatever you say. Water under the bridge now. I've got to get out of here, get busy on damage control if I'm going to keep my job."

Kearny waved a disinterested hand after him as he stormed out, and sat back down, thinking furiously.

The Baron had asked for him by name. Logically, the only place he could have gotten Kearny's name was Cal-Cit Bank. But only Stan at Cal-Cit would have mentioned Kearny. And it was the Baron who had told *Groner* to get DKA. Who else was there? Himself, he realized with a start. But where to begin? DKA did no work at all for overseas clients.

He gave a sudden grunt, as if someone had poked him in the gut. Then he gave a wry chuckle.

Staley Zlachi, King of the Muchwaya. He had all sorts of overseas contacts, and he had recently been a DKA client. The Gypsies had dropped out of sight when the Homicide cops had shown up with a warrant for Yana. Kearny was suddenly on his feet. What were the Gypsies up to these days? He had to find sly old Staley and shake some answers out of him.

On the sprawling grounds of the Villa Borghese in Rome, Freddie's facility was much like the one at Xanadu, itself based on Brantley's setup in Hong Kong. A box of a room with a cage inside it and a one-way glass observation window in the wall. Looking into Freddie's room through the window was Willem Van De Post. Thanks to the Baron, he had his beloved ape at last.

In Freddie's room, Robin Brantley, newly arrived from Hong Kong the night before, was outside the open cage door with a half-dozen sealed envelopes. Brantley was very British-looking, tall and almost gangly with a long horse face and a lock of greying blond hair hanging down over one eye.

They were teaching Freddie a new trick; Freddie loved new tricks. Even so, Willem's voice on the speaker said, "Once more to be sure."

Brantley carried the envelopes into the cage. Freddie selected one, slapped it against his forehead, held it there. He shut his eyes. He swayed. He opened his eyes and tossed the envelope, still sealed, into a waste bin attached to the wall under the observation window. Then he turned to his computer. After a moment of unmerciful mugging, he started punching keys.

Words appeared on the big monitor screen behind the computer.

RED DRESS WOMAN STOP SAD. BEATRICE HAPPY IN HEAVEN. SAY BINGO GET WELL SOON.

Freddie stopped typing. No more words appeared.

"Perfect!" exclaimed Willem's voice.

Brantley gave Freddie a handful of pumpkin seeds.

When Dan got back to the office, he asked Giselle, "Heard anything from the Gyppos lately?"

"*Nada* since the cops kicked us off the case."

"Find them for me, Giselle. And quick. It's important."

"Okay, will do, Dan'l," she said cheerfully.

Easier said than done. She could use none of the usual skip-tracing avenues—friends or relatives, credit or DMV applications, medical records—to find them. Gypsies left no paper trail, not even any Internet trail, because none of them ever used the same name twice.

Four hours later, she still hadn't found a single *Rom*. Staley's number at the hot-electronics shop was disconnected. So was Rudolph's East Bay number. So was that of Eli Nicholas, the Gypsy guitarist. So were all the other Gypsy contact numbers DKA had accumulated over the years. Her Rolodex came up empty.

Had Yana disappeared also? Not likely, with the cops after her and no access to a Gypsy documenter for a passport. And it was time for Giselle to make the decision she had been mulling over since Sunday night. She dialed the contact number Geraldine had given her. The phone was picked up but nobody spoke.

"This is Giselle," she finally told it. "Let's meet."

"Sappho's Knickers," said the phone. "Eleven tonight."

Larry and Midori were eating pasta with *mizithra* sauce at the Lakeside Café on Ocean Avenue just a few blocks from the Stonestown Mall.

"We one person short in menswear," said Midori. "Luminitsa taking leave of absence."

Larry asked sadly, "Old Whit?"

Her nod danced lustrous black hair around her face.

"She say he's"—she raised her eyebrows—"sinking fast?" Larry nodded. "So she gotta take care of him until he dies."

"Smoke Gets in Your Eyes" drifted from the old-fashioned jukebox. Red candles lit the tiny tables. Cozy little place, Sappho's Knickers. Giselle tried to imagine Ken Warren here. Or Larry, or even Rudolph. Orientation aside, few men would be comfortable in this place.

She barely recognized the woman waiting in a booth. Yana was now blond, but beyond that, by some subtle shift of attitude and skillful use of makeup, she looked just a whole hell of a lot like a very specific blonde. Giselle Marc, to be exact.

Deliberate? Very deliberate, Giselle decided, but didn't comment on it. She was committed. She hesitated, then put a manila envelope full of money on the table.

"If I'm wrong about you . . ."

"You're not," said Yana.

She met Giselle's eyes. Limpidly. She had succeeded in conning Giselle Marc! But she also had an absurd impulse of gratitude. Careful, Yana. That would show weakness.

"Where will you go?" asked Giselle.

"Wherever the first plane out takes me," Yana lied.

Because of a remark overheard the night she met Giselle at the House of Pain, Yana knew exactly where she was going. And what she was going to do when she got there.

It's better than the old turkey baster.

Corinne Jones, Bart Heslip's ever-loving lady, ran her own travel agency in the 400 block of Sutter Street. She had a classic Nefertiti profile, gleaming ebony hair to Giselle's spun gold, *café au lait* skin to Giselle's alabaster. The next evening she sat down at Giselle's table in the Jeanne d'Arc, a French bistro in the basement of the Cornell Hotel on Bush Street.

"Great place!" she exclaimed, looking about the narrow restaurant with its snowy napery and gleaming silver.

"The food's even better," said Giselle.

Then she launched into an explanation of what she hoped Corinne could help her with. Corinne listened, her almond-shaped eyes brimming with good humor and intelligence.

"Are these the same Gypsies you guys messed with over all those Cadillac cars a couple of years back? The ones that Bart's been working on in Vallejo and down in L.A.?"

"The very same. The whole tribe of them took off for parts unknown very recently, in a hurry, probably *en masse* by plane."

"Charter flight? No. I doubt they could find one in a hurry this time of year. They might use scheduled flights, individually or in small groups . . . You have any names for me?"

Giselle handed her a list. "These are the names we know them by. Look especially for Rudolph Marino under the name Angelo Grimaldi or something really Italian like that. He's been living over in Point Richmond, if that's any help."

"It might be. I'll get on the Net tomorrow with a bunch of other local travel agents and see what I can find out."

Scorning the creaky old elevator, Yana trudged up to her third-floor room at the Hotel Canada on Via Goito, just a few blocks from Rome's *Stazione Termini*, the central train and bus terminal built by Mussolini in the 1930s, where many of Rome's Gypsies hung out. She tossed her two suitcases on the bed, took from one a small carryall, and went out again.

Just after dark, the well-dressed young woman set her carryall down on the *stazione* platform. Instantly two ragged ten-year-old kids with shoe-button eyes approached her, one from either side. *"Signorina!"* exclaimed one of them. When she turned toward him, the other snatched the carryall.

Yana grabbed each boy by one arm, sinking her fingers into the flesh. "Muchwaya?" she demanded. They shook their heads. She let go, gestured at one boy to open the carryall. He boldly unzipped it. It was stuffed with cheap plastic toys, red and blue and yellow, silver and gold. Their eyes widened in astonishment.

"Muchwaya?" she asked again.

"*I* Muchwaya *Americani. Ma non sono qui, Signorina. Sono in* Trastevere."

"Trastevere?" she asked.

They both nodded and gestured vigorously. The second one said, "Trastevere, *si! Il Papa. Il Vaticano. Hanno fatto una bella storia, i Muchwaya Americani!"*

A pretty story? Back at the hotel, she used the lobby pay phone to call Geraldine in San Francisco and tell her about a rather astounding phenomenon that she thought might interest some of Geraldine's friends. She was sure some of them would want to take advantage of it.

forty-eight

Bart bounded into DKA like he was entering the ring. He leaned across Giselle's desk to point a demanding finger at her.

"That college roomie of yours, Sofia Ciccone, who works in Records at the Hall of Justice, has to get me a mug shot of Yana from the time she was booked for running a bogus mitt-camp."

"Who lit your fire?" demanded Giselle. Bart flopped in the chair across the desk from her.

"I've never had a picture of Yana to show to Etty Mae down in L.A. It's ridiculous!"

Giselle deliberated. If she was wrong about Yana, she would be in serious trouble for what she'd done. She sighed.

"I'll call Sofia," she said.

"I can't steal mug shots for you, Giselle!"

"Why not? Rosenkrantz and Guildenstern are flashing her pic all over town, why can't we?"

"They're cops, for God sake. I'm a cop. They got the right to show it around and you . . ." She paused, sighed. "Oh, okay. But next Sunday we go up to the wine country in your little red car for the entire day. Just you and me, with the top down. Chasing after any foxy guys we see."

Brother Bonaventura emerged from a rose-colored building on Vicolo della Cinque in Rome's Trastevere quarter, contemplating the fact that sin was not new in this world. For at least two thousand years, pickpockets and fingersmiths had dwelled in this short street close to the River Tiber. Pilgrims' purses from distant Anglia, *porte-monnaies* from Gaul, oversized fine Moroccan leather wallets, all had been emptied here, then thrown into the blond river to float down to the sea. The street's name, *cinque*, referred to the five fingers of a pickpocket's hand.

There wasn't time to stroll along the Lungotevere to the Basilica of St. Peter, so he cut across Piazza San Egidio past the large entablatured windows of Vicolo del Cedro, judiciously cross-barred with heavy iron grillwork not even a two-year-old could penetrate. The young Brother swung along at a thoughtful, contemplative pace, his summer robe flapping happily around his sandals, his tonsure, surrounded by black curly hair, growing warm in the sunshine.

After dropping Bart at the airport limo to SFO and his flight to Burbank, Corinne Jones drove against the grain of rush-hour traffic up into Marin. She crossed the San Rafael–Richmond Bridge to Point Richmond, soon was drinking coffee with Johanna Knudsen in the triangle park across from Johanna's office.

"I knew he was too good-looking and well-mannered to be true," Johanna lamented. "Alberto Angelini, Angelo Grimaldi, those names are close—and he fits your Rudolph Marino description to a T. I put his people on Alitalia's daily flights to Milan, spread over four days, ongoing to Rome."

"They probably went on phony passports and stolen credit cards," Corinne warned. Johanna shrugged.

"The bank and the feds and the airline can fight *that* one out. I've gotten my commission and I'm hanging on to it!"

Bart Heslip parked his rental car in front of Etty Mae Walston's white frame house on Marathon Street in L.A. Someone new was living in Ephrem Poteet's place next door; one of the fancy lightweight silver kid's scooters called Razors was lying abandoned on the porch beside the front door. He wondered if the tenants knew that a man had been murdered in their bed-room.

Etty Mae's front room curtains stirred, the door opened be-fore he could lay his finger on the buzzer. She dragged him into the sitting room for iced tea, then was disappointed when he took out the envelope that held Yana's mug shots.

"Aren't you supposed to show me a bunch of other women's pictures at the same time so I can pick her out by my-self?"

"I'm not a cop and this isn't a formal identification." They were going through the glossies of Yana's full-face and profile together. Yana glowed with beauty. "They're police mug shots, which should be pretty good for identifi—"

"This isn't her."

"What?" Bart was stunned. "Now take your time, Miz Wal-ston. It was night, it was dark—"

"I don't need any time. Remember, I saw that woman two nights under a streetlight with my binoculars. She's got more of a hawk nose, different-shaped forehead, fuller mouth, rounder face. She's not this woman. I'll swear to it in court any day."

"Well I'll be damned," said Bart Heslip.

"Have some iced tea instead," suggested Etty Mae Walston.

Incense thickened the air inside St. Peter's ornate Basilica. Great spiraled pillars supported the domed tentlike canopy over the main altar, which had been covered with red and white linens. Ramon Ristik, mating Gypsy adroitness with the respect his tonsured scalp and clerical garb demanded, had passed with many other pilgrims through the immense crowd to the end of the pew closest to the wide central aisle. Tears came to his eyes when the wail of a *bosh*—the Gypsy violin—rose to the vaulted dome. A soulful Spanish guitar accompanied the choir's traditional Latin chanting. The Pope wore unusually colorful vestments: fiery red, yellow, and orange that looked like flames.

During the processional the Papal entourage of bishops and cardinals in red robes and tall mitres walked right past Ramon. He was so awed he didn't even *think* of picking anyone's pockets.

Outside in St. Peter's Square, big as a couple of football fields laid out side by side with a huge fountain in the middle, was a different story. It was jammed with forty thousand people, which meant at least eighty thousand pockets. The sun was glaring now. Ramon wiped sweat from his tonsure with a handkerchief. In bringing his hand down, he jostled a fat balding tourist wearing plaid shorts and a T-shirt reading LIONS TEN—CHRISTIANS ZERO.

"Scusi, Signore," said the bogus Brother Bonaventura, using a tenth of his entire Italian vocabulary with those two words.

His handkerchief-shielded hand dropped the tourist's wallet into the long pocket of his *soutain* to join the dozen-odd other wallets already there. The pig deserved it, wearing an irreverent T-shirt like that to St. Peter's.

A long red banner unfurled from one of the top windows of the Papal apartment overlooking the square and the Pope's frail white-clad figure appeared in the open window.

"Viva il Papa!" thundered forth, and again, *"Viva il Papa!"*

The Pontiff, voice amplified by speakers hidden among the carved biblical figures topping the pillared walls, announced the canonization of the first Gypsy saint in the church's history. In 1936, Ceferino Jiminez Malla was arrested by Republican forces during the Spanish Civil War for defending a priest. When he wouldn't renounce his faith, he was executed.

"Ceferino Malla brought to all of us his heart, rich with faith. It is time to take up his journey, on which we are announcers and witnesses."

While the Pope spoke, Gypsies wearing bright bandannas worked the crowd. A score of them were selling Jiminez Malla's finger and toe bones. A dozen more were explaining that the fifth nail—the one meant for Christ's breast, which had been stolen by a Gypsy at the foot of the cross—had come down to the new saint in Spain and here was that very nail, right here, which the owner must now sell to be cured of his maladies.

All this activity made Ramon nervous. With so much going on, someone was going to get arrested, and he didn't want it to be he, unable to talk himself out of trouble because he couldn't speak the language. He drifted silently away to slip between the ranks of tour buses parked behind the square in Piazza Leonina. Someone grabbed his arm. He spun around, ready to run—but it was a nun in the brown and black ankle-length habit of the Franciscans. She put out her arms as if to embrace him. He stepped back, shocked and disoriented.

"Brother of mine, aren't you glad to see me?" she said.

"Yana! But . . . the San Francisco police—"

"This is Rome." She was leading him past the buses and away from St. Peter's Square. "You must find me a *boojo* room—and a *Romni* who does not know that I am *marime* to lend me her infant for a few weeks. For a small cut of the take, of course." She slipped her arm through his. "In the meantime, what's this pretty story about the American Muchwaya?'

He was confused, then beamed. "Oh Yana, wait till I tell you!"

Giselle buzzed Dan Kearny with the news from Corinne Jones that the Gypsies had decamped for Rome, and for some reason he didn't seem surprised. Two hours later, her private phone rang. She picked up.

"It wasn't her," said Bart's voice. "Etta Mae said she was definitely not the same woman."

Yes! Yana was innocent! Giselle leaped to her feet, trotted twice around her desk, and pounded her fist on the blotter with glee.

When she went to tell Kearny the news, his desk was empty. Jane Goldson saw Giselle and pulled off her lightweight headset phone.

"Mr. K? He left as soon as you told him the Gypsies had done a bunk." She pointed to a stack of files on the edge of her desk. "He said for you to carry on."

Giselle called Corinne Jones at the travel agency again.

"Round-trip to Rome, business class, no return res," Corinne confirmed. "He just picked up his ticket on his way to SFO."

"You wouldn't happen to know where he's staying, would you?"

"I found him a place called San Filippo Neri." Corinne added, chuckling, "A convent. Dan Kearny in a nunnery. They converted the upper floors into accommodations for paying guests. It's very reasonable and it's near St. Peter's where all the action is."

With his American passport and single modest suitcase, Kearny cleared customs at Fiumicino's sprawling Leonardo da Vinci International Aeroporto di Roma without breaking stride and was directed to a tall taxi driver with a fair command of English.

"The convent of San Filippo Neri in Prati," Kearny said. Corinne Jones had written the address in Magic Marker, bold print; he didn't even have to grope for his glasses.

"Seventy-five thousand lire," said the driver promptly.

Dan tried to lean back against the seat and relax, but it wasn't easy. He was just coming off eleven hours in the air, nonstop, and all the way in from the airport the hackie drove one-handed with his cell phone to his ear, talking nonstop. Neither he nor any of the other drivers had any concept of traffic lanes.

Once inside the city limits it was sirens and loudly buzzing motorcycle engines in every direction, inescapable as Muzak. At an intersection a bus, ATTACK written on the side in red letters, stormed through a red light a foot in front of them.

Half a block farther on a little kid wearing baggy jeans and tattered shirt and hightops was hawking watermelon from the sidewalk. Dan's driver said something into his cell phone, screamed to a stop in the middle of the traffic, and jumped out. He came back to put a watermelon carefully on the seat beside Kearny, and roared away again—never lowering his cell phone from his face.

Finally the taxi turned into a narrow tree-lined street made even narrower by angle-parked hordes of the small European cars Dan had already realized the Italians favored. They slammed to a stop in front of a narrow mid-block mustard-colored building with wide steps up to a formidable door. Dan stepped out stiffly to retrieve his single bag from the back seat.

"One hundred fifty thousand lire," said the driver. "You said near St. Peter's. This is very far *north* of the Vatican."

Kearny slapped eight 10,000-lira notes into the man's hand, said, "Keep the change," and started up the wide stone steps with his bag. At the top he turned to look down at the angry driver.

"You ought to pay *me* for *that* ride," he said.

forty-nine

Ephrem Poteet's dying words were, *It was my . . . wife . . . from . . . 'Frisco . . .* After a pause, he croaked, *Yana,* and with his last breath howled out her name: *Yana-a-a-a . . .* Etty Mae heard him clearly. Cut and dried. But on seeing Yana's mug shots, she said just as clearly that Yana was *not* the woman she had seen on those two fateful nights. So far so good. But none of it proved Yana's innocence.

Giselle had puzzled over this ever since Bart had reported it, but it wasn't until she was driving to work that she was able to catch the thought that had been tickling at her brain. What if after saying his wife had killed him, Ephrem called out to Yana, not in accusation, but in despair because she was his only true love and he was dying all alone without her there? What if there had been another, bigamous wife?

The Bureau of Vital Statistics was in the ornate newly earthquake-refitted City Hall. Behind the counter of the otherwise-empty office a large indifferent black woman in a print dress was giving someone a cake recipe over the phone.

"You stick a broom straw down into each layer. If it comes out clean, the cake is done." She gave a booming laugh. "I'm gonna get me *more* than *a* piece of that cake, girl!" and hung up.

She looked at Giselle sternly; no cake recipes for her.

"I need a vital statistic," said Giselle.

The laugh again. "Them we got plenty of." She shook her head, chuckling, "Yessir, got plenty of them. Whut you need?"

Never confuse a bureaucrat. Giselle literally spelled it out for her. She was looking for a marriage license issued to a Poteet, P-O-T-E-E-T, Ephrem, or to a Mihai, M-I-H-A-I, Punka.

"Ain't gonna be many, not with no goofy names like those."

There weren't. On Friday, March 3rd, Punka Mihai had married Nadja Gry in a civil ceremony right here at City Hall.

Giselle went out into the June sunshine to sit on a bench by the reflecting pool and congratulate herself a little and reflect on what she had. She had a start. A bigamous marriage. What she needed now was Nadja Mihai's current name.

Luminitsa Djurik sprinkled a careful measure of the magic salt Whit Stabler had mentioned to Larry Ballard into the chicken noodle soup and set it down in front of the old man. She used the cheery voice of caregivers worldwide.

"The magic salt will have you all well in no time, Whit!"

He began shakily spooning soup into his mouth. He mumbled valiantly, "I . . . think I feel stronger today."

She needed a power of attorney to get at his investments, and the house deed made over to her so she could make a quick sale. Once he signed the papers, the final dose of magic salt . . .

"You certainly are stronger," she said, taking the spoon from Whit's shaky hand. "Let Mama help you. And then maybe tonight you can help Mama by signing the deed to the house."

Ramon had found a house in Rome on the Via Tor dei Conti near the partially restored ruins of the Foro Romano where the conspirators killed Julius Caesar. Just down the street hulked the Colosseum, haunted by the shades of the countless thousands who died there to entertain the citizenry of Rome.

The hallway was lined with a dozen straight-backed chairs filled with women in obvious pairs. Some had their arms around one another, others rested their heads on the shoulder of their beloveds. They had paid in advance, very dearly, to be here.

The tall door of the *salotto* swung silently open. A tonsured monk in a simple brown robe stood in the opening.

"*Suora* Maria Innocente has composed herself sufficiently to receive you," he said gravely. "It is very difficult for her, as you can imagine. But you may enter."

The couples trooped into an echoing high-ceilinged room made dim by dusty crimson floor-to-ceiling plush drapes pulled shut across the windows. It smelled musty.

Beside the fireplace sat a slight nun in brown robes. Her bland face was framed by a stiff white headpiece under her black veil. Her slender throat was wrapped in severe white linen. In her arms was an infant. As the women took their places in the semicircle of chairs facing her, the silence was broken only by the scrape of wood on marble, the nervous clearing of a throat.

The pale nun suddenly raised her head to stare at them. Her eyes burned with the starved inner fire of the fanatic. How had they ever thought of her as bland? She spoke. The voice was harsh and cold. It sliced to their very souls.

"You are here today to bear witness to the martyrdom of an innocent woman."

She leaped up, thrusting the infant high above her head as if to dash it to the marble floor. Several women gasped. The child gurgled sleepily. Sister Maria Innocente was motionless.

"I am bound by my final vows of poverty, obedience, and chastity. I honor them. I am poor. I am chaste. I am a virgin. And I am mother of this child." She lowered the infant, cradled him to her bosom. "When I was a teenager, God told me my destiny was as a bride of Christ. I embraced that vocation."

But after she took her final vows, visions started to come. Of a child. She told Mother Superior of her visions. Mother Superior reproached her for the sins of pride and presumption.

One day, as she prayed alone in the motherhouse garden, a voice spoke to her in a strange tongue.

"I do not understand!" Sister Maria Innocente cried out.

"Listen . . . listen . . . and repeat . . ."

After three times she could recite the words perfectly, right down to their inflection—and suddenly she understood them. She never heard the voice again. Then she missed her period. When the morning sickness came, she went to Mother Superior with the whole story. She was ejected from the convent.

"I brought my child to Rome to seek wisdom of holy men and women assembled for the two thousandth birthday of the Church."

One of these holy men had a housekeeper who, like the women gathered here today, could not abide the thought of a man touching her. But she desperately wanted a child.

"I told her there was nothing I could do. Secretly, I was terrified. What if my visions and my voice had come, not from God, but from Satan? But she pleaded and pleaded . . ."

They prayed together, and Sister Maria Innocente spoke the words over the housekeeper three times. The woman became pregnant. She told others of the miracle.

Sister Maria Innocente slumped in her chair, exhausted. The monk told the women, "You have come from America, even farther away than Trieste. You have chosen to live your lives without men, yet you desire children. God has given Sister Maria Innocente the gift of immaculate conception. Only during this Millennium year can she perform this miracle for you."

The nun was on her feet, fatigue gone. The monk accepted the infant from her arms and left. This was women's work.

"At the moment I speak the sacred words, six of you will be impregnated by the Holy Ghost. There can be no turning back, no changing of minds. Do you wish your donation returned?"

No one spoke. No one moved. The pairs of women knelt on the hard marble floor in front of Sister Maria Innocente. She spread her arms wide and chanted:

"Káy me yákh som
Ăc tu ángár!
Káy me brishind som,
Ăc tu páni!"

She repeated it, then said it a third time in English:

"Where I am flame
Be thou the coals!
Where I am rain,
Be thou the water!"

Sister Maria Innocente lowered her arms. "Those of you who have chosen to be mothers are now pregnant," she said.

The monk escorted them out. That evening, the twelve chairs lining the hallway were once again filled with hopeful women without men, who wanted babies and who were there because of Sister Maria Innocente's fame, just in case, just in case.

They were yelling, sweat was flying, Midori's nails were raking his back. One last tremendous thrust took them right off the side of the bed. Even at that ultimate moment, Larry the karate kid spun them in a nifty one-eighty so he was underneath when they hit the floor. The impact made them both come.

They just lay there for a time, holding each other for dear life, laughing with the sheer joy of it, panting, spent, sated. Midori still had an hour before she had to get to work; they untangled and squirmed around to sit side by side with their knees drawn up, their bare backs against the bed.

Midori giggled and panted, "You . . . very bad . . . man, Rarry."

"And you . . . very bad . . . girr, Midori," he panted back.

When he said "bad girl," dark images of Luminitsa Djurik and the old man she was taking care of sprang to mind. Here were he and Midori, young and crazy in lust—maybe even in love—and there was that poor old geezer, on the way out.

"How's old Whit doing?"

She shook her head, bottomless dark eyes suddenly somber.

"Midori not know, Luminitsa quit her job, no work no more."

Larry jumped to his feet. "Jesus Christ!"

"What's the matter?" Frightened, Midori sprang up also.

He was pulling on his pants. "Whit said she sprinkled magic salt in his soup."

"Sure, he say it better'n Viagra. But . . ."

"What's Whit's last name?"

Midori paused, pulling on her wispy underwear. "Stabrer."

Larry grabbed her two-year-old phone book off the bedside table, muttering to himself, "Stabler. Whitney Stabler." On Portola Drive. He dialed the number. Not in service. She'd had it changed, sure as hell.

"Come on," he said. "We've got to get over there!"

fifty

irty Harry picked up the phone and heard, "Call me."

He sauntered out of the Bunco bullpen and down the hall to the bank of pay phones, tapped out the number, got Luminitsa.

"Last night he signed the deed and the power of attorney," she said. "I can list the house and close out his brokerage accounts this afternoon. With a good dose of magic salt in his breakfast, another at lunchtime, he'll be gone by nightfall."

"Shouldn't I be with you? All that cash . . ."

The greedy turd: eventually, he'd have to go, too.

"Relax, lover. Come around six, we'll drink champagne and hold his hand while he goes." Her throaty chuckle was like her hand caressing his groin.

Larry ducked in and out through the thickening clots of morning traffic on 19th Avenue, took a left into Sloat, squealed uphill into Portola Drive, stood on the brakes. It was a modest stucco two-story in the 900 block, but in San Francisco's red-hot real estate market probably worth close to a million bucks. Plenty to kill for, if you were the killing kind.

Midori was holding back. "Luminitsa my friend! She no do anything like—"

"You may not believe it, but Whit needs help. You stay here."

Midori, good submissive little Japanese girl, stayed. A short flight of terrazzo steps led to a minuscule porch. Larry put his finger on the bell and left it there, Ken Warren–style. The door was flung open. Luminitsa Djurik glared out at him.

Her magnificent body was barely concealed by a filmy negligee; he could see the sharp brown thrust of her nipples against the thin bodice. She really did look a lot like Yana, though she sure didn't sound like her.

"Go goddam away. I've got a sick fucking man here."

To the left was a stairway leading to the second floor; to the right a living room with a nice fireplace. Ballard strode through it to the dining room, through that into the small neat kitchen. Luminitsa was right behind him. No Whit.

"Where is he?"

"In bed, you goddammed fool! He's sick, for Chrissake!"

"Yeah, and we both know what made him that way."

Luminitsa grabbed a butcher knife off the rack and was only a dozen seconds behind him into Whit's room at the head of the stairs. Larry bent to scoop up the frail old man from his bed.

"I'm taking him to the hospital. They'll run blood tests and find out just what the hell you've been pumping into him."

With a shriek, Luminitsa leaped at him, sweeping down the foot-long razor-sharp blade over his shoulder and at his chest.

That's when stocking-footed Midori slammed her in the back of the head with the frying pan she had carried up from the kitchen after sneaking in despite Larry's order.

Twice, driving in to work, Giselle caught a glimpse of the same dark sedan behind her. Her phone was ringing when she got to her desk. It was Larry Ballard. When he hung up, she was no longer worried about being tailed. She counted on it. She called Geraldine, caught her going out the door to work.

Rosenkrantz spun off the wall to smash the heel of his heavy shoe into the flimsy door just at the latch. It flew back against the wall with a crash. He went in low and to the left,

Guildenstern, behind him, high and to the right. Two women were in the room. The cops holstered their pieces.

"Okay, you've had your little joke!" yelled Guildenstern. "Now, where in the fuck is Yana?"

Giselle Marc said to the round-faced Italian-looking woman with her, "The hairball is Guildenstern, the cueball is Rosenkrantz. They're supposed to be Homicide cops." To the cops, she said coldly, "I believe Yana has left the country."

"How? She doesn't have a passport, she can't get one from a Gypsy documenter because she's *marime*..." Rosenkrantz stopped to point at Giselle. *"You!* You gave her your passport!"

"My passport was recently stolen, yes," Giselle admitted haughtily. "I have reported the loss to the State Department and have applied for a replacement document."

Guildenstern grinned evilly. "You ain't gettin' away with that one, sister. We're gonna fry your pretty little butt—"

"Oh, grow up. Yana isn't your killer."

"I suppose you're gonna tell us who is," he sneered.

"I sure am. A woman named Luminitsa Djurik. She married Ephrem in a civil ceremony as Nadja Mihai. Together they murdered two old men with what she called magic salt."

Despite himself, Rosenkrantz was listening.

"But those two old guys died of digitalis poisoning."

"Magic salt is dried, crushed foxglove leaves. She would sprinkle it over their food like salt in small progressive doses like arsenic poisoning. Eventually they'd just ... waste away."

"Where do we find this mythical broad?" asked Guildenstern with a sneer in his voice.

Giselle smiled sweetly. "After she killed Ephrem, she started slowly poisoning a third old man named Whit Stabler—"

Rosenkrantz, obviously now a believer, was aghast.

"You knew this and you didn't report it so we—"

"Would you have listened to me? This way, Mr. Stabler is safe in the hospital and Larry Ballard is at his home on Portola

Drive right now, holding Luminitsa Djurik for you. She was trying to kill him and got knocked out with a frying pan."

Guildenstern sighed. "Let's go get her, partner. This lady
here is just too goddammed much for me."

When they were gone, Geraldine asked, "Can I tell Yana the
news?"

Giselle was a bit surprised. "You know where she is?"

"She calls me from Rome."

"Rome again," said Giselle. "Dan Kearny's in Rome. He's
staying at a place called San Filippo Neri."

"A convent?" asked Geraldine.

"Yes. How did you know?"

"I'm Italian, remember. I know my Italian saints." She
sighed. "I don't know anything about the world. San Francisco
is the farthest I've ever been from Dubuque."

An hour later, Yana called Geraldine from Rome. An hour
after that, she descended from her room at the Hotel Canada
with both suitcases in hand. All her sophistication of dress and
manner were gone. Her hair pulled back, her face without
makeup, she looked like a schoolgirl in Rome for the religious
celebrations. The thick-featured balding man at the front desk
looked at her in heavy-lidded surprise.

"Parte già, Signorina?"

"I'm going to my cousin's," she laughed. She shook her
hand in that very Italian gesture, with the limp fingers waggling
from side to side. "Everything costs so much!"

She caught a bus to the *Stazione* and after three streetcar
rides checked into the convent of San Filippo Neri.

Dirty Harry climbed the stairs silently. Already his one-eyed
snake was twitching in his pants in expectation of the sexual
delights to come. Whit's room was dim; the shades were down,

the curtains closed. A motionless form was just visible on the bed. The old fart must already have died.

Then *the dead man sat up*. Harry gave a strangled cry of terror—and the lights went on. Rosenkrantz was sitting under the covers, beaming at him.

"Harry my man, who makes the ideal groom for a murderess?"

Guildenstern said to Harry's back, "An old guy with a million-dollar house who dies on his wedding day."

"Except Whit didn't die." Rosenkrantz was off the bed.

Harry found his voice. "I don't know what you're talking about. I was just going to—"

"Shut the fuck up," Guildenstern advised him.

"Until we can read you your rights," explained Rosenkrantz.

And snapped the cuffs around Harry's wrists. Really hard.

When Dan Kearny returned to the San Filippo Neri convent, the chapel and kitchen were dark, the office closed and locked, the TV turned off in what had probably been the sewing room. The polite nun from India who had checked him in was nowhere about. He was vaguely disappointed. He enjoyed talking with her. Nobody else even knew he was in Rome and he was a little lonely.

He got into the tiny elevator, punched three. When it shuddered to a stop at his floor and he turned toward his room, a nun passed him in the hall. Her black veil and starched wimple were unlike the habits of the nuns of San Filippo Neri, and left little of her demurely downturned face to be seen.

"Good evening, sister," Kearny said as they passed.

"Buona sera," she replied in a muffled voice.

At his room, the heavy slatted wooden window shutters he had left open on the latch let in just enough light for him to see the unsealed envelope on the floor inside the door. He stepped back into the corridor to read the bold block lettering.

GIARDINO ZOOLOGICO
VILLA BORGHESE
AFTER MIDNIGHT
THIS IS FOR GISELLE

He had been wrong. Someone in Rome knew him after all.

fifty-one

Just north of the Aurealian wall lies the 17th Century Villa Borghese, six kilometers in circumference and still a place of harmony in the heart of the Eternal City. Twelve hectares are given over to the Giardino Zoologico. At 4:00 P.M., an iron-haired, stern-faced priest entered the zoo through the main entrance and did a quick tour of the grounds. Dan Kearny had noticed that the clergy seemed able to move around Rome without anyone noticing them; with his lack of the language, he needed any edge he could get.

The zoo seemed to have too many bears and large cats, not enough primates. But a new small modern-looking building caught his eye. A large sign on its locked door announced grandly, INSTITUTO DEI PRIMATI.

"This'll be it," he muttered to himself.

At four-fifty, when the zoo started closing for the night, he buried himself in a dense thicket near the new facility. It was a warm evening and the light lingered until nearly ten o'clock. After the voices of departing patrons died down, he dozed off.

Just at midnight, a dozen dark figures passing close by woke him up. He followed them discreetly.

Looking like a *Rom* was an asset for this scam. Nanoosh Tsatshimo and Wasso Tomeshti, dressed in Gypsy garb, let half a dozen of the English-speaking believers they had encountered in the bar in Piazza Leonina into Freddie's room after collecting their hefty fee. Rudolph was waiting outside Freddie's cage to give note paper and an envelope to each mark.

"In the thirties," Staley told them, "the Gypsy saint, Ceferino Jiminez Malla, traveled throughout Spain with Freddie's grandfather as his companion. Jiminez Malla could foresee the future and God let him pass this gift on to his beloved ape."

Make it mysterious enough and hard enough to believe, and the marks would fight to give you their money.

"Jiminez Malla's beloved companion finally died, but Freddie, last of the line, still has the gift of second sight. Seal your question about the future in the envelope, and be careful to let no one see it. Not even Freddie will ever see it—but he will answer your questions even so."

The marks did as directed. Rudolph presented the sealed envelopes to Freddie. He selected one and pressed it against his forehead. He shut his eyes. He swayed. He opened his eyes. He tossed the unopened envelope into the waste bin attached to the wall under the observation window. He went to his computer.

Freddie started hitting his keys. Unseen behind the one-way glass, Willem started hitting his, and the answer showed up on the screen in Freddie's cage. Freddie pointed at the words.

RED DRESS WOMAN STOP SAD. BEATRICE HAPPY IN HEAVEN. SAY BINGO GET WELL SOON.

In the observation room, Immaculata Bimbai retrieved the sealed envelope from the open back of the phony waste bin, tore it open, and handed it to Willem. She watched through the one-way glass as Willem quickly scanned the first real question and Freddie pressed the next envelope against his shiny black forehead. He grimaced and swayed. He typed. So did Willem.

LAURA LOVE YOU. SHE FAITHFUL. MARRIAGE BLESSED.

Dan Kearny had the impression that he had already met the receptionist. Dark eyes, arched brows, a strong-bridged nose, black hair pulled back to tumble down her back in a single twisted braid. No. He had been seeing that same classical Roman face all week long in the art museums on saints, angels, martyrs, Madonnas. This one, 21st Century instead of 17th, gave him a big smile. She gestured at the closed door behind her.

"Please go in. The curator can see you now."

Willem Van De Post, curator of the Rome zoo, was a large, fit man in his early 60s with ashy thinning hair. Piercing blue eyes looked up from the papers on his desk and widened in surprise as Kearny spoke without preamble.

"I was locked in your zoo last night by accident. At midnight some Gypsies . . ."

"Surely not, Father!" exclaimed Van De Post.

"Tell me about the orangutan, my son."

"It's a long story," said Willem. "Making this zoo a world-class primate center has been my life's dream. People don't come to the zoo to see hedgehogs and foxes, you know. Our board of directors supported the idea of such a center, but could not budget it. When I became curator I got a chance to buy an old silverback gorilla from the Munich zoo, but until now there have been only two great apes in the primate center."

"The gorilla and who else?"

"Myself, Father." Willem leaned back and waved a hand at the computer. "I was exchanging e-mails with Dr. Ulysses Seal, a medical doctor in Minnesota and a prodigiously energetic conservationist. He put me in touch with captive breeding specialists in many zoos. But I had no money to buy a large primate, and had no animal of like value to exchange."

"But then Our Lord sent you Freddie."

Willem looked at him quizzically. "I suppose you could say that. I've known Robin Brantley for years from various wildlife conferences around the world, and of course knew his work training Freddie in language skills. As the date for the Chinese takeover of Hong Kong approached, he learned that the Peking

Zoo wanted to take over Freddie. He flew my wife and me to Hong Kong as his guests to meet his pupil."

"And he asked for your help," said Kearny.

"Yes. Brantley made me an offer. If we could find enough money for him to get them both out of Hong Kong clandestinely, he would give Freddie to the Rome zoo. My wife's family are animal trainers, we both agreed that Freddie would suffer great psychological trauma if removed from Brantley's custody. For me it was the opportunity of a lifetime."

"How did Marr get into the picture?"

"Marr has the collector's disease. He heard of Freddie he wanted him, and he took him. The rest you know . . . Mr. Kearny."

Kearny shrugged. "I do indeed. It cost DKA ten thousand dollars to mount the Xanadu operation to rescue Freddie, Baron."

"How long have you known?" demanded Willem.

"Since a few days ago. When I learned that Marr had stolen the animal from a man in Rome, I knew you were either that man or his agent. When you stayed in the Observation Room rather than meet Freddie yourself, it was because *Freddie knew you.* You couldn't let him see you. I followed a hunch—and the Gypsies—to Rome instead of Berlin."

"Your reasoning is excellent and your team was excellent, Mr. Kearny. But . . ." Willem opened his hands, sadly. "I regret that I have no money to give you."

"Aside from the ten thousand," said Kearny, "what about that show last night? Is Freddie going to be doing carnival tricks the rest of his life?"

"No! No!" Willem was aghast. "Robin Brantley will be the curator of our new primate center. He will continue with Freddie's training. But last night I had a debt to pay. You were right about the Gypsies. My wife's aunt is Lulu Zlachi. Staley Zlachi did me the great favor of recommending you for the job."

Kearny got to his feet, walked over to the window. Freddie

and the silverback lolled in the sun in their temporary fenced enclosure. Looked like a nice life to Dan. He turned back.

"You zoo guys always need philanthropists. If you can see a way to put Daniel Kearny Associates on a bronze plaque in that new primate center, then I guess we can just shake hands and go our separate ways."

Ramon sat on the edge of the bed and watched Yana in her nun's habit interlard 100,000-lira notes between the pages of books, into brochures, journals, even empty audiocassette boxes. Then he helped her carefully pack them all into the sturdy yellow mailing box on the table below the window of her room.

"They're going to check this at the post office before you send it," he warned.

"At the Vatican? With hundreds of tourists sending off packages of Millennium year souvenirs? They'll just take a quick peek inside and seal it. Besides . . ." She gestured at the declaration of contents. Under CONTENUTO she had printed in bold block letters: GIORNALI, LIBRI, RICERCHE ACADEMICHE. "Books, journals, academic research. Sent by a nun in habit? What could be more innocent than that?" She met his eyes. "You've got to face the facts, my brother. The virgin birth scam has another month at most to run."

"No! It will last at least until the end of the year."

"When our first marks realize they aren't pregnant after all, the whole lesbian community will know it's just a scam."

Ramon left to ready the *boojo* room in the house on the Via Tor dei Conti for that day's operations, and Yana addressed the package. Then she threw back the wooden window shutters to sit on the sill and look down into the narrow sun-drenched street. Outside the convent-hotel kids played around a red metal trash can. A middle-aged woman in a shapeless robe watered the plants in her window boxes.

She loved it here, but what would she do when the con was

over. What then? She suddenly leaned farther out to stare down. The stocky grey-haired priest had just issued from the convent with a box of his own under his arm. She gave a joyous laugh and turned back into the room. *Baripe!* Perfect!

The branch post office just outside the Vatican walls sweltered under the noonday sun. Most Romans were behind closed shutters until the midday heat passed, but not the locust horde of sweating tourists who wanted the *Roma Porta Angelica* postmark on their packages. Among them was a stocky, hard-faced priest with a box under his arm and a fistful of garish tourist postcards in his hand.

"Excuse me, father, do you speak English?"

He turned. The pale slender nun with the heavy-looking yellow box in her arms seemed to droop under the heat of her full Franciscan habit.

"I do, my daughter," he said gravely.

"*Bene.*" With almost a little girl's gesture, she thrust her yellow box toward him. "I find I am feeling faint. Do you think you could mail this package for me, father?"

He accepted the proffered box. "Certainly, sister."

"Bless you, father."

The ghost of a smile might have passed over the lips of each of them. She laid a small clever hand on his black-clad arm for just an instant, as if in benediction, then was gone.

Dan Kearny looked at the address hand-printed in bold block letters on the box under DESTINATARIO.

> MR. DANIEL KEARNY
> DANIEL KEARNY ASSOCIATES
> 340 11TH STREET
> SAN FRANCISCO CA 94103, U.S.A.

He left the line. A few minutes later, in the secluded rear of a coffee bar across the street, he was not surprised to find bank-notes of large denomination between the pages of the books, Yana's thanks for DKA getting her off the murder charges. Enough to cover DKA's fee for the Xanadu caper. But where the hell was he going to be able to convert lira to dollars? He'd have to go to the Gypsies again.

Inside the square, the very last of the Holy Year pilgrims slipped out of the huge bronze Holy Door of St. Peter's Basilica just before it was sealed for the next twenty-five years. By passing through it just now they received a Plenary Indulgence—remission of punishment for all of the sins they had committed during the course of their lives.

After a moment of silent prayer, slowly, with labored effort, the 80-year-old Pontiff Pope John Paul II pulled shut the twin thirteen-foot panels. Later, they would be bricked up until another Pope declared another Holy Year in 2025. Thunderous cheers went up from the 100,000 people gathered in St. Peter's Square behind him to witness the event.

Among them was a slender pale nun, in full habit, who had been the very last person to slip through the Holy Door before the Holy Father closed it.

author's note

Con games are by their very nature cruel. They are also sometimes astonishingly inventive, and often amusing because the victims should have known better. Most of the cons, scams, and grifts in this novel are real; but if you feel that nobody in our sophisticated age would fall for them, consider that, since 1950:

An English businessman bought the Scandinavian fishing fleet in Norway. A South African company bought an RAF military airfield in England. An Italian consortium bought several U.S. Navy ships anchored in the Naples harbor. A Japanese investor bought a BOAC airliner during its three-day stopover in Tokyo. Several different buyers purchased the Eiffel Tower to tear down for seven thousand tons of scrap metal. An American tourist leased the Colosseum for ten years to stick a restaurant on top of it.

All paid cash to the putative owners. All received nothing in return. All were conned. None got any money back.

In this new Millennium, such hoary scams as auction fraud, adoption fraud, stock fraud, credit card theft, and trademark theft have gone online with a relative newcomer, identity theft.

During my years as a repoman at the real DKA, I took part in more than one split-second dealer raid like that on Big John's UpScale Motors. DKA always later recovered the pilfered demos.

Kearny's day in court happened exactly as in the novel; I merely substituted Dan Kearny for Dave Kikkert, Larry for me.

The novel's murderous "magic salt" long con stems from a 1993 San Francisco case of alleged digitalis poisoning: purple foxglove seemed to have been put into the food of five old men who died. Allegedly involved were corrupt cops, unauthorized cremations that destroyed forensic evidence, and members of the infamous Bimbo (as in Tough Guy) Gypsy clan known for its nationwide mayhem since the early 1900s. In 2000 a few slap-on-the-wrist sentences were passed out, none for murder.

I watched the fake-mentalist sealed-envelope gag nightly on a carny midway when I was a "roughie" with a traveling tent show touring the American Midwest in 1955. For the novel, I added a computer and an ape. Primate studies show that nothing Freddie does—including the use of sign language—is far-fetched.

The House of Pain stories are real.

Concerning Yana's Rome scam, I offer the following, without comment, from Leah Garchik's *San Francisco Chronicle* "Grab Bag" column for Saturday, March 27, 1999: "10,113 virgins bought insurance against immaculate conception next year."

None of the characters in this book are real, of course; I made them all up. Mere fictions, mere figments, every one. Having said that, I have to state that, as always, I owe profound thanks to all those who helped me write it.

First and foremost, always and forever, Dori. Wife, lover, best friend, best person (and best editor) I have ever known, who right down to the very last second worked much harder on this book than I did to make it right.

Henry Morrison and Danny Baror, my book agents, who labor long and hard all over the world in every medium on my behalf.

Bill Malloy, Editor-in-Chief at Mysterious Press, for being

such a good friend and dynamic editor. Also long-suffering Harvey-Jane Kowal, Executive Managing Editor of Time Warner Trade Publishing, who takes the time for my work.

Paul Sandberg, entertainment attorney and film producer extraordinaire (*Picking up the Pieces*), who tells the world's best jokes, many of which have found their way into these pages.

Novelist Michael Connelly for letting me borrow Harry Bosch (in name only) as a fun foil for Rosenkrantz and Guildenstern.

Rick Robinson for lending me his name and physical being for one of the novel's quasi-bad guys. In real life he is a gentle giant who edits the excellent mystery fanzine *The Perp*.

Sis Moeller of Global Travel in Mill Valley worked out how to get my Gypsies to Rome on short notice during Millennium year.

Jean Jong of Gold Dream Jewelers at San Anselmo's Red Hill Shopping Center gave me invaluable data concerning the color, size, origin, and price of emeralds I needed for my jewelry scam.

Bill Corfitzen supplied me with a great deal of material about Rome in Millennium year not elsewhere available.

Blair Allen did likewise for the "magic salt" case.

Stan Croner, one of the world's true good guys, lets me continue to bash him about as Stan Groner of Cal-Cit Bank.

Dick Mercure and Vicky McPhee opened their premises and their hearts to Dori and me during the novel's early stages.

Finally, many Gypsies told me their stories, their cons and scams and grifts, their folktales and spells and charms and legends, on condition they remain anonymous. And so they do.

This novel was begun at Frederiksted, St. Croix, American Virgin Islands, worked on in Arizona and New Mexico and Colorado, and completed in the San Francisco Bay Area.

Joe Gores
January 2001